SECRETS

Mixed Up Moods & Deadly Attitudes

JOJO MAC

ISBN: 0692419691
ISBN 13: 9780692419694

Website: www.jojomacmusic.com
www.firenicerecords.com
Youtube: www.youtube.com/thejojomac
Facebook: www.facebook.com/jojomac11
Twitter: www.twitter.com/badsingergirl
Reverbnation: www.reverbnation.com/jojomac

DEDICATION

This is dedicated to my hilarious, wonderful and caring husband Winston "Byia" Solomon. Thanks so much for being the wind in my sail, never letting up no matter what. I feel really blessed to have you in my corner. I love you big guy.

ACKNOWLEDGEMENTS

First I must say thanks to Almighty God for giving me life and light when my way gets dark, for the will to make me keep going no matter the odds. Without him being the source of all the different energies it takes to navigate through this beautiful thing call life I would not be here at this moment giving thanks.

Thanks to my wonderful, handsome husband Winston "Byia" Solomon. There are no words to explain how important you are to everything that I do, and I mean everything, from the music and so much else. I love the ground you walk on big guy and I will never be able to thank you enough for the love and support you give me; even those times when you are not sold on what I want to do you support it anyway. For that I thank you as well. You are my rock. I know it's not always peaches and cream for you because I am so hard headed but you smile through it all. You know you are "My Angel"…I love you baby. Keep me laughing.

My beautiful mom, Celestine "Laverne" Robinson do you know how much I love you for being mother and father to me all my life? I do everything with you in mind. I pray that you will be around for a very long time so I can spoil you the way you did me growing up I laugh now when I think about how I really thought I was a princess. Then one day I grew up. I think. Thank you.

My beautiful, courageous and quietly fierce sister Andrea Jones, you know my love for you is concrete. I love you like you are from my womb and I know you must love me too because you are always in my corner and lord sometimes my corner was just gangsta but you my beautiful sister was always a big supporter of all my endeavors and I thank you for that and being one of the most wonderful person I know. I love you loads. And let me not forget to commend you on your successes. You make us all proud.

To my sister Paulette Edwards Dixon you know no matter what I will always love you. I see you growing in ways that are new and wonderful and I commend you. Continue to work at being your best self. And yes, when you support you go hard. I love the relationship we have now. Whew! Let's keep it that way. You are beautiful. My nieces, Antoinette Bruce and Alicia Dixon and nephews Antonio Edwards, Damian Dixon and Hugh "Courtney" Dixon, I love you guys so much. I pray for you every chance I get that God guide you through these years along the right path as I am confident that you all have everything it takes to make a successful and fulfilling life. Don't be distracted. And let me not forget to send out love to my grandnephews Antonio Jr. and Lamar Andrew Bruce, I can't wait to meet you both.

Big love goes out to my aunts and uncles on the maternal side; I love you all very much. Aunt Jean you know your love is on a whole other level. Aunt Ruby, Aunt Gloria, Aunt Merva, Aunt Judith you know I love you, Aunt Ina I wish it was different; my uncles Trevor, Julius, Matthew and Neville, I love you. Uncle Ralph I honor you. On the paternal side, Claston and his wife Jackie, Uncle Lascelle, Uncle Winston, Brown Man and Godfrey, and my Aunts Joyce and Maxine (Ida), I love you all very much. Uncle Glen you are always there for me when I call on you for a photo shoot and I love you for that. Big up yourself Betty, you are still family to me, also Sonia Roberts Douglas. Linda and Valerie Douglas, I love you all.

Bless up to all my cousins, I am not able to mention all of you here but some of you that comes immediately to mind are, Shanna, Simone, Laura, Donna, Eva, Aldo, Stephanie, Paulette, Paul, Michael, O'Neil, Freddy, Lenny, Dwayne, Brian, Andre, Patrick, Steven, Chad, Sherelle, Little Neville. What's up Maurie B and Carol C. Shirley Lu, how are you? Sheldon and Simone, Clinton, CJ and Ashley, Janice, Sharon Daniel, Tammy and Howie, Sharon Allen, Karlene, my darling cousin Marcia over in the UK along with Nola, Nova, Clive and one of my all time newest favorite Adrian Stone (the real family man)...Cammie and Karbyne. Big ups to all of you and if I forget anyone, please note that I do not love you any less, but I need to leave some space for the content of the book. I love my family world without end ...All generations…Biggest love to all of you whether you were mentioned or not. Hey Morgan! What's up Hardy, you good?

To my sisters from another mother, the McKenzies; Barbara (Mummy), Hyacinth (Onie), whom I know all my life…I love you. To the ones I am yet to meet Andrea (Cookie), Vanessa, Kareen (Kay), Safia and my brother Simon, we missed so much already I hope I get the chance for us to truly find each other and make the proper connections..Really, I can't wait to meet you guys. Nonetheless, I am happy to have you as my sisters and brother from another mother. I can't wait to meet the nieces and nephews as well.

I love you Orville Samuels, Michelle (Annie) and Negreta. I am so sorry for the years we missed, there is a gap that needs to be filled and I think we should start filling it up by getting the link a little tighter. I have such great memories. I miss daddy too "Roy Samuels", the only daddy I knew.

Big ups to my brothers-in- law: Marlon Facey, Chris and Terrence. To my ready-made family, Crystal "Angel Eyes" and the beautiful Kaily, Shanna "Lot Solomon", Sharntay, London, Junior and Jordell, I love you guys. And how about my mother-in-law Ms. Madgoline Brown, I love you lady. You raised such a wonderful son and I am so happy he is in my life so I can be in yours. I love you loads.

Oh lord, my friends…Judith "Precious" Martin-Hopkins and Shirley "Marilyn" Richards you have been my friends practically all my life and there have never been any friendships that I find this easy. Precious you and I are so much alike it's uncanny. Shirley, you are always a big supporter of all I do. I love you both. Patricia Daley-Parham, don't think I forget you, look where our friendship came from and where it is today "and people thought you were fraternizing with the enemy"; remember that Pat? Hey Frankie Parham big respect. Alcia Evans, do you think I would forget you? Never that; I pray you achieve all you have worked so hard for (A yuh say hustle…lol). To the Whites and James' down there in Florida, Miss Pansy and the crew, I love you dearly. Thanks so much for being there for me during a time when I felt lost and beaten, big ups for that Julia. Corneita "Cecile" James I am waiting for you to finish your book now girl. I know you got it in you, just move to it. Don't think you got rid of me; you will always be family to me.

To all the people in the music that I have had the pleasure of working with Duckie Simpson, you are first on this list. You have been a force in my profession of music since the beginning and here we are again. Thanks for making me a part of this very legendary group "Black Uhuru"; I am certainly enjoying this run. Bless up group member Andrew Bees…Road we seh! Hopeton "Scientist" Brown, you were around during my early years as well and now you are back, how lucky am I? I get to work with you again. Big love and respect goes out to Fitzroy Francis and Empres Skortcher for ever being in my corner, you two are a force to be reckoned with. I am waiting for your book of quotes Fitzroy. Empres I am so at ease with you. You are a star. I wish you much success. Delroy "Phatta" Pottinger, Danny "Champagne" Grant, Sicka, Chaka Demus (I had a blast working with you), Lloyd "Pickout" Dennis...I think we may be on to something. Let's paint not just the town, but paint the world red…Phillip Gaad I have the biggest hug for you when I see you…and Bionic Steel, don't for one minute think you are escaping an equally big one. Color T, Baker, Tippa Irie and Jah Rain, Dan I (Issachar) what's up? Love you guys.

Joseph "Caesar" Frei, thanks for all the times we worked together in the studios, we have such chemistry, and how about the videos and photos, basically every darn thing, and let me not forget the wonderful artwork for this book... Luis "Faust" Matos my beat man…You know you are the best, right? Yes you are...Keep knocking out those beats for me. Hey Sess thanks for the link to those tow music masters I just mentioned…You will have to shoot a video for me soon. … SK Michelle big respect…you know the "ting", dem betta know. What's up Sista Barbee Dee (had to mention you for rinsing out my tunes the way you do), General Culture, Bevin "Doctor B" Walker mi doops, Chip Smith thanks for always championing my cause, Mr. Clinton Lindsay thanks so much for ever highlighting reggae with no bias, Dj Face Money thanks for the love, Fiba Don, Crown Prince, Ringo T, Tony "Father T" Mosley, Mr. Mighty and the beautiful Jodi, Mr. Speng, BiggaU, Papa Ray, King Mohican, Dj Wayne..My girl Jenny "Smoothie B", Girl power we seh … Bad Boy Satta Blue, we still love you. Tony Carr ever holding down D.C…Jutta Hessbruggen blessed love for you always, Wanda Thomas "Airm", Winston Francis and Keallie, bless up for the constant support. Thanks to all the people who played my music even once... Big up to Duque from Islandah, you are such an avid supporter, thanks for always looking out for me. Leroy Francis, you were the first to take me into the studio to record "Please Mr. Please" …and do you remember that Karen White cover I did for you "Superwoman" ...Can you even find that? …Troy Fenton, it was a blessed day when I met you. We have been busting it wide open since...We have lots of work to do pal. Lets Reggae and Roll into it. What's up Peter Blacks Super Dj, you ready to play the tunes dem? There are so many of you I want to thank, but I can't do it all here.

To my peers, yes I know we are all vying for the top spot but we take time to appreciate and show support for each other … Zabrick you are top of that list, always championing my music, I love you for that, I hope Clap it Like Thunder goes viral. The great Engineer Quata Don …you tuff no end! I love working with you. Rocky Persaud I love your work, you do it all, you are a master at the game. Roscoe Murphy how awesome are you? I love working with you. It's been a long time. Richie Harris, see I finally finish the book; you were always pushing me to finish since your first peek. I wish you the best as well in your music career. Déjà vu, I still have high hopes for "Baby You". Phrench Vanilla, we have to do another tune together. John I-Shenko McKenzie, I wish you all the success in the world cuz. To my Studio One family, Courtney Dodd and Vincent "Morgy" Morgan, My experience there was awesome. Clement "Coxone" Dodd and Mrs. Norma Dodd treated me like royalty; big love ... Courtney let me know when you are ready to drop the big Studio One tunes. Photographer Richie Williams, I so miss your photos. You are still boss. Teri International and Maxine Tomlinson big up yourselves.

I want to send some shout-outs to some of my face book friends and supporters as well as some of my pals (real friends)…Aaaww! Annette and Johnny Senior of Spicy Delight in Washington D.C., how did I get so blessed to be here calling you friends? You are such wonderful people and such big supporters…I remember when I did that show with Beenie Man years ago after I left D.C. for a while and you guys surprised me at the show with the biggest bouquet of flowers I had ever seen and today you are still supporting me. I love you. Sharon "Lady W's"Lindsay, you have been a good friend. You were the first to book me on a show when I first moved to Florida without even hearing a single song from me, you never even heard me sing until the night of the show. Thanks for the vote of confidence. Remember how they threw money at me that night, you picked up a ton of money for me, I felt like a stripper without a pole, but I had a blast. Remember how the MC invited me back three times to the stage to sing that Macy Gray song over and over again...And we still good after all this time. To Morais "Father Sonny" Witter, thanks so much to you and your family for being there for me when I moved to Miami, y'all can't get rid of me now. I love all of you. Thanks a million. To my other dear friends and constant supporters, the promoters of the Rachel One Love Fest, Vernon and Gayle Saunders and Andrea Benbow, you are family to me and I love you guys, thanks for always looking out for me. Doreen "Korean" Orlebar and Mark Orlebar you are both special to me, any friend of Byia/Writer is a friend of mine. Big up Mark Orlebar's brother Skeng and your hot-boy Rapper son R Money; to the world...Patricia Balfour, Donna Strachan, Valerie Ferguson, Charmaine Martin, Judith Daley, Marcia Stultz, Marlene Crowl, Ann McKenzie, Andrea "Melody" Williams, Jayjay Armstrong. Yanique "JaJa" Jackson-Wright, I will always love you. Melody Spriggs, Linda Brown Shuga/Philly Lin Lin my number one fan, I love you girl. My hair stylist Paris Hills thank you. I hope to keep you busier this year onwards. Patrice Wright I bet you are surprised that I mention you here, but I have to. One of the things that got me energized to get on this book was all the novels you sent me and brought to me personally. I read enough of them to realize it was time I finished my own. You are a big-hearted lady, stay that way. Ansel Livingston can we say a day late and a dollar short? Stay blessed pal.

And how about my video vixens, Crystal Reynolds, Lynn Caffee, Megan Tilghman, Majestic Fyah, Renee Glover, CJ the Barber, Sakia Ayanna Peck, Andrea Milton, Chantee Davis, Natalie LaPrade and my leading men Gary "Sir Fixx" Fennell (Hey Sir Fixx, what about those many trips to the studio, thanks for the support) CJ the Barber, Yardy Rico, Clever "Dox-Pert" Nyadongo and Neville Pinnock. Thanks to all of you.

Andre Porter, I have to tell you that while I was editing your work, it inspired me to finish this book that I started several years before.

Dar Stellabotta, I had to save you a special paragraph. Since the day we met you have been a force in my musical life, you are always there to take care of all my online and cyber needs. Though you are a singer yourself, you have taken up the torch for me in a way that no singer would for another. Thanks for believing in me and I do hope you will hang in there until we get to the light outside the tunnel. If only people know all of what you are capable of. You are my idol girl.

Porsha Alvarado thanks for lending me your beautiful image for this cover. I pray your dreams come true baby girl. This will make for a nice little tap up on your resume. Go hard, you can do it. Reach for the star baby girl. Hello Nadine Blagmon, Maureen Cox and Natasha Alicia (Ferryman), Maria Alvarado I love you girls. Special love goes out to my Godson Patrick Salmon.

To my long-lost and now newly-found friend Paulette Mendez (Vivienne) it's such a pleasure.

I picked three people from my face book page that are so hilarious that each time I get on face book I have to see what craziness they are up to next ..Though you all may not know me personally and may not even see this, I have to say shout outs to "Carlos Max Brown", Mishibu Di Riddim Queen and Keisha Koffee Freeman …You three have me in stitches every time I log on. If there was a face book Grammy the three of you would definitely be winners (yes, I am stalking)….Laughter is the best medicine.

And finally to those who have passed on that still lingers in my heart because you have all been a force in my life, my grandmothers Alice Robinson and Susan Campbell, there are no words to describe how I miss you both. I know you are both hanging out right now; I dreamt it. My Aunt Euriel Robinson, we miss our Prayer Soldier. I miss you loads. Conroy Robinson, gone way too soon, there is so much to say, I loved you so much and I miss you even more. Delroy "Chin" Davis rest in peace pal, you tried and it did not go down the drain, I am still here trying to make everyone proud. You are missed. Roy Samuels thanks for having been my Father, it meant the world to me. We all miss you.

And last but certainly in no way least…I must thank Whitney Parks, Nichol Lashley and the team at CreateSpace for taking me through the process of getting this book out there, for the wonderful artwork and the myriad of things it requires for me to be finally able to say "I released a book". Whitney thanks especially for the patience and the time you took baby-stepping me as I no doubt have you chuckling over some of my hitches. Thanks a million.

If I left anyone out who should really be mentioned please forgive me, who knows there may very well be a part two to this …. Boom!

Chapter I

NATASHA

I woke up this morning in a really good mood, because today is the day that I make my first big move toward the big times. It is only seven o'clock but I was ready to get it popping. I am not doing any back flips though because I feel it has been long overdue. Still I would not even begin to complain because the modeling and fashion industry is a very competitive one and so many gorgeous women who so badly wanted to grace the fashion runways or the magazine pages never even made it inside the doors of an agency.

Three years after graduating college with my bachelors in early education I still never even tried to get a job outside of modeling so my mom and dad decided maybe they should at least support that since I wasn't about to do anything else. Of course they still bitched about how I wasted their money on college. I constantly have to keep reminding them that it was not a waste because I could still fall back on it later, much later I hope.

Now I am finally scheduled to do a photo spread. It's already Monday and I feel like I am still living the weekend. I have a one-o-clock appointment with Margaret Mitchell who has been my agent for the past two years. She is a very close longtime friend of my parents and my mother had her sign me to her very successful self-made agency "Mitchell Models."

I managed to drag myself up and into the shower, as the warm water caressed my skin, I closed my eyes and think about the day ahead and wondered if this could finally be the break I have been waiting for. I am still trying not to get too excited, I do not want to be disappointed like I have been so many times over the course of what seem to be a career pending. I stepped out of the shower with water dripping from my light brown skin. I quickly dried myself off and with the towel wrapped around me I headed for the kitchen to start my coffee brewing.

I made myself a cup and sat on the sofa in the living room and watched the morning news, same shit different day. Today, like many others there is a story about another sex offender on the loose. It makes me wonder if all the sex offenders have set up residence in Florida. Lord knows we seem to have more of them in this state than all the others combine. After the sex offender story, I changed the channel just in time to see my best friend Kylie Mason promoting her new novel "Becca's Revenge." "You go girl," I screamed at the television as if she could hear me. She would have killed me if I missed it.

I felt a rush of pride fill my entire body, my girl is finally in the big leagues and I couldn't be happier for her. I watched the interview and when it was over my phone immediately rang.

I grabbed the phone, "Hello."

Melanie was screaming into the telephone, I could hardly hear a word she was saying, but she sounded really happy. Then I realize that she was just getting excited for Kylie, she had just watched the interview.

"Mel, slow down," I screamed back into the phone.

"Girl, I am so glad she finally made it with this one," she said after she calmed down.

"I am so happy for her," I said feeling good for my friend.

"Anyway, I have to go. I guess we will have to make this Friday night a major celebration."

"No doubt; I have to run, my photo shoot with Excell is today and I have major preparation to do, call you later." I said before hanging up the telephone.

Before I could walk away the phone rang again, I started to ignore it because I really needed to start getting myself together, after all it's not every day that I get to do a spread for any magazine, let alone Excell. I picked up the telephone on the third ring. "Hello." I said practically hollering into the phone

"Hello miss big time. What's it looking like for your big gig today?"

It was our newest major player, the big time novelist. This was her third novel, and her first published work, and it has been garnering some very good reviews from the media; both television, radio and print. Only this morning Matt Lauer on the Today Show called it the breakout novel of the decade as he welcomed Kylie to the show.

"Hello darling, congratulations baby girl. I am so damn proud of you."

"As I am you," she said almost gushing.

I laughed because she did sound so genuinely proud, but I was quick to remind her that the shoot had not actually taken place yet and for all I know it might not even make it to the stands, and if it does I might not make the cut. I know it sounds a little negative on my part, but after years of not doing anything quite so major I do have the right to get a little despondent from time to time.

"I do have to go sweetheart, but I will catch up with you later this afternoon, will you be available or will you be doing Oprah." I said with a giggle.

She was cracking up on the other end of the phone.

"I'll be free, no more interviews before Wednesday. So we can certainly get together." She was still laughing.

"Girl, it's not funny, you are finally on your way to being a best-selling author. But we'll talk later. Love you."

"Love you back. Bye."

I hung up the telephone and again it rang. This time I checked the caller ID before answering and thank heavens I did. It was my ever pathetic ex Marcus. He is the last person I want to speak with today I do not want anything or anyone to upset me and Marcus has a way with pissing off people. He and I spent two years shacking up in an apartment in Aventura and I could safely say that it has been the worst two years of my life thus far. I ignored the telephone and lit a cigarette, which I dragged on slowly enjoying every pull like it was about to be my last.

The shoot was not until two in the afternoon and it was only ten thirty, so I had plenty of time to prepare myself. Then I thought to myself "what preparation?" All I need to do is to show up with freshly scrubbed face. Excell will be providing the clothes and all necessities for the session. I suddenly start feeling super good about the upcoming events of the day, but I am trying to relax and not get too hopeful. I think I will just pray about it and leave it in the hands of God. Ever since I was a little girl I was used to praying and leaving things in the "hands of God."

As a kid I grew up in the church, I remember having to wake up at five o' clock Wednesdays and Fridays for a half hour prayer meeting with my mom and dad and my older sister, Tanya. There were days when I would pretend I was sick from the night before so I wouldn't have to join them the next morning. However, my dad believed that if you are ailing, not feeling up to par, then there's no better place to take it but to the lord. So a huge percentage of the time I would still have to get up and join them for what seemed the longest half hour in history. I use to think that even God didn't think it was fair to wake us up so early when we have to go to school, but as I got older I came to understand that it is never too early or too late to pray. So I prayed.

At twenty-six years old I feel blessed that I even still have a career pending. It is no secret that in the modeling industry twenty-six is considered old for someone getting their first break. At that age most models are established or looking toward new career goals. But not me, I am basically just getting started by industry standards and I feel I have a lot of catching up to do. However, I do have one thing going for me. That fresh faced youthful glow and it doesn't hurt that I am as thin as a rail. At five feet eleven inches and weighing in at only one hundred twenty pounds my friends would tease me about getting swept up and away by a big gust of wind. I would tell them that I didn't mind being swept away as long as it blows me smack unto the cover of People or Times magazine.

I guess I could classify this upcoming shoot as 'my gust of wind," though it's not People or Times. Excell is right up there in the top ten though, so that's good enough for me. I guess I could classify this as my best opportunity yet.

As I waited for the time to pass, I decided to brush my hair. You know that one hundred strokes process, that's supposed to make your hair more shiny and manageable, though it never seem to do much for mine. My thick jet-black hair hangs down the middle of my back and I was never able to achieve those one hundred strokes because my hands would be tired by the time I hit the fortieth.

I love my hair I just could never handle it myself so Karen, my hairdresser of four years would sit me down once per week in her chair and create miracles, miracles because she would make me look so much better coming out than going in. When she gets finished with me I always look the way a model should, ready for the runway. I call her my fairy godmother. She is the baddest white girl I know. She handles hair like no other, I think the girl have a Love Jones with black hair. It was just yesterday she gave me a shampoo and blow dry, leaving my hair straight and ready for whatever destructive process the magazine stylists would put it through. Thank God I could talk her out of leaving the shop where she used to work and start working in Melanie's shop. With Melanie being one of my best friends, I had an obligation to support her cause. That is what any good friend would do. So I told her about Karen and she hired her immediately. I later found out that Karen was not happy at that shop anyway, so it worked out well for everyone. Well maybe not everyone; I am sure they must be missing her at that other place. She was the best they had.

Ok, I think I am getting a little nervous now for I have no idea when I smoked as many as three cigarettes, but I guess it's a natural thing to be nervous when you have had so many false starts; photo sessions that led nowhere. The average person would probably think that every time you do a shoot it would most likely end up in print somewhere, but not always. I was one of those average people until I signed with Mitchell. I came to my senses really fast after my fifth shoot was shelved. After a while you learn not to even ask why, you just move on to the next one and pray.

I need to get off my ass now and head out the door, the time flew by so fast it was already noon and I have a forty-five minute drive to the studio. I need to get there ahead of time so I can finalize some last minute details with Margaret, before session time.

I walked into my oversize closet and pulled out a pair of Baby Phat dark blue jeans and Baby Phat altar top in gold and quickly dressed, finishing with a pair of louboutin brown boots. I stood in front of the mirror, just admiring myself for what seemed too long. I grabbed a pair of gold hoop earrings from the dresser to finish my look. "There," I said aloud. My purse and keys were on the hallway table so I picked them up on the way out the door and I was off.

I live on the fifth floor of a high rise condo on Collins Avenue so I took the elevator to the garage in the basement. Before I got to my car my cell phone rang. It was Margaret.

"Hi Natasha, you ready to go?" she asked.

"Oh yeah, I was just getting………"

Before I could get out all the words she quickly jumped in.

"Great! There is a limo waiting for you in front of the building, it will be at your disposal for the entire day, so if you have some errands to run or anywhere to go where you need to make an impression today would be a good day to do it."

I could not contain my excitement. Since my four years in the business this is the first time I have been offered a limousine for any reason.

"Oh Margaret, thank you so very much."

"That's nothing Nat you deserve it, now run along."

"Yes ma'am."

"See you soon."

I headed back to the elevator and when it opened I pushed the lobby button. I was happy for the limo ride for more than one reason. I hate driving on the highway and that would be the only way to get there. So that took care of the nerve wrecking drive I would have endured, but my main reason was it seemed to raise the bar for me. Maybe once and for all my career is about to take a turn in the right direction.

I got out of the elevator and Murphy the doorman greeted me with a wide grin and said, "You look simply gorgeous Miss Natasha," as he opened the exit door.

"Thank you Murphy, see you later'.

The big black limo was sitting right there in front of the building just like Margaret said. As I strutted toward it, with a sudden excess rush of confidence, the driver hurried to open the door. He said good afternoon, I said good afternoon back and got into the car. There was a bar stocked with numerous top shelf liquor, there was even a nice fruit cocktail, peanuts, chips and a cold shrimp platter.

"Damn!" I said aloud.

The driver did not hear me luckily. I would hate for him to think that I was not used to such luxuries, after all he doesn't have to know that I am not as huge as this limousine makes me look. So, I'll just relax and be the star he probably thinks I am.

The usual forty five minute drive took only thirty five and I was a little surprised when he pulled up in the arched driveway of the Mitchell Modeling Agency, a modern stoned building with huge bay windows on both sides of the entrance way. The red carpet lining the steps into the hallway, gives the feeling of success as you enter the spacious foyer decorated with early Victorian furniture and a huge luminescent water fountain in the center, all of brown and gold hues.

The building was an old movie theater that was deemed too small for the ever- growing population of moviegoers. When it went up for sale Margaret snatched it up and went to work remodeling until finally she got it exactly the way she envisioned. This building, this agency is Margaret's baby. She claimed to be still paying out of her behind for it. Though from the look of things Margaret seem to be managing quite well. She changes her Mercedes every two years and sometimes drives a customized Range Rover. Her only child Jenny is married to a senator and living in Ohio. Margaret was married to Jenny's dad for most of her life until he ran off with some young Italian girl from the law office where he worked.

Margaret was crushed, her agency was not doing well and she was just getting over her near fatal car accident that happened just the year before. But now she is having the last laugh, because shortly after the divorce business started booming for the Mitchell Modeling Agency and it has been upward bound since.

Now she is a multi-millionaire with some of the biggest names in the industry signed to her agency.

I walked to the far end of the foyer where her long time assistant, Mona Miles was sitting behind a huge desk that looked like it belonged in a hotel lobby, but with much more elegance.

"Hi Mona."

"Hi Nat, you look beautiful as always. Go on in, Margaret is waiting for you."

"Thank you Mona, so do you."

She laughed and waved me on my way. She was never good at taking compliments and it made me wonder why in the world not. She is as beautiful as any of the models at Mitchell and would certainly give them a run for their money if only she was taller. She was only five feet four inches tall, too short for the runway, but would certainly make a more than decent print model.

Mona is forty two and married to a very wealthy real estate mogul and is more than capable of taking care of herself, but she insists on working. Being an old friend of Margaret's, she chose to help her out at the agency. Which proved to be a big break for Margaret; having someone she can trust and depend on. Money was never an issue in Mona's life she has always had plenty, so Margaret did not have to pay her a huge salary. Actually Margaret said she had to force her to take a monthly check at least. The minimum wage was the maximum she would accept, just to make the relationship at work as professional as possible, although Margaret would be the first to tell you that they do not need lines drawn between them. They were the best of friends who respect and think the world of each other.

I knew my way around the building quite well. I have been here numerous times in the last two years since she moved the agency here from a basement office in a small building located in West Palm Beach. People say it's one of the most attractive and famous buildings in Coral Gables.

I walked through a huge double door that led into a hallway that leads directly into her office. As soon as I approach the door it swung open and Margaret met me with open arms. It is not usual for her to be personal, but there are rare moments when she would loosen up and let it rip.

"How was the ride down?"

"Fantastic."

"Come on in and have a seat, we have a few things to go over before your session. They are setting up in the East Studio as we speak."

I sat in one of the two high-back chairs positioned in front of her huge oak and glass desk. The entire office was decorated in glass and wood, in the same gold and brown hues as in the foyer.

She shuffled through some papers, all the time with a serious, almost tight look on her face. It was silent except for the rustling of the papers she was toying with and I could feel some nervousness coming on. I took a couple of deep breaths and she looked up at me with a half-cocked grin that left me even more nervous. I gave her a half smile in return, not sure what to think I focused my attention on the family photos on the mantel adorning the fireplace in the corner of the back wall to my left. I have never seen a fireplace inside an office before and suddenly it all seemed clear to me. Margaret was successful because she was creative and innovative and you could see it in the building from the outside in. There were pictures of Jenny and her husband the Senator and a photo of her late mother who passed away shortly before Martin left her for that Italian bimbo. She was the splitting image of Margaret only older.

Margaret finally looked up at me after what seemed like an eternity, I glanced at the desk clock and what seemed like forever was actually just a minute.

She smiled at me and said, “I know that since you signed with me you have not had what most of us would call a “breakout” career and I know from time to time you probably court the idea of breaking loose and signing with another agency, and I couldn’t fault you for that, so I thank you for sticking it out.”

I could feel my chest tightening as the words left her lips and I waited for the bomb to drop. The part where she tells me that she doesn’t think I can make the cut and the time has come for her to let me go. I must have drifted way deep in thought, because I came back to earth with Margaret saying, “Natasha, are you alright?”

“Ye……yes, I’m fine.” I faked a smile.

“I was telling you that the Excell people want to give you the cover of next month’s issue; that would be the April issue so they sent out their best man for the job. They thought you were spectacular in those photos I sent them.”

I felt like I was just pardoned from a death sentence minutes before my execution. I jumped out of my chair and dashed behind her desk to place a big wet one on her cheek.

"Oh Margaret! Thank you, thank you." I could not contain my joy. I knew what that meant. It meant I was now on my way to the big times.

Margaret was beaming with joy just eating up the moment, probably thinking how silly I look acting like a kid in a candy store. I gathered myself together and walked back to the chair I had so hastily abandoned.

"That's not all Nat, it gets better. You are scheduled to do a Ralph Lauren fashion show in New York only one week after the magazine hit the stands."

I let out what sounded like a big old yelp.

"Thank you, I don't know what to say, oh my God." I was speechless.

"This is just the beginning sweetie, your brightest star is about to start rearing its beautiful head." She paused for a moment and leaned forward looking me dead in the eyes.

"Do you really know what this means Nat? A Ralph Lauren fashion show is as big as fashion shows come. All the major magazines and network channels will be there. All the magazines will be carrying photos of the models and what they wore. So with all that you have learned the last couple of years and your charm and matchless beauty you are going to knock them dead. I want all the magazines to have a photo of you in there somewhere. With that and the Excell cover, the calls should be coming in from the morning and talk shows."

She leaned back in her chair. "So young lady are you ready for this?" she asked without blinking an eye.

I was beaming with confidence and I knew I was about to kick some ass on this photo shoot today, and then kick some even bigger ass on the New York show.

"Yes! Yes! Yes!" I screamed.

We looked at each other and we both started laughing like too teenagers, I wasn't even sure what we were laughing about. When the laughing finally subsides Margaret slid some papers over to my side of the desk and after going over fees and schedules, I signed on the dotted lines.

I spent the remainder of the afternoon in the East Studio on the East side of the Mitchell building in front of cameras and bright lights. By the time I got home I just wanted to crawl into bed and sleep and never get up till the next day or two but I couldn't do that because I promised Kylie we would go out and celebrate her newly found fame. Hell, I have a lot to celebrate myself, screw the bed. On second thoughts I will reserve my celebration for another day. I do not want to steal Kylie's thunder. Let me not get ahead of myself after all, because Kylie's thunder is way bigger and louder than mine. Yes, I've made up my mind I will hold off telling her and our other three friends my good news until we have bled all the life out of hers. Maybe I could delay telling them anything at all and wait till the magazine hit the stands, surprise them. Well, tonight we will not be getting together as a group. It will just be Kylie and I. We have been friends the longest of the five of us, truth is we have been friends since we were six years old, and it shows that we are closer to each other than we are with anyone else among us.

I picked up the phone and dialed Kylie's number and she sounded half asleep herself. We made arrangements to meet at Ginger Bay Café in Hollywood where we could have a nice spicy Jamaican meal and listen to a live reggae band. I usually hate to eat late but I did not eat all day and I could most certainly enjoy a nice big meal. I still have access to the limousine so we decided that I would pick her up at ten.

After I hung up the telephone I stripped down to my panties and bra, set the alarm for eight thirty and hopped into bed for a catnap. I was a little exhausted from the events of the day. We started at two thirty, after about an hour of hair and makeup. With touch ups and restyling and costume changes, the bright hot lights and dancing more than posing, I couldn't wait for it to be over. By the time it was over it was way after six and I wasted no time getting out of there.

Don't get me wrong, I had a blast doing it, it was probably one of the most exciting things I have done in a very long time. I liked being the center of attention, having everyone fussing over me like I was a star. But they are no idiots, they know that even if I'm not as famous as the people they are used to working with, they also know that my star is about to shine, so it would be in their best interest to treat me well. On the other hand that could be the way they treat everyone they work with.

I could not fall asleep no matter what I did. I counted sheep, I shut my eyes tight and dared the sleep come but nothing. I eventually fell asleep I believe because next thing I know the alarm was going off and it was time for me to drag my black ass up and get ready for our little pow wow.

I took my second shower for the day, picked out a little short black dress from my closet, a strappy Burberry boots and matching purse. I spent about fifteen minutes on my makeup and I looked absolutely fabulous. By the time I was all finished putting my beautiful conceited self together it was nine twenty five. I called the limo driver from the card he gave me when he dropped me off earlier and he told me he was already in front of the building. I had told him earlier that I would be leaving home about that time, so I was pleasantly pleased to know he was so reliable.

As I entered the elevator, a sudden rush of happiness overcame me and I let out a loud, long scream of delight. So many good things were happening today, and not just for me, but also for my very best friend in the world and together we are going to paint the town red. The evening doorman Jeffrey, the only black person working in the building, smiled a shy hello and hurried to open the door for me. When I got into the limo and waited for the driver to walk around to the driver side, I looked in the direction of the lobby and Jeffrey was still standing with his jaws dropped open and looking awe struck. It must be the limousine, because he had seen me many times before, looking just as scrumptious.

When the car pulled off he was still standing there looking until the car was out of his sight. When we pulled unto Kylie's street it was exactly ten. She lived on a street lined with beautiful palm trees and red brick houses. She bought hers just three months ago when she got her first big check from her publishing company. We were all so proud of her and we all five of us helped to decorate and pick out new furnishings. The house looked great from the outside but the inside was like something out of Home and Garden.

I was waiting for the driver to open my door but instead he asked if I wanted him to go and ring the doorbell and of course I said yes. I took my cell phone from my purse, dialed Kylie's number, she answered just as the driver rang the doorbell.

"I am ready miss hot shot," she said before I could say anything.

"Then get your famous black ass to the door." I said laughing back.

"Yes ma'am." Then she hung up and the door swung open.

She said something to the driver and he laughed all the way back to the car. Miss thing was also wearing a little black dress, but she topped it off with beige and black Liz Claiborne purse and matching black boots. She had her hair piled atop her head in a very conspicuous bun with a few tendrils hanging from both sides, just enough to make it look sexy and soft.

When she got in the car beside me I gave her a big squeeze.

"Congratulations Kylie, I am so happy for you."

"Thank you mama, I know you are; all of you." She said, making reference to Keri, Melanie and Amanda.

"Did you speak with either of them today?"

"Of course, they wanted to take me out to celebrate, but I wanted to reserve today for just us. I guess we can all celebrate again on Friday when we all get together."

"You'll do anything to keep the celebration going uh? I said teasingly.

We laughed out loud, reached over and gave each other a bear hug. We said very little the rest of the way and I didn't even notice when the car came to a halt in front of the club. The driver walked around to the sidewalk and opened the door for us. There were tables lining the side walk in front of the club and people of all races were sitting at tables sipping on whatever they were sipping on, smoking cigarettes, laughing and bobbing their heads to the music coming from inside the club. Reggae singer JoJo Mac's song "Dancefloor" was on the turntable and the energy was off the chain. I could see through a gigantic glass window at the back of the stage that the band was not yet playing, but their equipment was all set and ready to go. Great, I thought, we haven't missed anything.

When Kylie stepped out of the limousine all eyes were on her. There were cigarettes held in mid air and glasses that never made the entire trip to the lip. She was stunning and they were hypnotized. I could see one woman touching the other woman beside her and pointing at Kylie. Maybe they saw her on television this morning promoting her book. I felt proud to be her friend. Kylie walked to the front of the car as I exited immediately following her and the eyes found me and locked me in. I stood long enough to say a few words to the driver who insisted on walking us to the door before he left. He bade us goodbye as we walked into the tiny club. We stood near the entrance for a few minutes scoping out the place. The entire left side of the club was mainly bar with a small area reserved for seating between that and the deejay booth at the back of the room. To the right of where we were standing you could see the small stage to the front of the club. There were about seven or eight tables to the right all the way to the back of the room with enough space left in front of the stage for a small dance floor. The overall ambience of the place was good. A few people were occupying some of the tables and I spotted a table for two near the stage against the wall. I nudged Kylie and she followed me. I sat with my back against the wall while Kylie sat facing the stage and I looked up just to see that even though the lights in the club were a little dim the people inside the club were staring at us too.

The waiter came over to our table. "Good evening ladies!" he practically screamed at us with this self-important look on his face. Kylie said good evening back and I nodded and proceeded to order drinks. "A bottle of bubbly please." I said in my best British accent. "Cristal if you don't mind."

"Right away my lovely," and headed toward the bar. Kylie rolled her eyes and said "asshole," almost loud enough for him to hear were it not for the music, which seemed much louder than when we first walked in. The waiter came back in record time only to inform us that there was no Cristal. I asked him to bring me a bottle of Dom Perignon instead, they didn't have that either so we settled for a bottle of Moet. The waiter returned again with our bucket of champagne and two glasses. He placed the bucket and the two glasses on the table then he popped the champagne and poured us each a glass, placing the bottle back in the bucket when he got finished. "Enjoy, your night ladies," the waiter smiled still standing in front of us. "Thank you," we uttered in unison. He nodded and walked away.

I picked up my glass just as Kylie picked hers up and I raised mine.

"To my best friend turned novelist. I always believed in you and I hope this is just the beginning of many more novels and all the accolades that comes with it. To you Kylie!"

"Thank you," she said as she tapped my glass with hers.

The band members were making their way to the stage and I recognized the drummer. Melanie went out with him a couple of times but when she found out he was staying with a friend because he did not have a place of his own, she quickly dumped him. She never told the rest of the girls about him because she did not want them judging her. You see, Melanie is the only one in our little circle of friends that manage to date two or three men at the same time. I happen to be the only one who knew him because she took me to a club where he was playing one night in Fort Lauderdale. I thought he was cute. Still is, but unfortunately for him cute alone doesn't cut it with Melanie.

I didn't bother saying anything to Kylie about him. I had no idea that he recognized me until he stopped at our table.

"Hello Natasha," he said extending his hand.

"Hi, how are you?"

"Good, thanks." Looking at Kylie with that same knowing look like the woman sitting at the table outside earlier.

"I saw you on television this morning," he said turning to Kylie. But before he could say anything else I jumped in.

"This is Kylie Mason; her book "Becca's Revenge" just hit the stands.

"Congratulations! I am an avid reader myself I will check it out."

"Thank you," Kylie said. She was never much of a talker.

"I gotta go. Enjoy the night ladies. Good seeing you again Natasha," He said walking away. I had no idea what his name was. The other members of the band were ready to play.

As soon as he sat down the band started up and Bob Marley's "No Woman Don't Cry" was the first song of what turned out to be an exciting one-hour set. It is almost impossible to go into a reggae club without hearing a couple of Bob Marley tunes at least. He was and still is the King of Reggae.

Kylie and I chatted and ate chicken wings that we ordered when the waiter came back to our table to "see how we were" he said. The food was good, and the music was better. We got a second bottle of champagne and the waiter was doing his cork-popping thing when the band members once again entered the stage for their second set. Our little drummer friend took the microphone.

"Ladies and gentlemen," he started. "We have one of South Florida's newest Authors in the house. You may have seen her in your home via your television screen. Ladies and gentlemen, please welcome the Author of "Becca's Revenge" Miss Kylie Mason."

Kylie was so surprised she wasn't sure if she should sit there and wave or stand up and give them the commemorative nod. I gently kicked her leg under the table as all eyes were looking in our direction. Everyone was looking to see her. She stood up slowly and made a couple of nods, smiling as she did so. The entire club broke out into a huge roar and the drummer gave us a drum roll and the music played.

It was three thirty when we met the driver of the limousine at the front of the club where he dropped us off earlier. On our way out people were shouting "congratulations" and "I can't wait to read your book." There were other really nice things being said but I couldn't hear them all. I got into the car before Kylie so she had the curbside window. I suggested she rolled the window down and wave as the car pulled off. Everyone was looking, and I mean "everyone". They waved back as the car disappeared around the bend.

We laughed and talked all the way to her house. Kylie asked me where I knew the drummer guy from and I lied.

"Uh, Melanie and I went to a club in Fort Lauderdale where his band was playing and he was hitting on her all night. It was cute." Well it wasn't exactly a lie I just didn't give her the full hundred.

"Oh." Was all she said and I knew that she believed me. I hate lying to her, we usually tell each other everything but Melanie wanted it kept a secret and I didn't want to betray her confidence either.

We hugged each other and said goodnight and Kylie exited the car. The driver closed the door behind her and stood on the sidewalk 'til she got inside and closed the door behind her. The driver dropped me off in front of my building and I could see Jeffrey appear in the doorway out of the corner of my eyes. I handed the driver a crisp one hundred dollar bill and thanked him.

"Had a good night miss Natasha?"

"Yes, thank you Jeffrey." I responded.

"See you." I said as the elevator opened for me, and yet again he was standing there looking at me with his mouth hanging open till the elevator door closed shut. Now I really couldn't wait to get in bed, I was pooped. I went straight to my bedroom and kicked my shoes off. I had left the air condition on so the place was cool and pleasant. I took my dress off, went to the bathroom and freshened up and it was none too soon when I finally hit the sack.

It's the middle of March but the Florida heat was kicking ass. The sun was bearing down with a vengeance and the streets were shiny from its glare. You could see that most of the drivers had their sun visors down, blocking the rays. I've lived here all my life except for the four years I was in college at Howard University in Washington D.C., but I still haven't gotten used to the heat. I wonder does anyone really get used to it. I always wonder why white people would lay out in the sun all day then look all fucked up the next in chase of a tan. Well, I do not need a tan of any nature, but if I had pale ass white skin I would not be laying out in the sun either, I know that for sure. Thank God for my dark skin. I was never known for wearing much clothing. So today I had on a little pink mini skirt with big white buttons in the front, a white tank top and pink sandal with a huge white button on top that matched my skirt to a tee. My little pink purse was the bomb too. I got the entire ensemble at a little boutique in South beach more than six months ago and this is my first time wearing it. Knowing me it probably won't surface again for another six months, and definitely not in Florida, in another country maybe, I hate to be seen in the same outfit twice, especially now when my career is about to kick up its heels and make a mad dash for the big times. It's been a long time coming and I think I have been more than patient given the fact that I have not been making much money. I really shouldn't complain though and I usually don't because I was always well taken care of. I thank God everyday for providing for me. I drive a nice Mercedes Benz, gold in color with matching gold leather interior fully freaking loaded with a bumping stereo system. I live in my very own two-bedroom two-bath condo in a very affluent neighborhood and being a clotheshorse I manage to spend thousands on shopping sprees. Don't get me wrong I do make decent money but nowhere near enough to support my lifestyle. I should really say thank God for Miles Covington.

I met Miles two years earlier when I backed into his Jaguar outside a grocery store in Aventura. I was driving a hunter green Toyota Camry at the time and while it was good looking on the outside I was having a warm time with it breaking down and needing a new part every time I turn around. I hit his front passenger side door and literally fucked up his car. When he jumped out of the car I thought maybe he was going to act like an asshole, because he looked like a corporate asshole in fine ass Armani suit and what was clearly some of the best shoes money could buy. He had a nasty look on his face and I braced myself for a tongue-lashing. He walked around the car and went inside his coat pocket and pulled out a cardholder, handed me a business card and the only thing he said before getting back into his car and driving off was, "This is making me late for an appointment, call me on my cell phone and we can make arrangements for you to take care of the damages." Before I could utter a word he was gone. Just got in his car and drove the hell off. That was weird.

I just stood there for what seemed like minutes after he left, not knowing what to make of the whole ordeal. He didn't ask for my drivers' license, insurance, nothing. I wasn't even sure if he even looked at my tag number. Anyway I recovered from my coma and drove home feeling relieved that he was in a hurry and didn't bother calling the cops.

By the time I got home it was past seven and I wavered back and forth on whether to call him then. Well, I remembered he said he was late for a meeting so I doubt he even got to the meeting yet let alone finish, so I decided to wait until later that evening. I made myself a cup of tea and as I sat on the couch sipping it, the unthinkable came to mind. Maybe I wouldn't have to pay, after all he took no information from me, and I am positive that he did not get my tag number because he did not go around to the rear of my car and I did not have a front tag. That thought lasted only minutes, I decided against anything shady that might affect my career.

I fell asleep when I finished my tea and when I opened my eyes again the clock over the mantel had both hands on eleven. Too late to call so I went to bed thinking there's always tomorrow.

The following morning right after my coffee I took the card from my purse, I realized I never looked at the card when he gave it to me. I just threw it in my purse. So I was shocked shitless when I saw Covington Motors, Inc. Oh shit! No wonder he was not furious, He was Miles Covington of Covington Mercedes. The buck did not stop there either, no sir. There were also Covington Lexus and Jaguar dealers. This dude had money coming out of his ass. Any notion that I had of charming him out of involving my insurance just went out the window when I read the card and realized that he was "The Miles Covington". This guy had more money than God and usually they are the ones who guard their money with their lives so I know he won't even try to give me a break. And as for seducing him with my womanly wiles I can forget that too. This guy's money can get him any woman he desires. He probably already married his pick of the lot, a man like that doesn't stay single for long, unless he has "gay-ward" ways.

"Okay Natasha," I said aloud, then I allowed myself to pick up the phone and without a second thought, without giving myself time to chicken out I dialed his number. It rang about four times and I was hoping that maybe he wouldn't answer and I would get a chance to just leave a message and have him call me back instead, but he answered. I could feel my heart coming through my cotton camisole. "Hello! Hello." He said hello twice before I eventually got any words from my now very dry lips.

"Hello, Mr. Covington, I am Natasha the young lady who hit your car yesterday, I am sorry I did not call you last night but…"

"Oh, don't worry about it Miss Bell, Natasha. I did not get out of my meeting until after eleven so I really did not expect your call until today." He said, cutting me off mid sentence. How the hell did he know my name what was he, working with the FBI? As if reading my mind, he continued, "I saw your photograph in Margaret's office at Mitchell's. She is a family friend".

"Oh, really?" was all I could say.

I was starting to feel a little uncomfortable; I really didn't know what else to say.

"Hello, Natasha. Are you there?"

"Ooh...Oh ye-yes."

Shit what the hell is wrong with me, I was acting like a mumbling idiot. Good going Natasha, you are just knocking him dead with that stutter girl,

I thought sarcastically to myself. He unknowingly saved me from further embarrassment while I tried desperately to get my tongue back from the cat that had it.

"I have a meeting to attend in five minutes, how about we meet somewhere for coffee or a drink and work this out later?" He said with a little more cushion in his voice.

"Sure. What…where did you have in mind?"

"Well, actually by the time I get out of here it will probably be way past six. How about I pick you up at eight,"

"Sure, let me give you my address." I never even gave it a second thought, not because I was flattered by his celebrity or anything but more like I had no idea what else to say. I was about to give him my address when he interrupted once again.

"I know where you are, I will be outside your building, see you then." Then he just hung the phone up. He just hung the hell up. The more I thought about it though the happier I got that he actually did hang up, after all cat had my tongue through most of the conversation. What the hell did he do run a background check on my ass? Was he having me followed? What the fuck did Margaret tell him about me? Did he even talk to Margaret about me? All those questions were taking up their own little space in my head. Maybe tonight I will get my tongue back. My heart was beating unusually fast and I found myself looking forward to seeing him. I came back to earth when a little voice inside my headed reminded me that I was not going on a date but to be tried and fined for a crime. But that thought lasted but a few seconds, because the distinguished Miles Covington was permeating my every conscious thought.

The day went by pretty fast, I ran a few errands, had my nails done and I couldn't resist a little black mini skirt outfit that I saw in a window on Washington street. It was made of raw silk, the alter top was quite simple but a little more effort was put into the skirt that was lined with spandex with a wide band sewn in the back on both sides of the zipper and joined together in the front by a huge black buckle about four inches square. I picked up a simple pair of black leather knee length boots and decided that would be the perfect ensemble for the date, um….meeting.

He rang my cell phone at exactly eight to tell me he was downstairs, I was impressed. I took my time getting there and ten minutes later he was opening the door to a bad ass Mercedes Benz. I was not really very surprised because he owned half the freaking car dealerships in South Florida it would seem. We did not say much by way of conversation on the way to somewhere past South Beach heading towards the keys except for a mere mention of the weather and other odd topics. He got off the highway and drove about a mile before he turned unto a dirt road that appeared to be heading nowhere, then as if out of the blue the road came to an end and there sitting in front of us was the most beautiful cabin I had ever seen, built from hardwood and red bricks with red zinc roof. I was taking it all in when he stopped the car and got out and walked around to open my door.

"You look a little pale, I hope you are not getting the flu or something," he said almost sarcastically.

"Oh no, I'm just fine thank you," I managed without stuttering.

"Good, 'cause I wouldn't want to keep you away from your bed."

I thought it would be best not to respond as he opened the door to let me out of the car. We walked a few steps to the cabin and when he opened the door my jaws dropped to the floor. Most everything inside was dark wood with hunter green accents, elegant and earthy, rich to say the least. But it was not the decorations and carefully selected pieces of furniture and artwork that captured my interest. In the middle of the living room sat a table with two chairs, candlelight and covered serving bowls with God knows what. It was really the candles that got me. My mind fast forwarded from its numbed state and I wondered how he could have a fresh candle burning and hot food on the table when he was at work all day, and another thing, that was no less than a thirty minute drive. There was no way he could have come here did all that, drove back for me and come back here and find steam still coming from the food. He must have done some helluva planning for this. What is this anyway, I thought. It was more like a date than a meeting and a very intimate date at that I was more nervous now more than when I was on the telephone with him. I wanted to ask him why we were there, why all of this but I didn't. I simply followed his every lead like a little puppy dog on a leash. He must have seen me as utterly unsophisticated.

"Please make yourself comfortable, Natasha," he said signaling me to the huge green and tan sofa, so huge it looked more like a bed, there was a matching armchair and dark wood coffee table, a couple of humongous plants in opposite corners of the living room, just perfect. I did not want to get ahead of myself so I opted to go with the flow. I wasn't nervous because I didn't think he would try to rape or kill me or hurt me in any way. After all why would Miles Covington want to rape or kill? It was the not knowing for sure what he had in mind, though the candles and the general ambience was a dead giveaway. Jeez, I hit his car and he catered dinner by candlelight, what if I had totaled it, maybe I would get a trip around the world or something.

He opened a bottle of champagne and the pop from the cork jerked me back from my inner thoughts. I have a tendency to get lost when my mind focus in on something. He poured two glasses and handed me one and sat beside me all in one stride. He was far enough from me that I doubted he could hear the heavy thumping of my heart, but he must have bionic ears because what came out of his mouth next left me dumbfounded.

"Is your heart racing for the same reason mine is Natasha." He was staring me dead in the eyes. Before I could open my mouth to say anything, like, I had anything to say anyways, he raised his glass and said, "To beating hearts." I touched his glass with mine and without even being conscious of what I was doing I put the glass to my mouth and swallowed every drop before I removed it from my lips. A small burp escaped my lips and my light brown skin turned red all over.

"I'm so sor—burp---sorry." Shit, I wanted the floor to open and swallow me up. I couldn't fathom why I kept making such a fool of myself from the moment I encountered the man.

He sat his glass down laughing his ass off as he did so then he took my very empty glass from my grip and sat it down beside his then he turned to me, "Are you alright? Or are you just making it really quick so you won't have to spend time with me?" he said still laughing but not as hard as before.

"I'm so, so sorry, I have no idea what got into me, please forgive my behavior."

My heart was still beating fast but at least I was no longer stuttering or just being totally tongue tied, at least I was making full sentences and hopefully maybe a little sense.

"I'm not usually like this, I'm so sorry." I continued.

"No need to be sorry, you are perfect", and as he said those words from his lips his eyes pierced mine with the unspoken. I was captured by his charm and confidence. I thought maybe he would have come off as an arrogant fucker but not a chance, this man sitting beside me may be a fucker but I seriously doubt he would be the kind of fucker that I would object to.

"How much damage did I do to your car Mr. Covington?" I blurted out of nowhere.

"Well, you have forced me to admit that I did not take the time to get an estimate. "Will you forgive me?" He said faking a puppy dog look on his face.

"Then why are we here?" I was trying to sound serious, but I was none too sad about being there. Something inside me made me wanted to be there, though I wasn't sure what it was, but whatever it was sure made me numb. I was always big on conversation; generally you can't shut me up.

"I would much prefer if you called me Miles". He smiled at me looking me dead in the eyes again.

"Okay Miles, why are we here?"

"I was saving the good news for after dinner, but if you insist." He paused then added, "I have decided to forgive your debt." He said in a more business-like tone.

"But… why?"

I knew I was asking a question that I already knew the answer to but I wanted to hear it straight from the horse's mouth.

"You sure know how to put a guy on the spot."

"Really, I'd like to know why someone would hit your very expensive Jaguar and you just decide you are going to let them off the hook. Explain it to me." I leaned forward with my elbow resting on my crossed leg and my chin in the palm of my hand.

There was a brief wave of silence between us that lasted only seconds but seemed like minutes.

In a sudden motion, with the same fluidity as when he first sat down, he stood up and offered his hand to me.

"We should eat, I'm starving."

I took his hand and stood up, and like a true gentleman he led me to the table. Suddenly I too was starving and the sweet smell of something was overwhelming my taste buds.

After chowing down on lobster tails, baked potatoes and a mixture of steamed vegetables, we sweetened things up with warm pumpkin pie topped with whipped cream. Dinner was absolutely delicious, just what the stomach ordered.

For another two hours we talked about everything we could think of and the conversation was much easier. I suppose dinner was the icebreaker.

By the time he got back to my apartment it was almost one a.m. He insisted on riding with me in the elevator and seeing me to my door, and I had no interest in deterring him. I opened the door, then turned back around to say goodnight. He leaned in to kiss my cheek and I unintentionally turned and my lips met his. Neither of us moved we just stood there with our lips brushing, but he apparently came back to earth a litter quicker than I did. He stepped back and said, "Good night Natasha, thank you for a lovely evening. I'll be in touch." Then he just walked to the elevator and disappeared. I was still standing there long after the elevator door closed my hands were still shaking and my palms sweating profusely. I finally made it into the apartment. I immediately kicked off my shoes and by the time I made it to the bedroom I was down to my panties and bra. I went to the bathroom and freshened up some, brushed my teeth and went to bed with him on my mind.

The following day he called before ten and we made arrangements to meet again that day, and within weeks we were literally dating.

The appearance of Miles Covington in my life had changed me in ways indescribable.

Chapter 2
KYLIE

I could hear the cheers coming down the hallway as I got off the elevator toward my small office at the Doctors Medical Center where I worked as a billing coordinator. I had taken Monday off but I did not tell anyone what was happening. After what happened with the first book I wrote, or maybe I should say try to write, because everyone I sent it to sent me a rejection letter. Well, not just a letter, I learned fast that rejection came in big packages when all the potential publishers sent my manuscripts back with the letters. I was so excited when I finished my first book I told everyone who would listen about it, so of course when it did not surface in any bookstores, naturally everyone kept asking about it so of course I was forced to tell some of them about my rejections. I knew a couple of bitches in the office were laughing and talking shit, but look who is laughing now. The majority of my co-workers were happy for me though, genuinely happy, so except for those outnumbered few everything was just peachy around the office.

My boss Dr. Jim Armstrong came out of his office and met me with the biggest bouquet of roses I had ever seen. There were no less than five-dozen roses in five assorted colors. The cheering stopped and you could hear a pin drop, but everyone still had their smiles still plastered all over their faces. It was too much for me, and the tears started rolling down my eyes.

"No tears today Mason, today we celebrate," he paused for a moment and everyone applauded then he broke out into a speech like we all expected. Dr.

Armstrong was also a Professor at the University of Miami and was a well sought-after public speaker.

"Kylie you know we have all been rooting for you, and we knew that you would not stop with your first book, though you kept this one under wraps. We are all very proud of you." He paused briefly and the applause came again.

"We have come up with a little something that we hope will help, though it may only be a drop in the bucket of the full scope of things. We have each purchased a copy of your book and would love to have you sign them for us, if it's no trouble." He smiled and winked at me.

"Oh, thank you guys, that was so thoughtful of you, I don't know what to say, look what you all did, now I can't stop crying." I really didn't know what else to say, I did not expect anything like this. I had no idea they cared so much and I just could not keep the tears from coming.

I spent quite some time signing books and I was further overwhelmed when some people put two books in front of me on the desk they had cleared for me. They were making gifts to family members and friends. By the time we were done it was past ten, normally the center opens at nine in the morning. I asked about that and Donna who also works in my department told me that Dr. Armstrong had someone rescheduled all the patients for later in the morning so that they could throw me this little shindig.

As if the flowers and supporting me the way they did was not enough Dr. Armstrong generously gave me the rest of the week off with pay. I left the office around noon and spent the rest of the afternoon shopping. I found a really tough outfit to wear for my appearance on Kelly and Michael Live the following morning, but I certainly did not stop there, I just went all out and bought outfit after outfit, shoes, bags and accessories. By the time I got home I was exhausted. I had an eight o'clock flight to New York tonight for my appearance on the Kelly and Michael Show so I had just enough time to pack and get ready for the airport. The bigwigs on the show were providing me with first class service all the way starting with a limo to take me to the airport. I called each of the girls while I got ready, and promised to call again once I got to the hotel in New York.

The car arrived at 6:30 but traffic was a horrible mess so I got to the airport with just enough time to check in and run all the way to the airplane. Fortunately I had no luggage to check in or I would not have made the flight. The limo driver had suggested that we left earlier than we did but I insisted on leaving at that time, so I'd have no one to blame but myself if I had missed my flight.

The flight to the big apple was quite smooth thank God, because I have a phobia about flying and height. Then again I have quite a few other phobias if you ask me, like being afraid of large bodies of water and spiders and cockroaches, frogs, lizards you name it, I'm afraid of it. I wonder why they call New York the big apple may be because everyone would like to take a bite, I don't know. This was actually my second time in New York and that first time was so very long ago I barely remember anything. I did not go site seeing or anything, I think I went shopping or something like that, only for a day though.

I arrived at my hotel about 1:30am and thought about calling the girls, but it was so late I was sure they were already in bed, except for Natasha of course, who would not go to sleep until she heard from me and knew that I was in my hotel room safe and sound. I pulled my cell phone from my purse and dialed her number. She picked up on the first ring. "Hello." She answered cheerily.

"Hi Nat, I didn't wake you, did I? I just got to the hotel."

"Oh no, I was waiting for your call."

"Well, I won't keep you up any longer and I should go ahead and get some sleep myself, they are picking me up at a quarter to seven in the morning."

"You're right you should get your rest so you can be at your very best when I watch you on the show tomorrow. Not that you need it."

"Girl you're too kind, I need every bit of beauty rest I can get."

"Well, break a leg and call me when it's all over. I'll tell the girls you called. Oh, we are having breakfast together at Amanda's so we can watch the show together."

It made my heart happy to hear that, those four women are close to my heart I love each of them with all my heart, and it just made me feel good inside the way they support everything I do. We have a special bond that I have never seen or heard of with so many women in one place. A lot of people feel like wherever there are two or more women there is always tension, jealousy and backbiting, but not us. We love each other and it is more than apparent in the way we care about each other and feel each other's pain.

"I know I could depend on y'all, now I won't be so nervous knowing you guys are there together rooting for me. I love you Nat but I have to go, I'll call you after the interview."

I wanted to chat longer and I knew that Natasha was feeling the same way, but if I stayed up any longer I will probably wake up with bags under my eyes.

"Bye Kylie, Love you too. We'll talk tomorrow."

I hung up the phone and set it down on the nightstand and plugged in the charger. When I arrived at the front desk earlier I asked the front desk clerk to give me a wakeup call at five thirty so I wasted no time getting in the big king size bed with soft white linen. I have stayed in hotels many times before but never anything like this. This was the ultimate five-star hotel. It took a while before I finally went off to sleep but when I woke up at the sound of the telephone ringing in my ear I felt well rested. Did I mention the bed was ultra comfortable.

The limousine provided by the show picked me up at six forty five on the dot. It took only twenty-five minutes to get to the studio and they shuttled me straight to hair and makeup. I was wearing the outfit I picked up the day before and I thought it looked mighty cute. My thoughts were confirmed when everyone in hair and makeup couldn't stop gushing over how well it fitted me perfectly. It was a Versace two-piece pants suit, red with gray pinstripes and matching gray tank top with strappy gray sandals. It was a professional, fun look. The jacket was fitting in the waist and slightly flared at the hem, with long sleeves with flared hem. The pants were skin tight with flared hems to match the sleeves of the jacket. I dropped nearly two grand on that number so I had better look good.

The stylist pinned my hair up in a soft bun that coupled with the make up to make me look years younger than twenty-eight. I was happy with my look, I was confident. I admit there were butterflies in my chest mainly because the show was live and I was a little worried about how it might turn out. Maybe I shouldn't worry too much though, since my appearance on the Today Show turned out to be a breeze. The more I thought about it the more relaxed I became. If I survived Katie I could most definitely survive Kelly and Michael, they are a lot more fun anyway.

I met the new hot actor on the block Shane D'Marco who had a blockbuster movie that hit theaters only a week before. He looked so much better than he does on the big screen and he was like eye candy on screen so you can imagine him standing right in front of me in all his handsome, masculine glory. I was floored but I kept my cool. We chatted for a few minutes until it was time for him to do his thing, then he wished me the best and promised to pick up a copy of my book. When he finished and returned backstage I handed him a signed copy and he gave me a big hug and promised to let me know what he thought. I knew that I would probably never see him again, in person that is, but I told him that I look forward to it. After all, his world is a world away from the one I'm in so there's hardly a chance that I will run into him again. But something deep inside me made me want to see him again. I felt it the moment his back went through the door to the elevators. For a moment I totally forgot why I was there and wanted to follow him to the elevators, out the door and to wherever the hell he went. I imagine he never gave me a second thought, but why would he when he must certainly have access to some of the richest most beautiful women in the world. Chances are if he should for some reason run into me again he wouldn't have the slightest idea who I was. Kylie who?

I feel a light touch on my shoulder and was brought back to earth.

"Miss Mason you're on." The woman said in a very small voice

"Oh, thank you." I said making my way to the stage door that was pointed out to me earlier, even though it's right there for me to see.

Kelly and Michael took turns ranting about the book then finally called me to the stage.

"Ladies and gentlemen! Here in our studio; all the way from Florida; the Author of Becca's Revenge; Kylie Mason!" And the crowd roared as if I was someone famous, like they really knew who I was.

I walked out with my shoulders back and even managed to strut my stuff pretty well to the stage where I got the standard hug from both Kelly and Michael; even they acted like they knew me. I loved it.

My three minutes went by really fast but not before Kelly proudly announced that they had purchased copies of my book for all the people in the studio audience. I was so close to tears but I thought about the girls watching and my parents and my sister. I did not want any of them to see me crying, no sir.

I was asked to stay and sign the books for the audience members and they did not have to ask twice. I was so happy to oblige, there had to be at least two hundred people in the audience, so that's two hundred more units sold. I was overjoyed, everyone was so nice to me they made it so easy.

By the time I was ready to leave the studio it was noon, of course Kelly and Michael was nowhere in sight, but they had someone on hand to assist me with anything I needed. I finally made it to the elevator and down to the lobby where my limousine should be waiting to take me back to the hotel. I had the room for the rest of the day until check out time the following morning and the limousine was at my service until the moment I get on the plane back to my home in Florida.

When I got off the elevator, I was taken aback. Maybe that's too mild a term, I was actually blown away, for a second time today because standing directly in front of me as I stepped off the elevator, was that actor I met earlier Shane D'Marco and he was holding a bunch of white roses in his hand. I smiled at him and stepped to the side so he could get on the elevator, but he moved over and blocked my exit.

"These are for you." He was wearing a very broad smile.

"For me, what did I do to deserve this?"

"Maybe it's not want you did but what you didn't do."

He lost me there, I had no idea what he was talking about and was just getting ready to ask him when he cleared it all up.

"I was quite aware of your reaction to me telling you that I would tell you what I think when I read the book. I could tell you didn't think I would read the book much less take the time to tell you what I thought," he paused as if to challenge me to say otherwise then he continued.

"Am I right or am I right." He said handing me the flowers.

"I'm, I'm........thank you." I managed to say without embarrassing myself. I was in shock I couldn't see why he would go through all that trouble just because of what I thought.

"You've been here all morning. I thought since you were so kind to let me have a copy of your book the least I can do is to take you out for lunch. I understand you are not from New York, so you could probably use a guide for a little site seeing." He was almost whispering.

"Sure. How thoughtful. I came here once before but I didn't see much, just a little shopping trip." I was starting to loosen up.

What was there to be tense about anyway, I was going to have lunch with one of the hottest actors in Hollywood and possibly spend the rest of the afternoon driving around New York with him, really what was there to be tense about? I should be doing back flips. I haven't had a man in my life since that bastard Milo I was shacked up with walked out on me for some fat ass bitch because she had won a hundred thousand dollars in the lottery. But I am having the last laugh because now I am worth more than twenty times that now and counting. He has been begging me to take him back, but I changed my number and he has no idea where I live now. Good for his pathetic ass.

"Come on, let's go."

He took the flowers in one hand and held on to my arm with the next leading me out the door.

"I have a car waiting for me outside, we could take that." I said not sure whether that was what I wanted or not.

"Then we'll take your car."

We had a lovely lunch, Chinese. I was surprised that he was such good company. Actually I was surprised that I was not the least uncomfortable. We went to see the Statue of Liberty and we even visited ground zero. He told me one of his uncles died in that 911 attack and that was the first time I saw him look sad.

We spent the rest of the afternoon just driving around site seeing and I returned to my hotel about six p.m.

He was staying at another hotel about a mile away and we made plans for him to pick me up with the car at nine o'clock for dinner.

Riding the elevator to the seventh floor where my room was, I couldn't help thinking that maybe this could be more than just a run around New York and dinner. Why would he want to spend all his time with me, I'm sure he has lots of friends, specifically girlfriend who would be delighted to be in his company, so why me?

While we were visiting the Statue of Liberty he told me he wanted to ask me to lunch when we were waiting backstage but he did not want come on too strong and he wouldn't want me thinking he did that with every pretty woman he met. Yes, he said pretty woman. Not that I am objecting, I could be considered eye candy, or at least that's what I think. So what if no one else thinks that. But Shane D'Marco called me pretty and that was enough for me.

It was kind of weird though, when he said it. I barely mumbled a "thank you" because I was not sure if he meant it. Shane was a pretty boy, prettier than most women. It could be his mixed blood. He was definitely black but you could pass him off for a white guy, and he certainly didn't behave like your typical black guy, he didn't have that black pride about him. I guess it's because he grew up with the white side of his family. I read that in the tabloids somewhere.

He had a lot going on for him with his new movie out and being the new face, or should I say new ass for Calvin Klein underwear. With all his new found successes and being as hot as he was, I couldn't imagine why he would want to take me out. He was just on Saturday Night Live this past weekend. Well let me not get ahead of myself, maybe it is just what it is, dinner.

As soon as I got to my hotel room I called Natasha but I got her voicemail so I left a message and then dialed Keri's number and I also got her voicemail. What the hell is going on, I thought they were anxiously awaiting my call, then again what did I think, they were all busy with work just as much as I was only my work took a three hundred sixty degree turn into a whole other direction, the whole television bit and all. I am not complaining in the least, I am definitely happy with how things are turning out these days. I always thought that I was meant to do more with my life than the normal nine to five routine that I found myself in year after year. I was an English major in college and I graduated with honors. I wanted to be a College Professor but by the time I graduated I was no longer interested in that career. I eventually went back and got my masters only because my parents felt like I let them down. They wanted me to get my masters because none of her sister's children got theirs, even though my mother would not admit to that being the reason but we all know how she is about her children being the best.

I decided to call Melanie next and she picked up on the second ring.

"Hello my famous friend," she said answering the phone.

"Oh girl, you're too kind I've only appeared on two talk shows, for what, umm maybe ten minutes total. So officially I haven't yet had my fifteen minutes of fame, so you might want to hold off on the celebrity tag for now."

"Girl, stop being so modest now, you know it's upward bound from now on."

"Well I sure hope so."

"You were great this morning, you were so much more relaxed than when you were on the Today Show. Maybe you are getting used to the interview thing already."

"I should be a pro by now, don't you think? Think about how many times I sat on the sofa rehearsing the day when my book is finally published. Remember how I used to get on y'all nerves having you pretend to be Oprah or Ellen or any of the many talk and news show people I turned you into?" We both giggled.

"So you know you owe us a percentage of the millions you will be bagging?"

"Have your people call my people." I deadpanned, and we busted out laughing. I was happy that she was so happy for me like I knew all the other girls were. We had a real strong bond between us and I think it is safe to say that there were no jealousies among us. After all we all had wonderful lives, what was there to be jealous about.

We chitchat for a little while, but I never mentioned that I met Shane because I wanted to see how things turned out before I said anything. I stayed so long on the phone with her I did not have any time left to call anyone else, I did not want to be still getting ready when Shane got there.

I still had enough time to indulge myself in a nice hot bath, normally I would not, ever take a bath in a hotel, but like I said this was no ordinary hotel, it was "The Hotel." Those showbiz people sure know how to live it up. Maybe one day I will work my way up to the penthouse, thank God I don't think that day is very far away. Well, I stayed in a penthouse suite before when that fucker Milo and I were together, but that was no match for what they have going on here. What am I talking about? I am now on my way to becoming one of those people who get to enjoy the finer things in life.

I immersed myself in the bathtub with my eyes closed and feeling the water caress my skin felt like heaven, I could most certainly get used to this. I have a feeling though that from now on it will be first class all the way, I can't believe this is happening but who is complaining, I have waited for what seemed like all my life for this, ever since I was a child growing up I always dreamed of writing my own novel or being an actress. My Aunt Kate thought I should be more realistic and settle for a nice position in some company or another so I could be guaranteed a regular income, hut that was never good enough for me. I truly hated working for others, especially when they have you on their strict schedules. I realized that when I got my first job after leaving college. I was working for the local telephone company and punching the clock was a bitch because I was never early for work, by their standard that is. The workday started at nine as per most companies and if you punched in at 9:01 a.m. you were considered late. What kind of shit is that? I thought slavery days were over? So I really never got too comfortable under that sort of regime.

After my oh so soothing bath I put on a brown single breasted pants suit with a cream mock turtle neck sweater bottomed off with ankle length brown and cream stiletto heel boots. It's still winter so New York was actually like a big old freezer turned way up. I had brought along a full-length leather coat so I was well prepared for my night out in the cold. However, that may work in my favor because he might just be sweet enough to put his arms around me to keep me warm, but I know there is no chance that will happen because those big celebrity types are usually very cautious about what they do in public because of the forever lurking tabloid reporters. Then again the poor guy might not have anything like that in mind. I should really control my thought process or I am sure to be disappointed.

He had the front desk ring my room at approximately nine o'clock and when I got off the elevator he was standing there with a single rose waiting for my exit. I just stood there with a big smile on my face and he took a step toward me, handed me the rose, took my arm and we walked out to the waiting car. The poor girl at the front desk was frozen from being star struck.

I was ultimately comfortable in his presence, he was easy to talk with and I was pleasantly surprised by his sense of humor. That always got me, the sense of humor thing. I love a man who can make me laugh more than I talk and believe me I can talk the ears off of an elephant.

He took me to a little place in Manhattan that looked like a mom and pop restaurant from the exterior with a very tiny neon sign that read "EATS". When the car pulled up in front of the building, for a moment I thought maybe we were having car trouble, but that quickly straightened itself out when the driver got out and opened the door for us. He got out first then helped me out like the gentleman that he was but I was still wondering why we would stop in a place like this. I started thinking all kinds of disappointing thoughts as we walked toward the door. But my disappointment was short lived as a big black bouncer type gentleman opened the door for us. It was absolutely beautiful on the inside and he could hear the deep breath that I took when we entered.

"This is my father's place, some of the best Italian food you'll find in New York." He said as we continued walking toward the back of the room.

"This is absolutely breathtaking," was all I could say."

"This is the Italian side of the family; my mother is a black, English woman who still lives in England where she met my father."

"Oh, they are no longer together?" And I could kick myself for asking.

"Never was."

A young Italian girl approached us, and led us into a room that was apparently set up just for the two of us.

"There you go, big bother," she said with the biggest smile on her face.

"Thank you sis, good looking out" and gave her a huge hug.

Oh, my bad. Carmen meet Kylie, Kylie my sister Carmen."

"My pleasure, I am glad to meet you." I said stretching my hand to her.

Shaking my hand, "Oh my God I saw you just this morning on television." Then without missing a beat she turned to Shane. "I thought you said you wouldn't date a celebrity?" heading for the door as she spoke.

"Bye Carmen." He said rolling his eyes at her.

"Bye, nice meeting you Kylie," she giggled as she left the room.

"She can't wait to see me with a wife and kids. She is my only sister and we all spoil her. I have five brothers I am the youngest and the only one not married with children." He pulled out a chair for me to sit and made sure I was comfortable before he pulled out his own chair.

The only table in the room was set up with a huge variety of Italian dishes. Shane explained what they all were. We chatted through dinner and it felt so good just to be there with him, I wasn't even hungry anymore, though I was before he picked me up. Just seeing him was enough to fill me up. Boy, this trip turned up more benefits than I expected. Wait until I tell the girls about this. Natasha was always a huge fan of Shane D'Marco since his very first movie a couple of years back. I know she will be thrilled and totally jealous. She called him her dream man. The brother was just hot with a capital H. Curly black hair that comes all the way down his temples forming a perfect line down the side of his face, he was clean shaven with a million dollar smile, he was standing at a towering six feet four inches, I read that part in one of those magazines, he has been on so many covers since he evolved on the scene I forgot where I read what.

I had no idea how or when we ate all that food I just know that at one time the table was filled with food and then there were almost none. I may not know how or when but I most certainly know why I can't remember. I was so caught up in conversation with that fine, intelligent character that I hung on to his every word. I am sure the food was just delicious, but I can't remember how any of it tasted, but I could probably tell you every fine detail about Shane's features not to mention those beautiful lips masking the prettiest set of teeth I'd ever seen outside of a toothpaste commercial. He talked mostly about his family but didn't say too much about himself, at least not the things I wanted to hear. However, he did mention one thing that grabbed my interest, he was definitely single, well single but dating.

I did not say too much about myself for fear that I might bore him to death, I'm sure he was used to all kinds of sophisticated women with interesting backgrounds who were much more worldly than I was, actually I was not worldly at all. I wondered if what his sister said was true. The part where she said he prefers not to date celebrities. Well, he should feel safe with me because even if my book sold millions I wouldn't consider myself a celebrity. I thought that was usually reserved for the Hollywood movie, television and music people. A little writer such as me wouldn't exactly fit into that category, well maybe if my book is made into a movie but for right now I'm just happy that I am published.

In another two months I will have to start writing again because my publishers signed me to another three-book deal with yearly releases. It took me quite some time to finish my first book so I better get started soon. I have a whole month of promotional appearances and book signing lined up and after that I think I want some 'me' time, so the girls and I have a little trip to Jamaica planned. I will have to quit my day job in order to start writing full time but I opted to wait until my four weeks of vacation time is over. After that surprise party at the office when the good doctor gave me the week off I put in for my vacation that was long overdue before I left the office. So when it's time for my return I will just go ahead and turn in my resignation and spend another two weeks to tie up loose ends and say a proper adios to everyone.

When we got back to the hotel Shane suggested drinks in the hotel bar and I was happy to oblige, because I did not want to part ways with him just yet. The hotel bar was almost empty except for two couples occupying two of the booths and two men sitting at the bar and a woman sitting at a table close to the bar. We sat at the far corner of the bar where we were not easily detected should someone walk in, not that we were hiding or anything, well maybe he was but I was quite comfortable either way.

I had strawberry daiquiri and he had scotch on the rocks. I could manage no more than a couple since I could feel my head getting light and I found myself laughing more than usual. I was not a very good consumer of any kind of alcohol, but Shane seemed to be doing all right for himself. I really didn't give a heck if I got a little tipsy because my room was upstairs. After a couple hours I was exhausted, because it was almost two in the morning and I have a flight to catch at ten o'clock.

He insisted on riding the elevator and walking with me to my room. When we entered the elevator I pushed the button to my floor and the door closed. Immediately he took my hands in his and looked me in the eyes and said, "So will I see the beautiful lady again, or is this the end of the line for you?"

That question caught me off guard and also put me on the spot all at the same time, but I wasted no time responding.

"Would you like to see the beautiful lady again?" That actually came out of nowhere, and he smiled and moved closer to me, and before I could take the next breath his lips were parting mine and I was lost for a moment, I didn't even realize that we were already at my floor and the door slid open with his mouth still on mine. He stopped kissing me just as suddenly as he started.

"Does that answer your question Kylie?"

I was still reeling from the kiss but I got my breath back long enough to answer.

"I guess." was all I could get out.

He stepped off the elevator with me and walked me to my room. I opened the door and said, "I had a wonderful time, thank you for making my visit here interesting."

"Have a good trip back to Miami and please call me when you get there so I'll know you're home safe and sound."

"I will. Thanks again."

"I can't wait." He said as he placed one last tiny kiss on my nose and turned in the direction of the elevator. I stood there nonplussed and watched him as his feverishly masculine frame disappeared into the elevator. I was still standing there looking in his direction even though he was long gone, but I pretty much had no choice because I simply could not move my legs. I had no idea whether he was pulling my chains or not. I imagine he must do this a lot it seemed so easy for him. I willed my legs to take me into the room where I just kicked my shoes off and plopped down on the bed.

I will never, ever forget that trip to New York of course for so many wonderful reasons. Being on the Kelly and Michael show was the highlight without a doubt, but I could never forget the handsome Shane D'Marco. The way he wined and dined me and made me feel the whole time I was in his company like I was the only living soul around him. Like nothing else mattered but me. I was just bursting to tell someone, I could tell Natasha right away because she was my best friend and I felt like I couldn't keep that beautiful little secret to myself. But I decided to wait until I get back to Miami at least. Actually I should at least wait until he called me again. What if it was just a spur of the moment thing that lasted for as long as we both were in New York then forgotten as soon we got back to where we came from? I should wait until I hear from Shane again. That's it, I will wait until I hear from him again, that way I won't embarrass myself in case he never called.

Chapter 3
MELANIE

"Mel, Donna is here she is in a hurry as always." Jennifer my shampoo girl said whispering to me through the slightly opened door to my office. I had just returned from the long lines of the Department of Motor Vehicles where I went to get my drivers' license renewed and I really was not in the mood to deal with the likes of Donna, but she was one of my best customers who was probably responsible for referring close to half of our clientele, so we made sure she was happy. Donna was very popular and knew everybody who was anybody. She spent half of her life shopping and the rest between the hair salon and the gym. She is one of the most beautiful women I have ever seen and most people seem to like her except for a couple of jealous girls in the shop. But she didn't give a damn, she knew they were just jealous, and she loved it. I like Donna she is just real.

"Donna is just going to have a shampoo and roller set, so go ahead and do that and you can come and get me when she is dry."

"Okay." She said and closed the door.

Jennifer answers okay to everything, she never complained and is always on time. She is the best shampoo girl I have had since I opened the shop a year and a half ago and believe me I have had a few. She also assist a couple of the other hairstylists in the shop because I did not have a lot of clients myself only a selected few, because I hate to be tied down doing hair all day and then having to do the books, to be honest I was never that good at the hair styling thing, but I was very knowledgeable when it comes to the theory of the hair. Jennifer is well liked because she never said much and she stays out of other people's business. She is never caught up in the usual shop gossip and chatter that is so synonymous with beauty salons.

It is Thursday and I am exhausted, I have been taking only two clients per day since I opened the shop so I am never tired from working. Of course I made a lot of money because I had eleven hairstylists, two barbers and two nail technicians on commission and I just started selling my own signature products with the salon name and logo and sales are going through the roof. If I were to be honest with myself I would admit that it's the men in my life who were keeping me tired. You do not get to have three lovers and not be tired. I am not like a slut or anything I think I handle it all quite tastefully and I haven't heard of anyone gossiping about it, though if they were I would be the last to hear. But who gives a flying fuck anyway? Certainly not me, I never cared much what people said about me because if you are doing bad, good or indifferent people will always talk and when I look at it people don't just talk about nobodies, you have to be somebody to have them tongues wagging.

I plan to leave the salon as soon as I style Donna's hair. For some reason that's beyond me she like for me to hook her up when the rollers are out. Like I said I am not the best stylist in the shop but she doesn't give a damn about that she just will not have anyone else touch her hair, and if Jennifer is not there to shampoo or prep her for whatever she was getting she would wait until one of us was available even if she had to come back the next day. Girlfriend was that serious. So I will just hang around long enough for that and then I can go home and get some well needed rest before I see my newest man tonight. Jerry the drug dealer, yes I said it, the drug dealer.

Jerry Underwood was not everybody's favorite kind of guy because he was unorthodox in everything he does and is. He is a sharp dresser with a whole lot of blings and you could see drug dealer written all over him down to his custom-made Hummer. I met him one night when I was locking up the shop. I was pulling down the outside shutters when he pulled up next to my car in his big yellow hummer, rolled his window down and asked, "Do you do men?"

"We are gender friendly around here, so men are most welcome." I said as I finished pulling down the shutters.

"When can you do me? He asked with a sheepish grin on his face.

"That would depend on what exactly you want done, we open at nine in the morning you can stop in then for a consultation."

"Fair enough, but who do I ask for?" he said with a big smile like I had just given him a compliment or something.

Oh, just speak with the person at the front desk and she will assign you an available stylist."

I did not mention that we had a couple of barbers on staff because he was wearing dread locks so he would have no use for a barber.

"I think you are the one I would like to take care of me so you could go ahead and tell me your name and I will just ask for you when I get there." He was relentless.

"Fair enough; it's Melanie." And we both laughed in sync.

"I'm Jerry. See you tomorrow Ms. Melanie."

He drove off and I got into my car and headed home. I really didn't think he would show up, he was just trying to be a player, I thought.

The following morning I was late going in, I actually didn't get to the shop until about quarter after eleven and I was shocked to see Jerry sitting in my chair I almost tripped over myself. The man was gorgeous, decked out in designer clothes from head to toe. I must not have taken a good look at him, then again how much can anyone see with him sitting in that tanker of a vehicle. He was tall and lanky with bushy eyebrows, and now that he was in the light in plain view I could see that his dread locks were shiny and neat and boyfriend had perfect lips. I am a lip girl so that was really a big turn on for me. When we spoke the night before, I did not take a good look at him. I did not want him thinking I was interested in anything he was saying, but as a businesswoman I had to be polite for fear of losing a potential client. Every single one of them counts to me. If only I could get a couple of the girls in the shop to understand that.

I said good morning to the receptionist and she pointed to my chair and told me that he had been waiting since ten o'clock and insisted on waiting until I got there. She also told me that he told her not to call me on my cellular phone because he was an old friend and wanted to surprise me.

Well, he most certainly did surprise me. I really wasn't expecting him to show up much less wait over an hour for me to show up. I walked over to my station where he was sitting and greeted him just like I would any other client that did not have an appointment.

"Good morning, did we have an appointment today?" I said in my most pleasant voice.

"Good morning Ms. Melanie I did not know I needed one." He said with a sheepish smile one his handsome face. I hadn't noticed that he was so good looking, not that it mattered he was not my type anyway.

"Well I did say you were welcome to stop in for a consultation." My voice was much softer this time, after all he was a potential client and I never turn anyone away.

"You sure did." He said still smiling. Good thing he had good teeth.

"What can I do for you today um….?"

"Jerry."

He jumped in before I could say his name, but it was a good thing because I didn't remember his name.

"Jerry, what can I do for you?" I said with a little smile of my own.

"Actually, I just wanted to invite you to lunch, if you don't mind." He was no longer smiling.

"Lunch? I'm sorry but I do not have time for lunch." I was caught off guard and I could see from the corners of my eyes that some of the workers and even the clients were looking in our direction.

"Dinner then?" He persisted.

"Well, I work late and…….." he interrupted once again.

"Then how about drinks after work, you pick the place." He was smiling that infectious smile again.

Deep down I really wasn't sure that I should turn him down because the brother was looking good, smelling good and was just simply reeling me in. I took a card from my desk and wrote my cell phone number on the back and handed it to him.

"Call me in a couple of hours and I'll let you know." All eyes were on us by this time and I would do anything to get him out of there before I made a fool of myself.

"Fair enough, I will call you in a couple of hours then." He said taking the card from my hand making sure that his fingers touched mine. He wanted me to notice his sly little move because he made sure his fingers lingered a little longer than was necessary, but I pretended not to notice.

We said our goodbyes and he left. I watched him walk out the door and remembered that I did not see that big yellow hummer parked outside. My unasked question was answered when I saw him open the door to a red Mercedes convertible on the other side of the street. Brother was rolling heavy every which way. I cannot pretend that I was not impressed by how he was rolling. I guess I'm just as materialistic as they come.

I turned to walk to my office and everyone was looking at me smiling. No one dared say anything because they knew very well that I would have no part in their idle chatter. I was careful not to get too personal with my staff and especially the clients. I was the ultimate professional, I wasn't a stuffed shirt or anything, I just knew from my experience and other peoples that it wouldn't be in my best interest to get too familiar with the people who work with me. I was adamant about the avoidance of gossip.

Jerry called in two hours like he said he would and I politely turned him down again, but he insisted on calling me back later that day to see if I changed my mind. He called me another two times that day and I finally relented and took him up on his dinner offer, but I was way too busy to find time before Saturday evening. The busiest days at the salon were the weekend days. We are usually closed on Sundays and Mondays so I could definitely find some time for myself from Saturday night.

I kept my promise and went out with him and I have been hooked on him since. It has only been six months since we started seeing each other but I see much more of him than I do the Lawyer and the Preacher man that's rocking my other worlds.

My friends have no idea about him and the preacher man. I made them think that Jim, the lawyer was the only man that I was hooking up with. I love my friends, all of them but sometimes they can be judgmental and they would probably think I'm a slut for sleeping with more than one man, especially Keri she has the tendency to act like she is holier than thou and always get on my last nerve, she thinks that any woman who have more than one sexual partners should be an outcast, treated like vomit. It is such a double standard in our society, that when a man has more than one woman he's a stud or a player, but when a woman does the same she's a slut or a bitch. Well I refuse to live my life by their standards, especially Keri's so I will just have to live by my own. Seriously though, I wonder if Keri ever gets any dick. It doesn't matter that she has a husband as fine as Miguel, I still believe she is lacking in the dick department. The girl is just way too stiff.

I am a believer in the notion that a woman was born with her riches. When you think about it there is some truth to it. I am not saying that a woman should sell her body or even use it to get what she wants, that is not what I am saying but if she puts any value on herself at all she would want to make sure that the man she was laying up with is willing and able to take care of more than just her sexual appetite. He should be able to put food in the refrigerator, clothes on her back and most definitely a roof over her head. I think a girl's free-pussy-days should be over the moment she becomes a woman. I have known so many women who claim they have a man and still complaining about the bills that it made me sick. I made up my mind a long time ago that I would never claim any man or let any man claim me unless he was taking care of me lock, stock and barrel. I value my assets, especially the ones I was born with, the ones God so generously gave me. If I don't take care of them then who will?

I styled Donna's hair and she left me a huge tip, that girl can really spend money. I bet she is not one of those women who give up her goods for free. I think there was a song to that effect in the eighties; I think it was called something like 'No romance without finance' by Gwen Guthrie. Donna has a lot of money the girl drives a Hummer and a Mercedes Benz and some other shit I don't even recognize and she wears nothing but designer clothes. I wondered where she got her money from because I know she did not work, but she was never one to discuss her personal life so I never got answers. She is loaded though and everybody knows it.

Tonight I'm meeting Jerry. I am going over to his place. Usually we would go out and eat, or go dancing or something like that then we would always end up at his place. He has never been to my place because I told him I was living with someone, so he is under the impression that I am cheating with him on my man at home. That works very well to my advantage because I have no place for drama in my life.

Jim Monahan, the lawyer I only see him once a week because of our hectic schedules; his mainly. He is a family man who believe it or not loves his family, but that apparently is not enough to keep him from making love to me. He is the only white man I have ever been with and I am truly impressed. I've heard stories that white men carry a smaller tool kit than black men. Well this white boy owns the tool shop. Sex with him is awesome we seem to just jell so well together, that is also true in our personalities. But the first thing that helped me to make up my mind about him when we first started seeing each other was his generosity. It was just before Christmas, two weeks to be exact when we first met at the courthouse downtown, Miami. He was there doing his lawyer thing and I was there on a speeding citation. We rode the elevator together on our way out of the courthouse and he said hello and asked if I was a lawyer. I gave him some kind of smart answer and we had a big laugh about it. There was a hotdog stand nearby and he offered to buy me one, I accepted, I didn't even like hot dogs but I knew that the hot dog was just a way of getting my attention for real, and I didn't mind giving my attention at all, he was hot, so hot dog it was. Jim and I became an item shortly after that first hot dog together. The day before Christmas we met for lunch and he wrote me a check for ten thousand dollars and said merry Christmas. I almost choked on my dessert. I will never forget that afternoon.

My other lover, the preacher man, the Reverend Michael Langston, the leader of some big church somewhere outside of Boca Raton, he was my number one man. We have been sneaking behind his wife's back for almost three years and he too takes care of me lock stock and barrel. He was the one who funded my salon business, down to the last dime, and he also was the one who bought me my four-bedroom house in Pembroke Pines and was responsible for thousands of dollars in my savings account. The good Reverend knows how to take care of a woman. He was taking good care of his ailing wife as well. She was suffering from Multiple Sclerosis or something like that and it was in its acute stages by the time he started fooling around with me. Him I met at one of those big conventions where the Reverend T.D. Jakes was speaking, we were both fans of his and went to see him speak. We were sitting next to each other in the front row and we had our own little conversation going on between speakers. Nothing ungodly. We mainly talked about the topics that the speakers spoke on. He gave me his card, I wrote my number down on the back of one of his cards and he called me the next day. We saw each other for quite some time before sex came into play. See, his wife had not been able to give him any since her MS worsened right about the time we met. We saw each other for almost nine months before our bodies surrendered to each other and we have been showing each other a hallelujah good time till today. I see him twice each week. Seeing him only twice per week and Jim once per week I have a lot of time to be with Jerry. Actually I really don't have that much time for Jerry either, but I see him a lot more because he is the only one who would stop in at the salon to see me, neither of the others ever just drop in. They have both been there but not when the salon is open, I let them both stop in if they must on days when the salon was closed.

I left the salon about two in the afternoon and headed straight home and slept until my alarm woke me up at seven o'clock. I am meeting Jerry at 8:30 at his place. He was also living in Pembroke Pines only ten minutes from my home but I wanted to look really good for him tonight. Of all the men I have been with Jerry is the most uninhibited of them. There are no boundaries where sex is concerned and he does things to me that make me wonder about his mental state, but I love it all.

I showered and pulled on a little long sleeve yellow dress and matching nude pumps, and I had my hair pulled back in one. I have really long wavy hair that I sometimes blow-dried straight, tonight it was straight but I know what will be going down tonight so I may as well get it out of the way already. Jerry always joked about all the hair I have, both on my head and between my legs. He sometimes complained about not being able to go down on me to the fullest because the hair is always in the way. I trimmed it down some but if I try to shave or wax I would end up with little tiny bumps between my legs and believe me that is a lot less attractive than some hair. I definitely could not wear a bikini without getting rid of the hair. When I go to Kylie's home for her pool parties, she love to have pool parties, or just to hang out I will go into the water but I stay put at the shallow end of the pool and I normally ditch the bathing suit bottom for a sexy pair of shorts.

When I got to Jerry's place, a nice little two-bedroom condo in a gated neighborhood, I could smell something really good going down in the kitchen all the way from outside the front door. Jerry love to cook. I knocked. He opened the door and gave me a tight squeeze.

"I hope you are hungry because I made your favorite, shrimp scampi."

"Starving, you always know just what I want."

"And you always give me just what I need."

I laughed.

I took a chair at the small kitchen table and he moved about the kitchen doing his chef thing.

"What is that I always give you? I asked even though I knew what the answer was. "I sometimes wonder if I even begin to take care of your needs the way you do mine baby."

"You don't hear me complaining, do you? And you do know what it is you give me." He said putting a plate in front of me.

"But seriously, would you complain if there was something to complain about?" I asked.

He put his plate on the other side of the table and sat down. Boyfriend had garlic bread, salad and a bottle of wine to go with the shrimp scampi. But that was Jerry though he loved to cook for me and since I hate cooking so much, it is just fine with me.

He took both my hands across the table and leaned in toward me.

"Look at me." he said and waited for me to look him in the eyes.

"Melanie, you fill me up in ways you maybe wouldn't understand. You are the number one person in my life right now, you are the only girl I'm sweating, and you know if you were not with that guy you live with I would be more than honored to be the man in your life, girl you are already the woman in my life. Do you understand that?"

I had never heard him talk like that before. Jerry was a good man but there is no way I would consider settling down with him while he was still in the business of selling drugs. I have been lying to Jerry since I met him making him believe that I was living with Jim, he has no idea what Jim looks like so that made it easy. I like the arrangement that Jerry and I have so I hope his ass is not getting mushy on me. It's not that I don't care about Jerry, I feel much for him but I cannot afford to live my life looking over my shoulders to see if the police was coming or some other drug dealer with a beef. He has another place where he worked from and none of his cronies knew where he lived so I felt comfortable in that sense. We spend very little time together in public, whenever we want to go to a club or to dine, we would go to one of those out of the way places where it was unlikely we would run into my crowd or his. Otherwise we just chill out at his place and fuck each other's brain out. Quite like what we will be doing tonight.

"Is that how you really feel about me baby?" I asked in my most innocent voice.

"Every inch of me." Still looking in my eyes.

"Let's eat before the food gets cold." I wanted the conversation to go in another direction.

"Sure, we'll have plenty of time to talk when we are finished."

Dinner was delicious and we ate it all up. Jerry loves to watch me eat when he cooks. He thinks that he could be a chef for real, and I must admit that I do agree with him. He had skills all the way up and down his body.

We watched about twenty minutes of a movie that was on cable and we just had to stop to make our own movie. He had a hard on that rivaled the Washington Monument in both length and strength. I couldn't wait to have him inside me and I knew he couldn't wait to be there. I pulled my panties down and spread my legs and he wasted no time getting out of his pants. I had quietly pulled a condom out of my purse and I had it ready in hand. I used my fingers to place it over the tip of the dick and used my lips to roll it all the way down the shaft. He loved it and I could feel his dick pulsating between my lips as I rolled the condom all the way down or is that up. I just wanted him inside of me right away, he kissed on me a little and I begged for him to put it in me. He fucked my lights out. Sleep came easy.

I awoke again at around three in the morning with Jerry eating my pussy. He knew that was the only thing that could get me awake and keep me awake at that time of the morning. He devoured me like a man on death row having his last meal. There was a storm raging inside me and when it finally landed I hollered like a banshee and he just swallowed me up. He put on a condom; we never do it without a condom I couldn't take a chance like that because I still do not know much of what he did when he wasn't with me.

"Open up baby." He said breathing really hard now.

"Oh Jerry, take me, take me, take me Jerry." I cried.

"Oh yeah, yes mommy." He hollered back.

He was deep inside of me and I could feel him moving in and out, back and forth, and heaven came down on earth right there in Jerry's bed.

It is Friday morning and I am back at the salon but not for long. I was so tired from the night with Jerry that there is no way I could stay there all day. Jennifer will be staying until closing like she always did when I have to leave early. She was more than just my shampoo girl she was also my extra pair of eyes when I'm away from the shop. I pay her generously so she doesn't mind one bit. She was no doubt one of the better-paid shampoo girls anywhere.

Tonight is girls' night, the night we all get together and catch up. Kylie got back from New York yesterday and I cannot wait to hear how it all went. I saw the show but I wanted to hear what happened when she wasn't on television. How she spent the rest of her day that kind of thing. I spoke with her before she left New York but she did not have time to go into it, she was hurrying to catch her flight. So tonight we will all get to hear about it, I hope she has something juicy to tell us. I mulled around the salon and then left for the day. It's not very often that I take time off from work, even though I can whenever I feel like it, but I learned early that it would be in my best interest to spend as much time there as possible for the good of the business. Jennifer is the only one who knows I won't be coming back for the day. I prefer that the rest of the staff stay in the dark when it comes to my coming and going, because they sometimes have a tendency to slack up when I am not around, but if they are not sure whether I'll be back or not they will more likely toe the line.

Driving home my cell phone rang and it was Jim. He just wanted to tell me how much he missed me and wanted to know how I liked the flowers.

"What flowers?" I asked puzzled.

"What do you mean what flowers? He was also puzzled, apparently he sent me flowers but I did not receive any before I left the shop.

"Where did you send it?"

"To the salon, I didn't expect you to be home on a Friday."

"Well, I just left there and it did not yet arrive, maybe they are running a little later than you expected." I rationed.

"I specifically asked that it be delivered by ten thirty."

"Well, I'm sure it will get there don't worry, and thank you baby. You always know just what I need."

"You're more than welcome sweetheart, if I had time to deliver it myself I would."

"I know."

My other line was ringing. It was someone from the salon, Jennifer no doubt.

"Hold on baby, someone from the shop is on the other line."

"Okay, I'll hold."

It was Jennifer, just as I thought. She called to let me know that a couple dozen roses had arrived for me. I thanked her and asked her to put them in one of the vases that I kept there for just that purpose then I switched to the next line where Jim was still waiting patiently.

"Jim."

"I'm here. Is everything alright?'

"Couldn't be better; that was Jennifer letting me know that my two-dozen roses came. Jim you're the best no wonder I am so crazy about you."

"Like I am crazy about you? I have to run sweetness I will call you later this evening. I love you Melanie, but you must know that by now."

"I know baby, and I love you too." I was lying like a dog but he didn't have to know that. Sometimes I wonder if I really love anyone or even if I could love anyone in that way.

"Bye sweets." He said hurriedly.

"Bye baby."

I don't mind hearing from these men how much they love me but to be honest I didn't love any of them. How could I, Jim is a married man and so is Michael the reverend and as for Jerry I was just afraid to love him because he was definitely deep in the game. So love was not on my agenda at this time. Why should it be? I would only be hurting myself in the long run. What's the sense in falling in love with someone I may never have for myself? Of the three of them the only one available on a permanent basis would be Jerry and why would I want to tie myself down with him when he lived so dangerously. I would hate to spend any of my time visiting him in jail, that's not my bag. Maybe if he gets out of the business I would consider it. Actually there is no maybe about it, I would lock him down in the bat of an eye, but it is obvious that was all he knew. I was shocked when he admitted to me just a month after we met that he was a high school dropout and he never did get his G.E.D. You see why I can't tell the girls about him. With their hoity toity ways and all they would definitely think I went to the bottom of the barrel. Really I shouldn't give a fuck about what anyone thinks but these were my girls and we do care about each other. I love them all, even stuck up ass Keri who acts like her shit doesn't stink. I bet that bitch has a lot of bones in her closet. Of all the girls I think I have more issues with her because she is so fucking self-righteous. She carries on as if Miguel is the only man she ever slept with; I wonder if she forgot that we all went to college together. She was no saint then and I am sure she did not just evolve into one. I just wished she was not so condescending and judgmental all the time. I get the feeling that she more than likely would cheat on Miguel if she met the right man, and boy does she meet them. Girlfriend was making mad money from that flower shop she owns down on South Beach. She specialized in exotic flowers from all over the world and if you did not have a limitless credit card you have to think twice about walking into her shop. She caters mainly to the rich and famous, supplying them with flowers for their weddings, garden parties and all the other events you could think of that warrants flowers, even for their homes on a weekly basis. You know how the rich and famous roll, only real live flowers in their homes and all; and she would tell us stories about the men who came in to do business; how they would flirt with her and ask to take her out but she never took any of them up on their offers. I am not sure I believe that she turned them all down, but I guess I have to take her word for it. She can get on my nerve with that shit from time to time but I love her nonetheless.

Sleeping during the daytime was always a challenge for me, so I closed all the blinds and the curtains upstairs to darken the place so I could fool my brain into thinking it was nighttime. I had no idea how long it took for me to fall asleep but I did until the telephone rang and woke me up. I didn't bother answering it, I just turned it off and threw the covers over my head and went right back into my slumber.

Chapter 4

AMANDA

I awoke to the sound of R. Kelly on my clock radio. I had set the alarm the night before for 7:30am and I could have sworn I had no more than a nap, as I raised myself up and reached for the stop button. Seemed like only minutes since I closed my eyes. I sat on the edge of my queen-sized bed, legs stretched in front of me breathing the comfort of my ultra modern bedroom. The cream Italian lacquer bed had strategically placed mirrors on the head board that is stretched against the back wall of the room with two matching night stands one either side of the bed that appeared to melt into the headboard that made the three pieces more like one. To the north of the bed against the wall stood the matching dresser with a round moon-shaped mirror and just a hint of mirrored glass stretched across the width of the dresser, just above the triple rows of drawers. Occupying the south wall, about two yards from the foot of the bed was an oak computer desk with cubicles filled with papers, magazines, manuals, bills and other knick knacks. Burgundy lace curtains hung at the double window facing the west wall matching perfectly with the huge burgundy cluster of flowers on the golden rod feather down comforter on the bed. The look was completed with matching pillow shams and bed skirt. There were also two cushions in burgundy. The entire color scheme offsets the cream colored carpet and puts the room in total harmony with the cream paint on the walls to give the place a highly decorative look.

I wiped the sleep from my eyes and struggled to my feet. I walked over to the linen closet that is located just outside the bedroom door, reached in for a washcloth and fresh towel and headed to the bathroom. As an afterthought I hurried out of the bathroom to the kitchen where I started the coffee brewing. I gotta have my coffee. Minutes later the shower was running and I was singing as loud as I could off key, while the steam from the hot shower became a sea of fog engulfing me. A steaming hot shower is one of the staples in my life.

An hour later, having swallowed my first cup of brew and already sipping on my second; I hurriedly got myself together. I took one last look at myself in the mirror and was satisfied with the image that stared back at me. I was ready to face the world. Well, not exactly the world, I was actually off to see him again. My mystery man, he made me promise not to ever tell anyone about him. I have been hiding and sneaking into hotels all the way between South Beach and Orlando for a year and a half now and I kept promising myself that each time will be the last time but something about him just keeps me going back. I want to tell myself it's the sex but I know damn well it's the money. The man takes very good care of me. If only he was single, I would definitely be chasing that ring. His momma had him well trained. He makes me feel like a queen when we are together and he sends flowers and little gifts out of the blue. The cash flow is continuous and I find it quite refreshing to associate myself with a man who knows that a woman needs money and she should not have to ask for it. A man who really knows how to handle himself will make it his duty to make sure that the cash flow is continuous. At least that is my take on things.

His career would come to a halt if anyone should find out about us and with his wife being sick and all. I like it that way though, because I would hate to be tied down with a man that I would have to cook for and clean up after. I think I'll have a lot of time for that in the next ten years or so. No one should settle down at twenty-six, because here I am twenty-six and I still haven't experienced anything much. And I mean anything! I am not a virgin don't get me wrong. I am so not a virgin but I have not yet experienced anything to make me click my heels three times or take me to seventh heaven on cloud nine. Since I started having sex at sixteen I have only been with three men, Okay, make that five and I still have not yet gotten an orgasm without a tongue involved. That shit that I hear Melanie and them talk about. Not only does she get them, she's getting them from a white man, I thought they said the brothers had the key to open that lock, so how come no one is opening mine, are the locks rusted or something? What the hell is that? My mystery man can barely get his up and when he does he has just as hard a time keeping it up. So I usually don't have to worry about him causing me any pain, or bruising anything. When I said it wasn't the sex that kept me going back for more, that was not altogether true. I cannot live without his lips between my legs so I guess I could say that I have actually experienced the cloud nine thing, only I took a whole other route getting there.

Apart from all that, the money and all that other stuff I talk about I really enjoy being in his company. He has a way of making me feel like everything revolved around me and what I like and want to do. Though the knowledge of his wife at home ill, never leave my head. I guess that must be conscience. He told me I was the only woman who could make him cheat on his wife and go against all that he truly believed in, but he believes that God understands and will forgive him for what he was doing because he would not have done it if his wife was well or expected to get better. I guess I am also guilty of anything that he may be guilty of because he never lied to me about whom he was or why we had to keep our affair secret. Not that I would ever want to go public given the circumstances.

Today I am meeting him at some fancy hotel down on Coconut Grove and I really can't wait to see him. I am wearing a pair of black Guess jeans, white oversize cream sweater by no one special and some bad ass black leather knee length boots with an oversized Michael Kors bag thrown over my shoulder. I called and he gave me the room number, our usual way of doing things. We never enter the hotel less than two hours apart, that way no one will have a clue about who I may or may not be visiting.

Traffic on I95 can be a bitch sometimes and today is one of those times. I sat in traffic for I don't know how long only to find out that there was some kind of bomb scare incident that turned out not to be a bomb scare after all. While

I appreciate the government taking extra precautions against terrorism and all I truly could not appreciate them picking today to do it. I have not had any in a while, the tongue thing mainly and I am as hot as ten firesides so getting there fast is of ultimate priority. This is how we always do it, Mr. Man and I; that is my little name for him, Mr. Man. He would get to the hotel and check in and I would show up a couple of hours later making sure I was not seen by anyone. When I get in the lobby I would call him on his cell phone to let him know I was coming up and by the time I got to the door it would be unlocked and I would just let myself in. That way I would have no reason to knock and alert the other guests or draw any attention to us whatsoever. We had it all worked out and we never use the same hotel twice and if we did it would be months later. That was upon his insistence, not mine. Really I couldn't care less who saw me with him but I have to respect his wishes if I want to continue seeing him. I would not want to do anything to scare him off I need him around for more reasons than one.

After about forty-five minutes of not moving more than five hundred feet, the traffic started moving steadily until it picked up to a normal pace. I arrived at the hotel and followed our normal routine. He was on the sixth floor and the elevator could not get there fast enough for me. I have no idea why I was behaving like this, what had gotten into me, but I sure was horny in aching-kind-a-way.

I entered the room and he appeared from behind the door somewhere and shut the door behind me then gently pushed me back against the door, took my face in his hands and kissed me deeply and passionately. I could feel inside my panties getting wet and warm and my vagina was suddenly pulsating. There was a fire burning down there and he was fanning the flames. My keys and bag fell from my hands to the floor and my knees became weakened. This has never happened before. Not with him. I suddenly find myself regretting that he was married. Maybe, just maybe I could keep him with all his other accolades, if he could make me feel like this all the time I could be a happy camper. But how much longer can I go on seeing him when I know he will never leave his wife for me, for anyone. With his very affluent standing, just leaving his wife alone would be cause for major concern not to mention leaving her for another woman.

We devoured each other with a passion neither of us had ever shown each other before. I had no idea where inside me it was coming from, and I was even more baffled about where inside him he found all that he was unleashing on me. There were no words between us, our fingers tongue and eyes did all the talking.

He slowly undressed me and lifted me up with my legs wrapped around his back, walked over to the huge king sized bed and laid me down gently, He pulled my sweater over my head while kissing my belly. He slowly pulled my pants down, moved my panties to the side and slowly moved his tongue down the center of my mound slightly opening the lips as it slid down the length of it. I was burning inside. He quickly stepped out of his boxers, the only thing he was wearing when I arrived and slowly covered my body with his. He continued with slow, gentle kisses from my lobes to my breast then all the way to my moist middle where he lingered and lingered filling me with feelings and emotions he had never exacted from me before. I reached heaven and I swear I had no idea when he entered me all I know was there was a sweet pounding going on inside of me causing me to lose my mind. We met each other at a place where neither of us had gone together before and I knew then that I would keep going back for more for a long time to come. Not that I have anyone else to spend my time with. I had to take the shit back I was saying about his lousy dick game. I guess he wasn't lying when he said it was because of all he was dealing with. He was definitely on point tonight.

We ordered room service and spent the rest of the afternoon talking and watching television. I must admit each time we get together it keeps getting better and better and I am not necessarily talking about the sex, but everything else.

I told the girls I had to go out of town for the day and that I would be back the following morning, so lying up in the hotel with him was just perfect for me. I would not want to take a chance on running into one of them. I hate that I can't tell anyone about him. How do you keep such fantastic moments to yourself? I feel like I would want to brag a little sometimes but I have to be careful not to let my tongue slip. He would always say it's a small world and one does not know who knows who, so we have to be careful to keep it just between us.

The girls, especially Keri always ask how I manage to do all the things I do on a department store manager's salary and I always change the subject, until I couldn't evade the questions for too long so I lied that I made more than the sixty thousand per year I was getting. After college I did not do any work in biology for which I got my degree or I would be making a lot more money than I am now but once I left college I found that I was no longer interested in science, biology or any of that stuff. I just was not enjoying myself at any of the jobs I found myself in, so here I am the manager of a major department store and having the time of my life doing it. No weekend hours, except for once in a very blue moon around inventory time, good benefits and all the clothes I can buy on discount. Most people could live very well on sixty thousand per year with no children to provide for but not me, I live high on the hog, only the best for me. I am mostly happy with the direction my life is taking. In another eight months I will be looking to open my very own clothing boutique even though I haven't told anyone about it yet, except for my mystery man who will be carrying me on that venture. I will tell the girls about it once the space becomes available. The people occupying the space will be out in five months they are expanding and moving to another location. It should be ready to go three months after that. As soon as the current occupants' leave I will tell all the girls. They have been bugging me about doing my own thing for a long time so I know they will be happy for me. So many good things are happening for us, we are so blessed to have each other. I feel bad about keeping secrets from them but sometimes it is necessary.

Before nightfall Mr. Man and I romped and burned up the sheets with our newfound passion. Maybe I should start calling him Mr. Long because he had more than enough stamina for himself and a soccer team and there were just times when I truly forgot how to be a lady. I even think that at one point I was speaking another language, one that he understood very well, because he kept pressing the right buttons, playing me like a guitar, strumming my every pleasure leaving me sluggish as the last note echoed through the air that was my body.

We talked about the same things we usually talk about but tonight he opened up to me in ways I never expected him to. He talked about his life and the way that he chose to live it, and that he was grateful to God for everything, but that there are times when he felt like God was punishing him, by making his wife ill and leading him to the decisions that he made along the way. Then he talked about how he felt about me, telling me time and time again how much he loved me and cared for me and that he believed that God brought me especially for him. Of course I told him how much I love and care for him that I too wished the circumstances were altered.

Just as I thought that I had everything under control, I start feeling too good about Mr. Man. I could see him being my husband, the white picket fence and all. I knew all along that financially he could definitely take care of me, but now I also find that he could take care of me sexually if he could just keep up the same way he did tonight. But what in the world was I thinking. I know I can't have him because he will not leave his precious little invalid wife.

It is amazing what some good dick can do. Before tonight I was quite happy with the way things were between Mr. Man and me. I was even sympathetic to his wife's condition, whatever the hell that was. But after tonight, with him unleashing the full one hundred on my ass, I want him, all of him. Some girls do have all the luck. Then again, on the other hand how much luck could poor little wifey have confined to a wheel chair with a cheating husband. Maybe I am the lucky one here, what was I complaining about.

He emphatically denied having any other woman but me and I guess I have no reason not to believe him, after all a man of his status could not afford to be so careless and carry on too many extramarital relationships or he would be foolish. I know for sure that I would never tell anyone about us but some women just cannot keep their mouths shut so he would need to be careful. I should admit that I really have no idea what he does when he is not doing me, so I really just have his word to go on. But nonetheless I take him at his word.

We spent the night together and ordered in breakfast before we left the hotel. I left ahead of him and went out a side door to the parking lot to my car. I turned on my cell phone that I had turned off the evening before. I had several messages but I could wait till I got home. I was about to put the phone down on the seat beside me when it rang in my hand. It was him.

"Hello darling." I said happily.

"Someone is sounding bright eyed and bushy tailed this morning." He said sounding happy himself.

"I just wanted you to know that you are second to none."

I knew right away what he was getting at. I had said something to him about how disappointed I would be if I found out I was playing second fiddle to anyone but his wife.

"From your lips to my ears baby." I said smiling.

"I love you Amanda, you are my breath of fresh air.... how I love breathing you."

"I love you too baby." I said it though I was not sure if it was true or not.

"I'll call you tonight, be good."

"Bye..."

On the drive home I pondered on what he said about me being second to none, I guess he wanted me to feel like I was the only woman in his life other than his wife. But what if I wasn't? Could second to none mean that I am first of the other women? Maybe I am reading way too much into what he said, I was drowning in my own paranoia. He was a man of many words, very quick witted so I have to analyze his every word. What was I, shitting myself? I am sure that he lied to his wife about his whereabouts, there were times when we would spend a whole week together in some faraway hotel, and what about the time we went to Jamaica for a whole two weeks, what did he tell her about where he was and what he was doing, or should I say who he was doing.

It is a good thing that I am off from work this week. I took an impromptu vacation that was long overdue so I will be well rested for our girls' night out. I have to go to the bank and run a couple errands but I will have plenty of time to relax before I meet with the girls. I look forward to Friday nights because it is actually the only night that I get to let down my hair and throw all caution to the wind. I missed the last couple of Fridays because I had to go see my mother in Virginia. She was having another of her nervous breakdowns and as her only daughter I felt forced to go and be with her. One of my two brothers is in the army and is stationed overseas and the other one does not give a fuck about anyone but himself. He married some white girl and moved to California forgetting that he has a family back in Virginia. Sometimes I really can't blame him for the way he is because my mother was not there for any of us. She ran off with some white man herself when I was only five years old leaving my two brothers and I with her mother. All three of us were different fathers and none of them stayed around to see about us. My brothers were seven and nine at the time. Thirteen years later my mother returned a drunk with major medical problems stemming from drugs and alcohol. She has been a pain up my grandmother's ass ever since. That was one of the main reason I did not stay in Virginia once I finished college. I did not want to be saddled by her problems. Where the hell was she when I needed her? My visits are getting less and less. I tried to get grandma to sell the house and move here to Florida in a condo but she loves Virginia. She has lived there all her life and has no intention of moving anywhere else. She once told me that when she died she will leave the house to me and my brothers, but I think we would all agree to just let my mother live there until she dies or something. We would not want to see her homeless even though she did not give a fuck when she was leaving us those many years ago. My grandmother told us the whole story. I could maybe understand and try to forgive her if she was strung out on drugs or something, then maybe I could chalk it up to her having a disease that got the better of her, but she was very okay when she made the decision to leave. The man she left with was an up and coming politician and had a lot of money, she claimed that he loved her but apparently he did not love her enough to want her children around, so grandma said she just up and left one day promising to come back for us really soon. Really soon came thirteen years later.

I have been sending money to my grandmother to help out but I told her not to let my mother know about it or she would pressure her too much, plus I don't really give a fuck whether she thinks I am doing anything for her or not. If I were to be totally honest I would admit that it is really because of grandma why I really went there those last two weekends. I really wanted to take some of the pressure off her so she doesn't worry too much about my fucked up mother.

My life is full of issues. I have a mother who does not give a fuck if I live or die, a father I don't know, an asshole of a brother who abandoned us just like his mother did and a man that belongs to another woman. Is that as good as it gets? I should get a damn dog or something. Someone to love me; someone who won't run out on me when the going gets tough or just when they don't want to be bothered anymore. My life is a lot more dysfunctional than I thought, but is there any wonder.

I am sure my youngest brother Peter, the one in the army would be dysfunctional too if he was as weak as Anthony. He is the one who ran off to California without turning the black of his eyes to see how we were doing. It doesn't bother me as much that he has abandoned Peter and me but for him to just turn his back on grandma the way he did made me sick to my stomach. She was the one who had to work two jobs to take care of us after her no good daughter left. I doubt if she knew who our fathers were because none of the three of us have ever met our dads. Without grandma we would have ended up in foster homes, but as far as Anthony is concerned we may as well have because the asshole act like everyone moved out of the neighborhood or he no longer remember how to get there. Like mother like son. I hope his black ass doesn't show up one day like our mother did after the white man's world got too much for her.

Peter and I have always been in touch, he was only a couple of years younger than Anthony but he was way more mature than Anthony. Always was. He is stationed somewhere in Iraq and I worry about him every single day. He writes all the time and calls every chance he gets. He helps out grandma too so with her pension and whatever she gets from the government we both make sure all her needs are taken care of. Together we pay the cost of a live-in housekeeper so she wouldn't have to work anymore than she wants to. Lord knows she worked hard enough to take care of us and see us through college and all, so that's the least we could do given that she does not want to do the relocating thing. What is it with these old people anyway, why are they so afraid of change. I thought that the winter cold would get to her enough by now to make her change her mind and move to sunny Florida, but I could plead until the cows come home she would not budge. We are left with no option but to accept her wishes and do the best we can for her. She is a very agile seventy seven year old woman who has no problem doing things for herself but she was so good to us that we refuse to do any less. Peter and I promised each other that we would always take care of her. We made no such promise about our mother but we know that she benefits directly from the help we give to grandma. I guess if grandma should pass away, God forbid, we would have to continue helping our mother, though I have a feeling she will be gone long before grandma with her heavy drinking and stuff. I think it's only drinking, but who knows she could be doing a lot more than just drinking. Well, I guess we will just have to take care of her too, bad as she is she is still our mother, but she better get herself together and start helping herself even just a little. I am sure she knows that Peter and I help grandma out, there is no way she could live the way she does on her pension and social security. But I am not complaining I know that any good daughter, any good person for that matter would want to help their own mother out. I just can't help her by sending her money directly or I would be really helping her with her alcohol addiction because that is all she would do with the money, buy alcohol. So this way, giving it to grandma is definitely the way to go. She has a roof over her head, food on the table and clothes on her back. She will just have to do the rest for herself. I offered to pay for rehab a few times and she turned me down so I stopped asking, suggesting or even mentioning anything about it.

When I got home I cleaned up a little and made a few phone calls before I just hit the sack and watched movies until I fell asleep. I woke up in the middle of the night and could not go back to sleep no matter how hard I tried. I wanted to call one of the girls to chat but who else would be up at two in the morning. I turned the television on and channeled up and down until my eye caught Mr. Man preaching his ass off. I was taken aback because I had never seen him at work before. Ironically his message was about Adultery, and I just sat there open mouthed and took it all in, for I don't know how long, maybe a half hour or so. All I could think about as I watched him move around the podium was how good his dick was only hours before. All I can remember about the sermon was the word adultery, but I heard nothing else. I kept thinking about how good it felt when we were doing it, committing adultery. But to hear him talk about it made me feel like shit, like God was about to beat my ass with a two by four.

I really could not fall back to sleep after that I spent most of the night thinking what a hypocrite he was. I felt like his big accomplice but what was I to do. The man takes care of all my financial needs I can't just give it all up because of one sermon. I knew what he did before I got involved with him at least he did not lie about that. But to hear him preach boy, was a kick in my reality groin.

The last time I look at the clock it was four fifteen. I stayed in bed for most of the day, getting up only to take a shower and eat. Later I will be hanging with the girls. It is such a shame that I cannot share with them about Mr. Man. I promised to keep my mouth shut about us and I will damn well honor that promise, especially after I actually saw him on television with my own two eyes and see how the congregation latched on to his every word. You could see the dedication in their eyes as they amen their way through his sermon. I realized that I cared about him too much to even judge him. What was he to do anyway, every man need some good sex from time to time was it his fault that his wife was too sick to give it to him?

Whatever the reason he and I got together in the first place, it is certainly working out for me, and I have to be concerned with me first but I am sure that he is getting quite a bit out of it himself. After all he is only human and of course I make good company, which led me to wonder if I was the only other woman keeping him company. It would certainly bother me if I found out he had another woman separate from his wife. Since I am already putting up with the fact that he has a wife I do not believe that I should tolerate having to put up with another woman too. I most definitely want to be the only other woman in his life. The only other woman he makes love to. I guess that I would really be the only woman he makes love to if what he said about his wife not being able to have sex is true. I do believe I am falling in love with him, and I think it only just happened last night. There was something in the way that he made love to me, the way he felt inside me, the way he held me, and the things he said to me. He made me feel like the only woman in the world.

My heart is finally warming up to someone after my last relationship.

It was only four years before when I met Phillip and immediately we got close. I remembered very clearly the day that we met. I was on my way to the drug store to pick something up and I stopped at a red light and he pulled up beside me, looked over and said, "I have no idea where you are going but I am willing to follow you just so I can get your phone number." I did not know what to say so I just smiled. When the light changed he did get in my lane behind my car and followed me to the store, which was only a half a block away. I was a little nervous because it was dark and the parking lot was not brightly lit. So I got out of the car really fast and hurried into the store, there was security there so I calmed down my nerves. I was searching the shelves for hair color when he walked right up to me and extended his hand introducing himself as Phillip Grange. He said something about me taking his number since I did not care to give him mine and pulled out a business card with his name on it. He was the vice president of Grange Construction, a family owned business. I saw their advertising on television all the time. I was impressed, and he was over six feet tall and as handsome as they come with smooth chocolate skin. I took the card and promised to call and he went on his merry way.

It was two months later when I finally called him and he took me out to dinner one Saturday night and almost every night after. After six months into our relationship, six months of seeing each other almost every day, Phillip asked me to marry him and I wasted no time saying yes. I remember he wanted to get married right away but I wanted the kind of wedding that little girls dreamed of and that would take some planning. The wedding was to take place approximately six months after the engagement. That was as long as Phillip was willing to wait. So I spent that whole six months feverishly planning what was to be my most important moment, the moment I say I do to the man who had totally captured my heart. He was totally involved in the planning and insisted on paying for the entire affair. That was a blessing in disguise because I heard somewhere that the parents of the bride should pay for the wedding, and seeing I had no parents so to speak it was good that he wanted to pay.

Everything was going as planned until the night before the wedding. The girls had planned a bridal shower for that night at Kylie's boss' home and Phillip's friends were throwing him a bachelor party at a hotel on South Beach. My bridal shower was over by midnight and Keri, Melanie, Kylie, Natasha and I decided to crash Phillip's party. When we got to the hotel we took the elevator to the penthouse suite, which was where the boys were. We could hear the noise coming from the room as we stepped off the elevator. I was about to knock on the door when Keri stopped me and tried the lock. It was open. We walked in the door and stood there for a good fifteen seconds before anyone noticed us. They were busy with women all over the floor and couches, wherever there was a spot. I was not familiar with some of the faces, but everyone seemed to know who I was. There was a lot of babbling come from some of them but I was not listening to anything they had to say. My eyes were all over the room looking for Phillip he was nowhere to be seen. I was a little relieved. Maybe he did not want to be a part of all this nasty mess. How embarrassing would that be to have my friends and I walk in on my fiancé doing nasty shit like that the night before our wedding. I saw a door opened up and a tall skinny high color black girl walked out with a big smile on her face. I started toward the room and she stepped in front of me and said something about me having to wait my turn. Melanie walked up to her and said, "Excuse me!" and she was gone. The door was slightly opened and I could see two people moving around thru the mirror on the dresser in the room, but the room was dark and I could not see clearly. I wanted to reach inside the door and turn on the lights but I was afraid of what I might see.

"What are you going to do Amanda?" I heard Melanie said to me.

"Ah...ah, I don't know." I whispered.

"I would have to find out, if it was me in this situation." Keri said unapologetically.

"Oh my God, Melanie, what would I do?"

"I don't know Amanda, but if he is in there you should know."

"Otherwise you'll be asking yourself that question over and over again and never get an answer. If you walk out of here tonight not knowing, you will not be happy at the altar tomorrow." Keri said all in one breath; and she was right I had to find out so I did.

` I could see behind us that everyone was looking at us, but no one could get to the door to warn whoever was inside the room, because we were blocking all entry. I pushed my hand inside the door, switched the light on and swung the door open with my hip in one fluid motion and I could feel the champagne I had earlier creeping up my throat. I took a deep breath and tried to stop myself from vomiting.

The man I was supposed to marry in less than twenty four hours was in bed with not one, not two, but three women. He was humping the shit out of one of them while one was licking his ass and the third one had her pussy in the one he was fucking face. I was sick to my stomach. When the lights came on he could not even fucking move\ the way they were wrapped around each other like pretzels.

I did not stick around for any more, I ran out of the room with Melanie and Keri in tow. I ran all the way to the limousine that was waiting for us in front of the hotel. The girls did all they could to comfort me, but I knew that was the end of Phillip and I, so how could I be comforted. There was no way I would ever be comforted.

I called off the wedding, but it was too late for anything to be done about the food and flowers, cake all of it. There was a girl Maria who cleaned our store who was engaged for three years and desperately wanted to get married but her and her fiancé could not afford a wedding, they were both orphaned and have no family and I decided that since everything was already prepared I offered to let her get married in my place. Not to Phillip but to her fiancé of course.

Phillip agreed that since I would no longer marry him and his money would go to waste anyway then I should go ahead and let them get married in our place. That was after all the begging me to forgive him stuff, but there was no way I could forgive him for something like that, I would be a fool to spend another day in his company.

Maria and her fiancé were so grateful, and I was so happy that I could do something for someone that made them so happy even when I was so sad myself. They had no relatives and more than half of the two hundred people whom we could not reach to let them know the wedding was cancelled showed up and I braved the crowd and went up and announced the cancellation and ask that they stay for Maria's wedding and reception. No one left and I heard that the ceremony and reception went well. Maria cared zero that they did not yet have a marriage license. She wanted to walk down an aisle with her man and have the pictures to show for it, and that was good enough for her.

I broke up with Phillip and never looked back amid all his pleading and begging. I would never take him back he might give my ass AIDS or something. The stinker was not even wearing condoms when I caught him with his ass up in the air fucking that dirty bitch and having them sucking him and rubbing all over him. I never even wanted to imagine all the other things that he did to them, and what about that other girl who was leaving the room and telling me it was not my turn, I wondered how many more went before her and that group he was with.

There was no room in my heart to forgive Phillip for what he had done to me, to us. Till this day I still have that picture of him in my mind. I vowed never to try and get married again and I guess that is partially why I did not give a fuck that Mr. Man is married. I would hate to have to go through some shit like that again.

Men nowadays are so fucked up it's not funny. They want to have their cake and eat it too, and a lot of them do get away with that because of those pathetic little bitches with low self-esteem that believe they cannot get along without those assholes. But I have a new policy now since Phillip fucked with my head. Why buy the freaking cow when you can get the milk for free. I may end up being stuck with the cow long after it has ceased producing milk. Then what would I do with a worthless cow? Maybe I was spared from having to clean up after some man's nasty ass while he is out getting his groove on. Spared from having to do his dirty laundry and cook for him and then lay my ass up so he can have his way with me whenever or however he pleased.

I think this way is a thousand times better. This way I am not burdened with having to care for him in any way, except to fuck him and that's for me too. A girl has to get her sex from somewhere and her money as well.

There is just one thing I cannot do, no matter how much money a man has he must have good looks to go with it and I must definitely feel at least a little something for him. I cannot just be with someone without a little feeling involved on my part, but I do not need a whole lot of feeling in order to be with him if he looks and smells good and has a big bank account to boot.

I feel more than just a little something for Mr. Man, especially after our last time together, but not half as much as I felt for that jerk, Phillip. Sometimes I want to think that I am over him, but I really do not think I am truly over him or I would not still be angry and bitter. But what am I suppose to do, I had big plans for the rest of my life with that man, or maybe I should call him a boy. Then again, on the other hand I have met boys who are much more of a man than he could ever be in my eyes. That germ infested varmint.

I really should get him out of my system though, but it's not that easy to do when you had a man who seemed to make you his entire world, made you feel like no one else mattered, tells you he can't wait for you to be his wife and have you bear his children and have you believe it, then turn around and make you feel like a little insignificant piece of shit lost between the grids on the bottom of a shoe. That was how small he made me feel, almost nonexistent but stinking as hell.

The girls try not to bring it up but from time to time Phillip's name would come up and I can tell that no one is comfortable with that topic. For some strange reason I am the one who continuously bring up his name. Well, what else do I talk about when everyone is talking about the men in their lives all I can talk about is Phillip and how he fucked me over. Lately though, I have been talking about Mr. Man but I cannot reveal to my friends who he is, though I wish I could. If it should ever get out about us it would hurt him just as much as it would hurt me because when he is no longer around to finance my high life what will I do, just live like the others? No way, I must do everything I can to keep our little secret a secret.

I was still laid up in bed just looking at Lifetime, the cable channel when the doorbell rang. I wondered who it could be because no one is ever welcome to my home without calling first. I hate people just dropping by unannounced.

I got up and went downstairs to the front door. I looked through the peephole and all I could see was red roses. I opened the door to a very stocky white man hidden behind the huge bundle of roses.

"Good morning ma'am these are for ah…ah Miss Davis." He stuttered as he tried to read something on the clipboard he was holding in surprisingly tiny little hands.

"Yes, that's me." I said and quickly took the clipboard out of his hands to help relieve him of the burden, seemed his little hands were about to lose the load. I signed and handed the board back to him and took the flowers from him. He stood looking at me then it dawned on me that he was waiting for me to give him a tip.

"Oh, please give me a moment."

"Sure."

I put the flowers down on the coffee table and went to the kitchen and returned to see him waiting patiently at the door.

I handed him a five-dollar bill and his face lit up like Disney World.

"Thank you very much." He said and hustled off to his vehicle.

I walked back over to the coffee table and picked the card up, it was from Mr. Man. It read *"Amanda, I'm missing you something sick."* And as per always he signed it, or I should say have them write it in for him, *"Your Quiet Side"*. We always joked about how I am the quiet side of him and him the quiet side of me because of our very secret affair. He always sends flowers. I feel blessed because he did not have a stingy bone in his body. The man has money and he love spending it on me.

I went straight back to bed after a snack of cheese and crackers, I was determined to get me some rest so I turned off both the house and cell phones, turned off the television, put my head under the covers and got me some well needed zees.

Chapter 5

KERI

"Keri Cruz? The voice coming over the intercom, which sounded more like a bullhorn was just as crusty as the equipment it was coming through. I was sitting in the passport office renewing my passport. Miguel and I did not take a honeymoon when we got married two years ago because he had just made partner at his law firm and the timing was way off. I was busy myself at work with the accounting firm that I worked for, still work for. I was in my third year at Marshall Gordon Accounting and they were in the process of doing some major overhaul in the company, firing and hiring. Thank God my job was never threatened because I was one of their biggest producers of new accounts and I have not lost one major account since I set foot in the company. But even if I was fired I would not starve or anything because Miguel made good money and I own a flower shop in South Beach that was raking in a lot of money.

I guess I did not get up fast enough for the bullhorn lady because she hollered my name impatiently through that horrible thing again.

"Keri Cruz!" By this time she was looking at me like I stole something.

"I'm right here." I said taking long steps toward her little cubbyhole thingy.

She handed me my passport for which I was more than grateful after spending an entire morning waiting for it.

"Thank you, have a nice day." I said as I walked away from the window toward the door. I couldn't wait to get out of there because there was this rather annoying woman talking my ears off about her son who was about to be deported for something she said he did not do. I was happy that she did not give me a chance to get a word in edgewise because I have no idea what I might have said to all she was dishing out.

As I exited the building my cell phone rang. It was Miguel calling to let me know that he had to cancel meeting with me for lunch as planned. He was caught up in a meeting and would not be able to see me before dinner. That kind of thing has been happening a lot lately, Miguel canceling lunch, dinner and almost everything we plan together. I have not been complaining or anything, but it has started to get on my nerve. We do not spend as much time together as we use to and it's not that we have any more time than usual but we always made time no matter what, but since the last six months or so Miguel have been extremely busy at work.

It will be none too soon when we finally take that long awaited honeymoon. Miguel wanted to go to the Bahamas but I badgered him until he changed his mind and agree to go to Jamaica instead. I love Jamaica with a passion, I went there with the girls once and I swear to you I did not want to return home. I could be really happy there living in the mountains wearing long skirts and sandals with my head wrapped like Erykah Badu chomping sugar cane, drinking coconut water and smoking the good ganja weed every day. I do not smoke at all but living there I probably would. One of the many things we did while in Jamaica was attend a reggae concert, and I was blown away by how available weed was. It was an outdoor event like a lot of the events in sunny Jamaica are, and there were vendors walking around selling peanuts, cigarettes and whatever they could conjure up, but none of us were prepared to see weed vendors. I mean people walking around with foot long stalks of weed shouting "High grade, high grade." We were probably some of the few people that were surprised, because men and women were picking stalk after stalk of the stuff and rolling up their joints right there wherever they were standing, no one was even concerned with the few police officers that were moving around the fenced in venue. It was amazing. We also went up into the mountains with a couple of Rastafarians and were amazed how much weed was up on the hill. Melanie and Amanda smoked some of the good ganja weed just for the heck of it, because neither of them are smokers in reality.

But that is not the reason I want to go there with Miguel. I want to go there with Miguel because the place has an atmosphere of sheer romance. I want to experience Jamaica with my man. Even the way they dance there makes you hot and bothered. That time I was there I wished I had a man to share it with, because I am not the type to go looking for a "Dexter" like Eddie Murphy said in his "Raw" comedy stand up act.

Since lunch was cancelled I opted to go to the office and get some long overdue work done, nothing really that important just some filing, sorting and putting things away. I was planning to take the entire day but what would I do now. If Miguel and I had gotten together as intended we would have taken the rest of the day off for a dose of afternoon delight. I hardly remember what that feels like.

I needed to pick up a few things at the drug store so I stopped at a little shopping center about two blocks from the office so I would not have to do anything but head home once I was finished. I spotted two parking spaces directly in front of the drug store and quickly drove into the one closest to the entrance, which was not soon enough because another car pulled into the next space. I was half way out of the car when I heard my name coming from someone in the car that had pulled in next to mine.

"Keri! Keri McDonald?"

Before I could utter a single word he opened the door and got out. I almost passed out when I saw who was standing in front of me. "Oh my God!" I heard myself say in my head but nothing came from my lips. I thought I was going to lose my breakfast right there in front of him. Why was this happening to me? Why?

"Surprised to see me Keri?" He did not appear surprised to see me at all.

"Paul, how....how are you?" Even a blind man would be able to tell that I was nervous, actually I wanted to pee my pants, of all the people I would not want to run into Paul Lopez was definitely top of the list.

"Don't be nervous Keri; it's a pleasure to see you again. Maybe we could get together and have a drink sometime, uh how about that?

I heard everything he was saying but I was more than speechless, I was in a comatose state with one leg still inside the car. I just stood there looking at him not knowing what to say because something did not feel right about that encounter. Something in my gut was telling me that was no chance meeting.

"Paul, I am hardly nervous but I do admit I am a little surprised to see you here in Miami. How long ago did I last see you or talk to you Paul, what nine years ago? So yes I am surprised to see you, but I am sorry to inform you that I do not have time to stand here and reminisce with you, I have somewhere to go."

I had no idea where all of that came from. I didn't even know what I wanted to say until I heard it coming from my lips.

He was looking at me with a nasty little smirk on his face.

"Don't try to be a bad ass Keri, it doesn't become you. Is that a wedding ring you're wearing? What, you married to some big doctor or lawyer now, so you forgot the little people uh?"

I ignored his comment about my ring. There was a lump in my throat and my lips felt dry. I finally got my other leg out of the car and closed the door, but I could not move, I literally could not move so I leaned against the car and took a long hard breath.

"What do you want from me Paul?"

I was looking straight in his eyes. He wasted no time with his answer as if it was well thought out.

"You, Keri; I want you."

"What are you talking about?"

"I know what you did Keri. I know what you did"

Shit was getting serious. He looked serious. Why was this happening to me now, why couldn't he have shown up three years ago before Miguel and I met, when there was nothing at stake? I lied to Miguel and everyone around me about a big chunk of my past and I would do anything to keep him from finding out about that dark side of my not so proud past. The part Paul represents.

"Tell me Paul, what is it you really want from me and what the hell are you talking about?"

He did not look that great he must not have attained that NFL contract he was so adamant about back in the day. I never heard anything of him not even in his college years. The car he was driving looked like a rental car and his plain blue jeans and white tee shirt was not doing much for him in the looks department, but he was still handsome and tall as he ever was.

"I know what you did after I left Westchester." Anger was apparent in his tone.

"I have no idea what you are talking about." What the fuck.

"I couldn't find you till now. I went back to Westchester when I figured it out but I was told that you all moved shortly after you graduated. I still have the newspaper clipping." He had this scornful look in his eyes.

When he mentioned the newspaper I knew for sure that he knew. He knew what I had done because I had kept some of those same newspaper clippings myself for a very long time. I was speechless. The whole world just stood still for what seemed like ages. Then I eventually got my thoughts together.

"I have no idea what you are talking about."

"Yes you do. You know exactly what I am talking about, so don't pretend with me." He was getting angry.

"Listen, I have somewhere to go right now but I will be in touch. We have a lot to talk about Keri and I know you know what I am talking about. I know you think I fucked up but what you did take the cake."

"I did only what you wanted me to do in the first place Paul so what are you so suddenly upset about? Why now?"

"You did not do what we agreed you should do, you did not."

"What is it that I did then Paul?" I was dreading the answer he would give me.

"Like I said, I have to go but I will be in touch."

"What are you going to do Paul stalk me, follow me wherever I go?"

"Oh no Keri, I am nobody's stalker but I will be in touch with you."

He got back in his car and pulled out of the parking space. Before he drove off he leaned out the window and said, "You've been a bad girl Keri."

After he drove away I just stood there in a daze. I eventually gathered myself together and went into the drug store to get what I needed. But once inside the store I could not for the life of me remember what it was I needed so I walked right back out empty handed got into my car and drove home. After that very unfortunate encounter with Paul I was in no mood to go to the office again.

I thought that I had left that dark side of my early past behind me nine years ago and so I never talked about it with anyone. Not the girls and most definitely not Miguel. Why would Paul try to find me after all that time, what could he really want from me? Does he really believe I would want to be with him after all that time? And what did he mean when he said he knew where to find me, did he know where I work or worse where I live? And what was he implying when he asked if I was married to some big time doctor or lawyer, did he know that Miguel is a lawyer? Or worse, did he know Miguel? The questions kept coming in my mind and I was literally sick to my stomach.

If this should come out I can't begin to imagine the impact it would have on my marriage, my life. I could beat myself for not telling Miguel about that part of my past but I never dreamed that one day it would come back and stare me in the face. There was no way I could tell him or anyone about what happened back in Westchester because there was no way I could tell them the whole story.

It was 2005 and we were only a few days into our summer vacation when Paul who was the captain of the football team and my boyfriend for my entire junior year broke the news that his parents were moving to Texas. His father was promoted to CEO for some big company there and was required to move by the end of August. He said his parents would be taking trips back and forth before then to find a new home and to get him and his sister enrolled in new schools.

I was devastated. Paul said he would stay if he could but he had no other relatives there in Westchester so he had no choice but to go with his parents. He could have stayed with his grandmother who lived only about a mile from where they lived but she died only months before. When she was alive he would spend more time living with her than he did at his parents' house, they were very close. It was a big blow for him when she passed away because he was not close to his mother at all. He and his father got along great but he was never around because of his work.

Paul said it sometimes made him mad but he's usually encouraged by the thought that his father was always a good provider who was very generous and worked hard to make his family happy. He always had good things to say about his father, but he was never that kind in the way he spoke about his mother whom he said was cheating on his dad and stuck him with babysitting duties and made him lie to his father to cover for her. He hardly ever talked about her, but he never shut up about his dad. He loved his little sister too. Paula was her name. Weren't it for the fact that she was five years younger than Paul anyone would have thought they were twins because they looked so much alike. They look a lot like their father, tall with curly black hair. It was obvious that they did not get much of their mother's black genes but you could still tell they had some black in them. It must have been rather confusing in that household with those names. His father was Paul Anthony Perez, Senior and his mother's name was Pauline. What were they thinking?

Paul was mixed blooded because his father was a half white Cuban and his mother was a black nappy-headed woman from Panama. You would never see Pauline without her full head of weave and little tight outfits on. She was cool as shit, I liked her the very first day I met her and I could tell that she liked me too. My skin was just as dark as Pauline's but I had long curly jet-black hair that I got from my mother's side. She was always killing me with compliments on how beautiful my hair and skin was. She would say her son has good taste in women just like his father. "Like father like son" was another thing she liked to say. Mr. Lopez was nice too but he was hardly ever there when I was visiting. Their house was only about ten blocks from where I was living with my mother and stepfather but I never was a regular visitor even though I was more than welcome. Even his little sister thought I was cool so I could go there whenever I wanted to. I was a homebody though, I did not like going out much and my mother and stepfather was cool with Paul coming over to see me.

A lot of the girls in my class were sexually active and they would talk about it like it was something as simple as taking a walk through the park, but I was not one of them. Paul was my very first boyfriend, I was too busy trying to keep my grades up to be bothered with boys, and I was not sure that I would want to do some of the things that the other girls were doing to them. Girls were giving out blow jobs like confetti falling from the sky. I guess they thought it made them popular with the boys, the jocks especially. I had one single friend in school, Angela Laws, but she moved away the summer before the beginning of our junior year. Angela was also from the same small town in Georgia where I grew up with my grandparents. My grandfather died when I was seven years old and then it was just my grandmother and me. It was such a small town that we had only one police station and nothing bigger than domestic violence ever happened so there were only about ten or so police officers. The town was aptly named "Little Town". Population: eleven hundred. Everybody knew each other and each other's business, and the main thing on many young girls mind was to marry rich and move away to a big city somewhere. There were a lot of fine young boys there too who dreamed of someday sweeping some filthy rich women of their feet with their charm and good looks. The women there didn't look bad either, there were some very beautiful women in Little Town but they did not want the town men unless they had assets like a gas station or convenient store or some kind of business going on. Most of the women were dating men outside of Little Town.

When I was twelve years old my grandmother remarried. I remember feeling happy that she would not be alone while I was gone. I was also happy for me that I was moving to the Big Apple with my mother. Everyone wanted to experience New York and I was getting my chance. Even at twelve years old I knew enough to know that Little Town was not big enough for my dreams. Paul was my first boyfriend and that did not happen until the end of my sophomore year.

After we found out that he was leaving Paul and I began spending a lot more time together. We saw each other every chance we got. For the entire year that Paul and I were together we did not have sex. We kissed and fondled each other but never actually did it. Paul asked me once to give him oral sex, more than once actually but I refused and made a big deal out of it the last time he suggested it and he never asked me to do it again. But even though I would not do it to him he insisted on giving me oral sex on a very regular basis and I must admit that I was always blown away by how good he was. In reality I had nothing to compare it to at the time but when I finally did have something to compare it with I truly realized what a master he was at the art. Even now, the only person I have to compare would be Miguel because he is the only other man that I have ever been intimate with.

The first time Paul and I actually had intercourse my mother and step-father were going away for the weekend and I was going to be staying at the house alone so I asked if Paul could stay with me and to my surprise they said yes after much warning about how responsible I should be of course. I was a pretty good kid and they knew that they could trust me, but I guess the warning thing is pretty standard in the act of parenting.

They left the Friday morning and that night was our first night staying together in the same house or the same bed, it would also be the first time we went all the way. It was the first week of June and only one week after school let out. Paul did not have condoms but we felt it would be alright because Paul did not fool around and I was a virgin so we did not have to worry about diseases. That weekend was the best weekend of my life. Paul was gentle and patient and he cooked for me and waited on me hand and foot. We were closer than ever. We were in love.

Neither of us gave thought to the possibility of unwanted pregnancy until I missed my period.

When my period did not show up at least a week after the due date I went out and bought one of those early pregnancy test kits and it was positive. I still did not believe that I was pregnant so I got another kit from a different manufacturer and that also proved positive. I was devastated, what was I going to do with a baby. I had one year left in high school. I was on the Dean's List and was a member of the National Honor Society. I was pretty much guaranteed a scholarship to most any University of my choice.

Even though my mother did not encourage me, or cheer me along she expected me to do well in school so I can get a scholarship because she was constantly complaining about how hard it was going to be to paying for my college education if I did not get a scholarship. She and I never talked much about anything. I spent a lot of time in my room mostly in my school books and when I wasn't doing that I would be reading a novel or doing crossword puzzles. My mother and I were never close and still are not close to this day. We are not on speaking terms and have not since the last nine years. My stepfather and I got along great but he and my mother are no longer together. He and I kept in touch however.

After the second kit pregnancy test I got a fake ID card from this girl I knew. I told her I was going to visit my cousins in Chicago and they wanted to take me to the club with them so I had to have identification to prove that I was at least twenty-one.

I took the train one morning to Brooklyn and I went to a doctor that I picked from the yellow pages. I had the first appointment of the morning and I made sure I was early. Fortunately for me, I was in and out of there before anyone else came in. I did not give them my home phone number because I would be in big trouble if they called and my mother or my stepfather answered the phone. How would I explain going to see a doctor in Brooklyn when if I was feeling sick I could go and see our family doctor right there in Westchester? On the other hand, they would not ask for me, Keri McDonald, they would ask for Sharon Williams the name on the fake ID. However, I gave them my cell phone number.

They called that afternoon to inform me of my pregnancy. As I held the phone to my ear the tears started rolling down my face and I heard nothing else that the voice at the other end of the line was saying. I was just standing there and I could see my whole world and everything I worked toward in school crumbling right in front of me. I had no memory of when I put the phone back on the receiver. I knew I was pregnant from the early pregnancy test I did, but hearing it from the doctor made it real.

It took me a while before I told Paul because he was away with his parents and I did not want to tell him something like that on the phone. I had no one to talk to and I could not keep it to myself any longer or I would go crazy. There was no sign of it anywhere on my body, everything looked the same to me, so my mother had no idea anything was going on.

I was not prepared for the reaction that I got from Paul when I gave him the news. I can still remember that evening like it was just yesterday.

We were at my house on the swing in the backyard. My mother and stepfather were away in Maryland visiting his mother and Paul was staying over and keeping me company again. He wanted to have sex again as soon as they drove out of the driveway, but I was in no mood for sex even though I had grown to like it a lot. It was a cool evening and we were hanging out in the backyard enjoying the evening breeze.

"Paul I have something to tell you." My voice was trembling and I could not stop the tears from suddenly raining down my face.

"What's the matter Keri, why are you crying? He was very concerned.

I buried my face in his chest and cried like a baby, all the time with him asking me what was wrong with me. He even thought that maybe it was something to do with my mother or stepfather.

"Keri is it Mr. Thomas, did he do something to you?" He was holding me close.

"No."

"Are you and your mom having a fight?"

"No."

"Then what is it Keri, why are you crying?"

"Tell you what; let's go inside the house where I'll make you a cup of tea then you can tell me why you are crying."

It never even occurred to him that maybe I was pregnant. After all we had unprotected sex more than a few times.

He made me the cup of tea as promised and I took a few sips, by then I had stopped crying. I had to be a big girl and take responsibility for what happened. I should have insisted on protection but I didn't so there was no one to blame but myself. My protection should first lie in my own hands.

"I'm pregnant." I blurted it out before I lost the nerve.

"What?"

"I'm pregnant, according to the doctor I am now six weeks." I was nervous as hell.

"How could you do that?"

"How could I do that? What about you, you didn't have anything to do with it?"

My heart was racing and I felt like I couldn't breathe, so I ran out the door to the back yard where I threw up.

He did not even come outside to see how I was. I could not believe what was happening. I thought he loved me no matter what and maybe we could talk about what to do about the mess we got ourselves into but the way things were turning out I was not sure I could depend on him in any way.

After about fifteen minutes I went back into the house and he was sitting on the bed in my room with a photograph of us in his hand. I became a little relieved. Maybe the news was too sudden and he did not mean to act that way.

I went and sat beside him on the bed and put my arm around him and he brushed me off.

"So that's how it's going to be. You are just gonna behave like I was having sex with myself when I got pregnant, and stupid little me did not wear a condom on my finger or whatever I used to screw myself, now I am pregnant and want to pass it off on my innocent boyfriend who had sex with me without condoms? Is that it Paul?"

"You should have been on the pills or something, it was somewhat my fault not to ask, but you knew you were not on the pills. I did not know that, otherwise I would have used a condom. What am I going to do with a baby? I have plans for a football scholarship to college and to move on to the pros. I won't have time to take care of a baby and you. You are going to have to get rid of it." He was pacing the floor as he spit out his venom.

I could not believe he was being so cold to me. I had already resigned myself to the fact that I would have to get rid of it but to hear him say it the way he did broke my heart up into little tiny pieces. I decided right there and then that whatever happened I was through with Paul Anthony Perez, Jr. I thought he was a better person than that and to think I thought he was the only person I could talk to. Boy was I wrong. I had no one to talk to.

I would have asked him to leave the house that night and go home but I had to think fast and I did not want my parents suspecting anything was wrong between us, they might start asking questions. So I made the decision to have him stay as planned.

He spent the entire time trying to convince me to have an abortion. He was only concerned with Paul and the impact it would have on him and his future, he was not in the least concerned with the effects it would have on me or my future for that matter. I knew I was going to have an abortion that was without question, but I could not bring myself to tell him that was what I had in mind in the first place. He was acting like the consummate asshole.

I eventually agreed that he would give me the money to go to the doctor and get an abortion. I had no way other way of getting the money, It was over a thousand dollars, eleven hundred to be exact and I had absolutely no way of getting my hands on that kind of money. He assured me not to worry that he would come up with the money. I waited and waited and the time kept going and going and still no money. Finally it was the last week in August and it was time for Paul to move to Texas. He never gave me the money until the day before he left and it was only eight hundred dollars.

It took me two more long weeks to come up with the rest of the money. I would get a hundred dollars every other week for my allowance and I had a hundred dollars left from money I had saved up. Most of the money I saved was spent on pregnancy kits and going to the doctor. I had to go back for a checkup after I was told I was pregnant that was when the doctor told me how far along I was. I could not come up with a good reason to ask my mother or stepfather for money so I had to wait for my next allowance that was not due for another two weeks. By that time Paul was gone for exactly the same two weeks and I had not gotten even a phone call from him. I had to take the train to the clinic by myself because I had no one to accompany me. I was planning on taking a cab home when the procedure was over but it was not to be. The doctor told me that I was too far along to guarantee that there would not be any complications. I was over three months pregnant. He was not willing to do the procedure on me. He gave me the name and phone number of a couple of other doctors and I went to see them both and no one would do the abortion. I was just too far along.

It was the beginning of the new school year and I had to go back to school. Even though I was over three months pregnant there were no signs of my pregnancy. I was tall and skinny with a very flat stomach and I could see just a small swell but nothing to garner any attention. I went to school every day without drawing any attention from anyone. The time of year worked out just great for me though, because it started getting cold about the third week in September and all the kids were then wearing several layers of clothing and huge coats to cover themselves from the cold. For me it was a multipurpose effort. I was being sheltered from the cold while I shelter my stomach from the world.

I was in some serious shit and I had no idea how I was going to get myself out of it, but something had to be done. I knew it would be a hell of a task trying to keep my pregnancy a secret but I had to do everything in my power to do just that. Keep it a secret.

The winter coats and jackets and oversized jeans played a major role in masking the small swell of my stomach and the fullness of my breasts. My mother and stepfather had no clue. My behavior did not change much. I was always a loner and I was used to spending a lot of time by myself. When I was home I would be in my room all the time and it was not unusual for me to wear oversized t-shirts around the house. I never experienced any kind of morning sickness, and my eating habit was pretty much the same except that I was craving pickles. I never even liked pickles before.

In school I was always a loner, the only close friend I had was no longer at the school. I missed Angela but I was happy that she was not around for that drama. That was something I had to do on my own.

I was well liked in school but I never talked much. I got along pretty well with everyone but I never really socialized with anyone. Nobody seemed to notice any difference in me. My grades were still going through the roof, I was doing great academically. It became second nature to me to not look worried or bothered. Not once did anyone have to ask me if something was wrong because I had "normal" down to a tee.

Thanksgiving came and went and I still did not hear anything from Paul. Not a single call, not a single letter. I could not believe that he did not even call me once to ask how the abortion went. He had no idea that I was still carrying our baby inside me. I felt no emotional attachment to it whatsoever because I did not want a baby. My mom asked about Paul a couple of times and I lied that he was doing okay and that he said to tell her hello. There were even times when I would voluntarily tell her that Paul called and he said to say hi to her and my stepfather. I made sure that I had all the bases covered so there would be no slipups.

We spent Christmas with my stepfather's mother in Maryland and that night Paul called me on my cell phone. My mother was out on the town with my stepfather so the house was empty except for my step grandmother sleeping in another room.

"Hello!" There was no answer so I said hello again.

"Hello!"

I felt a kick in my stomach the moment I heard his voice. I grabbed my stomach with my free hand.

"Hello Keri! Merry Christmas."

I wanted to throw up for the first time since Paul left Westchester but I fought the feeling until it subsided.

"Merry Christmas to you too Paul."

I was as calm as cucumber. I did not want him to hear any stress in my voice. He was quiet on the other end of the phone and just as I was about to say something he spoke.

"How is everything?" he asked and I could hear that he was a little nervous.

"Everything is good." I was very abrupt with my answers but there was no sign of anger in my voice. I was not trying to make conversation, because whatever the reason he was calling it was way too late for me to be interested in it.

"Are you alright?"

"I am alright."

"Okay then, I will call you some other time."

"Bye." I said before I pressed the off button.

He had some nerve to call me to wish me a merry Christmas. What the hell did he think I had to be merry about? I knew he probably believed that I had gone through with the abortion as I intended, but any decent guy would call me immediately after to find out how it went. I could not blame him for not being there to go with me to the clinic because he had to leave with his parents, he really had no choice in that but he chose not to call me for four whole months. I was already six months into my pregnancy too late to tell Paul about it even if he was the least bit interested.

I had my mind made up about what I was going to do about the baby. I was not due until March and I planned on getting in touch with an adoption agency and see if I could make some arrangement to have them take my baby. Graduation would not be until May and so I could probably pull it off if I could come up with a fool proof reason to give my mother so she would allow me to go away for a couple of weeks or so. I had a little money saved up. I still had the eight hundred dollars that Paul gave me for the abortion and I have been saving up most of my allowance. My allowance was raised to one hundred dollars per week instead of every two weeks when I had my seventeenth birthday in September. I got over five hundred dollars from my mother and stepfather for the holidays and my step grandmother gave me another five hundred dollars that she told me to keep between us, plus my grandmother gave me some money when I went there for thanksgiving. She was always giving me money. So I already had about four thousand dollars saved up.

I wore my clothes a lot looser and since it was still cold in New York I continued to mask my pregnancy from everyone.

I found an adoption agency in the yellow pages and I told them I was twenty-two according to my renewed fake identification card with the name Sharon Williams. I told the woman that I was single and did not have any way to take care of the baby I was about to give birth to and she told me that they might be able to help me but I would have to come in and see her. I insisted that she told me what the procedure was before I came in or I would go to another agency. I said that because she was sounding so desperate telling me how many wonderful couples were waiting to adopt.

I stayed in touch with her for weeks, blocking my number each time I called. We made arrangements for me to meet her two weeks before my due date when she would have me examined by a doctor who would deliver my baby right there in his office, but that was not to be.

Exactly three weeks before my due date I was home alone again. My mother was away on business, she was the buyer for this huge clothing store chain and she was somewhere in California at some seminar that was suppose to last an entire week. My stepfather was out of the country on business for the company that he worked for so I had the house all to myself.

I was sleeping one night when a sudden pain in my stomach jerked me awake. I tried to sit up but I couldn't, not for a while anyway. Suddenly I was peeing myself, or so I thought. It was actually my water that broke and I panicked.

"Oh my God, this is not happening." I cried.

I had no idea what I was going to do. I could not call 911 or there would be a huge scandal. Everyone would hear about the baby. I could not call the adoption lady because I only had her office number.

I remember I had seen on television somewhere that I would need hot water and clean towels, so I staggered to the kitchen and put the kettle on then gathered some fresh towels. The pain kept coming faster and faster and more severe.

I got back in bed and I breathed like I saw them do on television. I knew I would have to have this baby all by myself. It was the middle of the night and I could not call the agency, if it was in the daytime I could have taken a cab there even though it was all the way in Brooklyn. But unfortunately it was not daytime and the agency was not open.

It all happened so fast. I had this brain crippling pain and I could feel the baby's head coming out between my legs. I breathed and I pushed, I breathed and I pushed until the entire thing came out. I had done a little reading on how to cut the umbilical cord and so I had to do that and separate myself from the baby. It was a little girl, but she was not moving, she was not breathing. She was dead.

I was planning to secretly take a cab the following morning and go drop her off at the agency but that was before I realized she was dead.

I had no idea what to do so I cleaned the dead baby and myself up and I spent the entire rest of the night trying to figure out what to do. I cannot remember ever feeling anything but anxiety to get rid of the body. I cannot remember for the life of me even feeling sorry for a second that the baby was dead. All I was concerned with was getting rid of the body. I could not believe what was happening to me. The way it was all playing out.

I had to think fast. It was going to be dawn soon and I could not get caught with a dead baby in the house.

My mother's car was parked inside the garage so I got the keys and went out into the garage to start the car. I went back inside the house where I had the baby wrapped up in a couple of large towels. I then put the baby inside as many as three garbage bags and took it to the car. It looked just like regular garbage.

I drove all the way from Westchester to the Bronx and dumped it in a large dumpster at one end of a dark alley. I looked around first and I was confident that no one saw me.

By the time I got home it was already five thirty in the morning. But I did not see anyone around when I drove into my neighborhood so I was home free.

That morning I got up and went to school as if nothing happened. Two days later it was all over the news that a dead baby was found in the Bronx and they were looking for the mother. They were giving a reward to anyone who could help them find the mother. I was not at all worried that they would find me because no one had the slightest idea that I was pregnant in the first place, I had no morning sickness and I did not miss a single day of school.

I went on to graduate high school with top honors and was given a full scholarship to Howard University where I met the girls. My mom and step-father moved to Atlanta where I would spend all my vacations but they ended up getting divorced by the time I was a junior in college. She stayed in Atlanta and he moved back to New York.

She remarried only five months after the divorce and her new husband tried to screw me when I went home from school, but when I told her about it she called me a liar and told me to get out of her house. That was the last time

I spoke with my mother, but I always kept in touch with my stepfather. He was the only real father I knew.

After college I never dated much I concentrated on my career. Don't get me wrong, I went out sometimes and had fun. There was even a guy or two that I could have settled down with but that experience with Paul made me literally afraid of men. All that changed when I met Miguel.

Though I could never admit to what I did I can't help but wonder how it would have all turned out if I had called the paramedics and let them see that the baby was born dead. I am sure if they did an autopsy on the baby they would realize that the baby was already dead by the time it left my body. But there was no way I could have done that. It would have surely ruined everything for me not to mention the scandal it would cause.

I felt sorry that I had to throw it away like trash but what was I suppose to do. I was only seventeen years old for God sake.

My day had definitely taken a nosedive after running into Paul. What in the world could he want from me? Didn't he have a life of his own?

Miguel called from his office to find out what I wanted to do for dinner. He wanted to go to Red Lobster it was one of his favorite places to eat. I told him I was not in the mood to go out. I told him I had a hectic day and would rather eat in so he opted to pick up dinner. We agreed that he would get dinner from Red Lobster. I had no real interest in dinner but he knew that I never turned down a good seafood meal and I did not want him suspecting that anything was bothering me. He had no idea how I spent my day so I would just keep that little episode to myself.

I was laying on the couch in the living room trying to forge some interest in a novel I meant to read a long time ago when Miguel got home.

"You look mighty relaxed. Are you waiting for Big Daddy Cruz?" He enjoyed playing little scenarios that would later lead to some hot love making, so right away I knew he meant business.

"For my food. Yes." I said smiling.

"Food for the stomach or food for the stomach?"

"The first one." I laughed and put the book down on the couch beside me.

"Why don't we just eat here?" I said clearing the coffee table so he could put the food down.

"Tell you what, why don't I just leave you to put it all together while I take a quick shower."

"Sounds good to me." I said all flirty.

I got us a couple of plates and set them up on the table and took out a bottle of wine and two glasses then I went to the bedroom and made myself more comfortable for my husband. I could tell he was in the mood and I did not want the likes of Paul Perez causing me to not pleasure my husband the way he needed me to. The way I needed to pleasure him.

I have loved my husband without conditions from the day I blessed eyes on him and I have never loved him any less. I also believe that he loves me unconditionally and I would do anything to keep him from stop loving me. I would not put my head on the block that he would never cheat on me or did anything to deceive me, but since I have no reason to believe either, I will give him the benefit of the doubt and say he was a faithful husband as far as I knew.

I felt like I had to put on a good face like back when I was in Westchester carrying that baby inside me. The only difference now is that it wasn't my parents and the people at school that I had to put on a front for but my husband.

I was really very nervous about the whole situation. I knew what I did was wrong. Throwing that dead baby in the dumpster and all, but it was already dead it was not like I killed her. But maybe Paul thought I killed the baby. One of the things that had me puzzled was why Paul connected me to that baby. What made him believe it was our baby they found in the dumpster in the Bronx anyway. Why would he link me to that particular baby when in his mind I should have long had an abortion? All those questions kept going through my head. What was the real connection there? He was right but how did he figure it out? Maybe he was just bluffing. The only thing I was sure of was that he knew something for sure.

"Are you ready to eat honey?"

Miguel's voice yanked me from my thoughts and I jumped as if he caught me doing something I should not be doing. Like he could see through my thoughts and know what I was thinking.

"Oh yes........yes."

"Is something wrong? You acted like you expected some axe murderer or something. Are you okay?"

"Don't be silly, of course I'm okay." I knew I had to be careful because he was quick to read into my moods. He knew me that well. I had to rid him of any suspicions he may conceive.

"Maybe it was that stupid movie I was looking at earlier." I lied.

"Little girls should not watch scary movies all by themselves; she should wait until her big daddy gets home so he can protect her from all those ogres and gremlins." He said playfully kissing my neck and nibbling on my ear lobes.

"And big hungry men should not nibble on body parts lest he gets carried away and bites something off."

"Well, this big guy is hungry for body parts Mrs. Cruz."

He straddled me on the sofa and pulled the thin straps of my little red nightgown from my shoulders pulling it down to expose my breast where he fed his appetite. All the time I was moaning and groaning. Neither of us paid attention to the food that was still sitting on the coffee table and we sure did not need the wine to put us in the mood. All thoughts of Paul and the past were erased from my mind as Miguel kissed my stomach and ran his fingers down the middle of my back. His lips found the center of my joy and I swore I had a peek into heaven.

My husband was in the mood for love. Or maybe I should say he was in the mood to love because when I tried to caress or kiss him, he would put my hands back to my sides and indicated that I just lay back and let him pleasure me. I obeyed without a fight. God knows I could use that kind of pampering and he sure knows what makes me tick. Just before entering my body he teasingly caressed the entrance with his hot shaft before slamming inside me with carefully maneuvered force. I lost all sense of pride and self and begged for more as he murder my pussy.

"Don't stop baby, give it to me. Give it to me, harder." I was shameless.

Just as I was about to explode he set off some fireworks of his own that met with mine, and the bomb dropped.

I rolled over so he could get on the bottom. We lay there hugging each other neither of us having the strength to move and it took quite some time for us to get back the energy to finally eat the food that we were now really hungry for.

I slept well; I did not think much about Paul and our little encounter. A whole week passed and I had not heard a peep out of Paul. Maybe he decided to leave me alone after all.

I still could not understand why he would be so mad at me even if he was right because he did not want that baby any more than I did so why would he care whether I got rid of it in a dumpster or in the toilet or wherever those people at the abortion clinic would dispose of it. The only thing that was important to him at that time was getting his football scholarship.

Another week passed and I still did not hear anything from Paul. All that time I was walking on pins and needles. Every time the phone rang at home or work I wondered if it was Paul. Since the day I ran into him in the drug store parking lot I keep looking for him to appear in my rear view mirror or in the aisle at the grocery store. I worried whether he would pop up when Miguel and I were out somewhere or even when I was out with the girls.

I just wished to God that he would stay away and never show his pathetic little face again. I would not allow him to ruin my life a second time. Yes I was as responsible for what happened to me as he was but he did not care enough to get me the money in time to get the abortion when he knew that I had no way of getting it. If he had kept in touch with me so I could tell him maybe things would have turned out differently. Even though I did not allow the situation to affect me getting my diploma and later my college degree, I still felt a sense of ruin because of what happened. I am the one who have to live with what happened for the rest of my life. I am the one who will have to keep it all locked up inside of me with no channel to rid myself of it. And just when I thought maybe I was coming to terms with it after all those years he had to surface and open that old and painful wound.

Chapter 6

NATASHA

The April issue of Excell is due to hit the shelves in a few days and I am more than a little excited. Little Natasha Bell the wobbly-kneed preteen whom all the kids used to call "pencil legs" was definitely on her way to the big times.

I always had a pretty face and beautiful hair and my smile boasted straight pearly whites but no one thought I could be a model because even though I was tall I did not come across as the model type. I had major self-esteem issues and you could not get me to stand straight for anything. When I was fourteen years old my mother decided that I should take etiquette classes and she also enrolled me in speech class and modeling class so I would learn to be a proper young lady who knows how to stand straight with her shoulders back.

I think her efforts paid off because I am no longer "pencil legs", I am Natasha Bell, Model and Cover Girl.

When I said I am more than a little excited I meant that I am going crazy out of my mind with excitement.

I went out with the girls last night to some new club that opened up on South Beach and we had such a good time we did not leave the club until the lights went out. Well only Kylie, Melanie and I went. Keri said her and Miguel had to go out somewhere and Amanda was nowhere to be found, but she has been pulling the disappearing act bit for quite some time now, she has been missing a lot of our Friday nights lately. As a matter of fact the circle seemed to be dwindling down to three from the usual five.

I got up pretty early for someone who got in at six o'clock in the morning. It was only twelve thirty and on top of that it was a Saturday morning. People should not have to get up on Saturday mornings until they are good and ready. There should be no jobs to go to, no grocery shopping to do, no laundry to do, just nothing. Some would say that's what Sundays are for but that's not true where I come from. You have to get up pretty early every Sunday to make sure the house is in peak condition, make breakfast, breakfast was a must on Sunday mornings in most every household, then dinner usually get started earlier than any other day, then when all that is done you take a shower, make it to church go home after church and finish dinner then go back to church again after dinner. What they should really do is let everyone stop working on Thursdays, okay then maybe Friday half a day so they can get the grocery shopping, laundry and whatever done, and the men do whatever it is they do. Then on Saturday everyone do whatever it is they want to do, stay in bed all day, watch television all day, Whatever. If I were a lawmaker that would be one of the first laws I would enact.

Unfortunately there are no such laws. Fortunately the only thing I have to do is Miles. He should be coming over later and I can't wait to see him, maybe it was that knowledge that got me up and moving. I always wanted to be at my best for him because he was ever at his best for me. He took nothing for granted. I think I am really in love with him but I have also conditioned my mind to the fact that he was someone else's husband and he could not really be mine. He and I never talked about his wife I made that subject taboo from the time we got serious. I wanted the time we spent together to be about us not about us and her or anyone else.

He will be spending the night with me. He started doing that only recently and I have not complained one bit. I love having him around. Whenever we are together we romp like little kids and make mad sick love like lunatics. Some women really do have all the luck. To have a man like Miles Covington for a husband was a huge milestone. It's like something your parents could be proud of even if you did not achieve a lot on your own, no college degree, no GED, they could be just as proud as the neighbor bragging about her daughter or her son "The Doctor". When they say shit like "Oh Susie is a doctor you know." Then your parents could say something like "My daughter is married to Miles Covington you know;" just as proudly. Unfortunately I am not married to Miles Covington. Though I wished I was.

I am not at all proud that I am hooked up with a married man but he was fulfilling all my needs and I had the need to keep him in my life. I don't believe that his wife knows anything about our affair and if she does she certainly turned a blind eye because Miles and I have been all over the place together.

I made sure the house was in tiptop shape and prepared a meal of baked chicken with cornbread stuffing, mashed potatoes, string beans, and cranberries topped off with Caesar salad and a strawberry cheesecake that I picked up just for the occasion.

I think I have a thing with cooking really fast, maybe it's because I hate cooking so much I can't wait to get out of the kitchen once I finally get in. I guess I could say that is one of the little perks to being single; I don't have to run home to make dinner for anyone but me. Who would want to cook then sit and eat by themselves? I eat out practically every day or otherwise pop a frozen tray of something in the microwave but no real cooking to speak of except for those times when I am entertaining; the girls mainly.

Being at my best for everything was like a mantra in my life but being at my best for Miles took precedence over quite a few things. It was important for him to always see me at my best because I was already at a disadvantage being the other woman in his life. We never discussed him leaving his wife for me and I doubt that he ever even conceived the thought. He would have way too much to lose I suppose, more than just his wife and possibly half his assets he would stand to lose custody of his two teenaged daughters and from what I know of him he loved his girls, he talked about Jessica and Julia more than he talked about anyone else. They were thirteen and fourteen respectively but he said they were way advanced in school and it was possible that by age sixteen Julia could be going to college; pretty smart. The two girls were his pride and joy and they were as beautiful as ever. He had pictures of the family at the cabin we went to on our first date, we still go there from time to time but he has been talking about getting one just for us because every time that we go there I would put his wife's picture face down on the mantel where he kept all his family photos. It would be nice that while he is getting one for us he just go ahead and put it in my name. That way when we are no longer together I could have it for old time sake or like I heard someone say once, for pussy pension. I think I will bring that up sometime when he is in one of his better moods, though I have never seen Miles in a bad mood, so to speak. He had a very calm demeanor; he did not allow a lot of things to upset him.

I am not trying to be greedy but I have to be sure that I have some security just as his wife does. What am I chopped liver. Yes, I may not be the one to take care of him at home, or the one he talks to about his business when he gets home from work but I sure add more than just sizzling sex to his life. Actually he does talk to me sometimes about business but mostly my business. He claimed that he hate to bore me with his business talk, maybe that was just his smart ass way of telling me that it was none of my business. But that does not bother me for a minute because we have much more fascinating things to do. Who needs talking anyway? We have a lot more satisfying things to do with our time than talk. Bottom line is; if the man should keel over and die I would not be left holding the shitty end of the stick. I have heard stories about women who never even get a chance to see the stick at all let alone get the shitty end after their lover; another woman's husband passed away or just simply end the relationship. Not me, if and when this is all over I should see something to make it worthwhile to have been there in the first place.

Don't misunderstand me, I do love Miles and he said he loved me though I can't tell if he truly loves me or just love being with me; but whatever it is that he feels for me cannot be all bad because the man takes care of me and respect me in a way that he could only if he loved me.

I should be honest and say that I truly adore him. Why else would I be so anxious to see him?

The doorbell rang and I was a little surprised that Miles would get here so early. I took a quick look in the mirror before I went to the door. There were butterflies in my stomach, happy ones.

Miles was the only person who would get pass the doorman without having to announce himself first and the girls never just drop in before calling so

I was utterly surprised when I saw who was standing on the other side of the door.

My heart skipped a beat but not in a good way, the happy butterflies fluttered and died. What the hell was she doing here and how did she know where to find me.

"Aren't you going to pick your face up off the floor and invite me in?"

"What are you doing here Donna?"

"I missed you, haven't you missed me Tash?"

"What are you doing here, what do you want?" I was working on being really mad but something inside me was not so upset about seeing her.

"I saw you last night at the club you and your friends but I was with someone and it seemed like an inopportune time to show my face so I waited until today." She was smiling as she spoke.

"Yes, but how did you know where I lived and how did you get pass Murphy?"

"I looked you up in the phone book darling. And who the hell is Murphy?"

"Never mind, I guess I should invite you in but I want you to know that whatever it is that brought you here is no longer in existence for me. I have a new life now." I opened the door wider to let her in then closed it behind us the second she was inside.

"Girl don't get your panties in a bunch, oh I forgot you don't wear those."

"I am sure you are not here to discuss my underwear habits."

"No, but it is still a hot subject." And she laughed.

All thoughts of Miles coming over had escaped me. I was at a loss at how to handle this very complicated situation that reared its ugly head at my doorstep. I was confused because I was secretly happy to see her but I did not want her knowing that.

"What is that smelling so good? Expecting dinner guest?"

"As a matter of fact I am, so unfortunately this will have to be a short visit."

"What, you got some new hot thing to replace me? Maybe we could all get together for our reunion, what do you think?"

"Listen Donna, let's cut to the chase here. There will be no reunion between us; whatever happened between us is over."

“Whatever happened between us? Is that what you just said? You make it sound like we had a one nightstand or like we were just experimenting or something. Natasha we had a relationship for almost three years. So how dare you just brush it off as something that just happened between us? We were in love with each other, or maybe I should just speak for me and say I was in love with you and I thought you were in love with me. Do you think it is any different from loving a man?”

“Donna, it is not the time for this right now, I am having a dinner guest any minute now and I’d prefer if you were not here when he shows up.”

“Are you kicking me out?”

“I am not kicking you out. You just popped the fuck up at my door and expect me to greet you with open arms after all this time what the hell do you expect?”

“Not this for sure.”

“Look Donna, I have company coming over so it’s very unfortunate that you dropped the fuck in, uninvited of course expecting me to be available but whatever it is you have to say to me will have to wait.”

I was still having mixed feelings. A part of me would have loved to have her stay while reality said she had to go. There was no way under the sun that I could have Miles show up while Donna was there because she was never one to want to hide anything and just the way she looked at me sometimes would tell a blind man that something more than just friendship was going on between us.

“That’s fair enough. When do I get to see you so we can talk?”

“Why don’t you leave a number where I can reach you and I will call you when I have some time?”

“Don’t be so cold Tash; you know I would not do anything to hurt you. I love you too much for that. I don’t have a number you can reach me. I’m between cell phones right now but I have your home number. I found it in the directory, same way I found your address.”

I suddenly realized how dangerous it was to have a listing in the directory. After all an axe murderer could get that information by just opening the phone book. Until today I had not given it a single thought, I will have to change that.

"Alright then Donna, go ahead and call me."

I did not respond to her comment about how cold I was being because the last thing I wanted was to prolong the conversation. I wanted her out before Miles show up. Even as I was dying for her to leave I could not help but notice how good she looked. She was tall and athletically built but slim. She had a perfect body that was covered in nothing less than designer duds. She was wearing a pair of tangerine and red stripe slacks low on the hips and a matching red sleeveless top that was fitting like a second skin. She had on a silver and black belt hanging on her hips and a pair of low heel black ankle boots. She was sexier than I remembered. I wanted to forget all the bad things that happened between us and just hold her close to me but I could not forget. Her golden brown skin was one of the many things about her that use to just set me off and made me want more and more of her. I wrestled with the thought of letting her stay, but it was a chance I could not take.

I walked her to the door from where we were standing from the moment I let her in. It did not occur to me that I did not offer her a seat until it was time for her to go.

"Bye Donna."

I was purposely abrupt because I did not want her to see through to my true feelings.

"Bye Tash." She blew me a kiss then turned around and walked away.

I shut the door and leaned against it thanking God that Miles did not show up before she left.

I sat on the sofa, mainly because my knees were weak. Donna still had that effect on me. I promised myself that I would never go back there with her or anyone of the female influence but I found myself wondering if I would keep that promise.

There was a knock at the door and I prayed it was Miles and not Donna finding some God forsaken reason to come back up.

It was Miles, this time I looked through the peephole. Damn that was close. He had to have seen Donna on her way out. Either that or he just missed her. She could not have left a moment too soon. A couple more minutes and I would be forced to introduce Donna to Miles. Not that I would have told him that she was an ex lover I just did not want Donna associated with or knowing anyone in my life that she did not already know. The way she said my name, her short version of it would be a dead giveaway. I use to love the way she said "Tash" with that sexy honey dipped voice. That was her special name for me. No one else ever called me that. It seemed like my lovers were big on calling me special names. Miles' special name for me was Nat. I wonder what's next; Tasha or maybe Asha? I don't know maybe soon they will run out of abbreviations.

"Hi baby."

"Hi sexy!" he said smiling hard.

He had his hand behind him all the time as he came in and shut the door behind him using his body.

"These are for you." He said handing me a bundle of flowers, those you see them selling on the streets at the stoplights.

That did not matter though, he could pick a single bud from the street side and I would be just as happy to have it.

"Thank you Miles; how was your day?"

"Better now that I am here."

He was never at a loss for words. But you cannot build a million dollar empire being at a loss for words so I was not surprised at his wit.

"I hope you are good and hungry because I am starving and about ready to have dinner with my favorite person in the world."

"You mean the whole wide world?"

"Yes, the whole wide world." I said pinching his buns.

"Ooh." Was all he said and grabbed one of my butt cheeks.

I slapped his hand and said, "No dessert before dinner Mr."

We both laughed and went to the kitchen. He helped me put the food on the table that was already set in the dining room. The dining room was separated from the kitchen only by two huge columns from floor to ceiling with a marble top breakfast nook between them. It was not yet dark outside though the sun had already gone down, but I lit the two candles on the table anyway because the inside of the apartment was much darker than it was outside without the lights so it gave the room a perfect ambience.

We talked about my Excell cover that was due out in another few days and other minor things while we ate. Miles was impressed with my cooking, it's not very often that I cook for him but whenever I do he would give me big compliments.

After dinner we skipped desert and headed to the bedroom where we lay up in bed and watched a repeat of the B.E.T. Awards from the previous year when they had the Reggae Segment with Chaka Demus and Pliers, Beenie Man, Dawn Penn and Elephant Man.

When Miles and I spend time together we never rushed into sex, except for a few times when we were both so hot and bothered we would rip each other's clothes off and behave like animals in heat.

We watched the award show from start to finish and Miles apparently thought it could not have finished any sooner because he immediately cut the television off and rolled over on top of me. I could feel his penis hard as a rock. I missed the opportunity to ask if it was a gun in his pocket because it felt like steel against my thigh.

"I'll never stop wanting you Nat."

"Really?" I was kissing his neck.

"Really, I swear I think about you more than I think about my own children."

I noticed that he did not mention his wife. I wondered how often he thought about her.

"I don't know what to say to that."

"Just say that you feel the same."

"That I think about me more than I think about your children? Of course I do." I was messing with him now.

"You know what I mean."

I got serious.

"I love you Miles, I think about you all the time too. And you know I don't have children so you get all of my thinking time." I was serious about that but as usual he thought I was trying to be funny.

"I'm serious Nat, I am going to try and make more time for us. Would you like that?"

"Of course I would darling. I love our times together. I impatiently wait for the next time I will see you. Each time I see you I miss you the moment you leave out the door. I thought you knew that."

"I think I do. That is one of the things I love about you, the way you love me."

"Well then shut up and let me love you."

"No objections here."

We kissed and fondled each other and I could feel the love I have for him boiling up inside me and I let go of any inhibitions I may have had, though I doubt there were any left where Miles and I were concerned. The man had seen me with my legs on my shoulders and my ass saying "how do you do?" more times than I would care to mention and that was probably one of the more missionary positions I have found myself in with him so there was hardly anything left to be inhibited about.

"Ooh, oh…"

He was licking my belly and working his way down to my vagina. He inserted a finger inside me and licked around my mound until I felt like I was going to explode. He used both hands to spread the lips of my vagina and when his warm tongue made contact with my clit, I totally lost it.

"Oh Miles, I love you. I want you in my life always. I want this….always."

He was not saying anything but, how could he. His mouth was busy making my catty purr.

Miles was a very thorough lover and he always made sure that when he made love to me I was totally satisfied. He is yet to disappoint me. Miles could make a quickie feel like a marathon session. He never failed to leave me sated and fulfilled. I only hope that I make him feel even half as good as he makes me feel. The man was a success with everything he touched including me. I am yet to find a single fault with Miles Covington. If ever there were a perfect man it would be Miles. But would a perfect man cheat on his wife?

I guess that's why there are no perfect men because it is my belief that all men cheat on their wives. I was watching Divorce Court on television one day and there was this woman who wanted a divorce because her husband was cheating. She said she felt bad about him cheating but when she thought about it, if a man could cheat on Halle Berry then they can cheat on anyone. I second that but it goes way deeper than looks or anything else that might have attracted them in the first place, men are just natural born cheaters and I also believe that a lot of women may have gotten the same traits because I know some women who would put some of those guys to shame.

Miles continued to put on layer after layer of sweet hot kisses where it mattered to me most and by the time he was ready for penetration I was so wet he had to wipe me dry.

"You taste so good I could eat you all night long."

"Mm," was all that came out of my mouth. But it was a language that Miles understood very well and continued to drive me crazy when he entered my body at a slamming speed. I brought my hips up to meet him and I immediately had what must have been my third orgasm since we started making love. Miles continued to lay it on me with excessive force and it was painfully good to the last drop when he screamed my name and shook so hard I thought he was having convulsions.

We spent the night together, which was also very rare and when I woke up the following morning he was gone. On the pillow where his head should have been was a single rose from the bunch that he brought me the night before. I told you the man was close to perfect, he was never at a loss for what to do to make me smile. His wife was a very lucky woman. I wondered if she knew just how lucky she was to have a man with such great qualities and to be filthy rich on top of it.

The whole time I was with Miles I never thought of Donna once. But from the moment I woke up she has been on my mind. It was easy not to think of her with Miles around because he so filled me up in every way that there was no room for thoughts of anyone but him. He had that effect on me.

Donna had a whole different kind of effect on me or maybe I thought it was different because she is a woman. I probably never felt as strongly about Donna as I feel about Miles but I had very strong feelings for her.

Donna and I met shortly after I left college. She was the Dental Assistant at my dentist's office and there were a series of work that I was having done on my teeth to properly prepare myself for my modeling career. I had root canals and fillings done among other things. I even had them straightened and bleached. It took quite a few visits to achieve the look I wanted and during those times Donna and I would make small talks.

I found her to be very funny and I used to tell her that she should quit her day job and go to Comedy Central and do standup. I firmly believe that she could be successful at it.

One day I got to the dentist's office quite some time before the dentist got there, he worked at a hospital so he was late coming in. Donna and I chatted for the whole time and she had me in stitches with her one-liners.

There was a lull in our conversation and I was flipping through one of the magazines in the waiting area when out of the blue Donna asked, "Would you like to go out and have a drink sometime?"

"Sure." I said thinking she meant a little friendly drink between two women but I later found out her proposition was more than just friendly.

She promised to call me up that weekend which was only a couple of days away and she stayed true to her promise.

I was home cleaning house that Saturday morning when my telephone rang, it was Donna.

"Hello." I said into the mouthpiece.

"Hi Natasha, this is Donna from the dentist's office. How are you?"

"I am pretty good, thank you; how about you?"

"I wouldn't complain. I was wondering if maybe we could go out for that drink later, I feel like I am taking the color of the walls in the house."

I had no plans for that day so I was more than happy to oblige as the only time I ever really get out was with Kylie and Melanie because the other girls were not yet doing the Friday night thing with us, so I was more than happy to get out.

"Where did you have in mind?"

'My sister owns a bar in Fort Lauderdale I thought maybe we could go there, it's not as crowded as some of the other places, and it has quite an elegant setting. I think you will like it."

"That sounds good to me. What time should we meet?"

"I could pick you up about eight o'clock. There's no sense in both of us driving."

"Okay, so eight o'clock it is."

"I'm looking forward to it. I will give you a call when I am ready and you can give me directions then."

"Alright Donna, see you at eight."

That night she picked me up and we had a wonderful time at her sister's bar. She was not a big drinker and neither was I but we finished one whole bottle of champagne between us and by the time we were ready to leave I was stoned. Literally stoned. The champagne seemed to have had no effect on Donna. Maybe I drank more of it than she did because I was drunk. It was a good thing that I was not driving because I do not think I would have made it home in one piece. On the other hand I don't think I would have so much to drink if I drove.

On the way home we were sitting at a stoplight when Donna reached over and touched my thigh asking me if I was okay. Even though I was as drunk as a skunk I could tell it was more than just a friendly touch asking how I was. I ignored it, just brushed it from my mind, I was not in my right frame of mind so maybe I was reading too much into it, plus Donna looked nothing like a lesbian. She was very feminine and showed no sign of being one.

I was living in an apartment complex in Miami Lakes at the time and before your spit could dry we were in my parking lot. When I got out of her car I stumbled so she insisted on walking me to my door. We made it to my floor and got out of the elevator. Donna took my keys from my hand opened the door and followed me in.

"Natasha, would you like me to stay?" She asked me with the same look she had in her eyes when she touched me on my thigh in the car, but I was still too tipsy to be sure what it meant. I thought maybe she had too much to drink herself.

"Oh, you don't have to do that I am going straight to bed anyway."

"I would love to stay." And she touched my cheek with a single finger.

"There is something I would like to talk with you about and plus it would save me the trouble of driving all the way back to Fort Lauderdale tonight by myself."

I was not sure if I wanted her to spend the night because I did not know her that well, though she seemed like a really nice person. I did not want to be a bitch about it and let her drive back all the way to Fort Lauderdale by herself so I relented.

She insisted on making me some tea and it helped tremendously. I could feel the champagne wearing off after I drank the tea. By this time Donna was sitting thisclose to me on the sofa.

She put her arm around me and asked me if I was comfortable. I felt like I was sitting there with a man and for the first time since that night I felt butterflies in my stomach because she was looking at me the way a man looks at a woman that he was lusting after.

"Natasha ever since the day you walked into our office I found myself thinking about you. Those feelings got stronger and stronger with every visit and I was not sure how to handle them so that was the main reason that I invited you out tonight. I am gay. Well, maybe I should not use the word gay because I do date men from time to time. There I said it. I have no idea how you might take this but I would love to spend some time with you and get to know you better. I know this is a lot that I am unloading on you right now but there's no other way for me to say it. I hope I have not offended you."

I was blown away but surprisingly I was not offended. I sobered up immediately, nothing like that had ever happened to me before. I have never had a woman in my face telling me she wanted to be with me sexually and I was not sure how to handle that. Though it was shocking I found myself thinking about what it would be like to be with a woman. Not just any woman; Donna.

"I don't know what to say, the thought has never crossed my mind."

I really did not know what to say, I was at a loss for words. I had no speech prepared for a situation as that and I was simply tongue-tied. Donna could tell that I was a tad uncomfortable and she removed her arm from around my shoulders and walked over to the window.

"If you are not comfortable with that I can understand but I just had to let you know how I felt about you."

She was back sitting beside me on the sofa but not as close as she was only moments before. I was no longer drunk but I found myself thinking that maybe I could try it once, just to see what it was like to be with a woman. The only thing that I was concerned with at the time was how we would do it. Would I have to do to her the things she was obviously trying to do to me? I was terribly confused. One part of me was aching to try it and the other part was asking me if I was out of my freaking mind, I paid no attention to the latter.

My mind was made up I wanted her to stay; I was getting hornier and hornier as the moments went by.

"Donna, I have no idea what I am doing or why. All I know is my curiosity is starting to get the better of me and I think its okay for you to stay."

I could not believe my own ears let alone what was coming out of my mouth. I had just told another woman who wanted to go to bed with me that it was okay to spend the night. Where in the world did that come from? I wondered because the thought had never crossed my mind, ever.

I was nervous as hell and I think she could see right through me. I suggested that we got ready for bed. I had a two bedroom apartment at the time but it made no sense putting her in the spare room because it was not one of those things where just another friend is staying over, this woman was gearing up to make love to me and I was about to let her.

That night was the beginning of my full fledge romance with Donna, my lesbian experience. I swear to God no man ever made me feel the way she made me feel that night and many nights after that.

After that night there was no turning back for me. I did not suddenly turn into a lesbian or anything like that; I was most definitely into men, strictly dickly. I was between boyfriends but I dated a guy now and again, but that thing with Donna was hot and it worked perfectly for me because I did not have to do half the things to her that she did to me. I wouldn't lie, I sometimes thought about how bad it probably looked in the sight of God but I would turn right around and justify it by the fact that none of us were perfect. The only perfect person was God himself. I grew up in the church and considered myself to be God-fearing, prayed every day and so forth. I really should read the Bible more though I don't do that enough, not since I went to college anyway. The point is that I knew it was wrong in accordance with my beliefs but I did it anyway.

Donna and I spent a lot of time together, mostly at my place. We would see each other at least four times per week which was sometimes a little much for me, but not enough for Donna. I loved her, but I don't think I was in love with her like I would be with a man, but she was crazy about me and became possessive to the point where it started to bother me.

She once invited me to go with her to Orlando to visit her sister. I was not surprised that her sister knew nothing of her lesbian tendencies because for all they know she was only into men, but the way she behaved it must have shown that we were more than just friends because when we were leaving her sister Monica said, "The eyes speak louder than words." Donna pretended she didn't hear it and said it probably meant nothing but I knew better. Monica's eyes were the dead giveaway, the way she looked at me, and it did not help that Donna kept eating off my plate at every meal. I hated that about her because she would do it just about anywhere we went. She said I worried too much, that women are naturally that way, but there were times when I would see other people looking at us, sometimes I even see them whispering and looking at us from the corners of their eyes. Donna had a thing with playing footsy under the table whenever we eat out and we ate out a lot. Sometimes I believed other people could see her doing it. I loved spending time with her but I preferred doing it behind closed doors because she became so jealous I was afraid that one day she would just do something crazy and expose me. I did not want anything getting in the way of my modeling career; not to mention my parents getting wind of what they believe to be nasty and unnatural.

Luckily for me Donna did not dress like a lesbian. Well she said she is not a lesbian she is bi-sexual. I did not put a label on myself because I knew that after Donna I was never going to let another woman get so close to me again.

We carried on our little affair for years and throughout that time Donna treated me like a queen, better than most men would and I was totally enjoying the way she showered me with gifts and money. One time I asked her how she could do all the things she did for me on her dental assistant salary and pay for that beautiful home she had and still wear all the latest designer clothes. She told me she was once married to a millionaire who died in a plane crash a year before we met and she got millions from his life insurance and later awarded millions by the airlines. She did not really need the money from working but the dentist was an old friend and she was bored having nothing to do so she took the course and began working for him until four months after we started seeing each other. I could see it coming that she was about to quit her job because when she stayed over at my place, she hated getting up to go to work and she was at my place a lot. She never missed work, she was very reliable but it was apparent to me that she much preferred laying up in bed with me all day than going to work so I was not surprised when she told me that she turned in her resignation. Because the dentist was a friend of hers she stayed for an extra couple of weeks and trained her replacement.

She was a very honest individual so she told me straight up that she quit her job because she wanted to spend more time with me. That was when the relationship started getting serious. We were spending all our spare time together and we had plenty of that.

Donna loved going to the theatre and we saw quite a few plays while we were together, I have not been to any since we broke up. When we were not behind closed door doing you know what you could find us out on the town somewhere or off on vacation to some exotic places. Kylie used to ask me where I found the men to take me on these vacations and I would just laugh. I could never let her know that I was seeing a woman because she had some very strong opinions on the subject. She met Donna but obviously the thought never crossed her mind, if it did, knowing Kylie she would without a doubt, say something about it. Kylie and I have been best buds since college and she met most of the people I knew so when she asked me when I met Donna I lied and pretended I knew her since high school.

I think she was feeling a little jealous over the friendship I had with Donna because we spent so much time together even though it did not affect my relationship with her in any way. We still saw each other as much as we used to but all the rest of the time I spent with Donna. I was careful not to talk too much about Donna when I was with Kylie and Melanie because I did not want them suspecting that our friendship was closer than it could ever be with either of them. They were my closest friends for years and suddenly Donna came into the picture and took center stage.

I was in lesbian heaven for thirty two months when it all came to a crashing end one night at a New Years Eve party in New York.

With her money Donna could get us into any party in any city and she usually did. This party was filled with celebrities like Cuba Gooding, Samuel Jackson, Steven Segal, Vivica Fox, Nicki Minaj, Arianne Grande, Jay and Bey and a few other familiar faces and they all knew Donna.

I wanted to just find someplace to sit down once I did the rounds with Donna and met half the people in the room. She knew so many people anyone would have thought she was the host of the party.

There was a little booth with a small table with two chairs that was empty and so I sat down after Donna got us both a drink. She wanted to chitchat with her friends so I sat by myself listening to the music and observing everyone. A woman came to the booth and introduced herself as Paula and asked if it was okay to sit at the table I told her it was reserved for someone but she could go ahead and take the load off until the occupant returned.

We were sitting there talking, I was not exactly in the mood to talk but I accommodated her anyway. I realized she was asking a lot of personal questions about me and when she suggested that we get together for a drink it took me back to the time when Donna suggested we go for a drink and it was déjà vu all over again, only this time I knew exactly what she had in mind and I understood clearly what the look she was giving me meant. Believe me I had no interest in anything the woman had to say but before I had the chance to say anything back Donna came rushing to the table like a raging bull, grabbed the woman and threw her out of the chair unto the floor. I wanted to die right there when she started lashing out at the woman.

"Why the fuck are you all up in her face Paula, you don't know she's here with me? Why are you all up on her?"

I could not believe what I was hearing I really wished I was dead then.

A couple of guys helped Paula up but you could see they were enjoying the drama. Warring lesbians, who wouldn't enjoy that kind of melee?

"Do you have a ring on her finger Donna?" She turned to me and I wanted the earth to open up and take me in with what came out of her mouth next.

"Are you Donna's woman, you belong to her?"

She asked that question really expecting an answer from me, I just held my head down and Donna lashed into her but did not help my situation any.

"Bitch yes and don't ever let me see you talking to her for the rest of the night." Then she grabbed my hand, pulled me up from the chair and led me out of the room like a fucking little puppy dog. I was already so fucking embarrassed that nothing she could do at that moment could make me feel any worse so in lieu of another scene between her and me I followed her without any fuss. I was never so embarrassed in my life, not before then and not since. I knew it was over between us then.

It was over before we could ring in the New Year together. I continued to see Donna but only at my place or hers never in public. I tried to break it off altogether that night but somehow I let her talk me into that new arrangement. I was no longer comfortable being with her because she was getting deeper and deeper into me. She even went out and bought a ring for me once that she wanted me to wear on my wedding finger. I remember her telling me once that we should get married in one of those mass gay wedding charade and she was serious about it too, it was shortly after that episode that she bought the ring.

The final straw came one night when I was staying over at her place. We had a big fight and I told her it was over, that we could be friends but I no longer wanted the kind of relationship that we had and she went ballistic on my ass and slapped the shit out of me. I was ready to kill the bitch because I pinned her ass to the floor and beat the holy shit out of her then went the hell home.

She called numerous times after that and I never once answered the telephone. She left messages apologizing for what she did; still I gave her no juice. I simply refused to have anything else to do with her. She popped up at my apartment a couple of times and I refused to open the door so eventually she stopped trying to contact me, and believe me eventually was a long time coming.

I moved from that apartment months later and changed my number and I never saw or heard from Donna again until she showed up at my door.

In a couple of days the magazine will be on the shelves and the following week I have the Ralph Lauren fashion show coming up in New York. Kylie wanted us all to get together the day the magazine hit the stands and celebrate so Melanie insisted on hosting a party. So on Tuesday night there will be a party at Melanie's and they have insisted that I invite Miles. I thought that was a good idea because they all liked him and he liked them too. Melanie's lawyer friend Jim will be there and Keri the only married one of the five of us will be taking her husband along. Amanda has been rolling solo for a while and so Kylie invited a couple of guys from where she used to work. I think Miguel also invited a couple of his lawyer friends to join the party. We have been trying to set up Amanda for some time now but the girl seems to have lost all interest in a relationship or a man for that matter. I did not mention it to the girls but I did not want to involve Miles in all my little get-togethers plus he was a very busy man. I did not bring Miles around my circle of people much because he was a married man and because I am fucking him does not mean that I have to walk around with him being the happy mistress.

I can't stop thinking about Donna how she just appeared at my door out of the clear blue. I still cannot understand why she did not call first since she also got my telephone number in the yellow page. When I broke off with her, for a long time I was unlisted but for the sake of my career I decided to keep a listing, it never crossed my mind that she would try to find me after all that time. I seriously thought she moved on.

I lounged around the house all weekend except for when Miles was there Saturday night through Sunday morning and my body felt totally rested but my mind was in a whirl thinking about Donna and Miles and how I would do anything to keep her away from the people that I love, the people who loved me. This was definitely not the time to fuck up, I am finished with that shit and I think I really want her to leave me the fuck alone and the next time I talk to her I'll let her know just that. Leave me the fuck alone.

I wondered what Miles would think if he knew that I fucked a woman. Some men would see it as a turn on and want to join in on the fun, 'cause that's what it is to them, fun. The typical man would want to share but they don't seem to understand that though the women are liberated enough to feel comfortable sleeping with each other, it does not mean that they would want to join in some cheesy little threesomes. I heard it somewhere that it is every man's fantasy. I wonder if Miles was one of those guys. We have never discussed anything like that but you never know what is going on in their heads, especially the little one. I do not believe that Miles is one of those guys who think mainly with his little head though; the man analyzed everything before considering anything. That's the way I've always known him to be. He sometimes get a little freaky but nothing major, don't get me wrong he drives me crazy in bed and the kitchen and the bathroom and wherever our body called but never threesomes.

Two days before the party both People and Excell magazine was finally on the shelves and that same morning I received a copy of both in the mail from Margaret. I almost peed myself, I could not believe what I was seeing. I was on the cover of two magazines on the shelves at the same time. The person on the cover of the magazines was extremely beautiful and oozing with sex appeal, I was blown away. A feeling of pride filled my entire being and the tears rolled down my cheeks, I could not believe it was really me. I have waited so long for this. I was so caught up with the photo I did not immediately see the caption above my head on the Excell cover and the tears flowed even harder. "*HERE SHE IS, MODEL AMERICA!*" screamed off the cover of the Excell and they were talking about me, little wobbly-kneed Natasha, pencil legs. That was the first time I actually thought that maybe I deserved the title "Model".

The People Magazine cover was just as beautiful but the caption was a lot simpler. "Natasha Bell....The New Face of Mitchell Modeling Agency". That was good enough for me. My face was on the cover I had no complaint.

I spent the day of the party preparing myself for the party. I did not plan on anything in particular to wear so I stopped in a little boutique and picked up something then spent two and a half hours with Karen my hairdresser getting my "Do" done.

She put a few platinum blonde streaks in my jet-black hair and the contrast was amazing. She made me look almost as pretty as the picture on the magazine covers. Karen subscribed to Excell so there was a copy in the shop that everyone was passing around and everyone was congratulating me and boy I felt like a star.

Throughout the day Kylie, Melanie, Amanda and Keri called to congratulate me; even Miguel got on the phone and told me how proud he was of me with Keri screaming in the background with glee.

My mom and dad called and said their congratulations and mom was even crying on the phone and saying how proud she was of me. My phone rang off the hook all day long. Margaret and some of the people from the agency called and Margaret suggested a party at the agency before the Ralph Lauren show. It was only a week away now and I need major preparation. Margaret will be sending along a chaperone and Kylie and Keri will definitely be there. Amanda won't be able to make it because of prior engagements and Melanie said she will try but was not sure she could get away from the salon that weekend. I will however have lots of support from all the girls and I feel blessed to have them as my friends.

Melanie had informed me that the guests should start arriving at eight o'clock so she wanted me there no earlier than nine so I could make my grand entrance while they were all there. Girlfriend was going all out on this one and it made me feel really special.

At one point I started feeling guilty because when Kylie's book was released we went out to celebrate but no one threw her a party. Maybe I should have opted to give her a party instead of taking her out to the club, even though we all got together for a bigger celebration later that week we did not do anything so elaborate. I know Kylie probably never gave it a second thought but I really feel bad now.

At exactly ten after nine I pulled up outside of Melanie's place and it was apparent that there were quite a few people inside from the number of vehicles that were parked outside.

I was wearing a simple red sleeveless tunic dress with diamond accessories and decided to mix it up with lime green mules and matching bag. I was looking the part of "the model" and it did my heart good.

When I rang the doorbell Keri answered the door and the entire room broke out in song. "Here she is, Model America" like the caption that was on the cover of the magazine and the tears started burning the back of my eyes but I successfully fought to hold them back.

When they were finished with their little ditty everyone shouted congratulations and applauded then people started taking turns hugging and congratulating me.

The party was much bigger than I anticipated both by the number of people that were there and the actual preparations. There was a live deejay and a huge congratulations banner with my name on it. How they found the time to do all that I have no idea? My feeling was that they had it planned long before they told me about it.

I thought that as nice as the party was it would have been even nicer if it happened after the Ralph Lauren fashion show, but what the heck.

The party was jumping and the music kept getting better and better as the evening rolled along. There was absolutely nothing that could put a damper on my spirit and by the look of things nothing was going to get in the way of the other people having themselves a good time.

Just as I was wallowing in that thought my eyes caught glimpse of Keri opening the front door. I could not believe that people were still showing up, it was almost midnight. What I really could not believe was the person that Keri let inside the door. What the hell was she doing here? Who the hell invited her and why? "Oh my God, I hope she does not come here and cause a scene like she did years ago." I prayed, silently.

She stood by the door for no more than a minute when our eyes met and I immediately held my head down, but she had already seen that I saw her. Oh God! She was walking right over to me. I hope she keeps her fucking mouth shut and don't even try to exalt like she did back when we were together.

"Hey guest of honor lady, congratulations."

"Donna, what are you doing here?" I was whispering so no one could hear me but her.

"Oh, you do not want me here?"

"No, I do not want you here. Who told you about this anyway?"

"Well if it matters that much I was at Melanie's shop getting my hair cut and I heard them talking about the party so I asked her if it was okay to come along and she said I could come. This is such a small world Tash, I had no idea she was a friend of yours when I first walked into the shop. It is such a small world."

"Apparently too small."

"Don't be mean Tash, I promise I will be at my best behavior."

The look on her face made me nervous.

"I won't be mean if you found some other party to go be at your best behavior at."

I was glancing around to see if anyone was paying attention to us. They were just dancing and having a good time, thank God no one noticed the exchange that was going on between Donna and me.

"Look, I…." I was interrupted before I could finish what I had to say.

"There you are!" Melanie was making her way over to us.

"Don't embarrass me Donna." I whispered before Melanie made it to where we were standing.

"Oh Melanie thank you so much, this is such a wonderful party. It's way beyond my expectations."

"Are you saying you expected less?" She was mimicking being mad.

"Oh no darling, I know you are quite the hostess I just thought it was going to be a lot smaller, and the decorations, absolutely gorgeous. I love it, I feel so blessed to have you for a friend, all of you." And I hugged her.

Her back was turned toward Donna so I as I hugged her I beckoned to Donna to go. Melanie must not have noticed that Donna left, not the party, I wished that she would. She was in the crowd somewhere being her beautiful charming self and Melanie never said another word about her, it was almost as if she totally forgot seeing her. That worked out pretty well for me. I have a feeling that it will come up again if not tonight then maybe later sometime. Donna did mention that she was Melanie's newest client and since Melanie had the most sought after hairstylists and the fact that her shop was hands down the most fabulous for miles it was expected that Donna would be going there for a long time to come. I wondered just how long. I should meet with Donna to find out more about what she is doing showing up now and why. I had no idea what became of her after our little fling. Yes, my mind is made up; before the night is over I will find a way to tell her to call me so we can arrange a meeting. She would love to hear me say meeting so she could tell me how cold I was being. She always called me cold but Donna was not the kind of person that you beat around the bush with; you will have to get straight to the point with her otherwise you have a beast of a time trying to end whatever involvement it is you have with her.

The remainder of the night turned out quite well and I did get my chance to talk with Donna long enough for her to understand that she needed to just ignore me and call me the following day. She was more than happy to oblige letting me know she would never do anything to hurt me again. I prayed to God she meant it because if she did anything to fuck with my life and my relationships with Miles and my friends I swear to God I will kill her.

I did not hear from Donna for a couple of days and I had mixed feelings about that. One moment I was hoping that she would just change her mind and forget about calling me or whatever little ideas she had in her head about me. On the other hand I was secretly hoping she would call and maybe even come over and rock my naughty little world. Really, I have no business getting involved with her again but something inside of me keep telling me that one more time would not hurt. After all I know how to handle Donna. If I didn't there was no way I could have gotten rid of her. Donna is like the lion of the lesbian jungle. Oh I forgot, she is not a lesbian she is bisexual, intimidating and sometimes downright rude, not to mention confrontational, yet so alluring and sexy. Just one look into her beautiful dark eyes and you are swept up into her whirlwind of seduction. I certainly was. The first time I really looked into her eyes was that night we first went to her sister's bar in Fort Lauderdale, after we got back to my place and she propositioned me. I remember how beautiful she was and when she kissed me her lips were soft and seductive; she sent shivers up, down and around my spine. She blew my mind and I just could not get enough. I kept going back for more, almost three years more.

But none of that stuff matters now, Donna and I are history and if she should call I will tell her there is no chance we could ever go back to where we were coming from. I was not that into women, only Donna when I was. I was not raised that way, there is nothing right about it where I come from; I just let myself get caught up in her little web of lust and pleasure. She does a body good; better than milk.

Three days after the party I was out on South Beach shopping for clothes for my trip to New York, I was heading to my car with my final purchases after four long hours of boutique-hopping and getting in and out of clothes when my telephone rang.

"Hello!"

"Hello back!"

There was no mistaking the voice on the other end of the telephone line. Donna was the mistress of seduction and she did so effortlessly.

"Donna! It's you."

"You sound surprise, maybe even disappointed." She sounded hurt.

"Oh no, it's just that I did not recognize the number and I thought it might be someone else. Anyway, how are you?"

"Not as good as I was when I last saw you. You were indeed Queen of the Night, I am really proud of you Tash; you did really well for yourself." She sounded sincere.

"Thank you Donna."

I was surprised at how my voice suddenly softened and when she asked if she could see me later that evening I was quick to comply but I warned her that I was not really in the mood to entertain, make dinner or anything like that. She said she would pick up dinner on the way and that I should just go home and chill. That was definitely what I planned on doing. We agreed to meet at eight o'clock and said our temporary goodbyes.

I threw my bags into the car and before I could get in to get out of there the telephone rang again. This time it was Miles.

"Hello Darling." The honey in my voice was eminent and he did not miss a beat.

"Someone is in a good mood today, but I guess you must have one "model" of a reason."

"Yes sir, I am just heading home from a little shopping spree. You know how new clothes affects me."

"Did you get anything special for me?"

"Oh yeah, I picked up a sweet little number for your next visit."

"Talking about visit, I need one with the newest and prettiest supermodel in America."

"You are too kind."

"So what's on your agenda for tomorrow? I was thinking we could go out to the cabin for the day and bring a picnic lunch or something. Think you might be up to that?"

"Of course I am. I would not miss the opportunity to spend an entire day with my favorite guy."

"Wait a minute! I thought I was your only guy." He joked.

"Oh sweetie, of course you are. You are a lot of guys rolled into one."

"Okay, you got out of that one." He said laughing.

"I am heading home now but as soon as I get in I will call you back. You know how I feel about talking on the telephone while I am driving."

"I love you." He sounded like he meant it.

"I love you back."

"Bye."

"Bye."

When I got home it was already past five o'clock. I put my bags away and took a quick shower, threw on a little slip dress and lay back and watch a little television. Though I did not get to see much of what I was supposedly watching because I decided to call Kylie, who in turn called Melanie who then called Keri. Keri then called Amanda and we had a little conference thing going on. We talked mostly about the party and my upcoming gig in New York. They made my day when they informed me that they would all be able to make the trip with me. I was so excited I could not contain myself. Four of the people I liked most in the world will be right there with me, front and center sharing one of the biggest moments of my life to date and being happy for me.

I was a little disappointed that Miles could not share it with me also, but who am I kidding; Miles would not dare show his face at such a very public place with me. He is a very popular man and it would definitely set off rumors neither of us would be willing to risk. He would have too much to lose, and so would I. I could not take a chance on losing Miles and all that he brings to the table. Sometimes the thought would cross my mind about what would happen if his wife found out about me. I wondered if she would up and leave, and if she did would Miles make me the number one woman in his life. The more I thought about it the more comfortable I get with what we have. I would not want to push the envelope then turn up the only loser in this very delicate triangle of love, lies and money. When I think about it I am now in a win-win situation. I am getting so much love from Miles, it does not matter to me one way or another the lies he must have to tell as long as I am not the one he is lying to and he would have no reason to lie to me, we have a very open and honest relationship but I am sure that he at some time or another, had to tell his wife a lie or two to cover for when and where he may be. And as far as the money thing is concerned I am getting quite a bit of that from Miles, so why would I want to screw up something so effortless.

So I have no other option but to count Miles out of that event. My mom and dad wanted to be there but something else came up that made them alter those thoughts. They apologized profusely but I assured them it was alright. I plan on seeing them as soon as I can slow myself. Maybe I will pay them a visit or just fly them to Miami to spend some time with me. I had more than enough room in my condo to accommodate them. I love my parents and I see them as often as I can and speak with them at least three times each week.

By the time I got off the five-way call with the girls it was already eight o'clock. I had not yet gotten a call from Donna which was quite odd. Donna was never late. The ringing of the telephone interrupted that thought. It was Murphy our night security guy at the condo. He wanted to clear Donna before he allowed her inside the building. I gave him the green light and within minutes Donna was standing on the other side of my most private domain.

"Hey! I said with the door flung open. I was a little nervous.

"He…ey. So that's your Murphy?" She asked in her signature drawl.

Her hands were filled with bags of food and she was wearing a huge tote bag hanging off her shoulders. She was feminine and sexy in a lime green and pink tank dress with pink slippers matching the bag. Donna has a way with fashion she could make a trash bag couture. I took a couple of the bags from her over-filled hands and used my foot to kick the door shut once she was inside.

We emptied the bags on the kitchen counter and there was enough food for four people at least. There was sesame chicken, steamed shrimp, vegetable fried rice, steamed rice and something that looked like spring rolls.

"What is all this, are you expecting other people?" I said that in my most pleasant voice.

"I wasn't sure what you would like so I bought a variety of things. I did remember though that you liked Chinese food."

"I see that."

I was keeping cool, I did not want to get into what I did or did not like when we were together. But I could not wait to hear what she had to say to me.

"The suspense is killing me. What is it you want to talk about so badly?"

We were piling loads of food unto plates that I took from the cabinets. I hated those flimsy little paper plates they put in the bag with your food at those Chinese carry-outs and I hate that my body was burning for Donna the way it was.

"Come on Tash, can we at least eat first? Do you want me gone so badly?"

Her eyes were suddenly puppy dog sad but I was not buying it. However I promised myself to be more hospitable from that moment, at least until we ate and talked.

"Okay, fair enough. How is life treating you?"

"Do you have to ask? Because if you have to ask I must not be looking as good as I think I look."

She had a mock frown on her face and we both laughed out loud.

"Still conceited, uh?"

"Confident."

"Well, that too."

By the time we finished eating and making small talks, it was well past ten. We spent some of the time watching sitcoms and having seconds. I had not eaten so much in a long time but never really noticed until the food was almost gone. Enough for four I thought, uh?

We set our plates on the coffee table in front of the couch. We sat on the carpet with our backs against the couch and our legs under the coffee table. It was something Donna and I did a lot of back in our time. Back when I allowed her to seduce me and take me places where no man had ever taken me before, both physically and emotionally. I am tempted to say spiritually but I don't want to get the spirit thing all mixed up in that affair.

When our plates were empty the second time around we cleared the table and I opened a bottle of red wine.

When I came out of the kitchen with the wine, Donna was already sitting on the sofa, her feet where the plates just sat.

"Get your feet off my damn table Donna, you never change."

"Oh girl, relax I can buy you any table off any showroom floor whenever you are ready. What's wrong with you anyway; since when did you get so picky? I know it is not really my foot on the table that bothers you, so tell me right now if you would rather if I leave."

I was feeling a little bad about my behavior; she was right I did not give a damn about her foot on the damn coffee table, she knew me enough to know that I did not trip over petty shit like that. Don't get me wrong, I do not just allow any old body to come up into my home and just put their feet and behind just about anywhere they please, but this was a little out-of-the-ordinary behavior for me.

"I'm sorry but I wish you would just say what's on your mind and get it over with. I know this is not as casual a visit as you are making it out to be, so get to the point." My voice was soft and considerate but very direct.

She just looked at me with the strangest look in her eyes.

"You know how I always loved you, still love you, never stopped loving you."

"Oh Donna, don't go there!"

There was a painful look in her eyes and a tear rolled from the corner of one of them, just one single tear. I do not remember ever seeing her cry the whole time we were seeing each other. She was such a tough cookie; no one or anything could reduce her to tears. I realized it had to be serious.

"I am not going anywhere Tash; at least not where you think I am going."

"What does that mean?"

"Please, just listen. This is really hard for me so just hear me out without any interruptions. Please."

I did not recognize the person sitting beside me when she spoke those words. She was covered in a blanket of grief. The Donna I know knew nothing about despondency.

I was not sure what was between the lines, but I was positive it was significant.

Donna took a deep breath then took my hands in hers and what followed changed my whole perspective on life and reminded me how precious it is; and how too many times we take it for granted thinking how some things only happen to other people, never us.

I spent the next thirty minutes or so just listening to Donna about the new developments in her life since we parted ways and I was blown away by the things she shared with me. I felt bad about the way I treated her when she first showed up at my door. But anyone who knew her would certainly understand how I could treat her the way I did, given her history.

First she told me how her entire family wrote her off when they found out she was sleeping with women. They are a very religious bunch and have zero tolerance for lesbians and gays. Her sister Monica stopped talking to her and told her parents and anyone who would listen, then they stopped talking to her. No one wanted to associate themselves with her; I guess they thought it would rub off on them.

Ten months ago she found out she had lung cancer. When she told me about the cancer I almost fell of the couch. I hugged her and cried with her and for what seemed like ages, I just held her and let her cry.

All the while she spoke about the cancer I was optimistic because of all the new technologies and medicines even surgical procedures that totally eliminate any sign of the deadly disease, but I was not prepared for what came next.

"Tash, the doctor gave me another six months to live, well five now."

"Nooooooo!" I could feel the breaking of my own heart and a strange numbness overcame me. I did not know what to say or even how to react to such horrible revelations.

I reached over and hugged her again; this time she laid her head on my chest and I cradled her to me. This time I was the only one crying, and she was the one assuring me that everything would be alright. But I knew nothing would ever be the same again; how could it?

Donna told me she had gone to several doctors, specialist, and the specialists for the specialists and they all had the same prognosis. The cancer was too far along. She only had another five months now and no one to help her through it but a shrink she started seeing just so she could have someone to talk to.

She talked about children and how happy she is now that she did not have any. She was concerned about who would take care of the children she did not have.

She purchased a home in Coconut grove sometime before she learned about the cancer, a six bedroom house with a huge swimming pool and even a tennis court in the back, but she disclosed that she hated being there because it was so big and lonely.

"What can I do to help you through this Donna?"

"I don't know just be here for me to talk to when I need it." She squeezed my fingers.

"Definitely, but I am sure that there has to be more. I want to be there for you Donna; I want you to know you can count on me to help you through this."

"Thank you Tash, but there is not much left to do now. I have my affairs in order; the house is on the market as we speak. I have a small condo that I purchased two years ago for investment purposes, I was renting it to a medical student and he moved out last month so I will be moving in there in a couple of weeks to wait out my time."

"Wait out your time? You won't be sitting up in no damn condo waiting for anything; if I have anything to do with it time is going to have a hell of a time catching up with you. And don't forget about miracles, fate sometimes throw one or two your way when you least expect it. I will certainly be on the lookout for one."

I really did not know what to say. What does anyone say to something like that? I promised myself that what happened between Donna and I in the past did not matter anymore; I will be there for her through this entire ordeal. She needed me and I will be there with her for the entire process. I prayed for that miracle over and over in my head.

Donna stayed the night and I just hugged her until we both fell asleep.

Chapter 7

KYLIE

I started my second novel, still untitled but I am elated with what I already achieved. I spend most of my time at home these days writing or going from one book event to the next. "Becca's Revenge" made it to bestseller status and my popularity was through the roof. I was very well accepted and everyone was talking about my book. I wondered why Oprah's people never called.

There was however one person who never stopped calling. Ever since I returned from my trip to New York Shane D'Marco the handsome movie star I met while I was there, the one I toured the city with then later had dinner with. The one I never told my friends about. I still did not say anything to the girls because I still did not want to jump the gun and take anything out of context. But now the time has come for me to tell them about him but I will wait until we all get back from the trip to New York with Natasha. She is modeling in a Ralph Lauren fashion show and we are all going to support her seeing it's her first big walk down the cat-walk. I am so proud of her and her achievements. She waited so long for this career to actually happen and now it's definitely on the way she could not be happier.

I spoke with Shane last night and he wants me to come and see him in California and I gladly accepted but told him that it would have to wait until I got back from that trip with Natasha. He was cool with it but wanted me to know that he was waiting impatiently. I still cannot believe that he would be so into me given the A-Listers he had to choose from. Women would give their left eye to be with this guy but he said he wanted to be with me. Kylie Mason. This guy was filthy rich from his movie deals and was apparently born into money so I was sure he was not after my little change. There were women out there who would more than likely spend millions on him just to be seen on his arm, even if he was not worth a dime.

The week went by so fast it was already Thursday and I did not pack a thing to take with me to New York. Natasha's show is Saturday and she must be in New York on Friday to prepare for the show the following night. Keri, Amanda, Melanie and I will be flying in Saturday morning.

I picked up the telephone and speed-dialed Natasha. She answered on the first ring.

"Hey girl, what's up?"

"Did you already pack for your trip?"

"I'm doing that now. As we speak."

"I haven't packed a thing yet but I guess I should get started. Do you feel like stopping by tonight?"

"No, I wish I could though. I have so much to do."

I knew she did have a lot to do but I also know that it is unlike Natasha to just blow me off. I invited her over the day before so we could chat and she turned me down then with the lame excuse that she was busy. I wondered what it is that is keeping her so busy these last couple of days and I know it's not the preparations for the New York trip or she would be more than happy to have me help her get ready. Something is going on and she is hiding it from me. I know Natasha, we are best friends. I know her almost as well as I know myself.

"What time is your flight tomorrow?"

"My flight is twelve thirty."

"Do you want me to take you to the airport?"

"I would be honored. Pick me up at ten."

"Sure. See you then."

"See you then."

I could not shake the feeling that something was happening with Natasha that she was not sharing with me. There was a certain aloofness about her that was not Natasha. I guess we all have little things that we keep from each other even if it is just for a while. Who am I to judge? I was hiding my friendship with Shane from everyone until the time is right, if the time is ever right. First I must find out all I can about him, the stuff that the tabloids did not tell me; maybe then I can tell the girls when I am certain that it is more than just a fling that will only end in sex. Maybe it is the same thing with Natasha, maybe whatever it is she is hiding from me she will decide to tell me when the time is right for her.

Shane called shortly after I got off the phone with Natasha and we burned up the phone lines for no less than three hours talking about everything and nothing. He did not talk much about himself, which I quite admired because at least ninety percent of the men that I met talked about nothing but themselves and that is such a huge turnoff. I imagined it maybe because he is a movie star and such a public figure that he was careful not to let anyone get too close to him that way. I suppose that's fair enough; After all he hardly knows me. I wouldn't expect him to just spill his guts about his private life. I bet he thought I already know enough from the tabloids.

He however, was very interested in who I was, where I came from and where I was going, but in a wholesome kind of way. He joked that I was the only real writer that he knew up close and personal and continuously showered me with praise. I could listen to him talk about me for hours on end. If he actually meant all he said about me then I must be a lot more fascinating, sexy, brilliant, beautiful and humorous than I thought I was. Whether he meant it or not, it sure did a lot for my self esteem because I was feeling like all of that. Why not, I am a woman on the rise and I am pretty good to look at, I make people laugh, I am confident and sexy and my first novel is on the New York bestseller list. I guess that makes me some kind of hot commodity now.

It has been quite some time since I dated anyone so this sitting on the telephone-for- hours-thing is sort of new to me. I keep asking myself how come he found so much time to spend with me on the telephone. Could it be true that as handsome, sexy and available as he is he still manage to keep himself free from the gold-digging clutches of the more than available and rich Hollywood women? Ever since Shane busted out on the scene he has managed to keep his personal life under wraps from the inquisitive ears and eyes of the media and his fans. I prayed his sister Carmen was right and that he did not care for the rich and famous especially. I prayed that he truly wanted a simple woman like me and I am sure that a little success of her own did not hurt as long as she was not from the world of movies, music or television. Well, if that is really the case then with all the right prayers I should be able to wiggle my way into his world. Maybe he did not want to be with anyone really famous because he wanted the spotlight to himself; then if that is the case I would be perfect for him because being a novelist is not nearly as iconic as being a movie star. I am sure he will clarify this whole thing up for me one day if we keep this up; tell me what the secret is to him keeping the gold-diggers out and staying out of the muddy claws of the tabloids. What keeps him eligible?

I could definitely use some sex in my life. Every other facet of my life is in full bloom but still no coochie action. All my friends were getting some. Natasha rattled on and on about Miles and how good he is in bed. Keri never shut up about how wonderful Miguel was in and out of bed. Melanie made no bones she was getting more than her share from more than enough men and Amanda has some secret lover she called Mr. Man that she is yet to introduce us to. So I was the only one not getting any, but with any luck that dry spell should be coming to a quick halt.

The following day I lingered at home until it was time to pick up Natasha and take her to the airport. I pulled up in front of her building and as I was pulling in as a Silver Mercedes Benz was pulling away and I could swear I had seen the girl driving the car at the party that Melanie threw for Natasha. I was certain that I saw Natasha talking to that girl. Maybe she lived in the building and Natasha told her about the party. I never really gave it much thought though.

I called Natasha from the car and before she could answer I saw her coming through the lobby so I hung up. I got out of the car to help with her luggage but the doorman appeared and took the suitcase from her and walked it over to the car where he put it in the already opened trunk. Natasha took the caryon she had in her hand and dropped it into the trunk and slammed it shut.

She palmed the doorman some money and he smiled and wished her a good trip; we then got in the car and headed to the airport.

We chitchat for a little while but I could tell she had a lot on her mind so I let her do most of the talking. She however talked mostly about the fashion show and admitted that she was a little nervous. I felt bad about not taking the flight with her instead of going later but there was nothing I could do at that point. I was somewhat relieved though when she told me Margaret would be there by the time she got to her hotel.

After I dropped Natasha off at the airport I went to Keri's flower shop and picked up a bouquet of fresh flowers for the dining room. I was hoping Keri was there so I could kill some time with her, maybe have lunch but she was not there. The girl behind the counter told me she would not be in until Tuesday so I went home.

I spent the rest of the afternoon packing for the New York trip. I was so excited and happy for my friend and her big break. I used to tell her that it would happen someday soon and finally that day was here. I was excited for myself too because I have never gone to one of those designer fashion shows before; I feel like we were finally getting in the 'know'.

The fashion show was the bomb and Natasha lit up the runway, she did not even look like a first-timer; girlfriend strutted her stuff with the best of them and they had nothing on her. At the risk of sounding bias I would think she looked better than all the other girls out there; and definitely fresher.

Margaret was there with her assistant Mona but the big surprise of the night was Mr. and Mrs. Bell showing up, sitting right there in the front up close and personal. The girls and I were in the second row immediately behind Margaret, Mona and Natasha's parents. After the show we all went out for food and drinks at some after-hours eatery to celebrate but mainly so we could all spend some time with Mr. and Mrs. Bell before they returned home.

Margaret had to get back to the Agency the following day with Mona in tow and Natasha's parents leave in the early morning. We were in no hurry to get back, our flight back to Miami was not until Monday so we spent the weekend in New York and boy did we have fun. We were all booked on the same flight back so when we got to the airport we each got a crossword puzzle book, the same issue and we challenged each other on the entire trip back. I won as always; after all I am the writer.

Immediately as I got into the house and dropped my bags I kicked my shoes off, threw myself across the bed and dialed Shane's number; he answered on the first ring.

"Hello pretty lady."

He seemed in a really good mood, even happy to hear from me. The whole time I was in New York we never spoke.

"Hello handsome. You sound mighty happy today. How was your weekend?"

"Miserable, I was missing you some kind of crazy, but I knew you were with your friends so I forced myself not to call so you could get your friend-time on."

"Oh, that's so sweet. I missed talking to you too."

"So how was the trip, did you have a good time?"

"I sure did, and Natasha was great, she was absolutely fantastic."

"I'm happy to hear that. So, tell me when you will be spending some time with me. Are you ready to come out to LA for that visit?"

"I sure am."

"So when will it be. I wouldn't mind if you came out on the next flight leaving Miami."

"Are you kidding me?"

"No I am not kidding you. I would love it if you could come right away because in ten days I will be leaving for Italy to start on my next film."

I was amazed that he was so anxious to see me. I was having a hard time trying to fathom what his real interest might be, but no matter how hard I tried I just could not wrap my brain around anything more than what it looked like. I think he really is into me.

"Right away?" I did not know quite what to say.

"Well maybe it's not fair for me to expect you to just up and go since you just got back from New York, but how about in the next couple of days, say……. Wednesday?"

"Well, I can't think of anything that would prevent me from coming out on Wednesday, so that sounds perfect."

"Great. So will you be staying with me until I leave for Italy? How does that sound?"

"Great. I think that sounds great."

"Well, I am going to get off the phone and make flight arrangements for you. Did you have any specific time that you would want to leave Miami?

"No, not really; anytime is fine."

"Fantastic, then I will make it an early flight, it is almost seven hours to Los Angeles and lady I want you here as early as possible; if you don't mind, that is."

"I don't mind at all, I actually like that notion."

I could not believe I said that. I should be careful about how vulnerable I make myself, at least until I was sure that all that stuff he was serving up was for real. I did not want him thinking that I was overly anxious, even though I really was; but he does not have to know that.

"Okay, I will make all the necessary arrangements then give you a call back with the details. I know you just got in so I could call you back a little later this afternoon after you get some rest if you prefer."

"I doubt I will be getting any rest so you can call me anytime. Thanks for the consideration though."

"You are more than welcome pretty lady. I will call you later."

"Okay."

"Bye."

"Bye."

I went around and around in my head trying to decide whether or not to tell the girls about Shane. At one point I even picked up the telephone to tell Natasha. I tell Natasha everything first; but I changed my mind. I eventually called her to talk and to tell her about an impromptu trip that I have to take to Los Angeles to promote my book, well at least that was my story. I knew none of the girls would volunteer to accompany me because after the New York trip everyone fell back into their normal swing of things. I called Melanie and made an appointment for the following day, with the same story about book promotions, and just so Amanda and Keri wouldn't feel left out I called once again with the same lie. They all bought it though and were very apologetic how at least one of them would not be able to go with me. I faked how sorry I was that they could not make it, and also lied about how busy I was going to be and that they would probably be bored to death anyway.

I spent the rest of the evening unpacking and repacking. This time I was a lot more careful about what I put in my bags. This was my chance to really impress Shane and maybe his friends if he had any; and even if he had some who said he would want to introduce me to them anyway?

I packed quite a bit of stuff for the time I will be spending in LA, a lot of which included sexy lingerie that I never got to wear but had to buy. Now I might finally get my chance to wear them. I knew I was saving them for special occasions with a special someone but I did not bank on anyone the likes of Shane D'Marco. Maybe I'm getting a little ahead of myself but I should be prepared one way or another.

I still am at a loss to the reason that Shane would want to spend his time with me when I am sure he could get any woman he chose, but the more I reflected on it the more I convince myself that maybe he was not one of the pretentious Hollywood type who just screw as many women as they can then throw them aside. I was starting to believe that he might be genuine. Then again, why wouldn't he? I am a beautiful, ambitious, sexy and now successful woman and any man would give their teeth to be with me, the only thing was that I had not met a man I truly liked since Milo.

For a while there I thought Milo was my soul mate, he was my rock; or so I thought. I met Milo while I was in college in Washington, DC. I was in my junior year and he was the manager of a men's store a couple of blocks from the school. I went into the store one day just to look around, looking for nothing really; I was simply killing time until my next class. I remember walking into the store not exactly paying attention to where I was going and bumped right into him.

"I'm so sorry…sorry."

I had knocked the clipboard he was carrying out of his hand and we both bent down to pick it up at precisely the same time and our hands touched and as if by some supernatural force we looked into each other's eyes and we both started laughing. Then his face turned serious, but in a pleasant kind of way.

"Oh, don't be sorry. I like what I am seeing down here."

"Is that so?"

"Yes, it is so.......how about dinner sometime?"

"I never accept anything bending down, especially from people whose name I don't know."

He broke into another laugh, then took my hand and helped me up.

"Good afternoon lovely lady. My name is Milo McNab and I am single, have no children, no longer lives with my mama and I would love to take you out to dinner some time."

"Well Milo McNab I am Kylie Mason and I am very busy with school and hardly ever find the time to go out on dates."

"Don't you ever eat?"

"Of course I eat."

"Everyone need to sit down at some point and enjoy and savor a delicious meal, so all I am asking is that the next time you want to sit down to one such meal, give me a call. Here's my number."

He pulled a card from the breast pocket of the nice fitting suit he was wearing and handed it to me. I did not even look at it; I just put it in the pocket of my jeans.

"Well alright, I will give you a call whenever I get the hunger for that kind of meal."

"That's fair enough."

We said our goodbyes and I never gave him another thought until it was time for me to do my laundry which turned out to be another two weeks later. That was when I saw the card he gave me, I was seeing it for the first time since he gave it to me and so I decided to call him. We went out to a seafood place somewhere out in Maryland, I think it was called Seafood House and the food was fantastic; but the company however, was way better than the food. The man was funny, charming and courteous. I was flattered and I stayed flattered for quite some time after that. I fell deeply in love with Milo within the first three months of our relationship and he was very much in love with me. I believed him when he said so because of his actions, the way he treated me and the number of times that he would tell me so. I had no complaints.

My parents both died in a car crash the same year I left high school and my Aunt Kate, my mother's sister moved me into her home to live with her. She had no children and always loved me like her own so I was very happy there. However, I did not spend a lot of time there because I went off to college. After my sophomore year I took a whole year off because I was going through so much with my parents' death I just could not concentrate on school. During that year I still stayed with my Aunt Kate in Georgia and just grieved I suppose; I went back to school the following year and it was during that year that I met the irresistible Milo. He was a dark skinned brother with black curly hair and the whitest set of teeth I had ever seen. He had that Blair Underwood type look. He was hot and he definitely knew how to treat a woman.

We had a really good relationship and got along great. It was at my graduation party that he asked me to marry him and gave me the most beautiful ruby, sapphire and diamond ring I had ever seen. I was sure he had to drop a pretty penny for that rock; you definitely did not require a magnifying glass to see the diamond, it was right there in your face. I use to wonder where the hell Milo got the money for a ring like that. I later found out that it was worth over twenty five thousand dollars and he financed a big chunk of that. By the time he ran off with his hundred-thousand-dollar lottery winner he had finished paying for the ring and I never returned it to him when I called off the wedding because he was the one who fucked up. You do not get to keep the ring when you fuck up. That is categorically against the rules of engagement. So now the ring is sitting at the bottom of my jewel chest.

After that episode with Milo, calling off the wedding and all I was not too interested in seeing anyone for a while; not seriously anyway. I get a little now and again I just don't tell anyone about it, not even Natasha. But now I believe I could go for someone like Shane D'Marco. I was never interested in the Hollywood type or maybe they just were not accessible to me, but even if they were I would certainly think twice about their real intentions seeing I am not one of them. Something in my gut however tells me that getting to know Shane might not be a bad thing after all.

Tuesday came without warning and before I knew it noon was raring its sunny little head. That was about the time I got out of bed. The first business of the day was a visit to Melanie's to get my do done. When I got there all the girls were there, their little surprise. They were all getting their hair done as well and we made a party of it like we did everything else. Melanie popped a couple bottles of Moet champagne and Jim, Melanie's lawyer lover brought us some of the best caviar I have ever tasted.

When we left Melanie's it was almost closing time. We said our goodbyes and they all wished me well on the "promotional tour" for my book. I really felt bad lying to them like that but I had to be sure what I was getting myself into before I go telling everyone and possibly make a fool of myself.

The next morning I took the shuttle to MIA and was on my way to see Shane. I was so nervous. I was flying first class of course; as I sat there I comforted myself in the thought that from then on I might never have to fly economy again. I still could not believe that I was on my way into the arms of Shane D'Marco. I slept for most of the trip until twenty minutes before landing when the pilot's voice woke me up.

Shane said he would be there personally to pick me up so I was hardly surprised when I saw him standing near the carousel where my suitcase would eventually emerge.

As I turned the corner to the carousel our eyes met and he hurried over to me with his now perennial flowers in hand. He kissed me on the cheek and took the carryon bag I had over my shoulder then handed me the bunch of red roses.

"Thank you, that was nice."

"Thank you for coming. How was the flight?"

"I suppose it was a good one, I slept through most of it."

I know he could not tell that I was sleeping because I made sure to stop in the rest room and freshened up my makeup before I went to baggage claim.

"Good girl, that is usually what I do on long flights otherwise I'd be scared out of my wits with every air pocket that the plane go through."

"Let me find out you are scared of flying."

"You just did."

The carousel lit up and the luggage started coming through the shoot. It took only minutes before my suitcase surfaced and I pointed it out to Shane who immediately grabbed it and we were on our way. As we walked out we realized all eyes were on us. Well, the eyes were really on Shane.

When we got outside Shane walked right over to a white limousine and the driver got out and set the bags into the trunk while Shane opened the door for me.

Inside the car he sat really close to me and took my hand in his.

"You are so much prettier than I remember."

"Thank you but it may be the lighting."

"What better light than the natural light of the sun."

It was early afternoon and the sun was beating down on the pavements. I guess the light could not get any more natural than that.

I laugh it off. We rode for about a half an hour before we got off the highway and into a neighborhood with nothing but Mansions and the whole time Shane was just killing me softly with compliments and just being so humble whenever the subject changed to him.

"Where is this?"

"Lovely lady, this is the famous Brentwood. My little nest is just blocks from O.J.'s old mansion."

"So this is Brentwood? Much more beautiful than what I'd seen on television."

The driver pulled into the driveway of a home that was so gigantic it looked like a five star hotel. He pulled up to the front door and a short, thick black man immediately opened the colossal double front doors and hurried over to the car. The driver opened the trunk after opening the door for us and the gentleman took the suitcase and my carry on out and headed back into the house.

Shane and I were already inside the lobby when he came in with the luggage.

"Hey Dunstan, put those in the room next to mine."

My heart dropped to my toes when I heard him say that. I guess I read too much into what I thought he may want from me. At that very moment I was glad that I lied to the girls because it was now apparent that Shane may not want more than friendship or a little fooling around. Why would he want to fly me all this way just to put me in a room by myself? I kept my demeanor and a little smile on my face, but I guess it did not work very well because he seemed a bit concerned that something was bothering me.

"What's wrong, are you okay?"

"Sure, I am just a little drained from the trip I suppose."

I was lying through my teeth, the only thing that was draining me was the thought that he did not want to sleep with me, or at least not in his own bed.

"Are you sure, would you like something to eat before you lie down?"

"Nothing to eat just yet but I would like a cup of tea if it's no trouble."

"No trouble at all. Let me show you up to your room first then I'll come back down and make sure you get that cup of tea."

"I appreciate that."

That Dunstan guy stole a look at me as he headed up the stairs with the luggage. I wonder what he was thinking.

I was a little nervous but I kept that well under wraps. I followed Shane up the most beautiful spiral staircases I had ever seen. At the top of the stairs there was a very long hallway and we went to the right where there were only two bedrooms but I swear my house could fit into one of them and my house is definitely not small.

"Thank you Dunstan" as Dunstan hustled his way back down the stairs. He said "No problem boss" and went on his merry way.

Shane showed me into the seemingly larger of the two rooms and it was fit for a king and his queen of course. I thought to myself, if that was the guest room

I could imagine what the master bedroom looked like. I looked around but did not see my luggage.

"I must be in the wrong room because my luggage is not here."

"I know; you are in the right room it's the luggage that's in the wrong room."

I was not sure what he meant so I asked.

"This is not the guest room, is it?"

"No, this is not the guest room it's my bedroom. I specifically told Dunstan to put your stuff in the guest room so he would not be all up in your business. I was not too sure about how you would feel staying in my bedroom and especially about them knowing about it."

"That was thoughtful. So where exactly do I stay now?"

"Wherever pleases you, but I would not mind you hanging out here in my room the whole time you're here."

I could not believe what I was hearing, he wanted me to stay in his bedroom and I almost had a heart attack earlier thinking he was banishing me to the guest room.

"I think I spend enough time at home by myself in my room that it would be illegal for me to give up such company and the chance to sleep in a bedroom as fabulous as this."

"I don't know about the bedroom but it would definitely be illegal to spend any more time alone than you have to."

We both laughed then he held me close, my face in his chest because he was so tall.

"Let me go see about that tea." He said pulling himself away from me. He gave me a peck on the forehead and left the room.

I was blown away by everything about the place, the color scheme the décor, the whole shebang, I must have gotten carried away looking around the room because in the shake of a cat's tail Shane was back with the tea, crackers and cheese and sliced pineapple.

"This is just a little something to keep you until dinner."

He pulled out a rolling tray from a closet and set the tray he was carrying on top of it.

"Okay pretty lady, go ahead and have you a little snack and your tea. I will leave you alone for a couple of hours to relax. Just roll the tray to the side when you're finished."

"Thank you Mr. Shane, you sure know how to make a girl feel special."

"You are. I'll see you in a couple of hours."

"Okay."

He left the room and closed the door behind him and I dug into my snacks because by then my stomach was screaming for something."

I ate everything that was on the tray then I called Natasha on my cell phone to tell her that I made it in one piece. We talked for no more than a couple of minutes because I told her I was going to a meeting. I had to keep up the façade and make it credible.

I must have been a lot more bushed than I thought because it was almost eight o'clock when Shane came into the room and gently awakened me.

He was sitting right next to me on the bed with his fingers stroking my hair when I opened my eyes.

"Hey." I said.

"Hey back. Are you ready for a proper meal now? Cause if you are I have reservations at one of my favorite restaurants."

"I'm game. But I will need to take a shower and change into something suitable."

"The bathroom is to your left, there are already towels and anything else you might need there. I took the privilege of picking up some things that ladies like."

"No you didn't. That's so sweet. Thank you Shane."

"You are most welcome pretty lady. Let me leave you alone so you can get yourself together while I go and do the same; but let me get your things first."

He turned and walked out the door and in seconds he was back with my luggage. He set my belongings down next to the bed then exited the room. Before he closed the door he turned around and what he said next just melted my heart.

"You know you have me feeling like a teenager in love, don't you?"

"Well I guess that makes us two teenagers in love then."

"I can't wait to show you off."

"In that case I better get ready."

He responded with a smile and closed the door behind him. I was indeed feeling like a naughty girl in love and I smiled at the thought of him melting in my mouth and in my hands.

A feeling of euphoria overcame me when I entered the bathroom; as if the bathroom wasn't enough to overwhelm me, he had a hot bubble bath waiting for me and a whole bunch of stuff from moisturizers to body essences, my favorite Dolce and Gabana perfume and just about anything a girl would need like he said. They were the good stuff too, the kind celebrities use and I was ecstatic because they were all untouched, brand new; bought specially for me. Perhaps he was really into me after all, why else would he go through so much trouble? I was certain he did not do all that just to impress me.

I wanted to just lie in the oversized tub and drift away but I thought twice about that. I had to make it a very short bath because I did not want Shane to wait too long before I was ready.

I made sure that the clothes that I brought with me were all just shake and go, nothing needed ironing. I selected a beautiful pink dress that was just above the knees and form fitting. There was just one strap from the left shoulder that ended at my right armpit and was matching the slanted straps on the matching pink high heel sandals. I had a black clutch purse to go with that and a pair of diamond hoop earrings and matching bracelet. My hair was still looking good from the day before and I just ran my fingers through it then did a little pinup number that Melanie would be proud of.

I applied very light make up, heavy on the eyes and light on the lips and I was more than happy with what I saw in the mirror when I was finished.

I was standing in front of the mirror taking a final look at myself when he knocked, then slowly pushed the door open and stuck his head inside.

"Are you.......ready?"

"Ready."

He flung the door open and in no more than two giant steps he was standing next to me with his arm looped. I had my purse in one hand and took the arm he offered me with the other and he led me out of the room, downstairs and out the front door. There was no one else in sight not even the seemingly available Dunstan.

The white limousine that picked me up at the airport was parked outside and the driver was standing next to it with the door open. Shane helped me in and in no time we were on our way. It seemed like he was always opening doors for me ever since the day we met.

When the driver pulled out of the driveway Shane pushed a button and the partician window rolled down.

"Roy we are going to Alfie's."

"Yes sir." Was all he said and Shane rolled the window back up.

Roy was a tall black man with thick wavy hair and brown skin. He had long legs and a strong muscular build. He more than likely doubles as a bodyguard.

All the way to the restaurant Shane was kissing the back of my hands and telling me how happy he was to meet me, and how much he looked forward to seeing a lot more of me. Little did he know I was anxiously looking forward to seeing a lot more of him; I mean a hell of a lot more of his handsome, charming and then-some self.

The limo pulled up in front of this quaint little building and Shane told the driver to hold his horses for a moment; he did not quite put it that way though, he was nice about it. That was one of the thing I was beginning to admire about Shane, the way he related to what was apparently his staff. Earlier when I was lying up in his bed recuperating from my coast to coast trip I heard him reminding someone to pick up his laundry the next day; then I heard a woman's voice, it sounded like an older woman but I could not hear clearly what her response was.

"I asked my only two friends to meet us here. I hope you don't mind."

"Of course I don't mind."

"They will more than likely bring their wives along."

"Their wives? Okay."

"Are you sure you don't mind?"

"Would it matter now?"

"Sure it would, they would understand; we could turn right back around and go somewhere else where you and I could have a quiet dinner, just you and me."

"Well, I don't mind staying here at all, I will be more than happy to meet your friends and their wives. And I really mean that."

"Thank you for allowing me the pleasure. I was hoping you would say that. Let's go."

He rolled the window down and told the driver that he would let himself out then rolled the window back up. He gave me a light kiss smack on my lips then opened the door and we exited the car with him helping me out. Not another word was spoken between us until we got inside the restaurant.

"They are already here." He said.

I was looking around but I did not see anyone befitting that group of two men and their wives. I was about to ask him where they were when a tall skinny white guy wearing a dark suit walked up to him.

"Mr. D'Marco! Good to see you. Your friends are waiting. Let me show you and the beautiful lady to the VIP room."

"Thank you William, it's good to see you too."

We followed William to the VIP room and when he unlocked the door and pushed it open I was blown away by the interior of the room. Everything was white, just pure white.

The room was empty except for the two men and two women sitting at the bar. There were white couches everywhere, huge white couches and white coffee tables sitting on white carpet. The only hint of color in the room was the beautiful red oriental carpet runners that were covering the areas most trodden.

It was absolutely spectacular and for a brief moment I could see me and Shane alone together in a place like that wrapped around each other.

He introduced me to his friends; Mark and his wife Anna, he is black she is white. His other buddy Simon is white and his wife Simone is black. They were a very good looking and pleasant bunch but I could not help the feeling that I was in fact there for more than just dinner. Well he did express that he wanted to show me off to his friends so I guess that was part of it. Still I believe that I was also there for their approval. The little get-together worked to my advantage however, because I learned a lot about Shane from listening to his friends. He apparently was not popular on the dating scene and has never been linked to any of the many beautiful actresses in and around Hollywood. Mark thought he was just too fastidious, but agreed that it didn't stop the women from throwing themselves at him.

The two women Simone and Anna seemed to get along very well and were very down to earth just like their husbands. I am no loggerhead so I fit right in and the evening turned out to be a very pleasant and enjoyable one. I left with the feeling that they all liked me, but then again these are actors and actresses we are talking about.

It was after one o'clock when we got back to the house and I was a little on air from the champagne that flowed like water throughout the night. We did a lot more drinking than eating, I even surprised myself with the number of glasses of champagne that I had.

Shane noticed that I was more than a little inebriated and thought that it was so funny. Boy was I relieved; what if he had a whole different reaction to the whole thing and was disappointed or even embarrassed. There was really no reason for him to be embarrassed however, because the effects of the champagne didn't really kick in until after I got back to the car so his friends had absolutely no idea I was walking on air.

Shane helped me up to the bedroom but once there I was semi-alright again. I went to the bathroom and washed up; I was not sure what Shane had in mind seeing he was a little enigmatic about his friends joining us at the restaurant earlier, so I did not put on anything too sexy, just in case he planned on being the gentleman for even longer. Personally I would not mind if he would just take me and rock the champagne out of me, but I guess I have to be patient. I emerged from the bathroom in a simple red nightie that was all lace and you could see the tiny black thong peeking from underneath if you looked closely enough.

There was a beautiful tan stuffed chair in the corner about four feet away from the bed and when I got out of the bathroom my eyes caught Shane sitting in a comfortable laid back position just looking at me. He was wearing nothing but boxers and I almost lost it when I got my first look at his awesome and well chiseled body up close.

"Mind if I join you?"

His voice was deep and sexy with just a hint of silkiness to it and I could feel my insides starting to get moist. What was he waiting for; I was screaming inside.

"You mean....ah...in the bed?"

"Sure, unless it would make you uncomfortable."

"I do not mind at all, after all this is your bed."

"Not while you are here. This is now your domain and I must ask your permission to share in it."

"That is so sweet of you, now how could I deny you when you have been so wonderful. Yes you may spend the night."

"I can only spend the night? I thought you said I was sweet and wonderful."

"Call it your orientation, then we'll take it from there."

"You go miss thing." He said and we both burst into laughter.

He got up out of the chair and walked across to the bed where I was standing and lifted my chin with his finger and planted a firm but quick kiss on my lips, I was about to comment on the length of the kiss when he brought his lips down on mine again, this time parting my lips with his and we had our very first deep, passionate kiss. I suppose that was the official commencement of intimacy between Shane and me.

That kiss led to a night of slow, tender patient and passionate love making. After his second nut he told me he was in love with me and that he hoped I was feeling the same way about him. Was he kidding? I am already so deep into him they will need a grave digger to get me out.

I have never felt so much so fast for anyone before and I was a little apprehensive. Milo did leave a bad taste in my mouth and there's still a little tinge of that still lingering. The saying once bitten twice shy was in full gear and it is kind of hard to just press the brakes and bring it to a sudden halt. When you have been heartbroken it is truly painful but when the heartbreak comes with such major embarrassment I believe it is even twice as hurtful and much harder to swallow, let alone get over. Shane is a very successful and available bachelor so it baffles me that he does not have a lot of women falling all over him. No secret phone calls or anything that would make me think that he had any other women in the wings. It's a possibility that even though I have not seen the signs that they could still exist, I must not forget how slick these men can be.

When I woke up the following morning Shane was not on his side of the bed. I opted to stay in bed knowing he probably was in the house somewhere; all I could think of was the night before, all of it but particularly the latter part of the night when it was just me and Shane and no one else. I can still remember him inside me, an absolute perfect fit. I wondered was that one of the positive omens that I was somehow missing. It was as if we belong together, like he and I had gone down that road before. The whole thing felt good from start to finish; It felt like a real connection.

Somewhere between thoughts of the sex and the wonderful way he was treating me, the bedroom door opened and Shane entered dressed in sweat pants and tee shirt. He was still so appealing and sexy. I still could not believe that I was actually there in his bed. Of all the things I dreamed of that was definitely not one of them. I somehow believed that men like Shane D'Marco were out of reach, out of my league; but I guess not, because there we were together, in his bed; with him inside my temple. I realized then that you only need to be in the right place at the right time and looking good never hurt either.

"Hey pretty lady, are you ready for breakfast?"

"Breakfast, did you make some?"

"I wish I could say yes I made some, but I must admit I am no good in the kitchen so I went out and got some instead."

"I could have made some and save you the trouble."

"It was no trouble and I will not have you cooking, not on your first visit anyway. I want you to just relax and have fun, nothing else. Well, maybe a little something else but I guess that would fall under the fun category."

He walked over to me while he was speaking and when he finished I had no time to reply because his lips were on mine and I could actually feel shivers going up my spine as he pressed harder and his tongue made its way into my mouth effortlessly. His kiss was deep and seductive and I could feel my insides erupting like a volcano and a rush of emotion surfaced and he could see that I was hankering for more.

"Are you still hungry?" he asked as he planted little kisses all over my neck and shoulders.

"Yes I'm hungry, but not for food."

"If not food, then what?"

"Do you have to ask?"

"I guess not."

He guided me to the bed and gently laid me down and opted not to undress me but instead pulled my nightie up above my breast and plastered my body with lithe, passionate kisses while he slowly pulled down my panties. I was out of my mind by then and had no idea when he got out of his clothes. What followed was a half an hour of pure delight. He explored avenues I never knew existed and made me feel things I imagined only happen in story books. When it was over we lie in each other's arms and fell asleep.

It was way past midday when we finally got out of bed and got dressed. We totally ignored the breakfast he bought earlier; he thought the bagel and cream cheese and vegetable omelet would be soggy by then so we opted to go out for lunch instead. We both had tasty lobster dishes and a lot of wine. We fed each other and even stole small kisses and I could see some of the patrons watching us. I imagined he saw them too because at some point he was having fun secretly watching them watching him. He made no effort to hide me from the curious eyes of the people around us so I started thinking that maybe he was not just fooling around with me after all; just maybe he wanted me as much as I wanted him. Shane uprooted feelings in me that were deep-sixed for what seemed like centuries. I was suddenly feeling alive again thanks to Shane. Becca's Revenge had something to do with my new found bliss but Shane D'Marco should definitely be credited for a massive portion of it.

After lunch Shane took me on a surprise shopping spree and boy did he drop some dough? Everything we picked out were designers, and I said we because Shane was right there telling me what he did and did not like and I was surprised to find out that we actually have similar taste. When the shopping spree ended we had a couple of bags between us but arrangements were made between Shane and the store representatives to have the rest delivered to the house later that day.

That evening when the deliveries arrived I was even more surprised to see that Shane had the store clerks slip in quite a few more pieces than I had actually picked out. So much that he had them deliver a huge suitcase to pack them in; and that was designer too.

I was speechless; I had absolutely no idea what to say. I was more than happy when he broke the silence.

"I took the liberty of picking out a few more things while you were in the dressing room. I figured you might get a little tired of slipping in and out of stuff so I went ahead and told the clerk to add them to your purchases and she was more than happy to keep my little secret. I hope you don't mind."

I thought that was the sweetest thing and it actually made my heart glad. He was so different from the men I was used to; but then again I have never dated a movie star before and I suppose they get enough practice playing romantic roles, so it would without doubt come more natural to them to be romantic in real life.

"I don't mind at all. Actually, I think it was a nice surprising gesture."

"I hope nothing else I do surprises you, because I want to do a lot more than just buy you clothes, shoes and jewelry. I think I am falling in love with you. What am I saying? I am in love with you."

I was about to respond to what he said but before I could say anything he spoke again.

"It is okay if you are not in love with me yet, I do understand that our emotions do not run the same course and not everyone fall in love at first sight, so it is alright that you go at your own pace. Just promise me one thing."

"What." I said in a whisper.

"Just keep being your sweet, sexy self."

"I wouldn't know how to be anything else."

"I'm happy to hear that. Now, I have some work to do in the office so I'll leave you alone to sort through your stuff or do what ladies do. Oh, my cook

Ms. Esther came by while we were out and I think she made us dinner. She had to run out and do some grocery shopping but she will be back by the time we are ready to eat. She's a nice lady; I want you to meet her."

"Alright, let me know when it's almost time for dinner so I can wash up."

"Okay, I'll be in the office."

The office was on the first floor, I knew that because when we got back from that surprise shopping spree earlier in the day he gave me the tour of the place and boy was I impressed. He had everything to his comfort including a gym, a mini movie theater, a party room that emulates a club setting and a very upscale one at that. The place even boasted an arcade with all types of pinball machines and games, there was even a couple of pool tables. I have never been in a house like that before, never even drove past one, I don't think.

I spent most of my time that evening packing my new suitcase with my new stuff; shoes, belts, not to mention the different variety of clothes. I thought about giving him a little surprise of my own and picked out one of the dresses that he selected. I was going to wear it to dinner. It was dark blue tunic dress that sits just above the knees with two slits way up on both thighs. The dress boasted a lime green band high above the waist. I selected a pair of lime green mules that matched the bow perfectly. All of which is courtesy of Shane D'Marco.

That night at dinner in the biggest dining room I've ever seen outside of a restaurant, I met Ms. Esther. She was a tall wiry woman with a face that had obviously seen some life, yet fresh and pleasant. She did not say much but the food she prepared spoke volumes about her skills in the kitchen. We had my favorite Caesar salad followed by chicken teriyaki and yellow rice, and the best corn bread I ever had, even the homemade cheese cake and coffee tasted deliciously different than anything I was used to. I complimented Ms. Esther on the food but she just nodded and squeezed a half-smile from one corner of her mouth. When she was out of ear shot Shane told me that he knew her since he was a child. Her only child Melvin was his best friend in high school and college, but he died in a car crash and she has never been the same since. He always stayed in touch and when things got a little hard for her and he tried to help her out financially she turned him down time and time again. She was a proud woman who would not accept handouts. She was never married and raised her son by herself; he was all the family she had. Shane eventually realized that she was adamant about not accepting what she called charity, so he offered her a job as his cook and she accepted. He said the arrangement was working out perfectly for him because as a kid he loved her cooking and he paid her enough money so she would not want for anything.

After dinner Shane wanted to take me out for drinks but I was pooped by then, so I settled for martini at home and he went out to meet with his agent which was the main reason for the drink out. It was quite alright with him that I didn't want to go and it was more than alright with me that he had to go because I needed some time to call the girls and tell them what was going on. I am finally comfortable enough to let them in on my big secret.

As soon as I got back into the seclusion of his massive bedroom I threw myself in the arm chair in the corner and dialed Natasha's number. She answered on the first ring.

"Girl, why can't anyone hear from you, what's going on, you okay?"

"I am fine, thanks for asking and I am sorry it took me so long to call but I can explain."

"I was just worried about you, because I know you are alone out there and you turned off your phone. We were all worried."

"Thanks, but no need. You won't believe what I have to tell you."

"What, Oprah called?"

"As good as that sounds this is better."

"What could be better than plugging your book on the Oprah show?"

"If you shut up long enough I'll tell you."

"Okay, I'm zipped."

"I met Shane D'Marco."

"You mean Shane D'Marco as in my Shane D'Marco. The Calvin Klein underwear-model-movie star, Shane D'Marco? Where did you meet him?"

"I met him in New York."

"New York, aren't you in California?"

"Yes I am in California I just did not tell you the whole story."

"What story? You're confusing me now."

"I met Shane when I was in New York doing the Kelly and Michael show, we met backstage, I gave him a copy of my book, I thought he left because I was there signing autographs for almost three hours but on my way out he greeted me at the elevator with flowers. We had lunch and dinner later that day, and actually this California trip was his idea, stemming from that meeting. So I am not actually here to promote my book but to spend time with Shane D'Marco."

"I can't believe you never told me about him, and then you lied to me, to us about the trip."

"I wasn't sure what would happen, so I did not want to put my hopes up and then get them dashed. You know how it goes with those Hollywood types, so I wanted to wait and check things out first. "

"I understand that perfectly, but Kylie I am your best friend."

"Yes you are, and as my best friend you will try to understand where I am coming from, won't you?"

"I guess, but I am still a little steamed that you kept such juicy secrets from me, but I love you anyway."

We were both acting like little school girls as I gave her the lowdown on the last couple of days, and I could tell she was happy for me. Before we got off the telephone we conference in Melanie and Amanda but Keri could not be found. They all cursed me out a little for holding out on them but they were very happy for me. I could not ask for better friends.

The rest of my visit with Shane was filled with little surprises, the biggest of which was the diamond earrings with matching necklace and bracelet. He gave me that the night before I left. We actually rode to the airport together the next day. He was headed to Italy and I was going back home to my life. I had the feeling though that my life would never be the same again.

Shane had unquestionably won me over and I knew I was falling deeper and deeper in love with him, but I was not as verbal about it as he was about being in love with me. I pretended not to be bit by the "love at first sight bug" but I emphatically was. I think however that he knew I was feeling a lot more than I was letting on.

The entire trip home I did not get a wink of sleep, all I could think about was how wonderful Shane was and the sweet, sensual sometimes hungry way we made love to each other. I prayed all Shane was dishing out was for real and not just something to do until he left for Italy, because I was in love.

Chapter 8

AMANDA

I arrived at work today in a really bad mood. Monday has never been a good day for me but I have been having a lot of days like that lately when I have no desire to do anything. I kept my distance from the employees because I really did not want to take out anything on them. One of the things I learned about management is that if you want the best out of your workers you must keep them happy. It seems to work very well for me because I have very hard workers who totally respect me. There is absolutely no one that I have to put a big stick to in order to get the work done; I guess I trained them well.

Just when I brought myself to thinking that my day would not get any better, it did. I was just sitting there in my office twiddling a pen, I knew that I should be doing something hut I just could not connect with work, so I just sat there looking in space. I could not understand why I was feeling that way because I had nothing to be sad about; but I could not shake the blues. Well that was until I got the telephone call. I checked to see who it was before I answered because by then I was not in the mood to talk to more than a chosen few. I grabbed the phone with swiftness when I saw the number. It was the woman who owned the store space I was waiting to lease.

"Hello."

I could hear the nervous tension in my voice and my palms started sweating. My day was already going downhill for no apparent reason so I braced myself for the worse.

"Hello Amanda; this is Linda."

"Hi Linda, how are you."

"I am fine, thanks for asking. I know you are probably busy but I just wanted to let you know of some unexpected changes."

"Changes, ah…aah.. What's wrong?"

"Oh no honey, nothing's wrong, quite the contrary. The store is empty now, the tenants moved out a couple of days ago so I was thinking if you want to start the process right away you are more than welcome."

"Definitely, I would like to jump on it right away."

"Great, then I will go ahead and draw up the lease."

"Thank you so very much Linda, you made my day."

"It's my pleasure honey, you are more than welcome. I will call you in a couple of days and we can meet at the store, so we can go over your floor plan."

"I appreciate that. I will be looking forward to hearing from you. Thanks again Linda."

"You are welcome Amanda. We'll talk in a couple of days."

"Okay, bye."

"Bye-bye love."

The moment I got off the telephone my day took a one eighty and I suddenly remembered what it was I sat down to do. There was something I had to do before I finally buckled down to some work. I had to call Mr. Man and tell him that the store became available sooner than we expected. That was a matter of urgency because he would be the one financing the whole project, start to finish.

When I called him he did not answer but I let the voicemail pick up and when the beep came I said nothing; that way he would know that I called because I always block my number when I call him. When he tried to retrieve his messages he would know the silent message belong to me; that was one of our many ways of connecting with each other.

I immediately called Melanie; of all the girls I was closer to her and Keri. Natasha and Kylie were best friends long before the three of us met them and therefore they have this bond between them that was deeper than that of the entire group, so it was natural that the three of us got close. If our circle of five should break up I think Natasha and Kylie would be one group and Melanie, Keri and I would be the other. We still manage however to form a nice bond between us and love each other dearly.

Mondays and Tuesdays are Melanie's days off so I called her cell phone instead of the shop where she could usually be found.

"Hey Amanda, what's up girl?"

"A lot, you would not believe what just happened."

"What?"

"You remember that place I told you about down on South Beach that was supposed to be coming up in a few months?"

"Yes, I remember. What about it?"

"Well, brace yourself....Its' available now. Right now, ready."

I could hear Melanie screaming at the other end of the line, but it was apparent that she had removed the phone from her ear. When she came back on the phone I could still hear the joy in her voice.

"Oh Amanda, I am so happy for you. I know how badly you want to start your own business, and now the chance is finally here. We have to celebrate. Did you tell the other girls yet?"

"No you are the first person I called. Well, make that the second; I called my friend, Mr. Man but I did not get him so you are the first to hear the news."

"Talking about your Mr. Man, when are you going to let us meet him? I'm sure he can't be that bad as picky as you are."

"When the time is right, and I am not picky."

"Yes you are picky. I think as one of your best friends you should at least let me meet him."

"Yeah, right! Anyway lady, I am at work so I will call you later."

"Avoiding the subject again?"

"Yes. I have to go we'll talk later."

"Okay, congratulations again. Catch you later."

Okay, bye."

I called the other girls, I got everyone but Kylie she was off somewhere with Shane D'Marco, the movie star. I still can't believe that she is really dating a movie star. She told us all about him after that trip she took to California and I swear girlfriend is in love. He is all she talks about since that trip. That was actually her first time in California but since then she went back so many times I've lost count. I am happy for her because she is really happy and the whole thing looks to be working out quite well for her; what with all the expensive gifts and jewels he has been lavishing on her. She deserves every bit of it. She went through some shit when that shithead Milo ran off with that girl because she won a little money in the lottery. I bet all that money is gone and he is somewhere regretting leaving Kylie for that skank. I am most certain that he had wind of her success and wait until she goes public with Shane he will definitely piss his pants then.

I got a lot of work in before I left the office because the news suddenly charged me up and got my motor running. By the time I left work it was way past eight o'clock and usually by six I am out of there.

When I got home that evening Mr. Man called and I gave him the good news. To be honest I was a little worried that he would say he wasn't quite ready or something but he was as elated as everyone else. He told me that he would be down to see me in two days when he would give me the check to take care of the whole shebang. I fell in love with him all over again. I guess money is never really an issue with these celebrity types, they just write a check and take care of the problem, sometimes before it becomes a problem.

I was overjoyed. When I got off the phone with him I called Linda and told her that everything is full speed ahead. She was happy to hear that, I could hear it in her voice.

Melanie called me back that night and was still talking about a celebration to kick off my new endeavors but I talked her out of it; well, you can't exactly talk Melanie out of throwing a party but I managed to convince her to at least wait until the store was ready to open. She hesitantly agreed and all was well with the world of parties again. Of the five of us Melanie throws the most parties. If someone's cat gives birth she wants to throw a kitty shower, the girl is incorrigible.

The next couple of days went by really fast because I threw myself into work like I never did before. Mr. Man dropped off a check for me like he said he would; a cashier's check at that. No chance of that bouncing, though I never thought that he would give me a bounce check anyway. He is a very rich and upstanding man.

He did not spend a lot of time with me when he dropped off the check. He had a flight to catch and he couldn't stay but a few minutes so I did not get a chance to look at the check until he left.

When I opened the envelope I had to take a second and third look because I could not believe my eyes. The check was for two hundred and fifty thousand dollars, I could not believe it. I was expecting something like maybe a hundred thousand dollars but never two hundred and fifty thousand. I had enough to pay a whole year's rent, prepare and stock the store with still enough left for a nice working capital. What more could a girl ask.

I will have to quit my job at the department store because my store is going to demand a lot of my time I know what it will take to make it successful and believe me letting someone else be in charge is not the way to go. At least not from what I learned in this business. People are never as honest as they seem and I know a lot about that sort of thing, being in the retail business for as long as I have, so being hands on is not even an option.

I met with Linda at the store and the meeting went well, I gave her the blueprints; I had it prepared a long time ago when Linda and I did a little mini contract to seal the potential deal. She was responsible for the reconstruction, setting the place up to my specifications. I also gave Linda a check big enough to cover the deposits and a whole year's rent. She decided not to start charging rent until the store opens.

The next order of business was to call Miranda. Miranda is the buyer for the store that I currently manage and she also buys for a couple of small boutiques in Aventura and Saw Grass malls. Miranda and I have a very good relationship, a friendship almost and we talked about her being my buyer once I got the store. I called her and arranged a meeting for the following afternoon and she was as excited as I was.

I put all my plans into gear and if all go well in two months I should be having my grand opening, but there is still one thing I have not decided on. I still do not know what I will name the store yet, I have a few ideas but I want to run them by the girls and see what they think or even get their take on things.

We are meeting again on Friday for our girls' night out so maybe then they'll help me come up with something.

That night I was so excited I couldn't sleep, so in the middle of the night I got up, started up my computer and wrote my resignation. I decided I would give them a month's notice and help in the interview process before I leave. My boss is a cool guy and he would definitely be happy for me and I will unquestionably miss working with him but I must move on.

When I got back into bed sleep came quickly but did not seem to last long at all. I got dressed and went to the office as usual and actually got a lot of work done, got everyone organized then left to meet with Miranda for a business lunch at Olive Gardens restaurant on Biscayne Boulevard. We discussed the lines of clothing I wanted to carry in the store, the age group that I was aiming for, everything down to accessories and estimates on what it would cost to stock up. The meeting was successful and by the time we parted ways I was already feeling like an entrepreneur. I was finally getting my own business, my very own. I had to literally pinch myself to make sure that I was not dreaming.

I went back to the office and got some more work in, but by five o'clock I was so tired I decided to call it a day and went home, which was not that unusual because most days I would leave hours before closing.

I was relaxing at home just making phone calls, putting the wheel in motion, at some point I turned the television on and the evening news was on. I wasn't really watching, just taking glances but I could hear everything. I was shocked out of my wits when Mr. Man's face appeared on the screen and the newscaster was sadly informing the world that Mrs. Michael Langston was dead; the wife of famed preacher Dr. Michael Langston. I felt like someone pulled at my heart strings and snap them. My thoughts went straight to Michael; I know he must be having a hard time with that because in my heart I knew he loved his wife. There were times when I wished I could have Michael for myself but I know that was only wishful thinking but now that his wife is gone I wondered would I be the next Mrs. Langston. I know it is fucked up to think that way but hey.

I got a hold of myself. How could I be thinking so selfishly when Michael was apparently going through so much? There were all kinds of thoughts going through my head. Why didn't he call me? I thought I would be the one he called when he was aching or going through changes. I was not sure if I should call because he was probably with his family and friends and that might make it a little awkward for him to even talk to me.

Another thing that kept going through my head was how mysteriously the man above worked. The store was not scheduled to be available so soon, and neither did we expect his wife's passing so soon, so I wondered if I would have still gotten the money if the death came before the availability of the store. Though I couldn't see why not because Michael had a lot of money, no matter the size of the funeral and everything surrounding it he had enough money to cover it all in style and it would not leave as much as a small dent in his financial status. Mr. Man is filthy rich.

I wanted to call someone, someone I could talk to about it but there was no one to talk to. I still have to keep our little secret because any public knowledge of our affair could still ruin his career. Deep down in my heart I was hoping with all hope that he would eventually make me his wife. Mrs. Michael Langston sounds good on me. I was feeling a little guilty that all I could think of during that time was snatching up that dead woman's husband even before her body got cold. But I got over that with quickness when the telephone rang and Michael's number came up on the screen. I answered on the first ring.

"Hi baby, I just saw the news on television, I am so sorry."

"I know. I wasn't sure you heard so I wanted to let you know."

"So, how are you doing?"

"I am doing fine, she was not doing so well over the last couple of months and the doctors told us that her time was coming, I just did not think it would be this soon."

"Oh, baby I am so, so sorry. I don't know what to say."

"You don't have to say anything sweetheart I know where your heart is and I appreciate you very much."

"Is there anything I can do for you to help make this easier?"

"Just continue to be your sweet discreet self for now and everything will fall into place. Just be there when I call."

"Okay sweetie, that goes without saying. I will be here whenever you need me."

"Thank you Amanda. I have to run so I will call you tomorrow I will have to go and make some funeral arrangements. Her mother and sisters are here at the house so they will help me through all the planning."

"Well alright then I will be here when you need me."

"I know baby, I have to run so I'll catch up with you later."

"Hang in there pal, we'll talk soon. I love you."

"I know. Talk to you later."

When he hung up the telephone I realized that he did not say he loved me like he usually does but I guess I understood. He would probably feel guilty telling me that when he was about to bury his wife, being a Christian man and all.

Sleep that night was even more far-fetched than the night before. I simply did not get any. I spent my entire night thinking about Michael and his dead wife and my new found project among other things. But the thing that hounded me most was whether or not Michael would want me to be his wife once the smoke cleared or if I would still have to play the game of hide and seek. In all honesty I do not expect him to just show up with another wife out of the blue, but when the time is right in the sight of God and man I expect him to make an honest woman out of me. I may not be a Christian but I am a good girl who wouldn't mind being a preacher's wife.

I did not bother going in to work the following day. I had a few things to take care of concerning my new project and I had a hair appointment with Melanie. In fact all four of us girls had appointments at Melanie's that day. Later we would meet for our regular Friday night get together. I spent most of the day running errands and getting permits lined up so I would meet my scheduled grand opening which was only two months away. I chose the last Saturday in September as grand opening day so I wanted to make sure there were no snags, I wanted that day to be smooth sailing.

I arrived at the salon about a half hour later than my appointment time but Melanie did not have any one else in her chair so I did not have any wait time. Boy was I lucky? I hate to have to wait when I go to get my hair done.

By the time I got there Kylie and Natasha were already sitting under dryers but there was no sign of Keri. She is always later than anyone else in the group so that was not quite so unusual.

I noticed that Melanie was not her usual talkative self so I inquired about her silence.

"What's eating you? You are not your usual self. Do you want to talk about it?"

"Talk about what?"

"What's making you so quiet? If I didn't know you very well I would think you are in mourning or something."

"Mourning, why would you say that?"

"Melanie, cut the crap. I know you and something is definitely wrong."

"Well, I guess you do not know me well enough because I am just fine."

"Okay then, I won't push but if you need me I'm here."

"That is good to know but I am fine Amanda."

"Well that's good to know, but you might want to erase that look of worry from your face."

"Girl, leave me alone."

The whole time she was doing my hair all I could think about was Mr. Man and his dead wife and how that would affect our quiet little relationship.

I knew Melanie had a lot more on her mind than she wanted me to believe but I left her alone like she asked and did not mention it again the whole time I was there. I was her last appointment for the day. She made it a duty not to take any clients in the afternoon on a Friday because that was the day all of us girls get our hair done. Melanie does all our hair except for Natasha who gets her hair done by Karen, a white girl that does black hair as well as any other I know. Karen use to work at another salon where Natasha use to get her hair done, but when Melanie opened her shop Natasha encouraged her to work in Melanie's shop. Melanie does not rent her booths out, all her employees are on commission and I have never seen a more dedicated bunch of hairdressers. Melanie once told me that they hate the idea of being called hairdressers, they prefer to be called stylists.

All four of us left the salon together that evening and Melanie mentioned something about Keri being tied up at work but mentioned that she would be getting together with us later that night.

When I got home I called Mr. Man to see how he was holding up and he seemed to be hanging in there and he managed a few laughs so I was not so worried about him as I was the day before when he called to give me the news about his wife. He told me that he wished I was there with him to help him through it but we both knew that was only wishful thinking, but it made me feel good that he would want me there with him if it were at all possible. When I hung up the phone, I was left with the feeling that I was still on his mind; and alive in his heart.

I know it's uncouth but all I kept thinking about is becoming the next Mrs. Langston. I felt sympathy for Michael but somewhere deep inside me I was relieved that he was no longer considered a married man. I felt shame for the way I was thinking but I could not shake the feeling. I would like to be the one he chooses if he opts to get married again. Well, he is a Christian man and I am sure he would need companionship, not to mention sex and if he wanted sex without sin in the eyes of his congregation, not to mention in the eyes of God from what I heard, then the logical thing to do would be to remarry. My mind was all over the place and I also wondered if I was truly the only woman that he was seeing outside of his marriage. Not that I don't trust him but I do have some reservations because he was cheating on his wife with me and I am positive she had no knowledge of it, so what would stop him from having a second woman on the side? Nothing from where I am sitting.

I called Keri and we chatted while I did some chores around the house and she assured me she would be meeting with us later that night. She also informed me that she spoke with Melanie earlier and she sounded like she was crying but would not admit to it citing that the air conditioning in the shop was getting to her sinuses. I never heard any such complaint from Melanie before and was convinced that something was wrong.

I chose a red tailored pant suit to wear out that night, we were going to some new place that just opened up on South Beach called Pros and we heard it's the in spot for professionals. Kylie told us about it a couple of months ago and so we finally decided that would be the place for the night.

We all arrived at approximately the same time, we planned it that way of course; and we parked in a twenty-four-hour parking garage only a block from the club. Kylie and I were the first to arrive and we waited but a few minutes when Melanie, Natasha and Keri pulled in behind each other like they were in a motorcade.

They parked and joined me and Kylie and it was on from the moment we left the garage. There were guys ogling and hollering at us from left right and center and we were eating it up. None of us had any interest in them at all but we enjoyed them drooling and carrying on over us the way they did.

When we got inside the club Kylie approached a huge black guy and said something to him, we were out of earshot so I had no idea what was said but she beckoned to us and we followed them to a secluded corner of the club that was roped off and furnished with huge couches and exquisite oversized coffee tables. VIP. I was impressed because we were the only people in that section of the club. He wished us a good time and left. Before we could even get ourselves situated a beautiful blond waitress made her way over to us, I was about to tell her to give us a few minutes when she spoke.

"Good evening ladies, welcome to Pros."

We said hello in unison and she continued talking.

"Miss Mason I was advised to tell you that all your drinks and food is on the house and that includes your friends."

"Really, that's mighty generous. Tell the house we thank them very much."

"We do appreciate that." Melanie said.

"What's your name?" Keri asked.

"I am Stephanie and I will be your server for the night."

"Well thank you Stephanie we appreciate that." Natasha said getting her two cents in. We ordered our regular Cristal champagne and some good smelling hot buffalo wings and the party was on.

While we waited for the waitress to return with our order I took the time to pick the girls' brains about what I should name my store.

Keri was the first to come up with something.

"How about Styles, I always said that if I did the clothing store thing that's the name I would use."

"That's pretty." Kylie said.

"I can't come up with a damn thing right now, I will have to give it some thought; maybe sleep on it." I laughed

"No need, I got it." Melanie said with a big smile.

"Let's hear it."

"Well I was thinking that since Miss Thing here is so secretive about everything that's going on in her life; specifically her man. The only appropriate name for the store, especially since he had so much to do with it becoming a reality for Amanda..."

"Oh cut the crap and tell us what you got." Natasha interrupted.

"As I was saying before I was so rudely interrupted." Everyone laughed when she said that.

"Okay this is it; drum roll please."

We all made a roaring sound and Melanie continued her little speech.

"And the official name of the store should be Secrets. What do you think?"

"What do I think? I think it's perfect. What you all think."

Everyone was in agreement with the name and as Melanie said, it was official.

"Secrets" if it worked for Victoria it will most definitely work for me. We drank to Secrets once our drinks arrived and for the rest of the night the champagne kept flowing, and I was never crazy about buffalo wings but they tasted pretty good and boy did we eat a lot.

Melanie seemed a little distant at one point and I was convinced that something was going on with her that she was not sharing with us. Or was it just me that she wasn't sharing with? I had no idea what it could be but I could tell something was definitely wrong. She was just not altogether her jovial self. Melanie was always the most buoyant of the five of us and the Melanie I was seeing was so not her usual self.

The club was jammed with patrons and I noticed that most of the couples in the club were of the same sex. There were groups of women and groups of men, with just a few mixes. Everyone was having a good time. Even Melanie got out of her funk long enough to get up and burn up the dance floor with some white guy who she later said was a doctor. She told us she took his business card that he offered to her and she told him that one day she might call him for a checkup. What is it with her and those white men anyway? Not that I have a problem with white men or any type of men in particular, but she was already dating Jim. Oh, well.

We all had a good time dancing but mainly among ourselves. Melanie was the only one that danced with someone. Most of the times when we go out together we pretty much stick with each other, no getting close on the dance floor with too many guys. We just do our girlie thing and have just as much fun if not more than all the people rubbing up against each other sharing sweat.

When we left the club that night we walked to the parking lot and hugged each other goodbye, got into our vehicles and went our separate ways.

The following morning I felt fried, I was so tired I could not get out of bed not to mention the hangover I had. I just dragged myself around the house laying up wherever the mood hits me. I called up Mr. Man to check on him and he was busy making funeral arrangements like I expected and there was a lot of people around him so we did not talk for long.

I called in at work to see how things were going like I always did on Saturdays and Sundays. Those were my two days off and that was by choice. I hate having to work on weekends but there are times during inventory that I would be there all seven days of the week working long hours, mainly to oversee what's going on but sometimes pitching in to help. I still can't believe that I was going to be my own boss, the captain of the ship, whatever I say goes and no one to tell me that I can't do this or that one way or the other.

Throughout the day that hangover feeling persisted and I even threw up a couple of times, but I chalked it up to all the champagne I had the night before, but when I was still throwing up on Sunday I made the decision to see a doctor the following day.

I was the first to arrive at the doctor's office and I was in and out of there in a flash. He gave me a complete physical including blood test and some other shit I was not too sure about but I trusted him. He has been my doctor for over four years and I completely trust him. I was not at all worried about anything but I was way past due for a physical anyway.

After leaving the doctor I went directly to work without giving a second thought to my health or the reason I went there in the first place. It was not exactly a normal day at work for me because I was on my way out and wanted to make sure that when I left everything would be in perfect order and easy to access.

The end of the day came fast and I was on my way home about six o'clock when my telephone rang, it was the doctor's office.

"Hello." I said as if I was expecting some bad news or something.

"Hello Amanda, this is Dr. Brock. How was your day; feel any better?"

"Lots, but I get the feeling that I am not as good as I feel. What's going on?"

"There is nothing to worry about, unless you do not want a baby."

"A….a...a... baby?"

"I get the feeling you weren't expecting this diagnosis."

"You are right about that. How far along am I?"

"Well, for that we will have to do another test, so you can come in and see me when it is convenient for you."

'I will, thank you doctor."

"You are welcome Amanda. Just come into the office when you get ready."

"Okay, I will. Thank you Dr. Brock."

"You are welcome Amanda. See you soon."

"Bye."

Pregnant! How could I be pregnant now? This is definitely not the time for a baby. What will Michael think? Better yet, what will he do? I know I am going to keep the baby because there was no way I would get an abortion, I just did not believe in taking a life no matter what stage it's in and having an abortion to me would be like committing murder. I do not believe that Michael would want me to have an abortion either not with his religious beliefs, but with the death of his wife and all I am nonplussed about how to handle this situation. I know though that I would wait until after the funeral and all before I let him know about our baby. This was going to be his first child unless there are others that he did not tell me about. As far as I know his wife got sick less than six months after they got married so they never made any babies together, but I wonder was there any other women out there who may have a child for him. I would not dare think that I was the only woman he ever cheated with.

How the hell did I get myself pregnant, Michael and I used protection all the time. Oh gosh, except that one time about a month and a half ago when we met in Georgia and we were just so hot for each other that we threw all caution out the window, but who would have guessed that I was so fertile that the one time he came inside of me it would turn into a baby.

I decided to keep my little secret to myself until I at least see the doctor again. I will not say a word to any of the girls until I tell Michael because I need a reaction from him first. That way I will know exactly how to tell the girls and when they ask about the daddy I should already have a story of some kind for them. Oh my gosh! What did I get myself into? The last thing I wanted was a baby. Maybe when I see Dr. Brock again he will tell me it was a mistake, that he had the wrong chart out when he called me or even the wrong piss cup. This is just not the best timing for a baby by any one, not to mention the famous preacher man.

Chapter 9

KERI

Nothing is the same since the day I ran into Paul. Just when I thought he would not ever show his pathetic face again, he popped up. This time Miguel and I were having drinks at Pros the new club on South Beach that the girls and I went to celebrate Amanda's new business venture. I told Miguel about it and he could not wait to get there. I guess I made a good sell. We were not there more than an hour when Miguel got up and went to the restroom when out of nowhere appeared Paul. I almost fell off the stool I was sitting on.

"Is that your handsome husband?" He had a nasty grin on his face.

"It is no business of yours. What the hell do you want from me Paul?"

If I wanted to piss my pants the first time I ran into him you can imagine how I felt then with Miguel just a stone's throw away.

"It is my business missy, or have you forgotten?"

"Look Paul, if you want to talk you will have to meet with me at another time. This is a very inconvenient time and place for whatever it is you want to say to me."

"Well then tell me when and where and I will leave you alone."

"Tomorrow; there is a little coffee shop around the block from here, on the corner of Washington and tenth I will meet you there at two, please just go."

"That's a lot better. See you then."

He walked off only moments before Miguel returned and for a moment I wondered if Miguel had seen him talking to me, but I guess he did not because he hadn't said a word about it. I made the best of the rest of the evening with my husband and finished the party at home but as good a time as I had it was turmoil in my head. I could not call Amanda or any of the other girls to tell them what had happened because they knew nothing about Paul and the baby or the stuff that happened back in high school. I was really worried that Paul could cause a major upset in my life and the more I think about it the more scared I got. This coming out could cost me my marriage. I told Miguel when I met him that I had never gotten pregnant in my life and if he should find out all that stuff about what happened back then he may even start thinking that I was lying about the baby coming out of me dead. Who would believe me now that I did not kill that baby myself? I kept the entire pregnancy a secret from everyone except Paul and if I had known how he would react then I never would have told him.

It was a Thursday night when I ran into Paul at Pros and I decided to meet with him at that particular coffee shop because they had a backroom where we could sit privately and talk without running into anyone. The guy who owned it was a friend and he was very discreet and really liked me. I called him before I left the office and told him I was meeting with the son of a very important client who needed to sign some papers so I would need privacy and he promised he would reserve the backroom for me.

Paul was there waiting in another rental car when I pulled up in front of the coffee shop and when I got out of my car I headed inside with barely a glance at him and he followed me. The tension was very thick between us and he looked even more evil than he did the last couple of times I saw him. I wasted no time getting to the point once we were seated in the backroom.

"So what is your problem with me now Paul?"

"No how am I doing, after all we were more than just friends once."

He reached across the table to touch my hand or whatever it was he was trying to and I made no mistake about how I felt about that with only one look at his sorry ass and he immediately got the message and put his hand back where it belonged.

"But now we are obviously less than friends so what is it that you have to say. I do not have all day either because I do have a job that I must get back to so if I were you I would just cut to the chase. What do you want from me?'

"Okay Keri, if that is how you want to handle it."

"Yes Paul that is exactly how I want to handle it."

A waitress entered the room and walked over to our table.

"Hi, I'm Missy. May I take your order please?"

Before I even had a chance to say anything he ordered quite a few items from the small menu that was already on the table when we got there.

"Nothing for me, thank you."

I did not want that jerk to think the occasion was a festive one in any way shape or form. I knew he was up to no good. He made that clear the last two times I saw him and I refuse to have even water with him.

"So that is how you keep that svelte figure of yours even after the baby."

"Fortunately for me I did not ruin my svelte figure at all because of the abortion, remember?"

I was desperately trying to find a way out of the mess I found myself in.

"Keri cut the bullshit the baby they found in that dumpster in Brooklyn was our baby. The timing was right on target and they printed that baby's picture in the paper and I know in my heart that was our baby."

"You know nothing. If I carried that baby all that time don't you think someone would have noticed? My mom and stepfather, or even the teachers or my schoolmates, don't you think someone would have seen me pregnant if I kept it? Come on Paul you are wasting my time."

He reached into his pocket and pulled out an old newspaper clipping that he laminated in plastic and laid it on the table and I could feel something move inside me much like when that baby was nine years before. I managed to look unaffected as if I actually believed my own lie.

"You are doing a heck of a job pretending you don't know anything about this." He was hitting the plastic encased clipping with the palm of his hand.

"You know how I knew this was our baby Keri? The newspaper article said that the baby had an extra finger on the left hand right next to the pinky. Guess what Keri? I was born with an extra finger on the left hand right next to the pinky. And you know what else Keri? The baby looks just like my little sister that died at two months old. I look at her picture and the baby's picture and they look like identical twins except one was lifeless at the time the photos were taken. So do not act all self-righteous and innocent, that was our baby."

"Okay Paul, this is what happened."

I told him the whole truth about what happened, how the fact that he did not care enough to get me the money on time put me in the predicament that I found myself in. He listened keenly without any interruptions and when I was finished he looked at me with such hatred in his eyes if looks could kill I would have keeled over and died right there and then.

"Keri, you killed that baby. You killed our baby."

"Killed...our baby?"

'You never wanted that baby no more than I did. It was your idea to get rid of it in the first place, now you are blaming me because I had to go through that horror all on my own at seventeen, while you were in "college" working on going to the pros. I was going to give the baby up for adoption but it came out dead Paul. She was born dead."

"I don't believe that and I bet the authorities back in Westchester County would want to hear about that. You know they never found out who the baby belonged to. You were good Keri. How did you do it?"

I could not believe what I was about to suggest to him but I realized I had no choice. Paul was evil enough to carry out his threat and even though they would be able to prove that the baby was born dead nine years ago, I was afraid of the repercussions it might cause if it should ever come out that I was involved in such horror. Miguel would no doubt want a divorce and I stand the possibility of losing my friendship with the girls. I could not allow Paul to affect me so deeply a second time in one lifetime.

"Paul, tell me what you want me to do."

"So you are finally coming around. I think that is your best defense; cooperation."

"Okay, what is it you want."

"I use to love you once and you seem happy in your little life so I will not do anything to upset it. Meaning I won't let the news leak to your husband or the Westchester Police Department. So because of that I only want money Keri. I am sure your handsome attorney husband has lots of it and with your job at that accounting firm in that fancy building you should have no problem coming up with one hundred thousand dollars."

"One hundred thousand dollars? Are you out of your mind? I can't come up with that kind of money."

"Yes you can and you have only one week to do it Keri. I must get back to my life. So the sooner you get started, the better."

"I do not have that kind of money Paul. Please don't do this. I am appealing to your decent side right now. Don't do this to me."

The waitress walked in with his food and he asked her to package it for takeout. I was relieved because I could not stand to look at him another minute. He borrowed her pen and wrote a number down on a napkin and handed it to me.

"You have one week Keri, one week. Call me at this number when you are ready. I will be waiting. Now, if I do not hear from you in seven days consider your life as you know it, over."

He walked out of the room and never looked back taking his carry out that I paid for.

I left the coffee shop minutes later and I cannot for the life of me remember how I got back to the office. I had no idea that day would be the beginning of unforgivable horrors and life-altering decisions.

That Friday night I could not face the girls for our usual night out, it was hard enough trying to put up a front for Miguel, but as close as my husband and I were he could not see through me like the girls could. They would see through that façade the moment they look at me, especially Amanda.

I went about my daily routine with a smile on my face each day for anyone who was expecting it and loved my husband just the same as always not missing a beat while I agonized over the dilemma that I found myself in. I went to the flower shop a little less but I knew Doris, the manager was holding down the fort so I checked up on things by telephone. I was between a rock and a hard place and I could not concern myself with much else. There was absolutely no way that I could come up with that hush money Paul wanted. I knew he did not deserve a dime from me and I also knew that I could not risk him digging up any bones surrounding that baby found in the dumpster in Brooklyn nine years ago. I had no idea what I was going to do but I knew I had to do something before Paul Perez ruined my life.

Three days before my blackmail deadline I called Paul to tell him I needed more time but he would not hear it. He told me that he had to get back to Los Angeles the day after the deadline because his wife was coming back from her assignment in Korea and she had no idea he was in Miami. He also let slip that he took a four month leave from his job lying that he was going to be with his wife in Korea so it was imperative that he got back that Thursday, the day after the deadline and not a day longer. He threatened that if I did not come up with the money by his departure date he would go directly to the police and tell them what he knew.

I had no idea he had a job much less a wife and I did not give a fuck about any of it, all I knew was that I had to do something to save my ass and I was going to have to do it alone. Coming up with that kind of the money was just impossible, it was apparent that Paul did not do all of his homework or he would have known that I did not have that kind of money, and even if I could how would I do it without Miguel finding out. If it was even fifty thousand dollars I still would not be able to put my hands on it without borrowing from all my friends and taking out a noticeable chunk from Miguel's and I joint account. There was no way it was going to happen but I can't just sit there and leave it all to chance because the look I saw in Paul's eyes was that of a more than desperate man. I wondered what kind of trouble he found himself in that he thought I could get him out of.

When I got off the phone with Paul that day I sat down in front of the television and found a movie that had already started but I watched it all the way through. Ironically it was about a woman being blackmailed and how she eventually got rid of her blackmailer with a plan of her own. They never found his body at the bottom of the Hudson River and she went on to live happily ever after. That entire day I could not get the movie out of my head, I kept seeing myself as the woman living happily ever after. That evening I devised a plan of my own. That night I made love to my husband with a hankering that I could not fathom and I knew I could not risk losing Miguel and the life I had with him.

The following day I called Adam the moment Miguel walked out the door for work. Adam was this drug dealer that lived in our neighborhood back in Little Town, Georgia. He was much older than I was but we got along great and when he went to jail for trafficking his mother got sick and my grandmother and I were always there to help her out. Adam was a small time drug dealer at the time so he could not come up with the money for a lawyer to defend him and neither could his mother so my grandmother loaned her the money and told her she could pay it back whenever she had it and it wouldn't matter how long it took. For years my grandmother did not get her money back but we still helped out until Adam was released. I think he spent five years. By the time he got out I had moved away to Westchester. But Adam was back to his old tricks and in no time after he got out my grandmother got her money back and then some even though she said it was not right for her to encourage that kind of behavior in Adam; but this time he got rich and opened a couple of businesses and life was good. I would see him around the neighborhood whenever I go to visit with my grandmother in the summer time and at Christmas and we got close. Not sexually but in a brother-sister kind of way.

After I graduated college and moved to Miami I ran into him in a convenient store and we chatted for almost an hour before we went our separate ways but not before I got all three of his cell phone numbers and a home number. He had moved his business base to Florida and the success showed in the clothes he was wearing and the custom built bad-ass BMW he was driving.

Adam and I call each other from time to time to shoot the breeze and talk about Little Town, his mom and my grandmother.

Today I have another call to make to Adam but this time it was definitely not to shoot the breeze. I dialed his number and waited for him to answer.

"Hello Keri, what's up?"

"Hey Adam, I need to talk to you."

"I'm all ears Ker."

He was the only person who ever called me that and I often wondered why because it is just as easy to say Keri but I liked it.

"No Adam, I mean in person. It is very important."

"How about this evening about seven, you say where?"

"No, No. I need to see you right away."

"Are you okay?"

"I'm alright, well sort of."

"Okay, meet me at that same store you saw me at that day in twenty minutes."

"Thank you Adam. I will be there in twenty minutes."

I hung up the phone and realized that even though I was going to Adam for his help I could not let him in on what I was planning to do so I had to come up with a believable story in twenty minutes. I had the feeling that maybe Adam would loan me the money, but one hundred thousand dollars is a lot of money and I probably would never be able to pay him back. I was also concerned about Paul coming back again when that hundred thousand was finished just like the guy in the movies. I decided against asking Adam for the money but there was definitely something else he could help me with.

When I pulled up at the convenient store Adam rolled in right behind me, this time in a big ass Land Rover looking like eye candy. I didn't remember him being so good looking back when he was living in Little Town. He got out of his vehicle and I opened my passenger door and he got in.

"Hey Adam, you're looking good as ever."

"Thanks, I try."

"I can see that."

"So what's going on?"

I took a deep breath and exhaled slowly, gathering my thoughts, even though I thought I had it all worked out in my head what it was I wanted to say. All the going around the bush thoughts escaped my mind so I went straight to the point.

"I need a gun."

"A gun? Why would you want a gun?"

"I need it for protection."

"So why don't you just buy one. You have a clean record and this is Florida, you can get a legal piece."

"I know but I am going camping with my friends tomorrow somewhere in the woods and it takes days for me to get one going through the proper channel so that would not work."

"I don't know Keri. Are you sure it's nothing more than camping?"

"What else could it be? I am definitely not planning to go postal at work or rob a bank. It is just for camping Adam. Having a gun there with us would make me feel safe and knowing my friends none of them thought of that. So here I am."

"Okay Keri how soon do you want this gun?"

"We are leaving first thing in the morning, so sometime today would be perfect."

"Alright then, I will do this for you but you can't let anyone know that I gave it to you no matter what."

"Gave me what?" I said smiling but he did not smile back.

"I'm serious Keri; you must never let anyone know about this."

"I would never do that to you Adam; you are like a brother to me."

"Okay I believe you." Then he smiled at me.

"Meet me at this address at seven this evening."

He was writing the address on a piece of paper he found in my car.

"Meet me at seven, no sooner no later. Make sure that you are alone so that I can at least show you how to use it if you are going to carry it."

I thanked him and he got out of the car then walked around to the driver side and I got out and gave him a hug.

"You are good people Keri. Don't think I forgot all you and your grandmother did for me and my mom when I got locked up. You were just a kid too. Anyway, see you at seven."

"Okay, bye."

That night at exactly seven o'clock I pulled up in front of a series of warehouses after Adam helped me with directions and he took me inside one that was equipped with an arsenal of weapons among other things. He went into a small room and returned with the shiniest piece I had ever seen.

He handed it to me.

"This is a 357 Magnum; it's the smallest piece I got that is still brand new. I don't want to give you anything dirty."

He spent the next half hour or so showing me how to load and unload and all the other intricacies that involved using a gun.

When I left Adam that night it finally clicked that I actually want to kill Paul, get him out of my life once and for all. I never could understand before how people could actually kill other people but now I truly understand how easy it is to harbor such feelings.

When I got home Miguel was already home so I turned all my attention to him and was actually in a good mood like nothing unusual was happening. I was more than happy when Miguel said he had to meet with someone and would be gone for about three hours. That gave me time to make contact with Paul when I thought the coast was clear. I dialed his number and he picked up on the first ring.

"Well, if it isn't my pretty little rich girl."

"I am not rich Paul. I do not have the slightest idea where you got your information from and I am in no mood for your crap."

"That's okay as long as you are in the mood to pay."

"I am only doing this because I want you out of my life Paul so don't get any new ideas and when you blow it up doing whatever it is that you do when you are not blackmailing other people, just remember you took it all and I have nothing left for you to come back for."

"Fair enough; let me tell you where I want you to meet me."

"You tell me where to meet you? I suppose you are assuming that I have even the least bit of trust in you. Listen, you have nothing to lose, I have everything to lose so for my peace of mind and security I will tell you where to meet me. I want to make sure that no one else knows about this."

"I guess I owe you that much."

"I will call you tomorrow night at seven and I will tell you where to meet me then. I will have all your money and hopefully you will have the decency to disappear out of my life forever."

"It's a deal. And you have my word on it." Pausing for effect he continued with his bullshit.

"I still care about you Keri I am just sorry it had to come to this and I promise I won't be back to bother you. You have my word on that."

I hung up the phone without another word. And without even thinking, I heard myself said aloud:

"I will see to that you asshole."

I took the gun out of my tote bag and just gave it the once over before putting it safely back in. Adam also gave me a case of bullets that were also in my bag. I still had some time to myself so I started putting my plans for the following night back in gear.

I locked myself in one of the guest rooms and loaded the gun. I cut up some newspaper the size of hundred dollar bills and packaged them in what seemed like stacks of five thousands then I placed a real authentic one hundred dollar bill at the top and bottom of each stack, just in case he decided to flip one over and inspect it. I had over four thousand in hundred dollar bills in my personal safe at the house and I took that to use in my plan. There was an old briefcase in one of the closets that I was planning on throwing out, so I used that to put stacks of so-called money in and it looked good sitting in there. My plan was on the way and the only thing left was to find a secluded place where I could meet with Paul without anyone seeing me. I could not let him ruin my life.

I hid the stuff under the bed in the guest room including the gun and went about the rest of the night without Miguel picking up any bad vibes from me.

I even called the girls and we all got together on a conference call. None of them seemed to detect anything unusual which made me even more confident that I could pull it off.

The following day, the day I was to meet with Paul and pay him his blackmail money was the longest day I ever experienced except for that night nine years ago when the baby came unexpectedly and lifeless.

It was so ironic how the worst days of my life always involved Paul in one way or another. The day I told him I was pregnant to the time I dumped the baby's dead body in the dumpster and so many days that followed, and now this blackmail shit. I have to put a stop to my nightmare and there was no other way to do it but to get rid of Paul altogether. I could not live down such a scandal and whatever legal retribution it carried.

I know in my heart that the baby was born dead and so does God himself, so my conscience is clear even though I regret having to throw that innocent little body away like it was garbage. Other than that I had nothing to be guilty about and I refuse to suffer because of it. I thought about what Paul said about the birthmark that the baby was born with and he was right, the baby had an extra finger attached to the pinky but I could not for the life of me remember now what the baby looked like. With all the information he had, even if there would be no legal consequences it would still make a great impact on my life and my marriage so there was no turning back.

I remember taking a coworker of mine to a site where they were putting up some new condo's down in the Opalocka area of the city. The condo project was stalled because of some licensing problems and she told me it would take months before they would resume building. The day I took her there she was meeting with one of the builders because she had paid money down on one of the units and she wanted to know what to expect.

I took a drive down to Opalocka and scoped out the place to see if it was suitable for my murderous plans. It was perfect. At night there was a minimal amount of lighting in that particular area and it was mainly businesses around the condo site.

I drove back home and made dinner for Miguel and when he got home we ate and made love then watched a little television. Miguel said he had to go to night court and I pretended that I was sad about it but deep inside I felt like God was really on my side. I knew Miguel would not get home before midnight and that would give me enough time to meet with Paul and get back home without him knowing that I had left.

I called Paul at exactly nine o'clock and arranged for him to meet at the condo complex in one hour. I had no idea how familiar he was with the area but he said he would be there. I gathered all the things I prepared the night before along with gun in the tote bag and left the house immediately. It took me only twenty minutes to get there and when I did there was absolutely no one around and the place was black with darkness.

I told Paul that he should park somewhere on the streets and walk to the last building in the back. I think he really trusted that I would come with the money and just let him have it so I could be rid of him, but he had another thing coming. I parked my car a block away and put on a blond wig that I bought specially for the occasion.

I waited in the darkness with the gun in my hand pointing directly at the door and I could see his frame in the doorway but he could not see me from where he was. As he entered the door and got closer, he whispered my name and sounded almost friendly doing it.

"Hey! Keri! Keri."

Before he had the chance to say my name a third time out of his pathetic blackmailing mouth I aimed the gun directly at his head and fired. He went down with a thud and I could hear him take his last breath. Something inside me moved and I took a deep breath.

I made sure he was dead then I looked around in the dark to make sure no one heard the shot. Then I thought the people in that neighborhood were used to hearing gun shots at all hours of the night so there would not be any immediate alarm, but I was still careful. There are a lot more commercial buildings than residences in that area.

I stood there for a while and when I was sure no one was going to come and investigate the noise I put on a pair of latex gloves that I put in the tote bag earlier and took his wallet and anything else that would tell the police who he was when they eventually found his body. I also took his cellular phone and crushed it under my feet then dumped them in a trash dumpster on the way home; but not before I tied them up with other trash, he had that haunting newspaper clipping with him and I tore it apart and ripped it to shreds but I was careful not to leave even a smidgen of evidence that would incriminate me. There was no way they would find those. In no time they would find themselves at the bottom of a trash heap somewhere.

I made sure my tracks were covered from A to Z and that meant getting rid of the wig. I put that in a plastic bag and disposed of it in yet another dumpster. I also dumped the cut-up newspaper less my real hundreds and the briefcase; that I took home and put back in the closet. The only concern I had left was what to do with the gun even though I took it back to the house with me that night. See, Adam said I could keep the gun. I got back home at least forty five minutes before Miguel got home and pretended to be asleep when he got there. He crept quietly into bed trying not to wake me. If only he knew.

That night I slept better than I did since running into Paul that day at the drug store. I got up the next morning and made my husband breakfast before he left for work.

Miguel has been working Saturdays now for the past few months because business started booming and he wanted to make sure it stayed that way and that meant putting in extra hours whenever he could. At least that's what he told me when I started protesting about us not spending enough time together. I have gotten used to him spending his Saturdays at the office doing what he does and I guess I have no real reason not to believe him because his paychecks are getting bigger and bigger. Just a couple of weeks before he was telling me that if I ever felt like not working anymore it would be alright because he was making more than enough to take care of me. I have no intention of taking him up on that offer but it is good to know that I have that option.

After Miguel left I turned all four televisions on in the house and put each one on a different news channel to see if someone found Paul's body but there was absolutely nothing about it.

I was certain that no one would link me with Paul because I never talked to anyone about him and I doubt that the one Spanish girl that was in the coffee shop got a good look at him. I am sure she is new because I had never seen her before and I am a regular at that place. However I do not want to leave anything to chance so I decided to take a little drive down to the coffee shop.

The Saturday traffic was flowing pretty smoothly so it took less than the usual time to get there and when I pulled up outside I could see the girl behind the counter, the same girl who served Paul a week before when we had our little meeting. I got out of the car and walked in and she gave me a rehearsed coffee shop welcome then asked if it was my first time there, I told her that I was a regular. At that moment the owner Mr. Gianni came in from behind a door and immediately acknowledged me.

"Hello Keri, you never come on a Saturday. Are you doing overtime at work today?"

I was about to tell him a lie and said yes I was but I had no real reason to lie so I stuck to my version of the truth.

"I had the taste for your special breakfast sandwich and I couldn't help myself."

"See Missy, I told you that my customers would go out of their way just to get a taste of my signature sandwich." He said to the new girl.

"Case in point." I said, still a little surprised that Missy did not recognize me.

"I haven't seen you in a while though Keri, busy at the office?" Mr. Gianni asked.

"Oh yes, but we are slowing down again so you will be seeing a lot more of me."

"Oh Keri, this is Missy my newest employee. Missy this is one of my best customers, Keri, make sure she gets the best service when she comes in."

"Yes Mr. Gianni." Missy said with a big smile then with outstretched hand she said.

"Nice meeting you Keri. You are very pretty."

"Nice meeting you Missy. Thank you."

"So how is the flower business doing these days, still good?"

"Yes very good. Thanks for asking."

"Thanks for coming in." He said with a smile

I saw a guy walking back and forth outside the store and took the opportunity to find out if the surveillance cameras were working.

"Mr. Gianni, do you see that man walking back and forth outside the store?"

"Oh yes, he was in here a little earlier and he and his girlfriend had a little quarrel and she drove off without him, so I guess he is waiting for her or someone else to pick him up."

"Oh. You know with all the crazy people out there these days one can't be too careful."

"You are absolutely right Keri. Which reminds me I need to get my surveillance equipment repaired, it has been a whole three weeks now since it shut down and I have not had the time to see to it. I have been here for six years and never had any problems but I guess you can't be too careful."

My mission was completed the moment Mr. Gianni mentioned the broken surveillance equipment. Three whole weeks he said which meant there were no records of me and Paul ever being in that coffee shop together and that Missy girl never even remember seeing me before. That introduction to her by Mr. Gianni was right on target and sealed the fact that she had never seen me before. I was more relieved now than I ever was. I prayed that they would not find Paul's body until it was so decomposed that no one would recognize him. I am sure no one will be looking for him in Florida. After all he lied to his job about going to Korea to be with his wife and his wife thought he was at home going to work as usual. His own sick game caught up with him once and for all. Who knows who else he fucked with and blackmailed. That bastard!

I could not believe how cold I had become. I killed someone, a human being and I was feeling absolutely no remorse, all I could think of was how my life would not be interrupted ever again by that louse. The more I thought about it, the more I thought he deserved it. That jerk got me pregnant and left me alone to deal with it then had the nerve to try to use it and blackmail me after nine years. He deserved what he got.

For four whole weeks I heard nothing of the police discovering Paul's body and I wondered if they ever would. I was at home one evening, the girls were over for a little impromptu get-together because they thought that I was avoiding them so they decided to all stop by with food and drinks and we had a girl's-night-in. Miguel was in New York and would not be returning for another two days so we had the place all to ourselves. We were sitting on the sofa, on the carpet or wherever we were comfortable just chatting and laughing away like all was well with the world.

I was about to go into the kitchen to get something when they interrupted the program on television with a newsflash. The newscaster was saying that the police discovered a dead body in the Opalocka area but it was badly decomposed and the entire face disappeared from animals eating the flesh. I had a glass in my hand and it fell to the floor. All the girls turned around just in time to see the mortified look on my face. Melanie was the first to speak.

"What the hell, you look like you just seen a ghost girl, what's up."

"Why you looking so frightened we see shit like that on the news every day." Kylie said.

I managed to keep my composure or what was left of it.

"You all don't think that someone dying like that is a horrible thing?" Pretending that the horror of it all was what I was concerned with.

"Of course but not so surprised that I would lose my glass, that sort of shit happens every day." Amanda uttered.

"If I didn't know better I would think she killed him herself the way that glass left her fingers" Natasha said and everyone laughed.

"Oh, that was just me being clumsy." I said seemingly unaffected.

Well they must have bought the clumsy excuse because no one mentioned that piece of news item or anything odd in my behavior for the rest of the evening, even though we saw the report a couple of times after that.

The news reporters all had the same story: *"An unidentified body of a male was found in one of several unfinished buildings from a condominium project in the Opalocka area. No identification or anything that would help to identify him was found on the body. The body was faceless from animals feasting on it. He had died of a single gunshot wound to the head and police are investigating. The police were alerted when one of the builders stopped by to do an inspection of the property and ran into the body that must have been lying there for weeks. The police have no leads.*

When the girls left and I was by myself I got down on my knees and asked God to forgive me for what I had done and hoped that he understood why I had to do such a horrible thing to a human being. But I had no other way to get out of the mess that I had suddenly found myself in. I could not come up with the hundred thousand dollars he was demanding and even if I could I was sure he would come back again for more. I could not risk getting caught in such an embarrassing and probable legal situation.

Miguel would never trust me again, he would leave me for sure and I doubt that my friends would want to be seen with me after my downfall, so I could not allow Paul to come in and change the course of my life. I already had one big secret that I must take with me to my grave and that was all because I met

Paul. Now the biggest and wickedest burden that I will ever have to carry was all because of him. I refused to let that bastard detour my life.

I doubt that anyone was looking for him anyway. I wondered what happened to his parents and what exactly he was doing in Los Angeles or whether he even had a wife like he said. Well I guess it doesn't matter now; whatever he was doing did not matter anymore, all I know was that he would no longer be doing it.

Fortunately for me I have never once mentioned Paul to any of my friends or Miguel so if the name should come up, should they identify him as Paul Perez he would not be connected to me in any way shape or form. The night I got rid of that dead baby was the night that Paul became nonexistent for me so there was absolutely no reason to mention him at all. I would not tell my friends about him because I was too embarrassed and scared that I would have a slip of the tongue and maybe say more than I needed to so I left the whole thing alone and as for Miguel I would not dare let him know that some man, no matter how young I was would treat me so shabby.

I was not at all worried that anyone would find out that I was the killer. I can't believe that I was even thinking of myself as a killer. I wondered was it in my blood because I had no remorse whatsoever and was relieved that my secret would stay just that; a secret.

It was not at all fair that I should suffer twice for something that was not even my fault. The baby was already dead when it came out of my body and I was only seventeen years old, what was I suppose to do? If it was born alive I would not have done something as cruel as throwing it in the dumpster. Maybe I was only thinking like a scared seventeen year old who was afraid to screw up her future and embarrass her parents. My heart was in the right place from the beginning, I tried to do the right thing when I contacted the adoption agency. Were it not for that unfortunate occurrence the baby would be with some loving family somewhere enjoying the fruits of life, but it was not supposed to be because she was born dead and there was nothing else for me to do at the time but what I did. At that stage of the game I could not tell anyone I gave birth to a dead baby because no one knew I was pregnant. That was a lot for a seventeen year old to go through all on her own and for Paul to try and use it against me the way he intended was just wrong so I will not think about that pathetic son-of-a-bitch, he got exactly what he deserved.

I never harbored any feelings concerning the dead baby, I expelled all emotions concerning that because I always believed that God worked it out and I will not harbor any feelings of regret for what happened to Paul. What I did to him. I think God worked that one out for me too. I did not deserve any of that mess.

Several more weeks passed and I heard nothing else about the body except that a rental car was found in the neighborhood not far from where Paul's body was found and it was reported stolen from the rental lot the same day that Paul met his death. I remember the date very clearly and when they mentioned finding a car in that neighborhood that was sitting there for weeks I put two and two together and came to the conclusion that Paul had stolen the car. If Paul was living all the way in California and came to Miami just to steal a car and blackmail me there is a possibility that no one would be looking for him there. I went about my daily business without any emotions outside the norm and lived my life without worry the way I did before Paul surfaced.

My only problem was that Miguel was spending more and more time at the office and it started to bug me. Nobody works that hard and look so well rested every day after getting home at midnight or later, then getting up at seven each day to do the same thing over again, six days a week. I know Miguel was not getting a lot of sleep but it seemed to have no effect on him whatsoever. It was only months before when he was only working five days per week and getting home by eight o'clock he was complaining about being tired all the time and now he is working six days, having a lot more business meetings and working later and later at the office and no complaints of being overworked or tired. I found that a little strange but this was definitely not the time to start any shit with all the shit that was popping off around me.

Chapter 10

NATASHA

My modeling career is up and running now and I am all over the magazines, I do not even get to spend as much time with the girls as I was used to doing because I am always at a shoot or a fashion show somewhere these days.

The majority of my spare time however is spent with Donna. I told all the girls about me and Donna's friendship. Only the friendship part of it though; the rest is still a secret, but I left them all with the impression that we knew each other from back in high school and they all bought it hook, line and sinker. They also know about Donna's cancer. Sometimes Donna would join us on our escapades but not very often, maybe once in a blue moon. Since that night Donna showed up at my door I have tried to be her pillar of strength, though if I should say so myself she has twice the strength I can muster. She is probably the strongest woman I have ever known.

She moved out of her house and moved into that condo she told me about but the house is still on the market to this day. Not many people can afford a house like that; it was like a mansion more so than a house. It boasted as many as eight bedrooms and Donna would joke about how when she decided to buy it she was planning to use it as a brothel and she would be the Madame. I would not put anything pass that girl she was as crazy as they come; but she had a good heart. That place was so huge I can't believe Donna lived there all by herself. She said she is a loner anyway, but I guess I knew that.

Donna went as far as making funeral arrangements telling me that she had not given up but was being realistic. She stayed in touch with her sister that owns the bar in Fort Lauderdale but refused to tell her about her cancer. No one in her family knows. She did not think they cared enough for her to tell them. I tried to convince her to change her mind telling her that no matter what they were family; but she would not hear it. She refused to talk to anyone but her sister Patricia, the one in Fort Lauderdale. They were not that close but at least they spoke, but I just can't get her to tell Patricia.

She bought a burial spot and paid in full for everything from the casket to the flowers and even recorded a tape that she want played at the funeral services or at the gravesite it did not matter to her where as long as it's played she said and she wanted me to be in possession of it but I was not allowed to listen to it until that day she is buried. I hate the way she keeps talking about her funeral, it is all so unsettling and the fact that she is putting me in charge of handling everything, well whatever little she did not yet or will not be able to handle on her own. I hate to think that in only months she may pass away never to be anymore. The more I thought about it the more I feel close to her because I could not even begin to imagine how she must feel.

Lately the cancer seem to be taking a toll on her though, she is tired all the time and sleeps a lot more than she used to and eat even less but she is always in a good mood no matter what she was going through from one day to the next.

I was coming from Keri's house one evening, the other girls and I went by for a little us-time and to cheer up Keri because she had been withdrawn and even looked sad. It was the second time we did that in as many weeks and we were a lot worried by then because she quit her job at the Accounting firm and decided to stay home, something Miguel wanted her to do for a long time but something she was firmly adamant about not doing.

Keri loved making money but she loved the business of accounting even more and that was the reason she said she would never walk away from that job. Her flower shop was doing well even though she was hardly ever there. Miguel made good money so that was not an issue for them but Keri just loved her job. So it was natural for us to get concerned when she quit her job. The girls and I surprised her one Saturday morning with everything one would need for a barbeque and decided to throw a little cheer-up-party for her in her own back yard but only with the five of us and Donna who was the life of the party, not surprisingly.

Everyone really liked Donna, but she made me promise not to tell them or anyone else about the disease that was eating at her body. If it was up to me I would tell them because I believe that at a time like that she could use all the support she could get but she begged to differ saying time and time again that she preferred to keep it a secret because she did not want people throwing any pity parties for her. I guess I could respect that. She definitely had a point so I did exactly as she asked.

I told no one about her cancer and I never let slip about the depth of our relationship. She promised never to tell anyone about us unless I wanted her to but she made it crystal clear that if it was up to her she would tell the world how good I really make her feel. I think the cancer changed the way Donna looked at life and mellowed her out some because the she had a whole new outlook and had very little interest in some of the things that made her tick in the days before the cancer. She eventually decided on her own to share the news with the other girls.

She told me stories about her two year relationship with an actress from a very popular soap opera and the A-list parties she was privy to because of that. That was how she knew so many Hollywood movers and shakers.

I tried to keep her in good spirits so we never talked much about the horrors of what she was going through but reminisced about the good times and the time that was ahead. Love making between us was at an all time high, well since Donna's return we did it constantly but only because she said that was one of the things she wanted to do while she still had time. I realized that I loved Donna but was no longer in love with her. However, I wanted to grant her all of her wishes and at that point I figured it was the least I could do for someone I was once in love with; someone who still loved me.

Everyone was in a good mood, even Keri, and she insisted everything was alright with her and that she quit her job because Miguel wanted her to but mainly because she got tired of working nine to five. She said she basically wanted to just concentrate on her flower shop and Miguel. None of us really bought that but we let it rest nonetheless.

It was after nine when our little barbeque at Keri's ended and I was taking Donna back to her condo when she suddenly started coughing up blood and I wasted no time taking her to the closest hospital. When we got there the emergency room people wheeled her back immediately on a gurney and it looked really serious. I had all of her information handy because that was one of the few things she asked me to take care of just in case something like that happened.

It took almost three hours before one of the doctors came out and sat me down. I could tell by the way he took my hand and asked me to sit that something was terribly wrong. Donna had instructed me that if anything like that should happen to her, it coming down to the wire like this, that I should call her doctor first, then her sister Patricia and let her know what was going down. She even gave me a letter to give to her if she passed away. The situation looked serious enough to me the moment the nurses wheeled her back into the ER and so I called the doctor, then Patricia.

She said she would be there as soon as she could but up until the time the doctor arrived at the hospital to the time he came out of the emergency room to talk with me in the waiting area she had not yet shown up.

He took my hand in his and he had this look in his eyes that told me what I did not want to hear him say aloud.

I wanted to scream, "Oh no!" but it came out in a barely audible whisper.

"She's alive. Let me confirm, you are Natasha Bell, correct?"

"Yes."

"I wanted to make sure because Miss Barrett left specific instructions to speak with you only and no one else."

"She did that? I did not know about that."

"Yes she did and so I wanted you to know that she is alive but I am not sure how much longer she will be able to hold on. Unfortunately the cancer has taken a toll on her body and now I am not sure if she has much time left. However, I've seen people go to that place where she is right now and came back to live another day; so we are doing everything we can to give her the best care possible."

"Thank you Doctor."

"I wish I had better news; however there is nothing that anyone can do right now but wait so I would suggest you go home and get some rest then come back in the morning. If anything changes I will contact you before then."

"Thank you so very much." I barely whispered.

He squeezed my hands and walked back into the emergency room but I could not move, at least not for a few minutes. I could not believe that Donna had asked him not to speak with anyone but me. She had him sign papers to that effect I later found out.

I eventually got some strength in my legs and got up to go home but as I turned toward the exit door I recognized Patricia talking to one of the nurses and I walked up to her.

"Hi Patricia." I said and she turned toward me.

"Hi Natasha, what's going on with Donna."

I explained to her how Donna wanted it all kept a secret and I had to respect her wishes and how I am sorry that she had to find out the way she did but Donna had cancer and had less than two months to live according to the doctors then I told her what happened that night to land Donna in the emergency room. She did not try to fight back the tears that started rolling down her cheeks. I sat her down and got her some water but did not tell her about the letter Donna asked me to give to her. She was beside herself but I finally managed to calm her down and told her to go home and come back the next morning because no one was allowed to see her then.

She was very cooperative and talked about how she loved Donna and how close they all were at one time. She went on and on about how she wished things were different but how hard it was on the whole family when they found out about Donna dating women and how it caused this distance between them and her, especially her parents and her sister Monica who stopped speaking to her altogether. She had an excuse for all of them, the parents she claimed was very active in the church and would go against everything they believed in if they accepted her way of life. Not accepting it of course meant that they would not have anything to do with her whatsoever unless she asked forgiveness and turned her life around. Monica's reason was a whole lot different she just could not let her husband know that she had a gay relative let alone a sister, so she cut her off and asked her not to call her house ever again according to Patricia. Patricia was not altogether with her either because she never called Donna at all but Donna would call her ever so often or even drop in once in a while, she cared so little about Donna that she did not even notice the difference in her appearance the few times we stopped by her bar since Donna broke the news about her cancer. Apart from the doctor and the people at the doctor's office the only other people who knew about the cancer were her therapist and me. I tried to talk her into telling Patricia but she wouldn't hear it; she just flat out refused to tell her about it.

Now here I am stuck with the job of informing Patricia now that the situation has worsened. I was surprised that Patricia was that affected by what I had told her and the more I thought about it on the way home the more I felt bad for her that she missed out on the truly wonderful person that Donna was in spite of her little faults. I did not buy into Patricia's tears but I appeased her by comforting her mainly because it was the humane thing to do. I could see why Donna insisted on keeping it all a secret. I knew all along that Patricia did not give a fuck about Donna; all she cared about was the money she would get from her after her many hard-luck stories. All she had to do was ask and Donna would write a check but even the blind could see that all she cared about was the freaking money. I proved it when I told her Donna was dying. Somewhere between her fake crocodile tears she had the nerve to ask me if Donna had made a will. I could not believe my ears. I pretended not to hear her and that was the actual moment I got up to leave.

By the time I got home it was way past midnight so I did not bother calling any of the girls though I felt like it. Sleep took a long time to get to me but it eventually arrived and put me out of my misery, but not for very long because at four o'clock the telephone rang and I could feel something in my stomach move because a phone call at four o'clock in the morning could mean only one thing; bad news.

It was the hospital, Donna passed away at three thirty in the morning.

I had no idea how long I had the telephone to my ear but it was quite some time before I hung it up and then dialed Patricia's number. She had asked me to call her the moment I heard something from the hospital. She actually tried to go in and see Donna earlier that night at the hospital but the doctor would not allow it. Again Donna had left specific instructions that I was the only person allowed in to see her should it ever come to that. Donna had a lot of money and could pretty much call the shots any which way she pleased.

When I got up in the morning first thing I called Kylie and Kylie called Amanda and so on until all five of us were on the telephone then I told them all about what happened after Donna and I left Keri's house to the time I got the phone call from the hospital telling me she was dead. They all agreed that I should not be by myself but I begged to differ, I needed that time by myself. The half about Donna and I have not been told. They have absolutely no idea about our history because the story I gave them was all a lie.

The last four months though were very special; Donna and I got really close and we made love aplenty throughout,but I did not feel comfortable with that anymore not just because of what happened in the past but because of her illness and the things it would put her through. It was almost one-sided because I would not make love to her the way she did me but I used the past as the only excuse, telling her that it was hard to just pick up where we left off especially after not being with another woman. I told her that my head was no longer in that place but I would be there for her whenever she needed me.

It hurt really bad to know that Donna was no longer. I feel so bad that that horrible disease would take someone so caring and kind and leave some other assholes who serve no fucking purpose in this world, but I know I did not mean that; it was just the hurt talking. I would not wish that on anyone.

Donna left me with an arsenal of information on how to handle her affairs should she pass and the first thing she instructed me to do after calling Patricia was to call her lawyer John Ashton. I called him later that morning before going to the hospital to take care of things there. He told me he would like to meet with me later that afternoon and I was shocked when he told me that I was in Donna's will that she wanted him to read after the funeral. He also told me that Donna had given him the job of informing her parents though I knew that Patricia must have called them to inform them of her death. They had no idea that Donna was ill so I can imagine the shock.

The lawyer wanted me to call him once the funeral arrangements were made because he wanted to come to the funeral. He spoke very highly of Donna and appeared to have liked her a lot.

Because Donna took care of all the arrangements before her death I did not have a lot to do but I had to make sure everything was done the way she wanted it done. I was a little pissed at her parents and her sister Monica because the cold mother fuckers did not show up until the day of the funeral, trying to justify it by saying that Patricia told them everything was taken care of. Assholes.

Donna left absolutely no stones unturned she even left an envelope with the list of people I should call to tell about her death and I swear every last one of those eighty people came including Ellen DeGeneres, Martin Sheen, some other big timers all the way down to Queen Latifah and Missy Elliott; just to name a few. Even Alicia Keys came. Her funeral was just the best, well put together and well carried out all the way to the cemetery. It was the first time I actually saw people wait around at the gravesite until the hole was filled up with the dirt. All the girls showed up and Miguel even accompanied Keri but the big surprise was Shane D'Marco showing up with Kylie. She did not tell us that Shane was coming she said because she did not see it as being important in the big scope of things. Yeah right.

I had no idea that Donna knew so many celebrities, I knew she was acquainted with one or two of them but she never talked much about them. She insisted that her repast be held at her condo because that was the last place she lived and that's exactly what I did. Her condo was no little place it was a huge five bedroom with enough space for a party so it was ideal for the number of people that showed up. I had a catering company to supply and serve the food and Patricia's husband insisted on manning the bar while her housekeeper Maria, a beautiful young Spanish girl hurried back from the church to the condo to help keep things in order. Girlfriend had a real bar in her condo. She owned the biggest unit in the complex because she bought two units and made them into one, it was awesome. Donna went on to heaven just the way she planned it. I made sure of that.

Everything was going well until Donna's parents found me alone in the kitchen.

"So you were Donna's lover?" I heard a woman's voice said from behind me.

I turned around to see her mom and dad standing there looking at me.

"Pardon me?"

"She asked if you were Donna's lover." The husband said.

"I think that's rude for you to ask me that and on top of that this is just not the time or the place for that right now."

"Well, she was our daughter; I do believe that we have the right to know." The mother said.

Her husband got in on the mess.

"Tell me. How do you feel knowing that Donna might not make it into heaven because of the lifestyle you and her chose?"

I was off the chain pissed at the motherfuckers talking to me like that and having the nerve to hold me responsible for what might happen to Donna's soul.

"Listen, I do not want to have to disrespect you both so I would suggest that you show even a smidgen of respect and leave that subject alone; at least for today. As you can see there are a lot of people here who loved Donna and if I have anything to do with it you will not ruin our celebration of her life by starting some shit up in here. So if I were you, Mr. and Mrs. Churchgoer I would eat some fucking food, have some drinks and keep your fucking mouths shut."

They could not believe their ears. They both stood open-mouthed until I finished then he took her hand and led her out of the kitchen pissing mad. I did not hear another peep out of them for the rest of the evening so much that I had no idea when they left. The repast went well and went on way into the night with people telling wonderful and funny stories about Donna.

Miles popped in for a moment but did not want to hang around for too long. However, he called a couple of times to find out how I was holding up. I had told him the same story I told the girls about Donna being my friend since high school and when he would eventually come to the apartment and see her there he never suspected anything more.

Donna's two sisters Monica and Patricia hung around long after their parents disappeared but I guess that was just to save face, because they were so uncomfortable you could see it from a mile away.

That night when everyone left except for the five of us girls and Miguel, Melanie suggested that we all spend the night at the condo so it wouldn't be empty for the night. I think she said something about keeping Donna company; but really so we could clean up the mess we made in the morning. I was surprised that Miguel allowed Keri to stay but he did and so we all spent the night together at Donna's place, less Miguel.

The Monday after the funeral John Ashton, Donna's lawyer called me to inform me that the reading of Donna's will would take place the following day and I was invited to sit in on the reading. I was curious to know why I would be invited to the reading. I know at some point Donna was in love with me and I thought I was in love with her and we had a marvelous time together at one time but I did not believe that she would even mention me in her will. Donna was a millionaire but I still did not expect her to leave me anything in her will even though I have been there for her in the last few months of her life when she needed me most. I was there with her on all her doctor's appointments since she told me of the disease and I made sure she did all the things she said she wanted to do before she died, and I was right there doing them with her but only because I really cared about her and wanted to see her through the whole ordeal. I did not expect any rewards for that. I was just doing what any good friend would have done. I wonder if her parents and her sisters were going to be there but I guess they would because they were the only family that Donna had and she had a lot to give so I am sure that she would include her family. Donna was the kind of person who would forgive them and let them have her money or whatever else she had.

I asked Kylie to come with me to the reading and she obliged but did not like the idea of coming along; however I was happy she did because I did not want to be alone with those people if they were planning to be there.

When we got to the lawyer's office, I was not one bit surprised to see her mother, father and two sisters. I said hello to her sisters but couldn't care less about the parents, they had some nerve. They disowned Donna and shut her out of their lives for years because they thought that her lifestyle was degrading; not good enough for them yet they show up at the reading of her will. What, they were accepting her in death now, or were it that her money was good enough for them but not her? I could not believe them.

I could not tell Kylie how I felt about Donna's parents because it would open up a whole other can of worms and I was in no mood for that. I doubt that I would ever be in the mood to tell them that Donna and I slept together. I prayed that her mother would not cause a scene in front of Kylie. That would be something.

Maria also showed up for the reading and a gentleman I saw at her Coconut Grove house taking care of the yard a few times, I think his name was Edgar, a Spanish man. There was also a young, pretty black girl who could not be more than twenty who walked in just moments before the lawyer invited us to sit in the conference room, I later found out her name was Beverly. He was hesitant about allowing Kylie in but he changed his mind when I quietly explained to him that I was a little nervous and need Kylie with me because I was not family and felt out of place.

The reading of the will was not a reading after all but a video that Donna made herself with the help of the lawyer. When he pressed play and Donna's face came on the screen I could see the disgusted look on her mother's face and the tears that started rolling down the cheeks of Monica and Patricia. The father was motionless and I could see his eyes welling up. I saw all that through the sunglasses I deliberately wore for the occasion.

The video was a very short one. I found out that Edgar and Maria were wife and husband who worked for Donna for just over two years and she left them her double unit condo. They were looking so sad but you could tell they were somewhat relieved when they heard about getting the condo. I was really happy for them; Donna must have really liked them. Donna left Beverly one hundred thousand dollars and a car. A Honda accord she had parked at her coconut grove home.

She also left her sister Patricia one hundred thousand dollars and all her gold jewels saying that she wished that they were closer and that she knew Patricia did not really like her but at least she did not stop being her sister. Donna suggested that Patricia should be more honest about her feeling towards people and accept them for who they are, then thanked her for not turning her back on her then apologized for not telling her about the cancer because if she told her then she would tell Monica and her parents and she did not want them to find out about it since they insisted on not speaking to her. She did not want their sympathy she said so that was the only reason she did not tell Patricia.

The big shocker came when she mentioned her sister Monica saying how she wished she had her to talk to because of how close they both were when they were kids and how disappointed she was when Monica turned her back on her, so she assumed that Monica would not want anything from her, so she left her nothing but good wishes. She went on to talk about her parents and how they turned their backs on her and no matter how she tried would not speak to her or even acknowledge her as their daughter. She said she was very hurt that when she did call to tell her parents about the cancer they hung up the phone when they heard her voice on the other end but not before they told her never to call back. She also said that she was sorry but she felt that if she left anything to them they would not accept it. She also wished them well.

The moment those words came out of her mouth on the video her mom and dad got up and left and only moments later Monica followed suit. The room was quiet for what seemed like forever, because the lawyer stopped the video when her parents got up to leave.

An even bigger shocker came when Donna said all her other assets, the remaining estate was left to me. The mansion in Coconut grove and a small apartment complex she owned in Fort Lauderdale that I had no idea about, her Mercedes Benz and a Hummer that she kept at the condo, everything including over two million dollars that was in her account. It was a lot to swallow and I did not know what to say or do. Kylie gasped but said nothing, she was just as surprised as I was. When the video ended the lawyer handed me an envelope and inside was insurance papers naming me the beneficiary of a five hundred thousand dollar policy and it was just too much to handle, I started crying.

I was overwhelmed by all that Donna did. I had absolutely no idea it would turn out that way. Okay, maybe when I got the news that I was in the will I anticipated maybe a little money, maybe a car or some cash but nothing like that. Kylie was blown away too by how much Donna left for me but she was even more surprised at how she treated her parents and her sisters. And finding out why she was estranged from her family at the time of her death. Her being gay shocked the pants off Kylie.

It was fortunate for me that Donna did not mention anything about our relationship beyond the friendship because I have no idea how I would have handled Kylie finding out. But I had a feeling she was wondering about that and no doubt had questions for later.

It has been a week since the reading of Donna's will and I am still in shock over my newfound wealth. I hate the way that I came into it but I knew that Donna's heart was in the right place. I take it she was being genuine when she constantly told me how much she was in love with me and that she would give me the world if she could. I use to laugh it off whenever she said anything like that, but if only I knew.

The house in Coconut Grove was paid off because Donna bought that cash and the lawyer told me that it was on the market for over five million dollars, I almost pissed my pants. What was I going to do with all that money and stuff that she left me? I will give some to the girls of course and some to my parents but I will still have plenty left to do anything I want. Maybe I will open my own modeling agency, I learned so much from being with Margaret that all I need are good people to work with. Or maybe I will open my own fashion house, get my own line of clothing. Yes that is it; I will open my very own fashion house.

Maybe I am getting ahead of myself. Donna's body is barely cold and there I was making plans to spend the money she left me. I still can't believe that Donna would leave so much to me. Actually I had no idea she would leave me anything at all, I certainly was not expecting anything much less millions, an apartment complex and a damn mansion, plus the cars and diamonds. Patricia got the gold and I got the diamonds. What was I going to do with all that money and stuff? There were moments when I did not think that I deserved it because of the way I treated Donna before she told me about the cancer. But for me that was a lesson learned. I realized how important it was to be kind to people and not allow little insignificant things to get into the way of a good friendship or any kind of relationship for that matter. It is important to tell the people you love and care about that you do love and care about them, and maybe more often than not we should find it in our hearts to forgive and move ahead with our lives. There is just not enough time to harbor vindictive feelings because you never know when will be the last time you get the chance to make amends, so it is imperative that we spend more time loving each other than wasting time hating.

Since Donna's death I have not had a good night's sleep. Miles spent the night a couple of nights ago and he just hugged me and let me cry on his shoulders because I was really missing my friend. After Donna dropped the cancer bomb on me I was more than happy to help make her life as easy as I possibly could and I treated her like a queen, not with any expectations but with the hope that if she died like the doctors told her she would in months then I wanted those last months to be the best she could have and so I saw to it that she did everything she wanted to do including a weekend in Montego Bay, Jamaica where she had a blast, rafting and climbing the Dunn's River Falls in Ocho Rios. She loved the theatre so we saw a play every week, sometimes the same play over and over again and she would laugh in all the same places. You could see how she lit up when she was in the theatre. Donna never looked to me like someone with any kind of health problems let alone cancer. She looked really healthy and she did not get chemotherapy because by the time they found the cancer it was already way too late to do anything about it. Donna said she did not visit the doctor much before the cancer. She said years would pass and she would go about her daily business feeling great, having no need to see the doctor. She barely got the common cold she told me; so when they hit her with the news about the cancer she collapsed and hit her head and was unconscious for three days. What a terrible thing for her to have to go through, if only I knew.

If only anyone knows what will really happen next we would deep-six it back into oblivion but that is not always how life is; some things just come at you out of the blue and you never get a chance to prepare.

She told me that she secretly wanted to be an actress but never really pursued it. She however knew a lot of actors and actresses and was even invited to some of their homes. Donna was a rich girl and money can get you in a lot of doors but her personality played a major part in the opportunities that came her way. She was mostly pleasant, when she wasn't being jealous and she had a sense of humor that was through the roof. She was sexy and beautiful but she could jostle with the best of them. Donna was amazing and I am really going to miss her. I was missing her already, I had no idea how I would feel when she died, even though she kept reminding me over the last few months how close she was to dying; but I kept telling her that miracles can happen, it wasn't over 'til the fat lady sings and other bullshit like that.

Where was Donna's miracle, how come we didn't hear the fat lady taking the stage? Life can be so unfair sometimes. I kept asking God over and over why Donna had to die but I am not sure that he even answers questions like that and if he did how would I know. Maybe I need to start going to church or something; get closer to God. I went to church with Donna a few times since she came back into my life and I really hadn't planned on going back after she passed but I guess I should rethink that thought and get a little closer to God. If there is a heaven I would most certainly want to go there as opposed to my other option and I prayed that Donna got closer to God before she passed. I think she did though because she was atoning for a lot of things in her life. I think she went home to God and her soul is in a good place.

The Monday after Donna's funeral I asked Margaret if I could get a couple of weeks off and she told me to take as much time as I needed, but I don't think that I should stay away for too long, even though I don't need the money as badly as I use to I feel like going back to work would take my mind off Donna some. I was thinking about her all the time and feeling bad that she passed away the way she did. She did not deserve that. She was a good person; a little crazy sometimes but she had a good heart. I thought about the things she said in that video about her parents. I was blown away that she did not leave them and her sister Monica anything. I think they were expecting something or they would not have shown up to the reading at all. I felt bad for them, but I guess Donna knew better than anyone else the reason she did it.

Donna had her entire affair in order before she died, down to the last detail. The morning before the barbeque at Keri's, Donna and I were having coffee at a little coffee shop in Aventura and she told me there was something she would like to say.

"What's on your mind sugar?" She was looking a little pale.

"I was just thinking how if you ask God for something and have faith he will give it to you, but I guess he only give you the things he thinks you deserve." Her eyes were sadder than I had ever seen them.

"Maybe I deserve this for some of the things I did in life. I don't think I did anything that would warrant something like this but then again, maybe I did. You have no idea how one little thing you may have done, one little insignificant thing could impact your life or even someone else's. I wonder about stuff like that lately. You know what I mean Tash?"

I wasn't sure what to say so I said the only thing that came to mind.

"Girl, there is nothing in this world that you could have done to deserve what is happening to you. You may be a little loco but you are harmless."

A big smile lit up her face and we both laughed out loud. People turned to look at us but we just laughed even harder.

"You remember that time we went to the mall and you thought that the gay guy in the eyeglasses kiosk was a lesbian girl and you called him a bitch and told him to keep his eyes off me? Yeah, yeah and he called you a butch and told you he liked dicks. Remember how all three of us busted out laughing and became best buds. Remember that?"

"Yeah, I was crazy then. Looking back how did you ever put up with me Tash?" She was looking directly in my eyes.

"I loved you."

"I know you did but I was just so damn jealous. I think I should have a jelly donut."

I got up and got us both a jelly donut and as soon as I sat back down Donna continued talking.

"Tash, I thank you for being there for me. When I found out about the cancer I thought about you, you were the very first person that came to mind and I set out to find you. I knew you were still in Florida somewhere or so I thought and it took me a whole month after finding your number to get in contact with you. I knew how you felt about what happened and after pushing me away so many times I finally got the message and wanted to respect your choice. It was hard because I never stopped loving you and I always hoped that someday you and I would meet again and you would find it in your heart to forgive me, but I never dreamed it would be under these circumstances."

There were tears in her eyes and I used a napkin to wipe them.

"That's water under the bridge honey. None of that is important now sweetie, I am right here with you and I think you should just eat up that jelly donut and let's go out and get new clothes for the picnic later."

I always knew how to get a laugh out of her. We left the coffee shop and went directly to South Beach shopping. I was happy to see Donna so happy. There was no way anyone could have known that would be her last day.

I found myself less energetic and a lot less motivated since Donna left us and I knew that I needed to get back into gear but it is really hard, feels like I need a good kick up the ass to get me going. Maybe the grand opening of Secrets, Amanda's store, will take me out of the funk I was in. It was only another two weeks away and we were all looking forward to it. Donna was looking forward to it herself telling me how she was going to spend so much money that day that Donna would have to restock immediately. If I knew Donna well enough she meant that; which gave me an idea. I will spend a lot more money than I planned on spending that day for me and Donna. I think she would like that.

Amanda was working feverishly to finish setting up for the grand opening, maybe I should start working on getting out of my funk right now by offering her some help. That is it, I will call her and go down and help her out.

Kylie was away on book business with a little Shane D'Marco in the mix. Melanie is always busy at the salon and we can all understand that, Keri is no longer working so she sometimes helps out Amanda. I haven't given Amanda much in the form of physical help because I was busy with Donna so maybe now I can offer a helping hand. I am sure she could use all the help she can get, and it would do me a world of good to stop thinking so much about the events of the past weeks.

Chapter 11

MELANIE

Since Michael called with the news that his wife died I must admit that I have some renewed expectations. Being his wife is a possibility after all. I was feeling his pain though. I was moping around the shop and everyone could see that something was wrong but I couldn't care less what they thought. Jennifer told me she was worried about me and I quickly advised her not to, that it was nothing but even though she left me alone without prying any further I knew she did not believe me, but I did not give a fuck about that either.

Michael told me not to call him because it might complicate things what with the both sides of their two families in and out of his house and helping with funeral arrangements and all the other people that was expected to show up he just wouldn't have the time to talk with me the way he would like to, so I respect his request but it has been a whole five days since we last spoke and I was crazy out of my mind.

I even lied to Jim that I was too busy preparing for a hair magazine's photo session to see him, and I have never missed a chance to see Jim. That was not really a lie because I was getting ready to do a photo shoot but it did not take much of my time to prepare for it. You just have to make sure that the day of the shoot you have all the models and the hairdos ready along with the outfits and as many makeup artist as you will need because it takes time to put that makeup on. I never understood why it would take as long as forty five minutes or more to apply makeup to anyone for any reason with the exception of those Hollywood movie makers making ogres.

Jerry was the only person I wanted to see at the time because he was the only one with whom I could spend an entire night unless we were out of town or something. I needed Jerry right now. I can stay at his place as long as I want day or night and whenever I am around him he treats me like a queen. I needed to have strong arms holding me all night into the wee hours of the morning or the long hours of the afternoon and Jerry was the only person I can turn to for that and he is always willing. I think maybe he really loves me like he said he does, but I do not really trust him like that. Not with my heart. I have been lying to them for so long I am sure someone must be lying to me too.

Love was the last thing on my mind, Money was definitely first. What would I be doing falling in love when I had as many as three men in my life? Three very generous men; I would be a fool to fall in love and complicate things. The guys can do it and so can us girls but a lot of women suddenly grow consciences and start feeling bad about it. Not the guys, they have a handle on that shit and if you are not a smart woman they drive you crazy with their lies. Well, that won't happen to me. I will do it my way and leave the love thing out of it. I could never wrap my head around that love thing anyway because more times than not it withers and dies.

I thought about going to Michael's wife's funeral just so I could see him, not to talk to him but just so I could look at him but I thought better of it. It would probably do no more than make him mad at me. I guess I just have to wait until he calls me. In the mean time I will just find comfort in Jerry he always fascinated me anyway.

All kinds of crazy things were happening around me. Shortly after Michael' wife passed away one of my favorite clients died as well.

Donna was my client for some time when I found out that she was an old friend of Natasha. Shortly after they ran into each other they suddenly became inseparable and I had even heard whispers from clients in the shop that Donna was gay but I never read much into it because she appeared quite normal to me and I knew that Natasha was as straight as an arrow. I never mentioned the whispers to any of the girls because I did not believe any of it. However, after Donna passed away and left almost everything to Natasha I couldn't help wondering if there was some truth to the gossip. Donna's death however did do a number on Natasha because they spent a lot of time together in Donna's final months so for a couple of weeks after the funeral we spent a lot of time at Natasha's to cheer her up and take her mind off Donna. But how could she? I am sure it is not so easy to just forget someone you cared about. I sometimes get the urge to ask Natasha to her face if there was any truth to the rumors, but I never brought it up because I was not sure that she even knew there was a rumor. It still puzzles me though how Donna left practically her entire estate to Natasha. I guess that would be enough to spark a rumor.

I know that Natasha was there for her in her final months but to leave her all those millions and all the other stuff she got baffled me. She did not even leave anything to her parents; I wondered why but I quickly evaded that thought, it was none of my business.

I knew Donna had to be rich but I had no idea how rich she was until Natasha and Kylie told us about the reading of the will. I had no idea she was worth millions, now my friend Natasha is an instant millionaire.

I heard that Donna gave her gardener and housekeeper a lot of money and an oversized condo, so what happen to her hairdresser, she never thought about me. I could kick myself for thinking that way but it would have been nice if she valued me enough to leave me a little suppen-suppen. I am happy for Natasha though, I guess her ship has really come in, what with the magazine covers, fashion shows and endless photo shoots, now all that money to go with it. I am not jealous or anything I guess I am still in shock over the entire thing. Well, maybe just a little. Everyone seem to be getting real personal breaks except for me, but I guess I should be grateful because I am doing exactly what I wanted to do. I have a degree in business and I am a business woman who is doing very well on her own. I should be further grateful because I had Jim, Jerry and Michael giving me a lot more than a lot of women get in their lifetime.

It is the first weekend in November and in only one day Amanda's store Secrets will be opening its doors for the first and as best buds we all went in and help with the final touches. Amanda wanted to hire a window-dresser to do the huge double glass windows in the front but Natasha and I took care of that with a beautiful thanksgiving theme. At first we thought it would be a little too early for that but by the time we were finished we were all transformed into happy little campers and the timing seemed perfect. There was no rule against getting a head start on the holidays. Kylie even tried to get Amanda to call the event a "Pre-thanksgiving Grand Opening" but she decided against it. It was way in the wee hours of the morning when all five of us left the store. It was worth every bit of effort put into it to see the way it turned out. Amanda really pulled it off, the place was top of the line. Crème de la crème. Secrets was stocked with high end fashion from all the popular designers and was so well put together with each designer getting their own little section, the checkout counter was at least twelve feet long and located at the back of the store, there were mirrors everywhere and her shoe section was just divine; girlfriend had it going on. I think it will probably be the only store in that part of Miami where people will be able to get all their favorite designers in one place. Amanda made us all proud with the way she put the entire venture together. The girl has class. The Kardashian's Dash store has nothing on Secrets.

We offered to help Amanda at the store on opening day but she flat out refused to hear it. We were all planning on doing a little shopping to help make the day a success so Amanda told us she had the floor and the register covered, she had enough people in place she said, so all we needed to do was be good customers, so we will be in to shop at one point or the other throughout the day. It was really nice that everyone was in town for the opening of the store. There's nothing like having the people around you supporting and encouraging what you do, sharing the moment.

I remember when I was opening my salon for the first time. I remember how proud I was when I looked up and saw the huge neon sign that read "Melan' Hair Designs". Amanda, Keri, Kylie and Natasha all came in that day to get their dos done and I think they drew a lot of attention to the salon from that first day. Natasha is responsible for one of the best cosmetologist I have on staff, but I am actually very pleased with the team that I have there. The stylists, the barbers, the nail technicians, the skin specialist all the way to the receptionist and the shampoo girls are all like a big family, so unlike a lot of other salons I was familiar with. Since day one business has been booming and each year proves better than the one before and I believe that Amanda will have the same success or better. I wish her the very best, she has a good heart and is quite a lady.

I get along quite well with the girls but I am definitely closest to Amanda. We had a special friendship between us, something a little beyond what we have as a group. I share things with her that I never shared with anyone else and I think she does the same with me. We do not keep secrets from each other, so sometimes I feel bad about not telling her about Michael but I promised him that I would not let it get out and I must honor that promise. I would not want to do anything to hurt or embarrass him. He is a good man and he was the one who gave me the money to open my salon so I owe him big time. The least I can do is keep my trap shut as promised. I really think that is the only thing I have not shared with Amanda. I even tell her about Jerry and I never told any of the other girls so I guess it is safe to say that Amanda was my best friend in the group. Everyone knew that Natasha and Kylie were indeed best friends, they've been that way since college and Keri is pretty much the floater but she floats mostly over to me and Amanda's side.

Michael told me he would see me tomorrow night because he would be in town for a meeting and was planning on spending the night with me. I was looking forward to spending time with him. Every time I see him he would give me money in the thousands or a piece of expensive jewelry. He is amazing. I wonder now that his wife is gone if he would ever ask me to marry him. I think I would jump at the opportunity. Jim is a white married man and I am sure he was not about to leave his white doctor wife for a black hairdresser, or at least that's what people would say because I don't brag about my degree so a lot of people probably think that all I have going on is a cosmetology license. And as for Jerry, he is straight up a drug dealer and I believe even if he did get out of the business his past will at sometime affect us in one way or the other, so if I am thinking straight I would say that is definitely a no-no. So that takes me back to Michael, the preacher man. He is a single preacher man now and I know that he has to do what looks good and continue to keep our relationship a secret but

I am thinking that after what is considered morally reasonable time I would not mind him asking me to marry him. After all I was the other woman while she was sick in her wheel chair, I provided him with all his extra needs. So I just hope he thinks I am good enough to stand by his side as his wife.

The morning of Amanda's grand opening I left early for the salon, I scheduled a couple of early appointments so I would have the rest of the day to run some errands and go shopping at Amanda's Secrets. The morning went by really fast and before I knew it we were approaching evening. I skipped some of the errands and drove to Amanda's. My cell phone was ringing off the hook and when it wasn't Natasha it was Keri or Kylie wondering what was taking me so long. They told me that they had all picked out what they wanted and was waiting for me to get there so we could gather in the backroom and break out the celebratory champagne.

Parking on South Beach is a bitch so I was more than lucky when I got a parking space directly across the street from the store. Walking across the street I could see that there were a lot of people inside and the four registers were just beeping away. A lot of the stuff we put out on the racks and the shelves the night before were gone. The store was buzzing and girlfriend had dance music coming from the speakers and the place was just jumping. It was like a party going on inside the store and everyone was friendly. There were ten and twenty percent off signs on everything in the store and people were just eating it up. They were spending a lot of money. When I walked into the store Natasha met me at the door.

"Where the hell have you been?"

"Working, or have you forgotten I have a business to run missy?"

"Excuse me. Amanda was asking for you a minute ago."

"Where is she?"

"I think in her office, she has been in there for a while now."

"Hey girl, you finally made it uh?"

It was Keri with Kylie next to her with a pile of clothes in their hands.

"I had no idea I was on the clock. What's this with everyone telling me how late I am?"

I know I was being a little snappy but don't they know I have a business of my own to see to. They were lucky to have the kinds of career they do that did not call for hard labor like standing on your feet all day and dealing with a bunch of mother fuckers from one day to the next.

"No need to get testy missy." Kylie said and nudged me with her elbow and we all hugged."

"So what should I make my purchases first or do we break out the champagne first." I said with a smile, trying to change my mood.

"Shop first, celebrate later." Amanda said from behind me.

"I am so happy for you." I turned around and gave her a hug.

"Thank you Melanie, thank you guys."

"Okay, that's enough. Now let's get back to our little shopping spree." Natasha said and slapped me playfully on my bottom."

"You don't have to tell me twice." Kylie said and walked off toward the Baby Phat section.

We were all going through the racks and the shelves when I saw Amanda peep out the door of her office and she looked like she was crying or something. I left the clothes I was looking at and went to the office. I was about to push the door open when I heard voices. One of them belonged to a man and it sounded quite familiar. I could hear Amanda telling him that she wanted to keep the baby. I could not believe what I was hearing. Then I heard the voice again and I suddenly recognized it. But it could not be. There is no way it could be him. The next thing that came out of his mouth confirmed his identity.

"Amanda, my wife only just passed. I am the minister of one of the biggest church in the country and people look up to me. I can't marry you right away, but eventually I will when the time is right."

Amanda spoke very softly so I could not hear clearly what she was saying but I think I heard her say something about keeping the baby no matter what.

I had no idea what I wanted to do, I didn't know whether to go back to the racks or just push the door and go in. No one could see me from where I was standing so I had time to think. I eventually decided to go with the latter; I had to see for myself. I had no idea Amanda was pregnant I wondered if anyone else knew.

I knocked and quickly pushed the door open and at that moment I realized I was not at all prepared for what I saw. Michael. My Michael was sitting on the edge of the desk with Amanda standing between his legs and his arms wrapped around her with her head on his shoulder.

When he saw me his eyes popped open as wide as his mouth did and he was speechless. Amanda quickly turned around and tried to hide the tears in her eyes.

"Melanie this is Michael." Amanda said.

He jumped up from the desk before I had a chance to say anything and stretched his hand out to shake mine. I could not believe that shit.

"Nice meeting you." He said.

I had no idea why I did it but I shook his outstretched hand.

"Nice meeting you too."

My head felt like someone was pounding into it with a hammer and my knees weakened. I felt like I was in a dream. I could not believe that Michael was seeing other women let alone my dearest friend and now she was pregnant with his baby. Where does that leave me? All the while Michael was telling me I was the only other woman in his life he was seeing Amanda. I guess he convinced her to keep it their little secret like he did me. Amanda had no idea what was going down ever so silently between Michael and I and I could see the desperation in his eyes, he did not want to be found out. I did not want to embarrass myself and look like a fool in front of my friends nor did I want to create a scene inside Amanda's store on the very first day she opened. I tried my best to keep a straight face and even managed a slight smile.

"Melanie, would you mind giving me a few minutes? And please lock the door on your way out I don't want anyone else coming in right now."

She had no idea.

"Sure Amanda. I will lock the door but I don't think that I will be here for much longer. I came in to tell you I have an emergency at the salon so I will just leave my stuff here and you can ring them up later. You can call for my credit card information when you get ready."

"Okay, Melanie and keep this between us please."

"Mum's the word."

I walked out without even taking another glance at Michael. So that was the meeting he had in Miami. I never discussed my friends with Michael just like I never discussed him with them. They had no idea there was a low down dirty preacher in my life named Michael Langston. If you can't trust a preacher who can you trust? So what now he was going to marry Amanda? I wonder what he was planning to do with me. There is absolutely no way I am going to sit back and be the sweet little girl who wants to spare everybody's feelings and get my very own feelings hurt in the process.

It was the longest walk getting out of that office. Pretending I had never met Michael. That hurts.

I stopped long enough to catch my breath then I looked around to see what the other girls were doing and was relieved because they were caught up in the shopping rave and that gave me the opportunity to slip out the door unnoticed. I hurried across the street where my car was parked and quickly got in. I spared no time getting out of the tight spot the car was in, some jerk had his shit all up on my bumper.

I drove for a while not going anywhere in particular; I could not believe that Michael would do that to me. How could he just flat out lie to me about having another woman in his life. I was not his wife, and I was more than happy with the arrangement we had but that was all a lie.

How in the world did he get to fuck me and one of my best friends without either of us knowing about the other? It was apparent that Amanda knew nothing about us. She had that look in her eyes that said she had no idea that I even knew Michael personally. She looked a little guilty but I could tell it was not about seeing Michael but more like guilt from not telling us who he was.

I did not feel like going back to the salon, they were not expecting to see me back there for the rest of the day anyway. I had no idea what to do with myself, I did not want to go home because I was not ready to face Michael and that would be the first place he would look for me.

I finally decided to go home because tears were rolling down my face and I was feeling like shit inside so I needed to be somewhere where I could just be a mess if I wanted to and the only place that I can do that without looking like a fool would be at home. It is so ironic that Michael is the one who actually bought the home I was running to after he broke my heart. That was exactly what he did, he broke my heart. I never thought I would allow any man to affect me so deeply, I pride myself on keeping the love thing at bay but it was apparent that it crept up on me when I was not looking because what I was feeling had to be because of love.

As I pulled in the driveway my telephone rang, it was Michael, I was not sure if I should answer, I decided against it. He called another ten times or more and I ignored him each time. Amanda also called, I thought about not answering her call either but I changed my mind realizing that I could learn more about her and Michael's affair.

"Hello." I answered trying to sound cheerful.

"Hey Melanie, is everything alright?"

"Everything is fine. Are you alright?"

"I don't know. I guess now that you know about Michael and me I can talk with you about what's going on, but you have to promise not to tell any of the other girls about it. Oh Mel, it is a big mess."

I remembered the conversation I heard between her and Michael outside her office door. I was blown away when I heard her mention the pregnancy, we had no idea Amanda was pregnant, and there were absolutely no signs of a pregnancy. Why was all this shit happening to me. Now I will have to sit through Amanda detailing her relationship with the only man that I would want to be my husband. Well maybe not the only man, because if Jerry were to straighten himself out and could guarantee my safety I would marry him. But it would have been an entirely different cup of tea if I got to be the wife of the rich and famous Reverend Michael Langston.

"Mel, are you there?"

"Yes, I'm here. But I will have to call you back in a bit. I am taking care of something right now."

"Okay, but can we get together when I close the store tonight? I really want to talk to someone if you don't mind."

"I don't mind at all Amanda. Would you like for us to go somewhere and talk?"

"Not exactly I was thinking about coming to your place."

I did not exactly want her to come to my place in case Michael decided to drop in unexpectedly. He never did anything like that before but with the wheels turning the way they were anything was possible.

"Okay, I gotta run just call me when you are on your way to make sure that I am here."

"Alright, see you later. Oh I almost forget; do you want me to ring up your stuff or what?"

"I'll get them later. Just keep them in the backroom until I get a chance to come in and try them on."

"Okay, later then."

"Yeah; later."

I was trying my best to sound normal but I wasn't sure that I was successful because deep down inside I was also a little pissed at Amanda even though it was not her fault that we ended up with the same lying, cheating son-of-a-bitch. I tried going back in my head to see if there were any signs that I missed that would have alerted me to the situation I was facing but I came up empty-headed.

Michael kept calling and I eventually answered his call. He said he could not leave without talking with me face to face. I was in no mood to talk to him and I definitely did not want to see him because I had no idea what to say to him and I was not really ready for what he had to say to me. I also thought it best that I speak with Amanda before I talk to him.

I had no idea what he could say to me to mend the broken heart he inflicted on me. In the back of my head I was thinking that if Amanda was not carrying his baby then maybe I would risk our friendship and fight for him but she already had a leg up on the competition.

What in the world could I do to make him choose me if it came down to that. I made the resolution that I would never tell anyone about that awful man and what he did to me, but I was not sure that I would still be able to continue my friendship with Amanda if he did eventually marry her. There was absolutely no way that I could bear to see them together knowing that I was cheated out of being his wife. That was a fucked up position to find myself in and while Amanda had me to talk to about him I had no one. I would look like a damn fool if I let it get out that Michael and I had an affair; then everyone would know that he choose another woman over me, and not just any other woman, my best friend.

I thought about how it would have played out if I did not walk back to Amanda's office at the time that I did. I think I know what would have happened; Michael would leave Amanda's store and later come to my place as planned, fuck my brain out and tell me nothing of another woman carrying his baby. He would pretend he loved me more than he ever did and tell me that in time we will be together for good and how we won't have to hide anymore. I would love to hear what he have to say but I doubt that the conversation would go anything like that with all that happened and the way I was feeling at this stage in the game, it can without doubt wait until my little talk with Amanda.

I was harboring a bit of resentment toward Amanda even though she was not the one who betrayed me. I was certain that if she found out about Michael and me it would hurt her just as much now that she was carrying his baby. When was she planning on telling us about this baby anyway? Was she even planning on keeping it? I am sure she had no idea that I heard the conversation between her and Michael because I stood by the door for a while before I went in.

My phone was ringing off the hook, Natasha, Kylie and Keri was burning up my phone lines but I was not in the mood to discuss what made me leave the store so fast or the wonderful pieces they purchased. Oddly enough though I could not wait to hear from Amanda because more than anything I wanted to see if she was going to tell me about the pregnancy and what she planned on doing with it. The devil on my left shoulder was hoping that she would decide to abort it and forget about Michael, but the angel on my right was saying that it was a real person growing inside her that deserved to live as much as anybody else. I couldn't wait to hear the things she was going to tell me about Michael. He was the one who financed her business the way he did mine. I wonder did he buy her that condo too. If nothing Reverend Langston sure knows how to take care of his women.

I was crying on and off and you would think that Michael was the only man in my life because I was feeling like I lost my husband, my life's partner.

Jerry and Jim were pushed way back into my memory. The only one I could think about was Michael. The more I thought about him the madder I got, but I know I have to maintain my cool around Amanda because there was just no way I could even give her a hint that I met Michael before much less tell her that we were having an affair of our own.

All kinds of questions started popping up in my head. Did Amanda get pregnant on purpose? Was it a plan to trap him into marrying her now that his wife was dead? Will he eventually marry her and if he did how would they explain the baby to his loyal and trusting congregation? I was driving myself crazy with questions that only they could answer. I would eventually get some of those questions answered when Amanda stopped by after closing the store.

Amanda called to say she was on her way to my house and that she picked us up some Italian food for us because she was starving. I guess she was, she was actually eating for two now, but I was not the least bit hungry. Food was the least of my problems.

When Amanda arrived at the house she was in a very good mood and my heart fell even deeper into the cracks where both her and Michael had shoved it earlier that evening but I had to put up a front and act like everything was about her and pretended how happy I was for her. I made sure not to touch the subject until she was ready but she was just bursting with excitement. I could not wait to hear what she was so happy about. Only hours before she was crying her eyes out then all of a sudden she was as happy as a lark.

With her mouth half-filled with Pasta she started babbling on about how sorry she was that I had to meet her mystery man the way I did and how she wished she could have shared him with us. All the time I was thinking if only she knew the irony to that because she was indeed sharing him with me, but now she will never know that.

"Melanie, I am so sorry that you had to meet Michael the way you did. But he insisted on keeping the whole thing a secret which was the right thing to do because he had a wife."

I wanted to just spill the beans and tell her that he had me too but I couldn't. I wanted to tell her that we had a secret affair that was not officially over yet but I couldn't do that either.

"Girl don't you worry about it, that is your business you don't have to share anything with anyone until you are good and ready. I admit I am in shock I never would have guessed in a million years. Tell me the whole story."

And she went on to tell me about the entire affair including the pregnancy and the financing of her new business. She told me how relieved she was that she found out about the pregnancy after the death of Michael's wife because if she had found out about it while the wife was still alive she didn't think she would tell Michael about it or even keep it for that matter. I found myself regretting that his wife passed away. Well if she didn't Amanda would not have a single claim on him and she would not put this baby up front and my life would be totally unaffected.

I listened to her go on and on about how good he was to her and how she believed that Michael will marry her because of his status in the church. All the time I just felt like screaming at her and tell her about us, but I couldn't. She had done nothing to me; as far as she was concerned I was still her best friend that she could share her little secrets with. She made me promise not to tell the other girls about any of the events of the last few hours and I told her I wouldn't.

The whole time Amanda was there Michael kept calling me constantly but I ignored him, even if I wanted to talk to him I surely couldn't do that in front of Amanda. He even called her once while she was there just to ask her if she was alright and it almost killed me when I heard her said "I love you too". He told her he loved her, I could hear him saying that the way he said it to me.

By the time Amanda left my place it was almost two in the morning but sleep was nowhere in sight. I decided to call Michael. He told me he was staying at a hotel not far from my house because he can't go back home until he explained things to me.

If I should go in accordance with the things that Amanda said, he shouldn't have anything to say to me because she believed in her heart that Michael is going to make her his wife. He must have given her a hell of a good reason for believing that.

I agreed for Michael to come by in the wee hours of the morning and the moment he walked in the door the fucking tears betrayed me and started rolling down my eyes like a waterfall.

"I am so sorry Melanie, I had no idea."

"You had no idea about what Michael? You had no idea that I would find out or you had no idea that you were fucking my best friend. Which one is it Michael?"

"Melanie calm down, I know I deceived you and I would like to make it up to you if you would allow me."

"And exactly how do you plan on making it up to me, because I can't seem to wrap my head around that one. Are you planning on abandoning my best friend and her baby?"

I could tell he was surprised to hear me mention the baby.

"You didn't know I knew about the baby, uh. Were you planning to lie to me about that too?"

"Melanie I am so sorry I have no idea what to say to you right now except that I am in love with you and after my wife's death the only woman that I ever thought about taking as my wife is you."

"Cut the crap Michael, I'm finding it very hard to believe anything that comes out of your mouth from now on. You told me time and time again that I was the only other woman that was in your life. You even told me how sorry you were that you didn't meet me years before. So tell me Reverend Langston was that all a lie?"

"Melanie please, I know I lied to you and to that poor girl but I will do the right thing by the both of you. I promise."

"You promised that you would never hurt me and you did. You promised that if your wife should pass away that I would become the next Mrs. Langston, but that was a big joke and the laugh was apparently on me. Why would you do that to me Michael? Tell me, and tell me how you could ever make it up to me." I was livid by then.

"Mel, the baby is a mistake I never thought that would happen. You know what; there is nothing I can say to justify the situation but I am so deeply sorry that you got caught up in it because I really do love you and I still hope that we can work things out between us without any animosity."

"What, are you afraid that I will go to the press and tell them what a dirty lying fake ass monster you are?" I was mad as hell and I could not help myself.

"Mel, please calm down." He had no fucking idea what to do at that point.

"Calm down, don't fucking tell me to calm down. So what, if I didn't walk in on you and my best friend you would come to me and tell me what was going on? Is that what you want to tell me?"

"No sweetheart, I ..."

I interrupted whatever lie he was getting ready to tell out of his lying mouth.

"Don't you fucking sweetheart me. You are a cruel man."

"Melanie, please hear me out."

I had no choice but to hear him out because by then I was totally breathless and I also realized that I was not giving him a chance to say what he had to say and up until that moment I did not know what his intentions were. I hope he did not think he could still see me after all that happened. I shut up long enough for him to say all he had to say without any interruptions. I at least owed myself that much.

"Alright Michael, I will hear what you have to say then you can leave."

"Fair enough."

'I'm listening." I said impatiently amid the tears and heartache.

He told me how he met Amanda before he met me and liked us both because we both brought different things to his life. He tried to convince me that he was not in love with Amanda but found her to be a good friend and that one thing led to another and they ended up in bed. He made it sound as if he was not in love with Amanda but however enjoyed her company. I wondered how many other women out there whose company he just loved. Were they all pregnant now?

He went on and on about how he hated himself for hurting me the way he did and how I should give him time to clear things up with Amanda. He said he would make sure that the baby gets taken care of and Amanda too, but he had no plans to marry her because his intention was to ask me to be his wife when the time was right.

Nothing he said meant anything to me because the situation was a lot more complicated than that. Even if his intentions were to marry me there was no way that I could agree with that because Amanda was my best friend and carrying his baby so all I could see was a lose, lose situation for me. The only way that would happen was if I was cold enough to just give up my friendship with Amanda and that would mean losing the other girls as my friends. They were all the family I had. I was between a rock and a hard place and I could not believe that I was even giving thought to that bullshit.

It was almost six o'clock in the morning when he asked me if it was okay for him to get some sleep. Something inside me made me say yes and he did not just spend the rest of the morning but we made mad passionate love.

I was happy that it was Sunday and I did not have to go work because I doubt that I could have handled that. The moment he left I called Amanda making sure my voice was normal and friendly.

"Hey girl" I said when she answered the phone.

"Mel, what's up?"

"You tell me. Are you planning on marrying your preacher man?"

"I have no idea girl he is talking about it being too soon after his wife's death to think about marrying someone else. Something about his image and the ministry but I am not hearing that shit. This baby is not going to be born out of wedlock if I can help it."

"I heard that."

I wasn't saying much because I wanted to hear everything she had to say.

"So did you tell him that?"

"I told him and he said he would do the right thing and it will work out for everyone in the end, but I reminded him that he and I were the only people involved now that his wife was no longer around. I get the feeling that he wants to do the right think but he made it clear he could not marry me right away. I wonder how long he expects me to wait."

"Well, you know he can't just up and marry you now or he would come under a lot of scrutiny that could destroy him, so don't be too hard on him Amanda because you had something to do with you getting pregnant too."

"I understand that but I have to think about the welfare of the baby inside my body."

"Did you tell anyone else about it?"

"Not yet but it not like it's gonna just go away or anything. In a couple of months my stomach will start showing and who will I say the father of my child is?"

"Girl you worry too much. I am sure this will all get sorted out. You said yourself that he said he would do the right thing. Just don't put too much pressure on him. Give him some time to think it through."

"Maybe you should also consider not telling the other girls just yet." I continued.

"You are right Mel, I will hold off telling them until it is necessary. I am so scared that I will have to raise this child all by myself."

"What would you have done if his wife was still alive?"

"I have no idea, but the fact is she is not alive so she is no longer an issue."

"But you can't be selfish Amanda, he still has the ministry to think about so try to calm down and don't do anything you will live to regret. Take your time to think the whole thing through before you do anything."

I had my own ulterior motive for encouraging her to take things slow. I even found myself wishing that Amanda would somehow suddenly have a miscarriage. I knew then that no matter what happened I could not stand the idea of her carrying and finally giving birth to Michael's baby. I will not have it. I could not stand to hear anymore about her and the man I love. I had no idea that I was so deeply in love with Michael until I found out about his affair with Amanda.

If he marries Amanda I could no longer be friends with her. I knew that for sure because I would not be able to stand seeing her with him. If he didn't marry her it would still create a problem because she had no intention of getting rid of the baby and even if she did and Michael chose me that would still open up a whole new can of worms. Whichever way I looked at it I was going to end up with the shitty end of the stick.

There was only one thing left to do. I had my mind made up I could not stand to lose Michael to Amanda. For the first time since we met I felt hate for her and I will not let her win.

I called her later that day to make sure that she kept this little situation from the other girls, I convinced her not to say anything to them at least not before she was sure of Michael's intention. I really did not give a fuck about her feelings at that time but I needed time to put my own little plan into gear. She will get Michael over my dead body. He was my man and I will not give him up without a fight.

I called Michael that afternoon to tell him I love him and that we could work things out if he so desired. I basically told him that I loved him too much to give him up to anyone and he said he would be back on Tuesday to discuss the situation with me.

In the mean time I have to make sure that Amanda keeps our little secret to herself so it would not affect the plans I had. I was not sure just what I was going to do but whatever it turned out to be I know it will affect our friendship in ways unimaginable.

Chapter 12

KYLIE

A lot was happening in my life these days and for the first time since Milo I think I am truly happy. Shane D'Marco has a lot to do with it. I was jet setting back and forth to be with Shane and he even spent a night at my place when he was held over on a flight from the Bahamas. The weather was really bad because of a hurricane that was rearing its ugly little head and there were no flights leaving Miami so in lieu of spending the night at a hotel close to the airport he chose to spend the night at my place. That was his first time there. He said he was impressed with the house and what I did with it but I did not read much into it because the man was living in no less than a mansion. My house could in all probability fit into his a couple of times with space still left over.

I was still on my second novel and was not the least worried about making my deadline because I was way ahead of myself. I truly feel like a writer now, it took a long time for me to essentially grasp the fact that I was a writer, a real writer with a bestselling book. Somehow that reality encouraged my resourcefulness in ways I never understood before and the stories kept coming, and the words kept flowing.

Amanda opened her store and boy did I shop my ass off. Well we all did, mainly to support our friend. Keri, Natasha and I hung around until the store closed and had a little champagne celebration in Amanda's office. Melanie had an emergency at the salon and had to leave, at least that's what Amanda said but I still cannot understand why she would just run out the way she did without saying anything to us.

I had a funny feeling that something went down between Amanda and Melanie but Amanda insisted that everything was as good as ever, but I could tell that something was wrong because that day Amanda was in her office for quite some time and I saw Melanie go into the office with a handful of clothes and accessories; I had no idea how long she spent in the office because I was busy going through the racks, but I remember looking through the glass window out into the street and I saw Melanie rushing to her car and she was looking really upset. I called Melanie's cell phone but she did not answer and so I called the salon but she was nowhere to be found and Jennifer said there was no emergency at the salon. I was sure then that something had gone down between Amanda and Melanie.

I asked them both later if something happened and they insisted that all was well with the friendship and made me feel stupid for even thinking the way I did. I still believe that even if they were right about all being well between them, that they were keeping something from the rest of us. Something happened in that office that day and I think it was something big. I dropped the subject but not before discussing it with Natasha and Keri. They too thought something happened in that office. But I guess we'll never know unless of course Amanda or Melanie decides to say something.

Our circle of five was dwindling lately, everyone was suddenly so withdrawn. Keri haven't gotten together with us since the opening of Amanda's store, she said she was really busy but I didn't understand how she would suddenly get so busy even though she quit the job at the accounting firm. One would think she would have more time on her hands but that was not the case.

The only time we saw Melanie since Amanda's opening was at the salon when we go to get our hair done. She has not been coming around either. Something was definitely going down with her because she was not her jolly old self anymore.

Amanda was a whole other subject, she spent all her time at the store but I guess I could understand that, it came with the territory. She dropped a bomb on us that was out of this world and we were all blown away. The day she told us she was pregnant Natasha and I had dropped in on her at the store, that was shortly after the opening and she took us in the office and just flat out told us she was pregnant.

Natasha and I had some time to kill and stopped by the boutique to surprise Amanda. She was back in her office as always and the four people working the floor and the registers were just buzzing away like busy little bees. Natasha walked directly toward the office and I followed but before we could break the corner to where the office was Amanda exited the women's room door. She was surprised to see us but looked happy about it.

"Uh, this is such a nice surprise." She was smiling from ear to ear.

"You look happy, business must be good." Natasha said and gave her a hug.

"Business looks good but I see a whole different kind of happiness, a sort of glow. Maybe someone is in love." I said taking my turn to hug her.

"Oh, be quiet the two of you. Let's go in the office."

We shoot the breeze for a while talking about business, Natasha's windfall, my book, her store. We even talked about Keri and Melanie, with me and Natasha airing our concern about them not showing up lately but Amanda was expressing the same concerns herself and gave us the impression that she was just as puzzled as we were. Maybe nothing really happened between Amanda and Melanie at the grand opening that day. Maybe Melanie had to take care of something personal. She was always the secretive one. She talked a lot, made us laugh a lot but she very rarely discussed her personal life.

Natasha and I were getting ready to leave the store when Amanda dropped the bombshell. I was already out of my chair and heading to the door and Natasha was admiring something on Amanda's desk as she reach for her purse.

"I am pregnant."

She said it with such nonchalance that I thought she was joking and I guess Natasha thought the same thing too.

"Girl, be careful what you ask for, you just might get it." Natasha said.

"What, would that make you the new-age Mary? I heard about the next coming of Christ but I had no idea that it would be that kind of rebirth." I was laughing and Natasha was just cracking up. Was she even fucking? I have never seen that man.

"That's a good one." All while she laughed.

We suddenly stopped laughing when we realized that Amanda was not laughing but just sitting there with this serious look on her face that said it was no laughing matter.

"You are serious aren't you?" Natasha asked.

"As a heart attack." She replied softly.

"Oh my gosh Amanda. Are you alright?" I felt like a louse for what I said earlier.

"I am. I am just a little scared."

"What are you scared of?" Natasha took her hand and asked.

"I don't know. It's a long story and I have to get ready to receive a couple of shipments but I will tell you all about it later."

"Alright, but if you need anything don't hesitate to call." I offered.

"We mean that." Natasha said

"I know. Thank you guys."

Natasha and I talked about nothing else the whole rest of the time we were together that day. We knew that Amanda was seeing someone way on the down low but we were puzzled as to why she would get pregnant for him when she could not even admit to anyone that they were seeing each other. From what she told us there was no chance of a future with him so I could not wrap my brain around the reason she would find herself pregnant. It had to be a mistake. I don't think she would knowingly get herself in that situation with a man that she could not even introduce to her closest friends. We had absolutely no idea who that mystery man was and I couldn't wait 'til she told us.

Natasha and I saw each other all the time but the other three girls seemed to be going in different directions with whatever individual mission they were on. Our group of five was not the same. It was safe to say that Keri and Melanie definitely changed and now Amanda with this baby thing will most likely fashion some changes.

I was at home just hanging out by the pool all by my lonesome when my housekeeper Julie came running from inside the house.

"Kylie someone is at the door to see you! He came in a limousine he looks just like that guy in the movies, um, um." She said in her thick Jamaican accent.

"Okay Carol you go ahead and let him in. Bring him back here." I said in my most pleasant voice.

I liked Carol because she had an innocence about her that made me trust her to take care of my home. She was a very homely girl but was quite intelligent. And she made the best Jamaican food that I ever tasted. She can cook her ass off. She was only in America four months when she started working for me as my housekeeper.

I was pleasantly surprised to see Shane and he was just delighted to see me. He was wearing jeans and white tee shirt and some tough ass Michael Jordan sneakers. I watched him walk toward me with those long sexy strides that he was so famous for in his Calvin Klein underwear ads and something inside me leapt for joy.

"Hi pretty lady; my pretty lady." He sounded sexy saying that.

"Hi Baby. I am so happy to see you I could cry." I stood up and hugged him.

I was wearing black bikinis and I had a red wrap around my waist. He gently pushed me away from him and looked at me as he pretended to drool.

"Looks like I am right on time for dinner."

"I guess you are if you prefer your dinner hot."

"Then I am ready to get started."

He took me by the hand and we literally ran into the house, up the stairs and into the bedroom where we ravaged each other and just enjoyed each other with a passion that was way past its release date. He was hungry for me and I was even hungrier for him but being in the same room with him was all I really needed to feel good. His mere presence was enough to make between my legs heat up. He actually being between my legs was just heaven on earth. He fucked me with sheer abandon…making my pussy hum. Doggy style took center stage and I could feel his dick all the way up in my belly…I felt like the luckiest girl in the world. Shane D'Marco smashing my back out. Yes, I am the luckiest girl in the world.

"Oh Shane, fuck me baby…aah, aah…ooooh!! Jesus."

"Ye...e…essss!! He was on the verge of explosion and I could feel his dick pulsating with a vengeance inside my womb.

He nutted just as a big rush of electricity ran from my toes then crashed and exploded at my hips in time to collide with his grand finale. I was in heaven.

I fell flat on my stomach and he crashed on top of me. It felt good.

We were actually in that room for over an hour when he remembered that his limo driver Roy was still outside in the car.

We got dressed and headed downstairs together. I heard talking in the kitchen so I went toward the kitchen while Shane walked to the front door.

"Hey, he is here." I called to Shane letting him know his driver was inside the kitchen.

Carol had him sitting at the counter with a thick slice of pie in front of him and I had never seen her so forthcoming before. They were apparently having a good time talking to each other. Shane told him that he would be spending the night and offered to pay for a hotel for him but I told Shane it was okay for him to stay in one of the guest rooms if he preferred. He was okay with staying at my place and so while Shane and I spent the rest of the evening before dinner upstairs in my bedroom burning up the sheets his chauffeur hung out pool side and was enthusiastically entertained by Carol.

One of the things I admired in Carol was that she could whip up a meal fit for a king in no time flat. She was not only good at making Jamaican dishes but just about any dish you could think of. Well she was no Wolfgang Puck but she could really throw down in the kitchen, something I was not very good at.

Dinner was baked chicken with pineapple sauce, mashed potatoes, asparagus cooked in garlic butter, yellow rice and dessert was fresh warm Jamaican sweet potato pudding topped with whipped cream.

Shane and I had dinner together in the dining room and Carol and his limo driver ate later while we hung out by the pool. The sun had set and there was a beautiful yellow reddish hue way out in the horizon. It was extremely beautiful and looked like a painting that I could reach out and touch. The evening was just the right temperature, not too warm and not too cool, just perfect. We swam together and played with each other in the water, we spent a lot of time kissing and touching each other and my heart could not get any happier than it was at the time.

Shane suggested we got out of the pool before he shriveled up into a little old man and I assured him that it would take much more than an hour in a pool to make anything of his shriveled. He thought I was being nasty, but he liked it.

He offered to take me out on the town if I wanted but all I wanted was to stay wrapped up in his arms and enjoy all the goodies that came with it. I was never tired of making love to Shane and I could tell that he enjoyed being with me as well because I could not get enough of the more than usual attention he was giving me.

The morning after Shane's arrival I got up to find him gone. I ran to the window and looked in the driveway and the limousine was still there. I exhaled and was about to go to the bathroom when he appeared in the bedroom door with a towel wrapped around him.

"You missed me?"

He had that knockout smile that just drove me out of my mind on his face and I could tell he was up to something.

"Of course I missed you. Did you go swimming?"

"Yep. You know what they say; the more energy you burn the more energy you'll have. Something like that."

"Oh yeah?"

"Oh, yeah."

We were back in the bed and he was back in me and I was back in seventh heaven, on cloud nine kicking my heels three times, four times, five times I actually lost count on the heel kicking. No man had ever made me feel the way Shane did and I have never given myself so completely to anyone like I did with him. I was head over heels in love with him and knew that I wanted it to last forever.

When I spend time with Shane I never really felt like I was with a celebrity. I felt so comfortable with him it was like being with the boy next door that you grow up with. He was so self-effacing, so humble and to me that was most refreshing. He had that natural sweetness about him that would make any woman bend over backwards to please him but he was just as happy to do the same for her. Hollywood definitely did not spoil him and I doubt that he will ever let it.

After our morning rendezvous we skipped the dining room and had breakfast in the bedroom, but he had to leave immediately after so I insisted on another little quickie before he left. He was more than happy to oblige and even joked that I was going to put him in a wheel chair before he turned forty.

He got dressed and picked up his overnight bag that he had taken from the limo the night before. I walked with him downstairs and when we got to the front door he rested the bag on the floor then he knelt in front of me and the moment he did that my heart skipped several beats and I could swear I was breaking out into a cold sweat.

"Kylie, I have searched for you all my life and now that I've found you I would love to have the pleasure of making you my wife. Will you marry me?"

"Shane, what are you doing? Are you sure about this"

I knew that was not what he was expecting to hear and I was not even sure that was what I wanted to say, but I was so caught off guard. He did not move a muscle.

"I am sure about this, will you marry me Kylie?"

"Yes, yes, yes."

He got up from his kneeling position and put a beautiful diamond ring on my finger.

"I am so relieved that you said yes, I almost left without asking because I was not sure if you would think that I was moving way too fast and I wasn't sure that I could handle hearing you say no or that you were not ready.

"Shane you have made me the happiest woman in the world right now. Though if I were to be honest I was already feeling like the happiest woman in the world just being with you. But I must say this ring is way beyond my expectation, not that I had any expectations."

I realized that I was babbling and so did he. He pressed his lips firmly against mine and laid a kiss on me that instantly made my pussy hot and moist. He told me he would call me later and that he was sorry he could not stay to celebrate with me but that he would be back in only a couple of days and we would celebrate then. Just like that, he was gone.

As soon as Shane left I called Natasha and told her to gather the other girls and come by the house because I had an emergency and I could use all their help. Everyone came with the exception of Melanie; she could not be found anywhere. That was not unusual though because Melanie was known for just disappearing into her own little world from time to time but she always made time for us. That was not exactly the case lately; I think she was deliberately staying away from us. I wondered why that was.

I had a bottle of Cristal champagne that I was saving for a special occasion. Well I had several bottles but I have had a lot of special occasions lately so I was down to my last bottle.

The girls did not notice the ring on my finger because I took it off just before they got there so I would not spoil the surprise. I put the ring back on just in time for the toast. They were all wondering what we were toasting to that was so urgent that they had to get there in such a hurry. They were pissed at me at first for making them think there was an emergency but all was forgiven when I showed them the huge rock on my finger and told them the entire episode about the proposal from Shane.

I could tell that they were all happy for me and I was happier than ever with the knowledge that I had such a wonderful group of friends to share stuff with. My life could not get any better. I have a bestselling novel flying off the shelves in the bookstores and online as well. A second one on the way and now I was about to become the wife of the most sought after man in Hollywood. God must really love me.

I was thrilled, they were thrilled and my heart sang songs that were long eliminated from my head. I knew in my heart of hearts that Shane was the man for me and when I thought about the way we met I was certain that God had a hand in it. Finding a man in New York was the last thing on my mind.

As a matter of fact men was not even on my short term agenda, my lone focus was on my career and nothing else.

Melanie called while the girls were still at the house and apologized for not being there but I told her it was not a real emergency and she felt better about it. She insisted that I tell her what the illusory emergency was and I was just too happy to tell her.

"Shane asked me to marry him and I said yes."

"Oh Kylie, that is the best news I've heard in a long time. Man, and I miss the celebration, I can't wait to see the ring. There is a ring, right. I'm kidding, Congratulations mama, I am going to have to come over and see it soon."

"Well you may get to see it sooner than you think because I have to get my hair done tomorrow."

"Perfect. Really Kylie you deserve to be happy and you sound so happy right now. I am so happy for you."

"Thank you Mel. The others are here, hold on they all want to talk to you."

She spoke with Natasha for a minute then Keri and Amanda before hanging up. Everything was just so sweet between us five. We were like sisters but closer than most, we had no secrets between us and I didn't know of any other group of women that were as considerate and caring as we were to each other. We had each other's back all the way, we were each other's protector and there was nothing that we would not do for each other. I felt blessed to be a part of something so special, so exceptional and filled with so much love. I would bend over backwards for any one of those girls and I knew they would do the same for me. I never worried that any of them would do anything to hurt me. We supported each other furiously and knew everything about each other.

I'll admit that I was a little worried about Amanda and Melanie but after that telephone conversation between them, though I had no idea what Melanie was saying I could tell that everything was honky-dory from the way that Amanda was laughing and talking with her. So I guess there was nothing to worry about. I believe though that it would be alright if there were disagreements between us, because we loved each other enough and respect each other enough to work them out intelligibly.

Shane called me last night and insisted that I set a date for the wedding. I told him that I would think about it and let him know today. It was already three week since the engagement and he said he was ready to get married right away. He warned me that he would be very heartbroken If I waited too long to meet him down the aisle and I assured him that the same thing would happen to me too so I would speed up the process to save us both the trouble. He always knew all the right things to say to make me laugh or just smile in my heart. Shane D'Marco was a sweet, wonderful and sexy man, not to mention rich. I was so lucky to have him. They say good things come to those who wait and boy was I glad I waited. I met more than my share of men since moving to Florida and I was never impressed enough with any of them to want to spend my life with them. I refused to waste my time with any of them the moment I recognize that they were not what I needed for me.

There was this guy Manuel, he was an Electrical Contractor who hailed from Cuba and he was the closest to what I needed. Actually he was everything I thought I wanted in a man or so I thought. He was handsome, caring, he had his own business and made a lot of money, he gave generously and the sex was good. I thought I hit the jackpot but after only four months I found out that Manuel was possessive and dangerous. He didn't want me to talk to anyone on the telephone when we were together and he wanted to know where I was every minute of the day. He once told me that if I left him he would kill himself. That did it for me, I hauled ass out of that one. Luckily for me he never knew where I lived or worked. I knew not to make that mistake; Lord knows I watched enough Lifetime movies. The girls were as disappointed as I was that Manuel turned out to be a psycho.

Amanda dropped by to chat, she was spending more and more time away from Secrets because she was confident that her staff had her back and was right on the money. We talked business as usual since the opening of the store and we talked about the pregnancy but she still hadn't told us who the daddy was. I tried pushing but she wouldn't budge so I dropped the subject. She insisted that it was better that way until after the birth of the baby and she was okay with it but I didn't think she was because no matter how hard she laughed and tried to look happy I could see the sadness in her eyes and it broke my heart that she was apparently in so much pain. Her eyes told it all, she was worried and the only thing that I could attribute to that worry was the pregnancy.

Later in the late afternoon, after Amanda left Natasha came by to see me. I had called her earlier and told her that I needed her help picking a wedding date. She was more than happy to oblige. I wanted Natasha to be the one to help me with things like that because she was actually my best friend. I ordered pizza and when the doorbell rang I thought it was the pizza guy, it was the pizza but there was no pizza guy. Natasha pulled up as the pizza guy was coming to the door and paid him; I was sure he left happy because Natasha was a big tipper. She handed me the pizza as she walked in the door.

"Girl traffic is a bitch out there."

She was looking fabulous in the sweat bottom and tight tee shirt she was wearing and I told her so.

"Well anyone looking as good as you would block any traffic my sister."

"Thank you honey but I had nothing to do with it I was just a hapless victim. Here's a nice little wedding gown catalog that I picked up for you." She said handing me the book.

"Let's have some pizza first, I'm a little peckish."

"Peckish, what the hell is peckish. I've never heard that one before."

"Remember when we went to Jamaica? People were always saying they were peckish and Amanda asked this Rastafarian man what it meant and he gave us this whole speech about where the word came from. Remember he said peckish means that you are just a little hungry, when it's not a burning hunger but just a little taste for something nice."

"Girl I don't remember any of that shit, but thanks for the patois lesson."

"Um this pizza is good."

I guess I was more than a little peckish because I was tearing into that pizza. Natasha wasn't doing such a shabby job herself she was already on a third slice and I was just about to finish my second.

"So when do you wanna get married?" She asked with her mouth full.

"Girl I have no idea, but Shane wants to do it right away. He is pushing for the next couple of months or so. I would rather wait another six or more."

"Wait for what? Girl you have to give this man his wish and marry him right away." She lifted my chin with her finger playfully.

"You think so."

"I know so. We need to come up with a date no later than two months away Mrs. Soon-to-be Shane D'Marco." She was so happy for me I could tell.

"Okay, I have a calendar right here." Pulling my cell phone out of my Chanel handbag.

We went back and forth, over and over, and I finally decided on a date. Shane told me the night before that any day I chose in the next two months would be fine with him so I chose Valentine's Day.

I was going to wait until Shane called to tell him that I had picked our wedding date but Natasha insisted that I called him right away and tell him. She thought that would be more romantic and I agreed with her. I dialed his number and he answered on the very first ring.

"Hi pretty lady." His voice was cheerful.

"Hi baby I've been thinking about you."

"That's nice. I hope you were thinking about when you want to marry me."

"I knew you were clairvoyant." I joked.

"So that's why you want to marry me, I thought you loved me." He joked back.

"I want to become your wife on Valentine's Day."

"Thank you baby, I love you." I could hear the smile in his voice.

"Is that a yes, Valentine's Day is good?"

"Couldn't get any better. I gotta run honey I'll call you later."

"Okay, later."

The whole time Natasha was just beaming with joy and was poking and touching me with excitement throughout the phone call.

"He said Valentine's Day would be perfect. He's going to call later so we can talk more about it, you know the wedding plans."

“Yep, you’ll have to jump on it right away because two months could go by really fast. It’s the middle of December now so fast and fabulous will have to do.”

“I guess you are right. I don’t want anything big and neither does Shane.”

“Who cares about big or small, fabulous is all that matters. You know what? Ditch that catalog I just gave you. You are going to have a dress made by one of the top notch designers, you can afford it, and better yet you deserve it.”

Natasha hung out at my place all night and we just went on and on about what I should or should not do for the wedding. I was definitely going to get someone big to design my dress. I really like that Vera Wang lady. A lot of movie and television stars had her design their wedding gowns but I wanted to find out what Shane thought before I made up my mind. I did not have to wait very long because he called me again later that night like he promised. He told me that it was going to be my day so I should do whatever I pleased and that I should not worry about how much anything cost because he would pay for it all. I could not believe what I was hearing it just kept getting better and better.

Natasha said she would call Margaret the following day and had her set up a meeting with Vera Wang and she did just that. I arranged to fly to New York two days later and it worked out wonderfully. I had an idea what I wanted but she knew exactly what would be right for me and so we signed a contract for her to design my wedding gown. With that out of the way I flew back to Miami to meet with a series of caterers and scheduled cake tastings with about four different companies; that would take place later the following week. I made sure that I scheduled them all on the same day so I would be able to make a clear choice. All the girls agreed to help me with the tastings and so I wanted to make it a one day thing so I wouldn’t take too much of their time.

There was no question in my mind that Keri would be the one to provide flowers for the occasion. She knew her flowers well and could get her hands on the most exotic ones from wherever in the world they originate and she had a knack for choosing the right arrangements for any occasion.

I was a little astounded that the planning of the wedding was going so well and stress free. I took that as an omen that the life after the occasion would probably be just as good and stress free. Shane was a wonderful man and spending time with him over the last few months has made me one of the happiest women on the planet. As rich as Oprah was I doubt that she was as happy as me. I was in love and I strongly believed that Shane love me just as much although I was sure that I would be just as happy if he loved me even half as much as I loved him.

I couldn't wait to become his wife; I don't know what got into me that made me think I could wait another six months to marry him. I was about to become Mrs. Shane D'Marco, what's to wait for?

Christmas was just right around the corner and Shane and I made plans to visit my aunt Kate in Georgia. For the first time in a long time none of us girls would be spending Christmas together, we were all going separate ways. Natasha was going to spend Christmas with her parents, Amanda was going to spend Christmas with her mother and grandmother in Virginia and I think her brother Peter will be home from Korea for the holidays. Keri and Miguel will be spending the holidays between his family in Miami and hers in Little Town, Georgia. Not so sure though what Melanie will be doing.

I never said anything to my Aunt Kate about Shane I just told her I would be bringing a male guest and she was as happy as a lark that I was bringing home a male companion. She said it was about time I found someone I was interested in and that she was looking forward to meeting him but I did not tell her who he was I wanted that to be a surprise along with the news of the engagement. Aunt Kate will be the only real family at my wedding to Shane and I was so happy to have her in my life but I was suddenly missing my mom and dad. They were just the best parents anyone could ask for.

My dad was Professor Kyle Mason he was tall, dark and handsome with beautiful hazel eyes and he was tough but gentle. He was born and raised in Mississippi and would tell my mom and I stories about the racism he suffered as a child. We could see the pain still in his eyes when he talked about it. He was very protective of my mother and he would take me with him almost everywhere he went; we were inseparable and he spoiled me rotten.

My mother's name was Althea and she was a beautiful half Indian woman with wavy black hair and even darker eyes. She never worked a day in her life because my dad would not have his wife working; that was a no-no. He believed that it is the man's responsibility to bring home the bacon. My mother never minded one bit because she hated working anyway even though she had gotten a degree in Business.

They were high school sweethearts and they continued their relationship even though my dad went away to Yale and her to UCLA. They got married a year after leaving college and I was born a year after that. I remember how loving they were all the time and they would tell me all the time how much they loved me; not that I needed to hear it because I knew how much they loved me without them saying it. I loved them just as much and it was truly devastating for me when they died. I remember that day like it was just yesterday.

It was the end of August and my mom and dad were out shopping. She wanted him to have a new wardrobe for the new school year even though he never cared one way or the other whether he got new clothes or not. He had a lot of clothes and was a very sharp dresser but he was happy with the clothes he had. My mother insisted that he should always be at his best and I agreed with her. My dad kept us in a lifestyle that was way beyond what most of my friends' parents could afford and so we thought that he should dress like the wonderful husband and father he was.

They spent most of that day out not just shopping but eating and going to the movies. I spoke with the two of them while they were having dinner and mom was really excited about their day together. After dinner they were heading home and they were only minutes away from the house when a truck ran a red light and slammed into their car. Dad was in the driver seat and his side got hit killing him instantly, the car ended up wrapped around a huge pole and they had to cut mom out, she died on the way to the hospital.

By the time the police got to the house to tell me the news it was already on the television but I had no idea that it was my parents. The car was so badly damaged that there was no way I could tell it was their car. I called Aunt Kate after the cops told me about my parents and she was there within minutes. She lived only about three miles away but she got there in record time.

My parents' absence took a toll on me from the moment I got the news and I had no idea how I even got through my first year of college. The second year was really hard and I could not concentrate on anything. I was not paying attention in class and I was not completing my assignments so I did the only thing that made sense and took a year off. Aunt Kate was a little worried about that but I assured her that I would take no more than a year and she supported my decision.

My parents left Aunt Kate a lot of money and they left me the house and I had a huge trust fund so I was not strapped for money and in that year I did nothing, no work, just nothing. Aunt Kate said it was good therapy to not have to worry about even the slightest of things and I proved her right because that year of doing nothing helped me to work through my feelings about my parents' sudden death. I did a lot of reading and meditating and just connecting with my inner self and realizing that life did not always give us what we want or even what we need, it gives us what is destined for each of us.

I will never get over them but I have learned to deal with them being gone and I feel like I have connected with them in ways that I never dreamed. I feel like they are ever present, just watching over me and still helping me to make important decisions. I just know they would love Shane if they were around to meet him.

I was saddened that they did not get the opportunity to see their only child walk down the aisle, that I was cheated out of having them share in the happiest day of my life. I realized that I did not have anyone to walk me down the aisle. I guess Aunt Kate will have to do because there was just no one else to do it and what better person to give me away than Aunt Kate, that's family and who says the person who gives away the bride has to be a man? That was settled, Aunt Kate would be my giveaway person I am sure she would not mind; I guess I could call her that, my giveaway person.

I could not believe that I was planning my wedding to Shane D'Marco. I never dreamed that I would meet him much less date him and now marrying him. That was never in the cards, or at least so I thought. The wedding plans were well on the way and I could not wait to walk down the aisle into his future.

Before I knew it Christmas was upon us. Four days before the big day Keri and Miguel left to go visit with his family. Natasha had flown out the day before that and Amanda, Melanie and I would leave for our destinations the day before Christmas Eve. This was only a day away. Shane was going to meet me in Florida and we would fly to Georgia together.

I was in the kitchen fixing myself a sandwich and the early morning news was on. The reporter was talking about a robbery that had taken place the night before and something about the story drew me to the television. My heart skipped several beats and a lump formed in my throat and I lost all feelings in my legs. I plopped down on the sofa and the tears started rolling down my eyes. I had no idea what to do; I realized there was nothing I could do that would ever change the reality of things.

The news reporter was standing in front of Secrets, Amanda's store, and there were police lines and police cars and police officers everywhere. She said that an employee came into work hours before and found the store owner dead in her office with a gunshot wound to the head, she went on to say that the day's cash intake was missing along with Amanda's credit cards and cellular phone.

I found enough strength to pull myself up out of the chair and went into my bedroom to get my cellular phone. I had all the girls on speed dial and usually the first person I would call at a time like this would be Natasha, but she was too far away and I did not want to spoil her time with her family just yet, eventually all of us would end up having a very bad holiday. Christmas will never be the same again for any of us, I was sure of that. I called Melanie and she was screaming so hard I could not understand what she was saying. Then we called Natasha and Keri together. I was hoping to spare them the horror for a while longer but I knew in my heart that they would want to know something like that right away.

Melanie made a mad rush to my house and we went down to the store to see what was going on. The police was still there and Amanda's body was still in her office while the officers moved about. I introduced myself to one of the officers and Melanie and I talked with him for a while. Melanie was very shaken up and I found myself doing the consoling even though I needed some consoling myself. I felt like I was falling apart at the seams.

The officer wanted to know how they could get in touch with Amanda's family and I gave him the number to the house where her mother and grandmother lived in Virginia. I immediately became worried about her grandmother and how she would take the news because she and Amanda were very close and she loved that girl out of this world.

I asked them please not to tell Amanda's grandmother the news by phone. I asked if they could send over a local officer to inform her and maybe have an ambulance on standby when they did so because her grandmother was very fragile and the news may just send her into the hospital. They said they would take that into consideration.

There was not much I or Melanie could do. We were not allowed into the store or anywhere close to it and I did not want to see them taking Amanda's body out; there was absolutely no way I would be able to live with that. I could not watch them wheel out one of my best friends on a gurney. Melanie had totally lost it by then and one of the female officers on the scene was trying to console her.

We left the crime scene and drove back to my house and just bawled. Natasha called to say that she was on her way back, that she was catching an evening flight and Keri called later to say her an Miguel was going to cut their trip short and come back the next day, Christmas eve.

I called Shane to tell him about what happened and he said he would be on the next flight out of Los Angeles and I was so happy that he would do that, I needed him by my side. I suddenly started realizing how much it would mean to me to have him there by my side in that terrible time. I also called Aunt Kate and told her about the tragedy and she asked if I wanted her to come and I was so happy that she asked. She said she wouldn't be able to make it until Christmas day because she had commitments at church and she did not want to renege on them. I told her not to worry that I understood and Christmas day would be just fine. She asked me over and over again if I would be okay and I told her that I was because I had friends with me and more were on their way. I finally convinced her that my safety was not an issue and that she should just go ahead and do what she had to do and I would see her on Christmas day.

That evening I called Amanda's grandmother and just as I thought she broke down when she got the news but Amanda's mother sobered up enough to take control of the situation even though she too was devastated. I could hear it in her voice when I spoke to her and then she just totally lost it. She just bawled "Not Amanda....not Amanda......not my Amanda!" I was at a loss for words, I did not know what to say to soothe the pain I heard in her voice, deep in her belly. Someone took the phone from her and told me that the grandmother was sleeping off medication that was administered to her when she heard the news about Amanda. Both Amanda's mother and grandmother were flying to Miami the next day to deal with the situation they had found themselves in. I did not get the opportunity to ask if her brothers were informed of her death.

The lady who told me about the grandmother's condition gave me flight information and the minute I got off the phone I called a limousine service but I suddenly remembered that Shane was flying in that day and he never went anywhere without his personal driver and body guard so I could have him pick them up at the airport. I was sure that Shane would not mind in the least having his driver collect them at the airport. They had to be going through so much that I wanted to give them the best in comfort. Not that it would help any but it sure wouldn't hurt.

Shane arrived that evening as planned and so did Natasha and everyone came directly to my house from the airport. Natasha's eyes were red from crying and she looked really tired so I asked Carol to make her some hot chocolate and insisted that she got some rest but not before she literally broke down on her knees and cried like a baby. Melanie and I held her and cried right along with her but Melanie was really shaken up. She was worried that whoever killed Amanda may want to kill the rest of us. She was very affected and cried constantly; I found that I had to stay strong so someone else could lean on me because everyone was too broken to cope. I was a little relieved that Shane was there. He just made me feel safe and secure but he could not take away the pain that was burning a hole through my heart. His presence was somewhat of a booster that kept me sane and a little more controlled.

There was no news about a capture; the police did not even have a clue to begin with. The only thing they knew for sure was that one of my best friends was dead from a gunshot wound to the head, her cash and credit cards were stolen and they had nothing else.

Shane and I sat by the pool for hours that night and just talked, he tried to comfort me but the tears just kept coming. Carol brought us hot chocolate and crackers that she insisted that I had because I never got the chance to finish that sandwich I was making when I saw the news on the television. She realized something was wrong when she got back from the market because the half-done sandwich was still on the counter with opened bottles of mayonnaise and mustard. She liked all the girls and when I told her about Amanda's murder she cried just as hard as the rest of us. I had to be stronger than I thought I could be. I literally forced down the hot chocolate and crackers because I did not want to make myself sick but mostly because Carol insisted on it.

Melanie and Natasha were upstairs in one of the rooms sleeping, finally. I could not stand to see my friends hurting the way they were, it broke my heart. Melanie took it so much harder than anyone else she just could not stop crying. I was happy when she finally got some sleep.

That night I cried and cried until I felt like my heart would explode. Shane held me while I cried and tried to comfort me the best he could but nothing could take away the pain that was tearing through my very soul. Shane did not get much sleep himself because he spent most of the night holding and consoling me through my many bouts of grief and depression. I was in total confusion. The whole thing was so surreal; there were times when I felt like I was not even inside my skin. Who would do such a thing to someone as good and caring as Amanda? I thought about how she must have felt and I could not begin to imagine what she went through. I wonder did she even see it coming. Did she beg for her life? Poor Amanda if any one deserved to die like that it was definitely not her. There was nothing that she could have done to deserve such a fate. Life was so unfair. How could God allow that to happen to her?

I knew I would probably never get the answers to those questions and we may never find out what happened that night. They were sure she died the night before and not that morning because the store clerk that found her said she was wearing the same outfit she had on the day before and Amanda would never wear the same outfit two days in a row, no matter what; and the coroner's office said something about the time of death being at least eight to twelve hours. I could not imagine how that poor girl felt when she saw Amanda slumped over her desk, dead. I don't know how I would have reacted to something as horrifying as that.

The police did not have a lot to say and that bothered me. They had no clue and the only motive they had was robbery. There was one thing that puzzled me though; if it was robbery how come the killers took only cash and credit cards? Why didn't they take any of the merchandise from the store? The store was stocked with all the latest designs from a huge variety of top designers, shoes, clothes, accessories from belts to sunglasses, bags to perfume but none of that stuff was taken. Didn't the police find that a little odd?

The following day Keri returned from her trip and her and Miguel stopped by my place. Miguel stayed a while then left. We decided not to go anywhere or do anything until the arrival of Amanda's mother and grandmother. Not that there was anything to do. Melanie's shop was closed for the holidays and Natasha and I had the holiday off and Keri's flower shop was also closed for the holidays so we had nothing to do but wait.

The news of Amanda's murder was still on the television, it was actually on all the news channels and the police still had no clue what happened that night she died. All they could tell us was that she was killed by a single gunshot wound to the head and that she was robbed of all her cash, jewelry and credit cards. They also said that she was shot execution style, in the back of the head at close range. I hope they find the mother fucker that did that to my friend. That was cold and senseless. Knowing Amanda she would not put up a fight she would let them take whatever they wanted. I could not understand why they killed her. She was so happy to have her own business she was already talking about opening a second store in the near future. Her grand opening was a major success and she was looking forward to great things.

Neither the news reporters nor the police mentioned anything about her being pregnant. I am sure they will find that out in the autopsy. It was not so easy to tell that she was pregnant because she barely had a little paunch, it was hard for us to see it and we were so close to her so I doubt that they would realize it right away. I was not sure if I should mention to her family that she was pregnant and so I decided to keep that little secret quiet. I suddenly thought about the baby's father, the man she was hiding from all of us. I wondered if he had anything to do with it. She never gave us a single clue to who he was. She constantly referred to him as her mystery man. Mr. Man she called him. I wondered If he saw the news or if he was the one who did that to her. I did not want to believe that because Amanda thought he was a good decent man.

We all had breakfast together including Shane, his driver and Carol. We talked about Amanda's murder but no one mentioned the pregnancy because no one else but the five of us knew about it. Shane had an errand to run and he promised to pick up Amanda's mother and grandmother from the airport. Carol went grocery shopping because we realized that if everyone was going to gather at my place we would need a lot more food in the house. I knew it was going to be a little hard on Carol doing all the cooking and cleaning for a house full of people so I suggested getting someone in to help her and she told me she had a cousin that was out of a job and could assist her so I agreed. She would pick up her cousin on the way back from the market.

Natasha, Keri, Melanie and I had the house to ourselves for quite some time while Shane and Carol were out and we tried to figure out who Amanda's mystery man was but we came up empty.

We were sitting poolside fully clothed because no one was in the mood for a swim or anything and I was surprised to see that Melanie had a glass of brandy in her hand.

"It's a little early for brandy, don't you think?" I said.

"Let her drink the whole bottle if she wants to, this is really hard on all of us you know but as close as we are, we are still individuals who have our own way of dealing with stuff like this." Keri defended.

"I feel like some of that brandy right now. Maybe it will just numb me to the point where I can't feel anything because I certainly do not like the way I am feeling. As a matter of fact, I am going to get a couple more glasses in the kitchen." Keri said and made her way inside the house.

"Well, I guess there's nothing to do until her folks get here." I said.

When Keri got back from inside the house she brought up the subject of the pregnancy.

"Do you think the baby's daddy might know something about the murder?" She said pouring brandy in a glass.

"Give me some of that." Natasha said referring to the brandy and without missing a beat she continued talking.

"I have no idea. See, that is why we should not keep secrets from each other. What if he is the killer, none of us have any idea who or where he is right now." Natasha said.

"Do you think we should say anything to the police about the baby or the mystery man?" I asked.

"I doubt that would help any because we really do not know who he is, we do not even have a name. I think we should leave that alone because from the little that Amanda said about him I doubt that he was a murderer. On top of that she had her reason for keeping him a secret. I think it is best that we leave that one alone." Melanie said.

"I agree. If Amanda kept it a secret for so long she must have had her reason, I think we should honor that and not say anything to anyone about it." Keri said.

"Well, it's not like we have a clue anyway so why bring it up. We have absolutely no information about this mystery man and even though I have no idea who he is I doubt very seriously that he would kill her. He did a lot for her from what she told me." Natasha said standing up and stretching her body.

"Let's just leave it alone. Amanda would want that; she never told me who he was either and no offence but you guys know that Amanda and I have always been extra close, like you and Kylie Natasha. She never gave me the impression that this mystery man was anything but good to her. What if we mention this to the police, it comes out in the open and cause a scandal and Amanda's name get dragged through the mud? I would not be able to live with that." Melanie insisted.

"I didn't really look at it that way but I guess you are right." I agreed because she did have a point.

"I didn't exactly look at it like that myself but Melanie is so right about that, let's just leave that topic locked up where Amanda left it. Case closed." Keri stated.

"Case closed." Natasha reiterated.

Carol came back from the market with her cousin Sharon in tow and they immediately made themselves busy. Carol wanted to make us lunch but I told her we would order pizza and suggested that she start dinner immediately. I wanted to make sure that when Shane got back from the airport with Melanie's mom and grandmother dinner would be waiting for them. It was already past noon and their flight was coming in at four o'clock.

After pizza Melanie went out for a while somewhere, she never really said where she was going and Keri went home but promised to come back in time for dinner and said she would see if Miguel wanted to come back with her.

Natasha and I remained at the house the whole time and Melanie returned just minutes before Shane's limo pulled in the driveway. I met the car outside and before the driver could get the door Amanda's mother pushed the door open, got out and walked up to me.

"I remember you, you are Kylie right?"

"Yes I am." I said with a forced smile because I could see the pain in her eyes.

"I am Amanda's mama, Rhonda and this here is Amanda's grandmother Mabel."

"Nice to see you again, I am so sorry that it has to be under such terrible circumstances." I gave her a hug.

"This is one of Amanda's best friends you know Rhonda, I remember that time you came home from college with Amanda, you were a pleasure that whole summer you were there. Thank you for being there for my granddaughter." She hugged me and started crying.

"It's going to be alright, God will take care of us."

I had no idea if that were true or not. I just knew that I had to say something to try and make her feel better but in the same instance I doubted that I would ever be alright again. Seeing Amanda's folks made the reality of things a lot more pronounced and I had to fight with everything in me to keep the tears from rolling down my face like they were with Rhonda and Miss Mabel. They were hurting some kind of bad.

Natasha and Melanie came out the front door together and everyone hugged and said how happy they were to see each other again, but we all knew it was not a happy occasion. Amanda's mother and grandmother met us all at one time or another but they knew the names better than they remember the faces.

Shane and Roy had long disappeared with the luggage and I suggested that we go inside the house where they could freshen up and get ready for dinner. I gave them the two guest rooms on the first floor that was reserved specially for guests who had a hard time climbing the stairs. Miss Mabel was in her seventies and she was troubled with arthritis and a heart condition so she was better off not climbing the stairs even though she said she would have had no problem doing so; but I doubted that. I put Rhonda in the room next to her so they would be close to each other. There was an adjoining door between the two rooms and I made sure that was open so they would be able to go from one room to the next without coming out into the hall. There was a master bathroom that is accessible from either room. I wanted them to be as comfortable as possible.

Miss Mabel and Rhonda wanted to go to the morgue to claim Amanda's body right away and so Shane asked his driver to take them. Natasha volunteered to go with them to the morgue and insisted that Melanie went with her. I wanted to stay at the house to oversee the final dinner preparations and take care of and spend some time with Shane. I think that was the real reason that Natasha dragged Melanie along; so I could spend some time alone with Shane.

Dinner was finished but I told Carol to keep it warm until everyone was back in the house then Shane and I disappeared upstairs and into the bedroom. I was exhausted both emotionally and physically I just wanted to lie down and relax for a while until the others got back from the morgue but Shane had other things in mind.

He laid me across the bed and slowly took my clothes off then proceeded to massage my body applying pressure in all the right places.

"I think you are a little tense baby, let daddy help you relax." He said then kissed me on the back of my neck.

"Yes, I need that." I whispered barely audible.

"I want you to think only about this moment that you are in right now, nothing else. Think about how much love is in these hands that are touching you; think about the man that these hands belong to and remember that he loves you with every fiber in him, remember that he will never leave your side and whatever you go through he will always be right there to go through it with you. Don't forget that baby. I want you to promise me that, okay."

"Okay, I promise."

"Now kiss me and tell me you love me."

I sat up and wrapped my arms around his neck and kissed him long and deep and passionate. He took his clothes off and pressed his body against mine and it generated a warm feeling inside my body that was so comforting. He made love to me tenderly and patiently and for a little while I escaped the excruciating pain caused by Amanda's death. Carol called me on the intercom to tell me that everyone was back and that Keri and Miguel was on their way over.

Shane and I took a shower together, got dressed and went down to the den where everyone was waiting except for Melanie who was sitting by herself out by the pool. Keri and Miguel arrived the moment I got downstairs and I told Carol to start serving dinner. Those of us who drink had a little wine before dinner and those who didn't settled for tea.

Dinner was wonderful as always because Carol had a way in the kitchen that was unmatched by anyone that I had ever known personally. There was chicken, fish, Jamaican ackee and codfish, rice and peas and even cooked green bananas. She had a big bowl of potato salad and another with cold slaw and as if that was not enough there was plain white rice and a garden salad, hot rolls and her famous sweet potato pudding. There was a huge jug of lemonade made with brown sugar and another filled with unsweetened iced tea and beet juice. I could not believe that Carol and her cousin did that much in so little time. My mom was an excellent cook but she could not hold a candle or in this case a spoon to Carol. She told me she used to be an assistant chef at a five star hotel back in Jamaica and that was where she learned to cook the delicious, tasty dishes that she has been whipping up for me and my guests for the last few months.

Shane loved her cooking and told me we should take Carol with us wherever we went so we would always eat well. I assured him that there were plenty other cooks out there that would please us just as well.

There was not much said at dinner, everyone was just too sad and too hungry to say anything much and I also thought that maybe no one wanted to talk about Amanda at dinner because it would be too painful for all of us but especially Rhonda and Miss Mabel. They were tired and hungry and I just wanted them to eat and get some rest.

That night after Rhonda and Miss Mabel's arrival I did not feel any better than I did when I first heard the news about Amanda but I slept a lot better than I did the night before. Shane was such a darling, he sang little love songs to me in bed and stroked my hair until I fell asleep. I knew that if I had to spend the night in bed alone I would have tossed and turned and wake up groggy but Shane was my comforter, he tucked me in like a baby and caressed me to sleep.

I got up very early on Christmas morning, got dressed and headed to the kitchen, Shane was still asleep so I was careful not to wake him. Carol and Sharon were already up. The house was clean and breakfast was well on the way. I was surprised to see Melanie sitting at the counter having coffee.

"You are up early, is everything okay." I was genuinely concerned.

"Aside from the obvious, I'm okay." Her voice was quieter than usual.

"Good morning ladies." I said to Carol and Sharon.

"Good morning Miss Kylie." Sharon said smiling.

"Good morning. Did you get some rest?" Carol asked apprehensively.

"Yes darling, thanks for asking."

Carol and Sharon went back to what they were doing and I sat across the counter from Melanie and took her hand in mine while I waited for Sharon to make my coffee.

"Mel, I know that you and Amanda were really close. As close as we all are, we know you and her had a stronger bond, sort of like me and Natasha."

She laughed when I made the comparison because she knew the real reason that I made reference to me and Natasha.

"But seriously baby, we just have to pray and be strong. We just have to hope that the police do everything they can to catch the person or persons who did this to our friend. But right now Mel you have to take care of yourself, you look like you did not get a wink of sleep; I have never seen you like this. Let's just be strong for each other and Amanda's mom and grandmother. I think about what they must be going through and it makes me hurt even deeper, but please take care of Mel. Okay?"

"Okay, but you have to promise me the same thing. You will take care of Kylie won't you?" She was smiling for the first time since the news of Amanda's murder.

"I promise."

"I thought I heard voices, good morning everyone."

Natasha entered the kitchen wearing pink sweat bottom and matching top, she looked like she got a little sleep.

"Good morning." We echoed.

"I want to have a little talk with the two of you, but before I do that where is the coffee?"

"Carol, make that two cups of coffee please."

"Okay Kylie, two cups of coffee coming up." Carol answered.

We took our mugs of coffee and went out to the pool. Melanie had herself a second cup and Carol offered us muffins but we passed on those. We sat at one of the umbrella tables and sipped our coffee and enjoyed the cool morning breeze.

"I want to pay all of Amanda's funeral expenses." Natasha informed us.

I admit I was a little taken aback but I was not really surprised that she would want to do something like that because Natasha was by nature a very generous person and since she was now a multimillionaire I could see why she would want to pay for the entire funeral.

"Are you sure Natasha, because I could chip in?"

"Listen, I have all this money now. Let me pay for the funeral on behalf of all four of us. I know you guys would want to be a part of it that is why I called Keri this morning and told her about it. Let me pay for the funeral for all of us. That is if Amanda's folks will accept our gesture."

"Well, you are right about having all that money part, you are richer than God now." I kidded.

"Fine with me, especially since I have hardly any money at all." Melanie uttered.

"So it's settled then. We will talk to Rhonda and Miss Mabel after breakfast." Natasha's eyes lit up for a brief moment then suddenly sadness set in.

"Man I still can't believe that Amanda is gone." She said and put her head down on the table.

"I know sweetie, it is hard for all of us but we will help each other through it."

Melanie was very quiet and I was very worried about her because we had no idea how she was dealing with Amanda's death. She was not saying anything about how she really felt, she was bottling it up all inside and that made me a little more concerned about her than I was about the others.

I got up from my chair and positioned myself between my two friends and hugged them reassuring them that we still had each other no matter what and that we would do something in Amanda's honor when the time was right.

My Aunt Kate was going to arrive at the airport at one in the afternoon and Roy was supposed to pick her up at the airport but I opted to go along for the ride because I thought it would be nice if I met her personally.

I brought coffee up to the bedroom for Shane and he was already showered and getting dressed. I told him I was planning on going to the airport with Roy to pick up Aunt Kate and he said he would go with me. I thought that was a good idea because that way they could get a head start on getting to know each other. The ride from Miami International Airport to Pembroke Pines was quite a distance so they would have plenty of time to break the ice. Knowing my Aunt Kate though I was sure there would be no ice to break and with Shane being his charming self I was sure they would just hit it off instantly.

We got to the airport only minutes before Aunt Kate came out the exit door pulling her luggage. I pointed her out to Shane and he got out of the car immediately with me in tow and he walked right over to Aunt Kate and took her luggage. I ran up to her and wrapped my arms around her and she gave me a big warm hug and a kiss on the cheek.

"Hi Aunt Kate; it is so good to see you. You are looking fabulous." Excitement was oozing from my voice. I was really happy to see her, she was my favorite aunt, well she was my only aunt but I would bet all my money that if I had other aunts she would be my favorite.

"Hello sweetheart, how are you holding up?"

"I'm doing okay, you know how it is."

Shane was putting her luggage in the back of the limousine with some help from Roy.

"So who is that fine gentleman that was so nice to take my luggage? And what's with the limousine?"

"Oh, I'll introduce you. That's Roy the limo driver." I said pointing to Roy.

"Hey Roy, this is my Aunt Kate." I said when we got to the car.

He rushed over to her and shook her hand.

"Good to meet you Aunt Kate." He said in his deep Barry White sounding voice.

"It is nice meeting you too Roy."

Roy walked away and stood by the door and Shane walked up to us with a huge smile on his face and I was surprised at what came out of Aunt Kate's mouth next.

"Kylie, I pray you are going to tell me that this fine specie of a man is the man that you will eventually marry?"

I was even more surprised at what came out of Shane's mouth in response to Aunt Kate's prayer request.

"I think you have a psychic in the family Kylie. Aunt Kate, I heard so much about you. Pardon my manners I am Shane and yes I am the man she is about to marry."

"Shane! Aunt Kate I was going to tell you when I visit for Christmas. This is Shane D'Marco and we just got engaged a few days ago."

"Shane D'Marco? Shane D'Marco, oh I know I heard that name before. You are that movie star that everyone is talking about?"

"I don't think everyone, but yes that's me."

"Tell me all the details on the ride to your house Kylie. I knew the right man would come along and sweep you off your feet. Good thing you were so choosy, just like when you were a child, you were a very finicky eater and you were picky down to your toys not to mention your clothes." She rattled on.

"Oh stop, I wasn't that bad." I said that but it really didn't bother me at all.

"You should tell me more about it later. I want to know everything about this beautiful woman." Shane said pinching my bottom.

We eventually got in the car and were on our way back to the house. Aunt Kate and Shane chatted the entire ride and by the time we got to the house they were best buds with Aunt Kate promising to make him one of her many varieties of cheesecakes before she return to Georgia.

When we got to the house everyone was in a somber mood and after the necessary introductions everyone perked up a little because Aunt Kate immediately changed the tone with her perky personality and even Melanie was talking and laughing a lot more than she did in the last few days.

Aunt Kate insisted on all of us stopping what we were doing and held hands for prayer and she prayed and everyone cried with the exception of Shane and Roy. When she finished praying hugs were passed all over the place and the mood changed yet again. For quite some time we were all laughing and talking and it was not as dismal at the table as it was at dinner the evening before.

After dinner Keri dropped by at Natasha's request. Natasha wanted the four of us to talk with Rhonda and Miss Mabel to let them know that we would like to take care of all the funeral expenses if they would allow us.

Amanda's folks were very relieved that we offered to pay for the funeral because Miss Mabel was just living off her pension and whatever help she got from Amanda and her brother in the army and Rhonda did not have a penny to her name. Miss Mabel said that she thought it was best to take Amanda home to Virginia and lay her to rest near her family and Rhonda wanted the same thing. We just wanted to help them do whatever it was they chose to do. Amanda had enough money to bury herself but we did not care about that.

I could not believe that we were really there talking about burying Amanda. I was having a hard time just listening to everyone talking about

Amanda, dead. I excused myself from the room and walked out the front door for a moment just so I could get some fresh air and to hide the tears that were streaming down my face.

A few minutes later I went back into the room and Miss Mabel was telling the girls that both of Amanda's brothers would be going home to Virginia for the funeral and she wanted to be back there two days after Christmas.

Amanda's grandmother knew for a long time how close the five of us were and so she knew that it was more like a sisterly relationship between us and not just a friendly one. She knew about the bond that existed between us and she also knew that we were each other's protector so when we told her that it was alright for her and Ronda to go back to Virginia to meet her grandchildren she trusted us enough to allow us to make all the arrangements for Amanda's body to be flown to Virginia while she made the necessary arrangements there.

As agreed between us earlier Natasha gave Ms. Mabel a limitless American Express black card and told her that she should use it to take care of everything that she thought was necessary. Miss Mabel was flabbergasted and Rhonda was equally blown over by that gesture. Natasha made it clear to her that it didn't matter one bit what she bought as long as Amanda got the most beautiful funeral that anyone could have and she was kind enough to tell them that all four of us were doing it together. We all insisted on refunding some of the money she would be spending but she would not hear of it.

Aunt Kate made herself busy in the kitchen helping Carol and Sharon with dinner. It was really more like her bossing them around and telling them what to do on every turn but they found it hilarious, thank God. They just thought she was so sweet and funny that nothing she did offended them. The sweet smell of Christmas was oozing through the place from the kitchen but there was a very obvious silence as everyone drew into their own little space. There was no Christmas tree because the plan was not to spend Christmas at home but Amanda's death changed everything and after all that, even though I had time to get one it just did not seem appropriate to me. I believed the others felt the same way about it as I did because no one mentioned a tree. Matter of fact no one even mention the word Christmas. I knew in my heart that Christmas would never be same for me again or at least for a very long time.

Aunt Kate suggested at dinner that we eat and be merry and consider it a celebration of Amanda's life rather than a mourning of her death. She always knew how to take the not so good and make them better, that was one of the things I loved about her.

I insisted that Carol and Sharon get out of the kitchen and get dressed then joined us for dinner. I wanted them to feel like they were with family and not just someone they worked for so all the food were brought to the table with the exception of a few dishes but Aunt Kate insisted on acting as a server, just making herself busy putting food on everyone's plate. The conversation was light and the only time that Amanda's name was mentioned was when Miss Mabel blessed the food.

The occasion was gloomy but we made it through dinner without anyone crying or too depressed. Melanie and Natasha never said much at dinner but neither did I. I knew that they were missing Amanda as badly as I was and it broke my heart that my friends were hurting so deeply and there was nothing that I could to stop the pain.

Shane and Carol had their own little conversation going on most of the time. She was telling Shane about Christmas in her country and he was shocked to find out that like in America turkey was not a Christmas staple in Jamaica.

Rhonda's mood was up and down and I could tell she was still having problems with her drugs or drinking and I felt awful for her. I don't give a shit how much drugs you are on if your child dies it does not hurt any less than when you are sober. She was doing her best to look good for her daughter's sake and I could see her trying.

Christmas night we just hung around the house, swimming, playing French dominoes and drinking. Even Rhonda got in on the dominoes and the drinking but Miss Mabel made sure she did not overdo it. She was like Matlock on Rhonda's case; keeping her in check. Quite a few well-wishers stopped by to offer their condolences and between Aunt Kate, Carol and Sharon. No one left without having at least a piece of pie, one test and they were begging for more. Carol's Jamaican potato pudding was a big hit as always; everyone wanted a piece of that as well, even Aunt Kate.

Keri and Miguel stopped by after dinner at Miguel's sister and it was almost midnight when they left. Everyone went to bed shortly after they left and I was glad Christmas was over.

Amanda's funeral was the last day of the year and we all flew to Virginia to pay our final respects. Shane insisted on being there with me and Roy came along with Shane. I doubt seriously that Shane ever went anywhere without him. A few of the girls from Melanie's shop went and Natasha was nice enough to pay the airfare for a couple of Amanda's employees who wanted to go to the funeral but did not have the money to go. Natasha had a heart so big she never stopped doing good for people and strangely enough she don't even have to really know them to do something good for them. She was really special and she has been that way since I met her, not just since she inherited all that money from Donna's estate.

There were a whole lot of people at the funeral. Most of them were from her hometown in Virginia but I was surprised to find out that so many of the people there actually flew in from all over the United States to see her for the last time and pay their respects. I didn't have the slightest idea that Amanda knew so many people. I looked around to see if there was any one that stood out that might be the father of the baby Amanda was carrying, but I could not put my finger on anything or anyone for that matter.

Amanda's mother and grandmother broke down and her brothers even had a hard time being strong because they too were broken and suffering deeply inside. They however tried to stay strong for their mother and grandmother.

Shane and I checked into a hotel the night of the funeral, so did Miguel and Keri but Natasha and Melanie stayed at the house with Amanda's family. Shane's driver and body guard Roy did not attend the funeral, Shane said he mentioned something about not liking funerals and that he wanted to take the time to visit with his family. The following day we all spent the entire day at the family house until it was time to catch our flights back to Miami.

The Amanda debacle took precedence over everything over the last couple of weeks and all thoughts of my imminent wedding eluded my mind. I was still deeply disturbed by Amanda's murder and even more disturbed that the police had no clue, no suspects, no motive, just nothing to go on. I needed answers, we all needed answers and it was tearing up our insides that there were no new developments.

I had to force myself to go back to planning my wedding. I had always dreamt that when I got married my four best friends would be there to share that day with me, now I realize that there were no guarantees that any of us will be around from one event to the next. The other girls are pushing for me to go on with my wedding as planned and I know that I should, and I will but I think that I lost some of the joy in the planning and therefore I found myself dragging, being very lethargic.

Shane was ready though because he kept pushing me to move along with the plans he even convinced me to ask his sister Carmen to be one of my bridesmaids. I guess with Amanda gone it would be okay to let Carmen fill in the blank space, though no one could really take her place in my heart. Initially I just wanted my four very close friends but I am now down to three so I asked Carmen and she was more than happy. She told me she would love it if I would allow her to help with the planning but I told her it would not be necessary because there were people being paid to take care of all the details.

I met with Vera Wang in New York for a fitting. Natasha accompanied me and I was confident that my dress was in good hands and I would be looking most fabulous on my wedding day; she would also create my after dress. While in New York I purchased shoes and jewels and everything I could get my hands on. I wanted to make sure that I had all the things I would need for that day I even bought my something blue. I picked out a really beautiful baby blue pair of strappy shoes that would be perfect for walking down the aisle.

Shane and I decided that we would get married in Miami and even though I did not get to church much I knew I wanted to have a church wedding. I did not have any particular pastor in mind and so Melanie told me that she knew the Reverend Michael Langston from television and that she thought it would be nice to have someone famous perform the ceremony. That did not sound like such a bad idea at all; after all I was marrying a famous movie star and I was well on my way to owning my own celebrity.

I had no idea that Melanie had friends in such high places and I was really impressed when she dialed his number and let me talk with him on the telephone. He was a very pleasant man and said he would be very happy to perform my nuptials. When I got off the phone with him my curiosity got the best of me and I could not help being nosy so I asked Melanie where she knew him from and she told me that she met him a few months back and that since the death of his wife she had been seeing him on the down low.

My days found me running around from one place to the next and I swear I was not prepared for the huge amount of preparation that a wedding would take, I only intend to do this once and that will be it for me. If I thought preparing for a wedding was hard constant work then I was really shocked to find out that a wedding to a celebrity was twice the work. I wanted to have everything just right; I absolutely wanted a perfect day.

Chapter 13

MELANIE

I have not had one good night's sleep since the day of the grand opening of Amanda's store and it started to take a toll on me; there were bags under my eyes and the energy was totally sucked from my body. I was still in shock over finding out that Amanda was pregnant for the same man that I was having my secret affair with. It made me wonder how many other women he may be actually involved with. I came to the conclusion that there were probably others that neither Amanda nor I knew about.

The thing that bothered me most however was Amanda's pregnancy. With her being pregnant and Michael pretending not to know me when we met up in Amanda's office it left me in a very heartbreaking situation and I found myself having evil thoughts.

That night after the encounter at Secrets, Michael came over to see me at the house and he told me he had no idea that Amanda and I knew each other. He even tried to convince me that he was involved with Amanda before he met me and that he did not intend to see anyone else until he met me. He told me that he was not in love with Amanda but at the time they met he was desperately in need of female companionship and she was there for him and they truly cared about each other but he was never in love. I did not know what to believe, all I knew was that I did not want to give him up and now that his wife was gone I thought more and more of what it would be like to be his wife and I liked that prospect. To be the wife of the great Reverend Langston suddenly became my mission in life but with Amanda and her unborn baby in the way that would most likely lessen that vision. I made up my mind that night after Michael left the house that as much as I loved Amanda I could not stand to see her with the man I loved. I knew then that I had to do something drastic. Michael was a good man in spite of the infidelities and I was sure that eventually when the smoke cleared from his wife's passing he would want to get married again. They never had children and I was a little scared that the baby Amanda was carrying inside her would more than likely be the deciding factor and I knew in my heart that if he had to choose between us that he would choose Amanda. The fact that he pretended to meet me for the first time in Amanda's office would make it even harder for me to put any claim on him whatsoever, especially since I never ever mentioned him to any of the girls it would make it difficult for me to suddenly talk about him. I am sure that they would all believe that I stole him from under Amanda's nose. Whatever happened I was determined that I could not let Amanda take from me the only man that can give me the life I've been dreaming of. The other girls were lucky, Kylie's book was a best seller and on top of that she was marrying a movie star. Natasha's modeling career was rising at a rapid pace and she became an instant millionaire when her friend Donna died; I still wonder about that friendship; and Keri's flower shop was the best on South Beach so business was soaring and her other ace in the hole was her husband Miguel, the hotshot lawyer. I was not in the least jealous of my friends but when I looked at the big picture I was at the bottom of the earnings pole. The salon was doing well but I did not have half as much as they did even with Jerry and Jim in the picture. I was feeling some kind of inferiority complex coming on and the only person who could change that was Michael.

My mind was made up, I wanted Michael and I was going to do everything in my power to have him. I had no idea when I decided it was in my power to kill Amanda. I just knew that it was the only way I was going to have even the slightest chance of being Michael's wife. He and I had something special and it was more in the way that I felt than in the things that he did that attested to me that he was the man for me, and believe me Michael did a lot for me but not enough to make me feel like I can measure up to the other girls.

A couple of days before Amanda's death I called up Jerry and told him I was lonely and tired of being at home by myself and he told me to come over and stay as long as I wanted, it was just what I wanted to hear. I packed a little overnight bag and headed to his place; on the way over I stopped at the liquor store and picked up a bottle of champagne.

When I got to his door it was half open and I did not bother knocking I just went in and locked it behind me. I could smell something cooking so I went directly to the kitchen where I found Jerry in his apron cooking.

"Hi sweetheart, what's cooking?" I asked as I entered the kitchen.

"Just a little something special; for someone special."

He wiped his hands in the apron and walked over to give me a hug and long lingering kiss. I could feel my knees buckling but I managed to contain myself.

"What is that you've got there?" he asked when he finally pulled his lips away from mine.

"Just a special bottle of something to go with that special something, for that special someone."

"Oh, that's good I like the way you put that. So I guess we are both in for a night filled with special things."

"I can't wait."

We ate a nice meal of Cornish hen and mashed potatoes with gravy, asparagus and broccoli. I was very impressed and ate a lot more than usual. After dinner we opened the bottle of champagne and Jerry rolled himself a joint. Jerry was a heavy marijuana smoker and he never once looked high to me. I smoked once in a while but only when I was around Jerry and so I took a few puffs and it made me really horny and before we could get through that first joint I was all over Jerry, burning for him to enter my world and put out the fire that was burning.

That night Jerry told me he had to make an early morning run to Tampa and said it would be alright for me to stay at his place until he got back and I took him up on the offer. I could not believe what was happening it was just too easy. I needed time to myself at Jerry's place because I wanted to get my hands on one of the many guns that he had hidden all over his house.

That morning after Jerry left I went directly into a room with a secret door that led to another room that was a little bigger than an average walk-in closet. I knew about that room because Jerry showed it to me once and he also showed me the arsenal of guns he had stashed away inside. There were at least twenty guns and they were all brand new. I looked through them and decided on a silver nine millimeter magnum. I knew where he kept the bullets and I loaded it and put it in my overnight bag.

I drove home and hid the gun under my mattress and then returned to Jerry's without him ever knowing that I even left the house.

The day I killed Amanda I woke up with my mind totally made up that I would not lose the opportunity to be Michael's wife to Amanda. I knew it was not her fault because she had no idea that the good old Reverend was seeing the both of us. Now I understand on top of every other reason he gave that it was just another way for him to have his cake and eat it too. When I thought about how he had the nerve to act like he did not know me at all it really made me mad. I did not expect him to say hello lover or anything like that but he could have at least acknowledged me and not pretend about that.

I convinced Amanda not to tell the other girls about him and that it would be best to wait and see how he felt about marrying her before she told anyone and she took my advice. However, I did not advise her for her sake but instead had my own motive. If no one else knew about Michael and Amanda it would certainly leave the way clear for me to be with him once Amanda was gone. I had it all figured out and she trusted me as her closest friend so that made it ever so easy to execute my plan.

Although it was easy to physically put my plan together, emotionally it was a whole other story. I was planning on killing one of my very best friends it was not bothering me much, at least not as much as it should. Deep down inside of me I was trying to reach for that one thing that would bring me to my senses, that one thing that would tell me that I did not have it in me to kill anyone, but that thing never surfaced. All I could think of was yet another one of my friends moving up into the big leagues and little me still getting left stuck in the salon. All the other girls have had that big break that they were looking for and I was the only one still on the same level as I was a couple of years back. I love the hair and beauty business and that's where I intended to stay but I want more than just a salon; I want an empire and Michael was the man who could give me that and the life that I really want.

Killing Amanda became an obsession in only a few days and the thing that bothered me most was how I would make a clean getaway, but by the time I got out of bed my confidence level had grown and I knew that I would be committing the perfect murder.

That morning I went to the salon as always and did my thing there then I pretended to be ill because I wanted to make sure that Jennifer and the others at the shop would have it riveted in their minds that I was sick and went home. I did not have to give any reason why I was leaving but being sick became part of the plan and I needed witnesses to that. If I were to pull the whole thing off I had to make sure that every single minute detail was taken care of. I had no idea how I got through the few hours I spent there at the salon because all I could think about was how Amanda was set to reap what I was sowing all along. I kept asking myself why life was so unfair; why did it have to be Amanda; couldn't it have been some other random bitch that I did not care about in the least? I was planning on killing my friend and it was finally bothering me but there was nothing I could do at this point, I did not want to lose the chance of being with Michael. I swear I could not find it in my heart however hard I tried to stop the plans that I had already put in gear.

I remember having lunch with Amanda and she went on and on about the baby and Michael and how she could not wait to be his wife. She even told me that he said he would marry her a year after the baby was born and then pretend to adopt it. All the time I could feel myself hating her but wearing the biggest and broadest smile I could muster; while at the same time knowing that she would not be an obstacle for much longer. We both had tuna sandwiches and lemonade and it was apparent that Amanda was eating for two because she ate her sandwich in no time and had a half of mine that was sitting on the plate un-touched. I had absolutely no appetite because I was so consumed with thoughts of Michael and Amanda, the more I thought of them being together as man and wife the less hungry I got. Amanda was concerned about my lack of appetite because I was never one to shy away from food. As a matter of fact I was sure that I ate the most of the five of us, everyone was always watching their weight and picking on their food, not me, I eat and I eat a lot. I think I have a secret love affair with food but fortunately for me I never had to worry about my weight, no matter how much I ate I never gained an ounce and the girls would always give me a hard time about that, but always in good fun. Amanda knew something was wrong and insisted that we talk about it.

"What's wrong Mel?" Amanda asked after swallowing the last drop of lemonade from a Styrofoam cup.

"Nothing is wrong, I just feel a little under the weather."

That was not exactly a lie because it was December and it was a little cold even for Florida.

"I can see it in your eyes and for you to pass on lunch speak volumes." She said with a giggle.

I giggled back and agreed with her on the latter.

"You know I never miss a meal uh? I had breakfast though." I lied.

"Well you should just go home and get into bed and sleep it off." Amanda suggested.

"That is definitely the plan, but I did not want to miss out on the chance to see you before we all go our separate ways for Christmas.

We hugged and kissed each other saying our goodbyes but Amanda had no idea how permanent that goodbye was going to be.

I went home where I stayed for the rest of the afternoon and at approximately seven o'clock I drove to South Beach and parked in a garage about two miles from Amanda's store then walked down the street where I caught a cab to a store only two blocks from Amanda's. I went inside and browsed around for quite some time, then finally picked out a pair of Gucci glasses and belt along with a Prada wallet. I asked the clerk to hold them for me and told her I would be back with my credit card before the store closed. All the stores along that strip including Secrets closed at nine o'clock. I had only twenty minutes before all the stores closed and so I inched closer to Amanda's and when I was sure that all her employees had left I called her on the store telephone from a pay telephone just to make sure that no one else was there. See, Amanda never answer the store phone as long as someone else was there, that was just one of her little rules. She had a direct line that she alone used. I was relieved when she picked up the phone on the second ring.

"Hello." Amanda answered.

Usually the phone would be answered in a very professional manner during store hours but after closing a simple "hello" was the norm.

"Hey you sound lonely, you by yourself?"

My voice sounded a tad nervous but I doubt that Amanda picked it up.

"Yes, actually I closed a little early today at eight so I was just about to leave."

"Well, I am in the neighborhood, actually just down the alley so leave your back door unlocked for me so I can just get in without having to linger out here. You know how Christmas can bring out all the worst elements, the predators and all."

"Okay sweetheart, come on in the door is open." She giggled.

Using the backdoor to the alley was ideal because there were no cameras there yet in that area of the store. I knew that because Amanda and I discussed that before. Only the front of the store and the sales floor itself had surveillance so I was sure that I could get in and out of there without being noticed.

I did not even look my usual self. I was wearing black sweat pants and top with a baseball cap. I never wear baseball caps but this one was pulled all the way down barely showing my face. When I walked into Amanda's office she was sitting at her desk and she had the day's earnings in a money bag in front of her on top of her handbag.

"Why you dressed like that, planning a heist." She laughed.

"That's very perceptive."

"What are you doing down here anyway?"

I walked over to the back door and made sure it was locked.

"Amanda, get up from behind the desk and sit over there on the couch."

"What do you have up your sleeve now? You know how I hate surprises."

"I know, just sit on the couch."

"Okay, anything you say. I hope this is good."

She had a big smile plastered on her face as she got up and moved to the couch.

"Okay Miss Melanie, hit me with it."

I pulled the gun from my waist hidden under the huge top and I could see the horror in her eyes as she realized that the surprise was nothing like she had expected.

"What the hell is going on Mel?"

"Amanda, I want you to know that I hate to do this but I can't let you rob me of my future. You have pulled the rug from under me in ways you do not even understand."

"Mel, what are you talking about?"

The tears were running down her eyes and she was literally shaking but I could not allow myself to get soft. It had already gone too far, if I change my mind now I could go to jail and all the girls would know that I tried to kill Amanda, nothing would be the same anymore so I had no choice but to carry out my plan.

"Michael."

"Michael, what's he got to do with you holding a gun on me Mel?"

"Michael and I have been seeing each other for a very long time now and he told me that when his wife passed I would be the woman he would marry when the time was right."

"Oh my God! You and Michael? But that day when you met him here….."

"Yes, he pretended not to know me and yes I pretended right back."

"Oh my God, why didn't you say something then? Oh no, so you have been planning this ever since."

"I'm sorry Amanda."

"So you are going to kill me for Michael? Mel you don't have to kill me I will stop seeing him, whatever you want."

"It is too late for that now Amanda. Much too late."

"Melanie please, don't do this. I promise I will walk away from Michael. No one will have to know about this. I still did not mention him to any of the other girls and I never told them about you meeting him either. Please Mel, you are not thinking straight, you and I love each other, we are best friends it's not in you to kill anyone Mel."

"Shut up!" I heard myself holler.

'Lie down, face down on the couch, now!"

'Mel ple..."

"Now!"

I did not want to hear her beg because I did not want to get soft. I could not allow myself to get soft at this point so I pulled out the silencer I had brought along with the gun and I attached it to the gun. There were a couple of cushions on the couch and I placed one over her head, more because I did not want to see the damage the bullet would cause. Before I could lose my guts I fired into the cushion and I could hear a deep groan from Amanda as the bullet pierced her skull. She was dead, I was sure of that.

I took all her credit cards and the kind of stuff that a regular burglar would, including the money bag filled with the day's revenue and her cell phone and stuffed them in a plastic shopping bag that I got from one of the little shops I had stopped in before.

I made sure no one was in the alley, then I walked at a normal pace over a couple of streets where I got into a cab and headed back to my car. I got into my vehicle and pulled out of the garage and went directly to my house. The entire trip home I felt like I wanted to throw up but I found some hard candy in the glove compartment of my car and that seemed to settle my stomach for a while until I got home where I let it all loose in the toilet.

I had no time to waste, I had to get rid of Amanda's things and I had to get the gun and its apparatus back to Jerry's. That was going to be a feat in itself because Jerry was not easy to get around. There was over eleven thousand dollars in cash in the money bag along with numerous checks and credit card receipts. I took the cash out and stashed some in a safe that I had secretly locked away in my bedroom and stashed the rest in a couple of secluded places. I was not even sure why I did that but it seemed like the safe thing to do. I cut up the credit cards into very tiny pieces and threw them along with the rest of the paperwork into the fire place that I had lit the moment I walked in. I put the cell phone into a plastic bag then used a hammer from the garage to crush it into little pieces then I threw the tiny pieces into the fire place and watched them turn to ashes.

I was acting on pure adrenaline, it was after midnight and I still had to get rid of the gun. I took the bullets out and put them into a paper bag I would get rid of them later but I had to concentrate first on getting the gun back to Jerry's because in a couple of days it would be Christmas and he was planning on going away for the holidays. I picked up the house phone and dial Jerry's number, he answered on the first ring.

"Hello baby, you missing big daddy?" he said in typical Jerry fashion.

"More than you can imagine." I answered.

"So you wanna come over and rid yourself of that feeling?"

"I thought you'd never ask. I'll be there in twenty minutes."

"I can't wait."

"Me either."

I hung up and got everything I needed then made my way over to Jerry's. The moment I walked in the door I started taking my clothes off and Jerry followed suit. We attacked each other like two dogs in heat and before long he had me moaning and groaning literally forgetting that I had just murdered my best friend and left her body lying there for someone else to find.

The sex was totally unbridled and sent feelings through me that only a man that you love could make you feel. I knew I was not in love with Jerry but the whole time he was making love to me I would think of him as Michael. It was Michaels face I was seeing in my mind, it was Michaels dick I was feeling inside me and it was Michaels hands that were touching me in places that made me shiver. I was in a sea filled with love for Michael. When we both finally came up for air we were exhausted and sleepy. I could not allow myself to go to sleep so I waited until Jerry started snoring before I continued on my mission. Sex was the only thing that could knock Jerry out and it usually does. Putting the gun and the silencer back turned out to be a piece of cake and I even managed to put the rest of the bullets back where I got them. I made sure my prints were no longer on them of course.

With all that done I got back into bed with Jerry but could not fall asleep. I tossed and turned for hours then eventually got up at seven and drove back to my house. I went directly into the shower and into bed where I was when Kylie called to give me the news about Amanda's murder.

I had the feeling that Amanda's body was found because it was already ten o'clock and the store normally opens at nine. I let the phone ring a few times before I picked it up.

"Hello."

"Mel, are you sitting down?"

"Why do I have to be sitting down, what's wrong Kylie?"

"I was just watching the news, channel seven and they found Amanda dead inside her office this morning."

"Oh God noooo.... No, what happened?"

"She was shot in the head and all her money and credit cards were taken. No one knows who did it."

I could hear the shock and the pain in Kylie's voice and the tears became real because it finally hit home what I had done. By killing Amanda I have caused so much pain to so many people but there was nothing I could do about that, it was just too late. Amanda was already dead and I could not take that back.

"I'll come over there right now. Oh gosh! Why Amanda?"

I had to fake the shit. A lot of it was really not faking though. I was really hurt that I had to kill my best friend.

"I'm here asking the same question. Will you be okay to drive?" Kylie asked.

"I'll be okay, I'll be there shortly."

"Oh, Melanie, just one more thing. I have not called Keri or Natasha as yet; I want to call them on the phone while you are still on it. It is really hard for me to do this alone."

"Okay sweetie, I'm right here. I'll dial Keri's number right now."

I called both Keri and Natasha and together Kylie and I told them the bad news and it truly broke my heart that I hurt so many people including the ones I loved the most. That was what made my tears so real. Deep down inside that was my only reason for remorse. I started thinking about the monster that I had become and every time I was ready to go into remorse mode I thought about the prize that was Michael.

That morning when I got off the telephone with the girls, I had to pinch myself to make sure I was still feeling. I could not believe how cold I was, the only remorseful feeling I was carrying was the fact that all my other friends were hurting so much and deep down inside I wanted to feel the same way about Amanda but I couldn't. Amanda was the only thing that was keeping me from the one thing that could make me happy; being with Michael. I could not risk losing Michael to Amanda. It turned out to be a good thing that neither of us told the other girls about Michael and I am glad I did not cause a scene that day at her office when I happened upon her and Michael. If I had caused a scene I am sure that all the other girls would have known about it and it would be that much harder to kill Amanda. This way with all of our secrets still intact no one would come up with any motive involving me.

I got to Kylie's place in record time. I had no idea how I got there, except that I got into the car and started driving. All the way there I was just thinking about the night before, and hoping that I did not make any mistakes or leave any evidence that would lead the cops to me. I had it planned down to the last detail but in these times of forensic evidence and all one cannot be too sure. I was aware that my prints were all over Amanda's store and office because of the number of times that I had gone there since she opened, but so was all the other girls. No one would ever think that I was the one who killed Amanda. Of the five of us she was closest to me and so I would be the last person they would think killed her. What would be the motive anyway? No one had any idea that we were both seeing the same man, no one at all except for Michael himself and I am sure that he would not be quick to volunteer any information about who was dating who because if he was found out he could end up in a whole lot of trouble.

Kylie and I headed to the store as soon as I got to her place and she saw me as being so devastated that she offered to drive even though we took my car. Luckily for me I was smart enough to park my car miles away from the store the night of the murder. There was no chance of anyone pointing me or the car out. I looked totally different from the night before, actually the night before I dressed a lot more boyish. I was confident that no one had seen me. When we got to the scene I cried like a baby, or at least so it seemed to those who were watching, poor Kylie was so distraught but she was so there to help me through my pain. There was actually pain but not the kind that I should have been feeling. I realized that I was not at all sorry that Amanda was dead, but I had to make myself cry hard enough that everyone else would believe that I was.

The next few days leading up to Amanda's funeral in Virginia I spent most of my time with the girls at the house consoling each other. That was all real though, I was really hurting for them because all of us loved Amanda. It was just such a terrible twist of fate that Amanda and I was seeing the same man and it was even a crueler thing what the devil did when I walked in on Amanda and Michael in her office discussing baby plans.

Since that night I saw little of Michael, as a matter of fact it did not take a rocket scientist to see that he was avoiding me and when Amanda told me that he actually spent a couple of nights at her house I knew I had to do something fast. Losing Michael was definitely not in the cards. After all that time I spent with him, keeping his little secret so his colleagues and his wife would not know about his extramarital affair I would be damned if I went through all that to just let Amanda have him.

I spoke with Michael the day after Amanda died. He called and said he wanted to talk with me and so I left Kylie's to meet him at my place. When I got there he was already waiting for me in his car that was parked in my driveway. He was wearing baseball cap, tee shirt and jeans; that was the first time I actually saw him in tees or even baseball cap for that matter. I had seen him in jeans many times but mainly with button downs.

I got out of my car and he followed me inside the house. As soon as we got inside and the door closed behind us he grabbed me and hugged me with such urgency and was trembling almost violently.

"Michael, what is it? I asked.

"Oh Melanie; why is this happening to me?"

"I don't know why this is happening to any of us Michael."

"I'm so sorry. I know you must be devastated; you and Amanda were very close. I know, she told me that after you saw us both together."

"Listen sweetheart, I know how you must feel she was carrying your baby."

"That is another thing that was on my mind. Melanie if anyone should find out about the pregnancy and me everything I worked so hard for could just get blown to hell."

"Well, you won't have to worry about that. Your secret is safe with me. None of the other girls know about you and Amanda, we have all decided not to discuss that subject ever again. As a matter of fact I will make sure that no one else knows whose baby she was carrying."

"Thank you so much Melanie, I do not know how to thank you. I know that I am not in your good graces right now because of what happened last month. But I swear to you I had no idea you and Amanda even knew each other let alone be best friends."

"I guess even best friends keep secrets from each other because even though we told each other practically everything, we never discussed you. Our mystery man."

"Is there anything I can do to make this a little easier on you?" He asked genuinely.

"Well yes and no. Nothing will ever take away the pain of losing my best friend, but if you assure me that you will be there for me long after this is over that would certainly help to cushion the blow."

"You've got it."

We hugged and kissed and before long we were making passionate, unbridled love and for those few minutes when our bodies were one I had no thought of Amanda. All I could think about was how wonderful it will be to eventually become the wife of that rich and famous preacher man and that added to the excitement of the moment.

Michael was worried sick that someone might at some point connect him to Amanda. I reassured him that if he kept his secret affair with Amanda as well-guarded as he did our affair together then he would have absolutely nothing to worry about. He knew what he was doing, he had a handle on his situation with Amanda and I and God only knows who else. He made damned sure that we were so well taken care of that we would not risk the chance of opening our mouths to anyone about him lest we lose. He had it all worked out and made sure that we promised never to mention a word to anyone about him no matter how tempting.

Amanda had confided in me that Michael was the one who gave her the money to start Secrets. I was truly happy for her that someone would be so good to her, but little did I know then that we shared the same man. She never mentioned him by name, only as her mystery man and I never mentioned him at all. The number one reason I did not mention him to the girls was because he asked me not to, and I did not want to jeopardize anything on my part. The other reason was the same reason I did not mention Jerry, I simply did not want them to know that I was seeing so many men at the same time. They all knew about Jim and they did not pass judgment on me about him but I am sure they would be more than judgmental about me seeing more than one man at a time. I guess they did not mind me seeing a married man because Natasha was seeing one herself. Not that I care so much about what they thought, but every girl should have a secret or two as in my case.

That night when Michael left I was convinced that the thought of me killing Amanda did not even cross his mind. He kept saying he was praying that they found her killer soon because it would be detrimental to his ministry and his reputation if the investigation led to his affair with her. Amanda's grandmother refused to let them do an autopsy on her body because of religious beliefs and so the cause of death was simply a gunshot wound to the head. I guess Michael got lucky there because they would be looking for the father of the baby by now. I guess it was also fortunate for me too that they did not do an autopsy because if the investigation led them to Michael it would probably lead them to me. I guess the Gods were looking out for me.

I convinced Michael that I would take that secret to my grave with me. In actuality I was keeping it as my trump card in case he later decides to marry someone other than me. I knew then that he would be my husband. I knew I had to give him time to get over his wife and now Amanda but when the time is right I am sure he will do the right thing and marry me after all he put me through. If he should think about marrying someone else then I would have to pull out that trump card and force him to marry me or risk losing everything. I guess that's what Jamaicans mean when they say "by the hook or by the crook." One way or another Michael is going to be my husband. I will just wait patiently for him to get through his little mourning period and time enough for it to look morally correct in the eyes of his congregation and everyone else watching.

At Amanda's funeral I was just as sad and distraught as everyone else. It was the first time that I felt bad about what I had done and I cried so hard the pain became physical. I hated having to do it but I also realized that I could not take it back and I did not want to spend the rest of my life crying about it.

After returning from Amanda's funeral we were all forced back into our daily routines, Natasha went back into the photo studio to shoot her numerous layouts for several magazines, Kylie was back to planning her wedding and putting the finishing touch to her book, Keri went back to running her flower shop full time I went right back to running the salon. Amanda's store was put up for sale and Natasha suggested we come together and purchase it so we could carry on Amanda's dream. But with the help of Keri and Kylie I managed to talk her out of it. I told her that there was no way I could go back in that store knowing it was the place that my best friend was so brutally murdered. Kylie was the first to agree saying that it was hard enough to think about the police lines around the store, there was no way she could go into that office where Amanda was killed and eventually Keri agreed and Natasha dropped the subject.

Kylie was back to planning her wedding and we all had our own little duties assigned us in regard to putting the whole thing together, because even though she could afford one of the best wedding planners in the business she wanted to have as much input as possible and she already had ideas of her own. Her wedding planner, a queer black guy named Adrian was top of his league and you could tell by the way he was putting it all together but he left enough room for Amanda to play around with some of the things she wanted to do specifically.

Our regular Friday night out had not taken place since Amanda passed and I doubted that anyone wanted to do it without Amanda. We thought that it was best that we buried the tradition with Amanda. It just would not be the same anymore with her gone. Somehow a circle of four just seemed too square.

Chapter 14

NATASHA

I took my first working trip to Paris and it was fantastic. There is something about Paris and the fashion world that just clicked and it was a major milestone for me. I have always dreamed of going to Paris to be a part of the fashion frenzy. It was not my first trip to Paris though; Miles took me there on a weekend rendezvous once but it was a whole different type of trip. I felt like a star and was treated as one with everyone running at my beck and call. I liked the idea of being a Super Model in Paris.

I tried throwing myself into work to get my mind off the horror of losing two of my best and closest friends and that was a task in itself. The police still had no idea who killed Amanda, they had no clues, no suspect, and no motive except that the killer took her credit cards and money which made it look like a robbery. But everyone is still puzzled that no clothing or anything else from the store was taken. The killer never used the stolen credit cards either and that seemed a little suspicious, unless he or she just thought it better not to leave trails. Why would they take the credit cards and not try to use them?

Amanda was murdered only weeks after Donna passed away and I still had not wrapped my head around Donna's passing. I was happy that I was the one that Donna turned to when she found out about her disease. I was glad that she gave me the opportunity to be there for her in her final months. With the two of them gone I felt like a big chunk of me was missing.

Since Amanda's funeral we have not gotten together as a group like we normally would on Friday nights but I guess that is not the normal anymore.

The only thing that was bringing us any joy was the planning of Kylie's wedding to Shane D'Marco. The wedding was only two weeks away and everything was going smoothly and according to plan. I spend a lot of my time helping Kylie with the arrangements when I was not doing a shoot or a show. Miles have been complaining lately that he was not getting enough time with me and I promised him that after Kylie's wedding we would take some time to ourselves on an island somewhere and we could make up for all the times we missed over the last few months. He was excited about that and said he would start making the arrangements for only days after the wedding. I guess that would be good timing; with Kylie off on her honeymoon and Melanie and Keri so withdrawn lately I thought that would be a good time for a getaway so I agreed to a trip to Jamaica. I love Jamaica; I can't go there often enough. I like Jamaican men too, I think that while a lot of them may not be your typical lover, most of them know how to handle that coochie; it must be an island thing. When I was in high school and college I dated mainly Jamaicans and so far they are the best I've had when it comes down to the wire, less the romance, and it's like pulling teeth for a Jamaican man to come out and say that he loves you. Those three little words do not come that easy for them. But that is on the real. The flip side is there are some that will use the "I love you" to death, just to get what they want from a chick. But don't get tricked and believe it.

I can feel the February chills. This shit doesn't feel nothing like Miami. I am on my way to meet with my realtor, Anthony Martin. I had him put the house that Donna left me on the market.

I was shocked out of my wits the first time I met with Anthony about selling the house. I had no idea that it was worth quite that much. The asking price was a whopping three point five million. Today's meeting is at his office and when he called me to schedule the meeting I got the feeling he had good news.

I got to his office on Biscayne by 183rd street. I pulled up in front of the high rise office building and parked my Range Rover. I made my way into the lobby and walked directly into an already open elevator and pushed the button to the 18th floor. I got off the elevator and walked the spacious hallway to the reception desk that was immediately visible as soon as you get off the elevator. Martin Realtors occupies the entire 18th floor. Anthony's Grandfather started the business many years ago and when he died Anthony's father inherited the business. Now, as an only child Anthony is next in line to the Martin's multi-million dollar empire.

I walked up to the receptionist who was ever so gently filing her fingernails.

"Good morning. I am here to say Anthony."

'Your name please?" She was still filing her nails and never bothered to even look up.

"Natasha Bell."

I was in no mood for that disrespectful bullshit, but I held my tongue. She stopped filing long enough to notify Anthony of my presence.

"He said to come right in. It's the first door on your right."

I didn't bother to say thank you or anything polite like that. I just strutted toward the door she pointed out. When I got to the door it was already open and Anthony was standing inside the doorway waiting for me.

"Hey Anthony, how are you? Any good news" I got straight to the business at hand.

"Matter of fact I do." He said as he gave me a hug then led me to his desk where he asked me to sit as he plopped himself down in a huge leather chair.

"Tired, are we? I joked

"I'm a little tired, yes. But I'm good." He replied.

"So, what's the good news?" I asked.

"We have a buyer" he smiled.

"Great. What's the final price?

I guess there were no negotiations because he never called me to haggle me on the price. I was eager to hear what he had to say.

"Brace yourself….." He paused for effect.

I was like a kid in a candy store waiting to taste the new candy. He started talking again and I was all ears.

"We got full asking price but you will have to pay closing. How is that?"

"How is that? That's fantastic." I was elated. Anthony and I chit chat for a while after taking care of the additional paper work brought on by the sale of the house. He told me that I would have the check in only a few days. I was in heaven.

I left Anthony's office walking on cloud nine. I did not even give a glance at the rude receptionist as I made my way to the elevator. Like luck would have it, the elevator was right there waiting for me.

I got off the elevator and out the front door to my car that was parked conveniently in front of the building. I hurried to open the door and get in so I could sit and let it all sink in. All that money from the sale of the house along with the apartment building and other assets and cash money that Donna left me has me overwhelmed. Tears started rolling down my eyes and it took quite a few minutes before they finally stopped. I missed my friend.

I dried my eyes and started the car and was just about to pull out of the spot when I saw Miguel, Keri's Miguel with his arms around a woman's waist heading into the same building I was coming out of. The woman had a baby in one of those baby carrier things. He was way too cozy with that lady.

I sprung into action straight. I jumped out of the Range Rover and ran up to the entrance to the building. I slowly opened the door just in time to see the elevator door closing. The only thing visible to me then was the baby in the carrier.

I stood there in the lobby and watched the elevator as the floor numbers changed. It made one stop. The eighteenth floor.

I had to think fast. The only business on the 18th floor is Martin Realtors. Who is that woman and what is Miguel doing with her at the realtors office.

I called Keri immediately. She answered on the fourth ring.

"Keri, where are you right now? The urgency was apparent in my tone.

"Whoa, slow down lady. What's going on?"

"I don't know for sure but you need to hurry your ass down to my realtors' office on Biscayne and 183rd right now."

"What' going …."

"Keri, I don't have time to explain it, but you need to be here. Trust me on this. And hurry please. You know where it is. You've been here before."

"Okay. I am only five minutes away. I was just about to go inside the DSW over here by Aventura Mall so I will be there in a flash.

I sat in my car and waited for Keri to show up. I prayed the whole time that Miguel would stay inside the building long enough for her to get the heads up. My worries ended as I saw her BMW pulled up next to my car. I rolled my window down and quickly told her what I had seen. I told her to move her car so that he would not see it when he got out the building and I followed suit. We both parked further to the left of the building and I got out of my car and joined Keri in hers.

"Keri, Listen. I have no idea what's going on so like I told you before, please don't say I called you. Tell Miguel that you came with me to see Anthony, but you waited in the car."

Since Anthony did not see Keri with me, I did not want anyone, especially Anthony thinking that I called Keri. So her saying she waited in the car and saw Miguel go in with the woman and baby would be the only thing that would save me from looking like a snitch. As far as Miguel is concerned, the way things look, I don't think I will give a fuck if he finds out. But I would still prefer that he didn't.

"Where the fuck is he? Why isn't he coming out? You are sure it's Miguel, right?"

I wondered if she heard a damn thing I was saying.

Keri was steaming. I only prayed she did not bust me out when the shit goes down.

Before I could say anything to calm her down the door to the building opened and out came the woman Miguel went in with and not far behind was Miguel with the baby in the carrier.

The driver side of the BMW swung open with quickness and Keri jumped out of the car and made a mad dash toward Miguel and the woman. He did not see her coming as they were headed to the opposite side of the building. I in turn swung my door open and ran behind Keri.

When Keri caught up with Miguel who was still a few steps behind the woman she gave no thought to the baby in his hand. She grabbed him in the collar of his shirt almost flipping him over backwards. He balanced himself and almost shit his pants when he saw that it was Keri. I had no idea who he thought it was but the look in his eyes said he would have much preferred if he was being jacked for his car keys or even the damn baby.

"What the fuck is this Miguel?"

That motherfucker just stood there with his mouth wide open, but nothing was coming out. He gave the woman who had just retraced her steps the baby.

"K....Ker....Keri" She cut him off.

"K...K...Keri my ass. Who the fuck it this woman and why are you carrying her motherfucking baby. Is that your baby Miguel?"

Just when I thought it could not get any worse for Miguel, Anthony's receptionist come running out of the building. Very unaware of what was unfolding.

"Mr. Cruz, you left the keys for the house?"

If you think Miguel was pissing his pants before, you should see the sweat running down his face in the early February chill.

I was expecting Keri to unleash some more of that rage on Miguel, but instead my friend just fainted. Miguel quickly caught her before she hit the pavement.

He gave the keys that the receptionist gave him to the woman with the baby and told her to go home and he will call her later. She obediently did as he ordered. Not a word other than "yes".

While Miguel leaned against the building with the passed out Keri, I ran to my car to get a bottle of water to splash on her face. Miguel sat on the concrete with Keri's head in his lap slightly raised. I could see the tears running down his face. I splashed the water on Keri's face, and it took a few splashes before she came back around.

Miguel was quickly begging for her forgiveness.

"Keri, I am so sorry. I can explain. It's not what it looks like."

I was surprised at how calm Keri had become.

She pulled herself up away from Miguel. He stood up and they were eye to eye.

"Just answer me two questions Miguel. No explanations; Just yes or no."

"Okay." He managed to get out.

I still had not said a damn thing throughout the entire thing.

Keri spoke.

"Miguel, is that your baby?"

"Keri, let me expl...."

"I said motherfucking yes or no. No motherfucking explanation."

"Is that your motherfucking baby?'

"Yes....but"

"No buts Miguel. Did you just buy a house for that bitch? The truth Miguel."

"Yes."

Without another word Keri walked away from Miguel.

"Come on Natasha," was the only thing she said as she headed in the direction of our cars. When we got to our cars Keri asked if I could follow her to her house and I did just that.

Chapter 15

MELANIE

I can't exactly say that killing my best friend has not been a burden on my conscience. Some days I feel really bad about it and other days I just chalk it up to life. Or should I say death.

I think it made me cold. Before killing Amanda I never thought I could even cut someone for real, much less shoot them. Love, or should I say greed, can make a woman insane and a man as well. Between love and greed I am not sure which could be the more dangerous.

The shop kept me busy and I have been spending a lot of time with Jerry and still doing my thing with Jim but I have not been hearing much from or seeing much of Michael. He is probably going thru hell on earth with his wife and his baby mama dead. What the fuck, it's not the end of the world. I am still here. Or has he forgotten.

The girls and I picked up our dresses for Kylie's wedding which was now only days away. My damn car has been giving me a hard time. I am not sure what the problem is but I am on my way to the dealership so they can take a look at it for me.

I got to the dealership and they did some diagnostics shit and told me something about my alternator that I did not understand. I didn't give a damn about understanding the mumbo jumbo. I just wanted the damn car fixed. Good thing I gave Kylie my dress to take with her, just in case I have to leave the car. We will all be getting dressed at her house anyway.

They told me I could pick up the car the following morning because I had taken it in too late to get it back for the same day.

I took a cab home and as soon as I walked in the door my cell phone rang. I closed the door behind me and hurried to get the ringing phone out of my oversize Hermes bag that Jerry bought me only days before. I pressed the talk button as I walked over to the couch in the living room where I plopped myself down.

"Hello" I barely whispered. I guess I was more tired than I thought. It's Kylie.

"Hey Mel, I tried calling you earlier but couldn't get you. Did you see the news today?'

My heart skipped sixty beats. What the fuck is it now? Should I be worried?

"No, what happened?'

I grabbed the television remote from the coffee table and started surfing the channels to see if there was anything on that was supposed to be of interest to me.

"They said that a surveillance camera from another building caught someone going in the back door of Amanda's shop on the night she was killed."

My heart stopped. But I had to recover real fast before Kylie got suspicious.

"Oh, my God; do they know who it is Kylie?'

"Well they said it looked like a woman, but they couldn't say for sure."

"Damn. Who could that be?" I was shitting my pants.

"The Chief of Police was there saying that they have a timeline and if they can't get anything from that particular video, they are going to trace the steps of the person after they left the store and see how many more videos they pop up on. You know, check with other stores in the vicinity and follow the person on the camera to see if they can get a clearer picture of the suspect."

"Wow, I never thought of that."

I could kick myself for saying that. Kylie did not catch on because she ignored my comment and continued talking.

"Mel, do you think one of her workers did it?'

"Girl, anything is possible. We live in a fucked up world."

"But why would anyone want to kill Amanda. What the fuck could she have done that was so bad. I hope they catch whoever the asshole is and fuck him or her with a blazing hot motherfucking iron."

I never heard Kylie talk like that before. I was speechless, more from my quilt than her rant.

The silence between us was deafening. Kylie broke the silence.

"Mel, go get some rest, you sound tired. I am pooped myself with the wedding only a few days away. I'll call you later if I hear anything.

"Okay Kylie. And don't worry we'll get justice for Amanda."

"I pray we do. Talk to you later babes."

Okay, bye."

For the next couple of days leading up to Kylie's wedding I became a recluse. I took phone calls only from the girls and Jerry. I know they would not be too worried as I am known to just take off for days. Though, with the wedding it would probably be a whole different ball game. I had left Jennifer in charge at the Salon since the day I took my car in the shop so I did not have to go there. I told her I wouldn't be in until after the wedding. She knows not to tell anyone ever about where I am or when I will be back. It was an understanding we had between us since she started working with me. She has not let me down so far. However, this time she has no idea where I am and when I will get back.

I realize that I cannot just sit around and wait for the ball to drop. I feel like the walls are closing in on me and I have no escape.

Jim called several times and so did Jerry but I did not answer Jim's calls. The only other call that I was willing to answer was the only call I did not get. The call from Michael Langston, the one I was no longer going to get.

I have barely eaten in the last couple of days. I feel weak inside and I have this constant headache.

I however did not just waste my time moping. I packed two suitcases with some of my best clothes and some necessities just in case I have to make any quick moves. I went to the bank and got money that I was saving in my safe deposit box at the bank that I moved to a safe in a hidden compartment in the bedroom along with another nice stash.

I can't believe my life has come to this. And to what end. Michael is not answering my calls and he is not calling me.

I killed my best friend and her baby for that motherfucker and he just threw me to the fucking dogs, just like that. I should have killed him and let Amanda live.

The evening news was all about Amanda. The police held another press conference and this time they said that they had some big help from other surveillance cameras and are waiting to speak with a taxi driver that transported the suspect. However, the taxi driver was away on vacation and will not be back until Monday. Three days after Kylie's wedding. The police said they were close to making an arrest.

My mind was made up. There is no way I am going to stick around to be thrown in prison. I had to put my plan in gear.

I sometimes feel like the other girls don't see me as their equal so I don't tell them everything. I keep a lot of little secrets because you never know when bitches will cross you. When we all went to Jamaica over a year before, we had gone up in the hill where they plant marijuana; A lot of marijuana. The Rastafarian man that owns the marijuana field took a liking to me and he quietly slipped me his number. Everyone call him Hollywood. I was surprised how well dressed he was and when he invited us to a party at his house on the hills, I was floored to see how elegant it was. Damn, I did not know they balled like that in Jamaica. He likes me. He told me so. I called him a few times since I got back so when I called him to tell him I wanted to come to Jamaica but I did not have anywhere to stay he said I can stay with him. Matter of fact, he was elated. He said he is single so there is no woman to worry about. That was music to my ears.

I called Jerry and for the very first time I invited him to my house. He was curious about the man I said I am living with and I gave him some cockamamie story about us not being together anymore. Jerry took no time getting to my house.

I hate having to involve Jerry in my getaway plans but he was the only truly unscrupulous person I know that I can trust.

He has a passport connection. Matter of fact, whatever it is you need Jerry has a connection to it.

The boy came over with fried chicken and macaroni and cheese. He said he had just finished cooking but did not want to take the time to eat because of the urgency in my voice. For the first time in days I was hungry, so I chowed down on the macaroni and cheese while I told Jerry some exotic lie about why I needed a fake passport.

I could not believe he bought it. I made him promise never to talk to anyone about it no matter what. He promised. I already knew I could count on him.

Jerry made a call to one of his cronies who even gave him the name the passport would be in. Jerry told me that he would be back with the passport in less than three hours.

Soon as Jerry left to go get the passport I called the airlines to check on flights to Jamaica. I called my Rastafarian friend and put some plans in motion. He was overjoyed. I guess he can't believe his "beautiful American gal" like he calls me; is coming to spend some time with him.

Little did he know I was running from a murderous reality. I can't believe I turned out to be a murderer.

Jerry came through with the passport and a drivers license, which I had totally forgotten about. I guess that's why he had asked me for two passport pictures. One of the first things I did after seeing the news conference was cut my hair short and colored it blond. I also had the good sense to get some new passport photos because I knew Jerry would need them.

He did not ask too many questions. I guess being in the streets for so long has taught him to leave other people's business alone. He however told me that whatever happen, I did not get the passport and drivers license from him. I understood fully.

I in turn insisted that he talks to no one about me and my little vacation I told him I was planning on taking. I did not give him the impression I was running away from anything but I got the feeling he knew.

I did not want to take a cab from my house to the airport so I asked Jerry to take me and he obliged, but not before we made mad, passionate love for the last time.

We were on the way to the airport before Jerry even thought of asking me where I was headed.

"So where are you going to on such a short notice Miss Melanie, or should I say Miss Robin Goodison?"

Robin Goodison is the name that's in my new passport and Georgia State drivers license that he provided me.

"Aaww! I am taking a trip to Canada. I have family there. I just want to get away from all the noise for a minute."

I was lying my ass off. Though I know Jerry has love for me and would probably do anything for me, I still did not want to tell him the whole truth. Plus I would not want to make him an accessory to my crime. If I had a way to get the passport and drivers license without his help I would have kept the whole thing from him.

"Well, don't just run away from a brother. Make sure you call me. I'll even pick you up from the airport on your return, so feel free to call me."

Thanks Jerry. You know I will."

"You better. I will be missing that good pussy the whole time you're gone."

"Like I will be missing that good dick?"

"I don't know that you will be missing me and my dick, but I will sure miss that pussy."

"Boy, please; you know you have a series of pussy out there in the streets just waiting for you to pop open."

"That's the reason I want your pussy, it's not out there in the streets."

"Whatever."

We got to the airport a little over two hours before my flight and we kissed and said our goodbyes for now. Or so he thought. Traffic was crazy inside the airport so we could not linger for long. As he drove away the regrets started to set in.

I am gonna miss that man. His cooking, his money, his humor and his love for me, but most of all I am gonna miss the way he makes my kitty purr. Sex with Jerry is out of this fucking world. There are times when I just sit in my office or lay in the bed and all I had to do is close my eyes and think about the many times and different styles that Jerry would lovingly torture my pussy and make me wish I could take that dick with me in my purse, or carry it inside me; you know, sit on it all the way to Jamaica. Oh well, I guess I will just have to find me another champion lover when I get to Jamaica. I hear they got plenty.

Jerry dropped me off at American Airlines and when I was sure he was gone I headed over to Caribbean Airlines. I had to stay on top of shit. I can't have him knowing too much of the real.

Chapter 16

KERI

All hell broke loose in my life since the day I caught Miguel with his mistress. As the drama unfolded it was revealed that Miguel had been having his extra-marital affair for over two years and the baby was indeed his. He confessed the whole thing to me that same night I caught him with his skank ass bitch.

I did not waste a single moment putting his lying cheating bitch ass out. The only reason I have not filed divorce papers on his ass right away is because I have been so busy with getting ready for Kylie's wedding. Girlfriend has us all in a last minute frenzy running around like headless chickens. Today is the wedding and I am all packed and ready to head over to Kylie's new home that Shane shelled out a few millions to buy just in time for the wedding.

On top of all the shit that has been happening in our personal lives we are worried to death about Melanie. We have not heard from her in a few days. She has not been to her salon. No one heard from her at all.

Melanie sometimes just vanishes into thin air then surfaces a few days later. We are used to that. But it is very puzzling that she is not here for Kylie's wedding. That's a problem. She would not just back out on Kylie or any of us for that matter. Something is just not right.

The other girls have been ringing my phone off the hook, as I theirs and no one has a clue where Melanie could be.

As I prepared to leave the house, I walked into the living room to turn the television off. I was just in time to see a breaking news report on Amanda's case. I still can't fucking believe that they killed my friend; and for what? A few dollars and some credit cards?

The news reporter was saying:

In the case involving the senseless murder of Amanda Davis, the police finally have a suspect and could be making an arrest sometime today. We will bring you more on this case in our news at noon. Now back to our scheduled program.

I wanted to call the girls, but it was just not a good time. I'll tell them when I get to Kylie's house. Natasha is already there because she spent the night. We are all worried about Melanie. Where the hell is she anyway? I hope she is alright. She would not just skip Kylie's wedding like that. Maybe she plans on showing up just in time for the ceremony. I don't know about that girl.

I hurried out the house and got to Kylies in record time. The wedding is not until five o'clock but we have a lot of catching up to do and making sure that Kylie is good.

I pulled up to Kylie's and Shane's palatial mansion. They were balling like motherfuckers. Damn. The place is as huge as the flipping white house. The yard on both sides of the house was a sea of beautiful well-manicured lawn. It has a double driveway and lord knows I cannot give justice to it by trying to describe it. Suffice it to say its fit for royalty. I parked my car behind Natasha's truck then walked up to the huge double front doors. I was just about to ring the doorbell when the doors swung open on both sides. It's Natasha.

"Hey girl, she said" with a big hug to boot.

"Hey ma, you guys heard anything from Mel yet?"

"Not a word. We are really starting to worry now. Where could she be?"

"Girl I wish I knew. I pray she shows up before the wedding starts, but just in case she doesn't I hope Kylie has a back up."

"Yes she does. Hopefully Melanie shows up, but if she doesn't one of the girls at the office where Kylie used to work is a perfect fit for that dress."

"You have Melanie's dress?"

"Yes. It's upstairs. Come on; let's go upstairs where Kylie is."

I could see the deep concern etched in Natasha's face. She seemed really worried about Mel. I followed her to one of the many master suites where Kylie was chilling out sipping on something.

"You are here." Kylie said as soon as she saw me.

"You best know it. You ready for that walk down the aisle into the arms of that hot masterpiece you will be calling husband before the day is over?'

"I could not be any readier if I tried." She said with the biggest smile I have seen on her in a long time.

See, we have not had a lot to smile about since the death of Amanda. I especially have not had a lot to smile about since I found out my husband is fucking another bitch and had a baby by her. Then to top it off; bought the bitch a house. But today I am gonna have to put all of that aside to be perky and fun for Kylie.

"Good. Nothing is going to spoil it for you today baby girl."

"Nothing is right; not even Melanie's trifling ass." Natasha chimed in.

"I am worried about her though. Where could she be?" Kylie said.

"Listen Kylie, today is your day not to worry about a damn thing. So just pour some more of that Cristal and let's drink to your fabulous life." said Natasha, grabbing two champagne flutes.

Kylie poured the champagne and we made a toast.

"To Kylie and Shane; may you live a long happy life with plenty of little Shanes and Kylies running around your beautiful mansion" I said.

We all laughed. Something I had forgotten how to do of late.

"Here, here." Natasha chirped.

We drank two whole bottles of champagne in no time. We left Kylie in her room when her stylist and makeup person came in to do their thing. Still no Melanie.

I did not mention what I heard on the news about Amanda's killer. I just did not want to fuck up Kylie's day. There was just too much going on for me to add that to the equation at this time.

Natasha and I had separate rooms which was a good thing because my shit was all over the place. Being in a room by myself also gave me time to think about stuff I did not care to think about. Like Miguel and his bitch and that bastard baby. I know it's not the baby's fault but fuck that baby too. I had no space left in me to give a fuck.

Miguel called me like a damn stalker after I put his ass out that night but I never once answered the phone. He left over a dozen messages and I have not listened to a single one. He can kiss my ass as far as I am concerned. The only talking we will be doing is through our motherfucking lawyers. If he thinks he is gonna take what we build together and share it with this bitch he has another thing coming.

I met Miguel almost six years now and we have been married for five of them. When I met him he had just landed a job with the state. He worked for the state for only a year and a half when he decided to start his own practice. I gave him more than half the money. I took out a loan for God sakes. Now he is running around with some bitch thinking he is gonna have it all. Over my dead motherfucking body he will.

There is a knock on the door that jarred me out of my thoughts.

"Come in."

It is Natasha.

"What's up, you not ready yet?'

"Shit. What time is it?'

"Time for your ass to get ready; the makeup girl is coming to you next. She just did mine. You like?"

"Love it."I said with a big grin

"Good. Get that dress on. She should be here any second now."

Natasha turned and walk out of the room leaving me to get ready.

Here I am getting ready to walk down the aisle as Kylie's bridesmaid at the very moment my marriage is crashing around me.

When did my life get this messed up? It was not suppose to end up like this. I did all the right things. I did everything for that man and this is how he repays me.

I have absolutely no luck with men. First it was Paul; now it's Miguel. I hope I won't have to end up killing this motherfucker as well.

Chapter 17
KYLIE

I stood at my bedroom window and watched as the wedding guests filled up the chairs in the backyard that was transformed into a sea of beauty for the wedding. The water in the twenty four by forty eight foot swimming pool was colored red with several dozen white roses floating on top. The pool was then covered with a thick giant sheet of glass and you can see the roses floating below that on top of the red water. There are rows of chairs set up along both sides of the length of the pool and the far end as well. The minister marrying me and Shane, the famous Michael Langston was already outside checking out the place where I will meet my man at the end of my walk down the aisle. It is simply breathtaking. There are two huge white tents adjoined to each other housing the dance floor, the deejay booth and two bars. The weather is beautiful. Fit for an outdoor wedding. Deejay Twitch who is a regular on the Ellen Show was already there pumping music that was floating all the way to my bedroom window. I could hear Biggie Small's Big Poppa coming thru the speakers. There are people walking around waiting for the nuptials to pop off.

There are white roses everywhere that were provided by Keri from her flower shop. Everything is just like I dreamed it would be. I am so lucky.

There is a knock on the door and I walked away from the window to open it. I had it locked so no one would just come in without knocking. I opened the door to see Keri, Natasha and Miguel's sister, Carmen standing there looking as beautiful as ever in their beautiful white dresses. We were all wearing white. The entire theme of the wedding is white…You could say I am having a white wedding.

Natasha's dress is a one sleeve off the shoulder with the sleeve fitted all the way down to the wrist, form fitting and just above the knees while Keri's was the same form fitting and same length except she has two sleeves with both off the shoulder. Carmen is wearing the same dress but with no sleeves and a mock turtle neck.

"Hi ladies" I said all excited and grinning from ear to ear.

"Hi." They said in unison sounding all Kardshian-like.

"So still no Melanie, uh?" Natasha said as they all entered the room.

I was really worried about Melanie, but I refuse to let her absence spoil my day. If she is not dead or laying up in the hospital somewhere she should be here and since Natasha and Keri called all the hospitals and she is not at any of them she should be here. So I will just push her to the back of my head and leave her there until after I am Mrs. Shane D'Marco.

The three girls and I are just shooting the breeze. It was only about twenty minutes to my walk down the aisle into the arms and life of the most romantic, generous and caring man I have ever met.

There was another knock at the door and Carmen got up to open it. This time it is someone from the office I worked at before my big break as an author.

"Hey, Marcia, is everything good?" I asked as she walked into the room in her white dress with cap sleeves. It is actually the dress that Melanie should be wearing. It fits Marcia to perfection.

"I am fine girl. Hello everybody" She said all bubbly.

Everyone said hello to Carmen and I took the opportunity with all of them there to thank them for being my bridesmaids. I handed them each a little jewelry box with their thank you gifts. I gave each girl a beautiful diamond tennis bracelet.

Each bracelet cost over two thousand dollars. They were delighted and wanted to hug and kiss me, but I backed them all off. I did not want to ruin my dress or makeup.

Just as we were about to leave the room, there was another knock on the door. Assuming it was someone coming to tell me it's time for the ceremony, Natasha walked to the door and opened it. It was Carol my housekeeper.

Before I could ask what she wanted two men in suits appeared behind her. They did not look dressed for the wedding. Carol spoke.

"Kylie, these detectives are here to talk to you."

"Detectives? Why?"

Carol moved away from the doorway and one of the men, a white older man that looked like he has seen his better days spoke.

"Sorry to bother you at a time like this maam. I am detective Martin Donovan and this is Detective Raymond Jones."

"What is this about?" I asked still standing in the doorway.

"It's about your friend Amanda." The black detective said with his beautiful grey eyes looking right through me. I think he was flirting a tad.

"Have you found her killer? Cause I swear, if you are here for any other reason than to tell us that you have arrested someone I am gonna be really pissed." And I meant every word.

"That is exactly why we are here." The old white guy said.

By this time all the other girls were at the door.

"Where is Melanie?" One of the detectives asked.

"What does Melanie have to do with this? Do you know Melanie? Are you a friend of hers? The questions were coming that fast."

"I am Kylie and this is …." The black detective cut me off in mid sentence.

"I know who you all are. Can we all sit down and talk Kylie."

"We are about to get started in a few minutes so we don't really have time to sit. I hope you understand." I was getting irritated now.

I guess maybe I shouldn't be. He probably just wants to make sure we all got the news. We were all close to Amanda so of course with the investigations into her death they would look closely at all of us as well. On the other hand here it is that no one heard from Melanie and now the detectives were asking about her.

I opened the door wider and told them they have to be quick because I was due to walk down the aisle in only minutes. I also informed them that with all that was going on we did not have time to sit. It was almost time for me to take my walk down the aisle to the best thing that ever happened to me and hearing that they captured Amanda's killer would be a wonderful gift.

The old white detective spoke.

"Is Melanie not part of the wedding party?"

"I thought you were here to tell us about Amanda. Why do you keep asking about Melanie?" Natasha asked.

"Yeah, what does Melanie being here or not have to do with what you have to say about Amanda's death?" Keri asked getting irritated.

"Well ladies, we have a warrant out for her arrest in the murder of Amanda Davis and her unborn baby." Detective Jones, the black one said.

All of us in the room barring the two detectives gasped almost in a chorus. The room got so quiet you could hear a pin drop on the three inch thick white carpet.

Natasha was the first to break the silence.

"There must be some mistake; Melanie and Amanda were very close."

"And Melanie could not kill anyone" Keri jumped in.

"There has to be some kind of mistake." I said as I dared the tears to stay at the back of my eyes.

The detectives told us all about how Melanie entered the back door of Melanie's shop and shot her in the head. They told us about the surveillance camera trail and how they found a bullet matching the one that killed Amanda in Melanie's car that was at the repair shop. They had an arsenal of evidence against her.

We were all in shock. The detective said their goodbyes, apologized for interrupting the most important event of my life to date and said they would get back in touch with us as they continue the hunt for Melanie.

It was all starting to make sense. Melanie's absence that is; but I was still finding it hard to believe that Melanie is actually the one to have murdered Amanda. That shit is just not possible. What reason would she have for killing one of her best friends?

After the detectives left we did not even get a chance to discuss it among ourselves because it was time for me to meet my man at the altar. I should be thinking the most beautiful, pure thoughts as I walked down the aisle but all I could see in my mind is Melanie killing Amanda. I was still finding it hard to believe. And what would be her motive anyway?

Chapter 18

MELANIE

"Damn, it's hot out here." I said aloud to myself while I waited for Hollywood to get his car. I landed in Jamaica at the Norman Manley International Airport in less than two hours. Going through customs was a breeze. The people with Jamaican passports and green cards were in one line and American citizens in another. The line with the American citizens moved really fast while the people in the other line looked like they were having a warm time with those customs officers.

"Damn. Hollywood, you are a baller? That's a nice Hummer you are pulling down bro." I said to Hollywood when he pulled up and got out of the vehicle.

"I like it." He said quietly in that deep, sexy accent.

"Welcome to Jamaica."

"Thanks."

There was a short awkward moment when I could almost hear him asking me how long I was going to stay even though he did not say it. He asked me that before I left the house and I skirted around it. He asked me again when I called him from my burner phone at the airport and I changed the subject. I did not want to lie to him. Not even a tiny white lie, because I need for him to trust me. My life depends on it.

I broke the silence.

"You asked me how long I will be staying here. I need some time away from Miami to think."

"To think about what?" he questioned.

It was obvious that he wanted answers and he wanted them now. His jaws were tight his shoulders were tense. He was not buying the just want to get away bit.

"To get away from the hustle and bustle" I said lying my ass off. The very thing I said I would not do.

"And that's it. No grand scheme or anything like that?"

"No. No grand scheme."

"Then in that case I guess I don't have to worry about aiding and abetting."

Why would he say some shit like that? Maybe I am just paranoid. I was reading too much into every little damn thing.

"Stop playing." I said laughing a little too heartily.

Nothing else was said between us the entire trip to his house in a place called Golden Spring somewhere in the hills of Kingston.

He pulled into a huge gate and drove up a long paved driveway to a beautiful white house with big bay windows. The house is two story and massive, nothing like I remembered it from before. Then again, when we were there that time we visited Jamaica I think we entered from the back. We did not see the front of the house.

We got out of the vehicle and I walked toward the back where my luggage was.

"Never mind the luggage. I' will have somebody get it." Hollywood said.

"Okay. Cool."

"Are you hungry? I had them fix you some real Jamaican food." He said as he took my hand and led me inside the big ass foyer.

"No, I am a little tired. I have not had a good night's sleep. Can I just go to sleep and eat later?"

"Sure sis. You can do that. While yuh doing dat, I will just go and run some errands."

One of the things that puzzled me about Hollywood is his good English. Most of the Jamaicans I know do not speak good English and I can hardly understand that Jamaican language that they talk; Patois. But surprisingly,

Hollywood speaks like he is well educated and somewhere within his Jamaican accent, you can hear a bit of foreign accent as well.

He took me to a huge, beautifully decorated room. Everything was in white except for the curtains and the carpet which were both army green and two oversized green and white striped chairs in two corners of the room. The furniture was all Italian white lacquer. Very interesting.

There was a brand new white bathrobe on the bed with a note on it. I took the note up and read it; "Welcome to Jamaica Beautiful - Make Yourself Comfortable". That was rather thoughtful.

I threw myself across the bed and for the first time since I got off the airplane I thought about the girls and wondered how Kylie's wedding went, feeling bad about copping out the way I did. But what was I suppose to do, just sit around and wait for my hell to break loose? Fuck no, I couldn't do that.

There is no doubt that I regret killing Amanda. I wish I could go back and erase that whole episode. All the way back to the motherfucking day I met that Michael Langston. I knew from a long time ago, since I was a kid that a fucking preacher is the last person you should trust. Yet, at the end of the day I have given so much more than trust to this man. I gave him my life. I gave up my flourishing business, beautiful home and yes all my worldly belongings, not to mention the best friends in the world to become a fugitive, literally running for my life.

I have no idea when I fell off to sleep, but I had the worst nightmare, in the middle of the day. I dreamt that the cops came for me with helicopters and machine guns and as I was running outside the house with my hands over my head, bullets started flying from everywhere and I was hit all over my body. I was screaming and rolling around on the ground and they kept firing.

I felt someone grab my foot and I began kicking and flailing my arms.

"Hey, it's me, Hollywood. What's goin' on wit you girl?"

I jumped up and was relieved that I was only dreaming. I made a nervous laugh.

"Oh, I just had a little nightmare; daymare in this case." Another nervous laugh escaped my lips.

"You were saying, I'm sorry, I'm sorry; what is that about?"

"I can't even remember what the dream was about." I lied.

Before he could say anything else I quickly changed the subject.

"So what's for dinner?"

"You have to come and see. It's a surprise." He said smiling like he won the lottery.

"Ok. I am gonna take a quick shower and I will be right down."

"Cool. Your luggage is inside that closet over there." He said pointing to a double door which I now discover is the closet.

"Thank you."

"No problem." He said and walked out of the room closing the door behind him.

We had a really nice fish dinner with okra and carrots and something called festival made from flour and some good tasting stuff. They know how to cook in Jamaica. I later found out Hollywood has a full staff, a male chef; he said he did not want any woman cooking for him if she was not his woman. He has a woman who does the laundry, iron and takes care of the house, and then he has one that comes in just to take care of the grocery shopping and stuff like that.

After dinner Hollywood and I talked into the wee hours of the morning. He told me all about how the woman he had in his life messed up by bringing a man into his home while he was abroad on business. She did not know that that particular trip was only for one day; she thought he would be gone for at least a week like his other trips before.

He told me that when he got home from the airport that night, He knew something was wrong the moment he pulled up and looked at his bedroom window from the car. The entire room was illuminated in red. He could see how red the room was thru the window curtains. He was more than familiar with that scene. What he did not understand was why that scene was set while he is away.

He said that he and his girl got a special lighting system that they turn on when they are making love or fucking or whatever they do. So it was baffling to him why it would be on in his absence, but not for long.

He said when he quietly walked inside the house and got to their bedroom door, a little young dude no more than sixteen or seventeen was banging out his girls belly. She was moaning and oohing and aahing with her eyes closed so she did not see Hollywood standing at the door and neither did the young boy whose back was turned to the door. Hollywood told me that he calmly walked up to the boy and tapped him on the shoulder and he jumped off the woman so fast he fell over on the floor. I was waiting to hear about the bloodshed that followed but to my surprise there was none.

Hollywood said he simply told the youth to put his clothes on and leave, which he gladly did. I nudged him on enjoying the drama. He told me that he asked his girl to put her clothes on, and then told her to pack and leave his house that very night. He said she has called and apologized many times and begged for a second chance, but he flat out refused.

Everything Hollywood told me was what I needed to hear. Here is a fine ass man in his early thirties, tall, light and handsome and standing about six feet with a body to die for. He has that "good hair" all black people talk about, and that made his dreads really shiny. His locks hang all the way down the middle of his back and are well groomed. He does not have much hair on his face, and it was naturally that way. He is intelligent and very successful albeit ganja. Well, at least that's what I thought.

Here is an opportunity to put into action my plan B. Finding permanent residence in Jamaica was of utmost priority and Hollywood can definitely provide that. I am sure he could use a good woman in his life and I can be that, so it is indeed a perfect situation for both of us. Problem solved.

Now all I have to do is get Hollywood to fall in love with me or even fall in love with my sex, then I can pretend that I want to stay because of him. He may not ever have to know about the life I am running away from. I already start the work on that; I told him that I hated being called Melanie and gave him some cockamamie story about why only my friends called me that and how I much prefer to be called by my real name, Robin. Robin Goodison. The bullshit I fed him was real to me. It had become my new reality.

He immediately started calling me Robin and told me he liked it a lot better than Melanie anyway. So that was already in the bag. Now I just have to let him fall in love with me. But tonight would not be the night. I have to take it slow if I want to make it work.

I eventually went to bed with Hollywood on my mind and for the first time since I killed Amanda I slept like a baby.

Chapter 19

NATASHA

It's been almost two whole weeks now since Kylie's wedding and the revelation that Melanie is actually Amanda's killer. No one has any idea where Melanie could be. We have not heard from her. Jennifer is running the salon and said she has not heard anything from her either. I guess that means the police are right. Melanie killed Amanda. But the one thing that has the police and everyone else close to the case puzzled is her motive. The police can't seem to find any reason in the world why she would do such a thing. I guess only Melanie can answer that question. Somewhere in the back of my mind I still hope that it is all a big mistake and Melanie is not the one to have killed our friend. But I know that's just wishful thinking because why would Melanie just disappear if she was not guilty. I don't think she is laying down dead someplace. I just know in my heart that's not the case.

Kylie just got back from her honeymoon only a couple of days now and we are about to meet up together with Keri. It is so odd now that our happy group of five has dwindled down to only three. One dead, while another is the killer.

I got dressed in a cobalt blue Versace three quarter sleeves mini dress with side pockets in the front, very chic, with golden rod yellow Christian Louboutin boots and matching Hermes handbag. I was feeling myself.

We are meeting at a reggae club and restaurant called The Gardens in Fort Lauderdale so I hit the I95 from Miami rocking to a badass club banger by reggae singer JoJo Mac called Time of My Life, when I wore that out by playing it over and over I played another one of her songs Learning to Win and gave it a sore back all the way to the club. I love her music. That reminds me I have been meaning to get Keri and Kylie a copy of her cd.

I got to the club and immediately saw Kylie's and Keri's cars parked side by side. I was lucky to see an empty spot next to Kylie's car. As soon as I pulled into the spot they both got out of Kylie's car and walked over to my car as I got out.

"Hey hot mamas." I said grinning from ear to ear.

Kylie was wearing a flowing cream baby-doll-like dress with sleeves and matching Jimmy Choo boots with a Hermes bag as well, cream and black.

Keri was no slouch, though she is usually a little more homely than any of us were. I must say she has been stepping up her game since the break up with Miguel. She was wearing skin tight jeans, and even though it was a tad chilly for the beginning of March in Florida she was wearing a Givenchy fitted long sleeve crop top with her entire midriff bare. She topped that off with some signature Gucci boots. She looks fantastic. We are a boot-loving bunch.

"Hey Nat. What's up?" Kylie said giving me a big hug

"Hi baby girl. You ready for this?" Keri said joining the hug fest.

"I was born ready."

We chit chat all the way to the entrance of the club and was laughing and carrying on. I think it is actually the first time we laughed this way since Amanda died. I was laughing and talking but my mind was heavy with Amanda and Melanie.

I still can't get over the fact that one of us is the killer of our best friend. That is something I think will fuck with me for as long as I live. I know it's affecting Keri and Kylie as well. Who would have known that Melanie could do such a horrendous thing? I know of the five of us she is usually the most aggressive and she is quick to fight and argue, but I never once thought that there was a killer lurking inside of her.

We got into the club and there were quite a few people there in spite of the fact that it was only 10 o'clock. Most of the patrons were standing so we immediately got a table for four with a clear view of the stage and dance floor. We ordered two bottles of Cristal from the waitress who wasted no time getting to our table. She must have seen big tips written all over us, and if that's the case she is right on the money. We are big tippers, and not just for the flossing effect but we think when someone does a service, especially when they do it well they should be compensated accordingly. We may be a bit excessive but it's all good.

We partied like our lives depended on it, dancing to reggae all night. We did not do much talking except for the few times we shouted something to each other across the table because the music was really loud. The strange thing is the louder it got and the more the bass lines thumped the more exciting it was. We had a great time and by the time we got out of the club it was almost three in the morning. We l.eft the club after having a too long conversation in the parking lot as far as I am concerned, so I suggested we cut it short and head home. We said our goodbyes and left for home.

I got home and usually we would call each other to say we made it home safely. I called both the girls and did not get an answer. I went to bed thinking that they probably still have their phones in their bags, where we always keep them. I fell asleep without effort and did not wake up until way past noon the following day.

I had my phone on the charger and I could hear it vibrating so I picked it up and realized I had over twenty missed calls. Most of the calls were from Keri and Kylie. I decided to call Kylie first. She picked up on the first ring.

"Oh my God! Natasha. Melanie did kill Amanda and you will never guess who the reason behind it is."

"What you mean who?"

"Yes, I said who." She went quiet.

"Kylie, what's going on? What did you hear and where did you hear it? I don't understand."

"Listen, it was on the news all morning. They have been showing Melanie's picture and calling her a fugitive who is armed and dangerous. But now they have a motive."

"So what is the motive?" I am bursting with curiosity.

"You better be sitting down for this one. It is so damned far fetc…."

I cut her the hell off; I want her to give me the short version but she was taking this shit all around the block in laps.

"Get to the fucking point Kylie and stop beating around the damn bush. Why did Melanie kill Amanda?"

"Damn, you need to calm down."

"Fuck calm. Why did Melanie kill Amanda?"

I was shocked out of my fucking mind when Kylie told me the whole story about how the famous Pastor Michael Langston was fucking both my friends. She told me that when the police found out Amanda was pregnant they wasted no time trying to track down the father. Since the big reveal at Kylies wedding when the police came to arrest Melanie every chance the police got they called us to ask more questions about who we think the father of the baby might be.

There was no reason to lie because we really did not have a clue that he was Michael Langston. All we knew was that Amanda called him Mr. Man and was very discreet about who he was. Now to find out it's the famous pastor has just blown the lid off the whole thing.

As Kylie told me the story we got on the internet and there were pictures of Amanda, Melanie and the famous pastor Langston.

Apparently Melanie was also having an affair with the famous pastor and when the authorities got all the information they needed through cell phone records the connection was made to pastor Langston. According to the reports, when the police confronted Michael Langston, he spilled his guts and told them the story from A to Z, and is now begging the forgiveness from his congregation. A lot of people on the internet believe he should get a second chance to keep his church and continue to preach because everyone knows about his wife being in a wheelchair for years and how well he took care of her until she died.

I read how Melanie found out about Michael and Amanda when she walked in on them in Amanda's office the day of the grand opening of Amanda's store. Pastor Langston told the police that he pretended not to know Melanie. So Amanda had no idea that her man was also Melanie's man. But all along Melanie was a woman scorned and did not want to see Amanda with the man she wanted for herself. The way the report read and the statement from Pastor Langston finally told us what drove Melanie to such depth where she would kill her best friend over a cheating motherfucker.

My heart broke in several little pieces. How could Melanie just kill Amanda over a damn man? I thought we were better than that. I thought our love for each other and all we went through together since college would be a deterrent to anything vaguely resembling that bullshit. We never even have petty quarrels. How did it ever get to this?

Even with all that I now know, I am still confounded. Kylie and I got off the phone and the internet and I broke down crying. My heart was truly shattered.

For the first time in a long time I got down on my knees and I prayed to God for forgiveness for Melanie and I prayed that Amanda's soul rest in eternal and heavenly peace.

There was just so much going on inside me. I stayed on my knees so long, just crying and praying that they started to burn, but it was nothing like the searing pain inside of me.

I finally got back in the bed and got under the covers. I did not brush my teeth or get anything to eat. Not even a cup of tea.

I decided to give Keri a quick call since she had called so many times but I really did not feel like talking anymore. I just wanted to get under the covers, go into a deep sleep and wake up to find that it was all a dream. I got Keri's voice mail and I was happy for that, I really didn't feel like talking. I left a message promising to call her later in the evening.

I heard my phone ringing and ringing and I thought I was dreaming for a moment. I glanced at the clock and saw that I was sleeping for way longer than I was feeling. I was actually sleeping for over four hours. I jumped up and answered it. It's Miles.

"Hello." I said in my sexiest smoky voice.

"I miss you."

"You don't have to." I said sitting in the middle of the bed.

"I don't want to anymore." He had this seriousness to him.

"So what are we gonna do about that sweetheart." I said.

"I don't know. Can we talk about it face to face?" He asked.

"Of course we can. You know that."

"Open the door."

"What you mean open the door, where are you?"

"Open the door."

I looked out the window just in time to see his car pulling in the driveway. I ran to the front door and right into his arms as he came up the walkway to the front door. I started kissing him passionately, he lifts me up and I wrapped my legs around his waist and we kissed all the way inside the house.

I hadn't taken a shower all day so I jumped out of Miles arms and told him I wanted to get a quick shower. He insisted on joining me and I let him. We washed each other's body and Miles fucked the shit out of me as I pressed both hands against the wall with one leg up like a peeing dog, giving Miles all of the pussy. He fucked me till my pussy ached but I wanted more.

Miles got out of the shower and dried the excess water from his skin then he reached in for me after I turned the water off and lifted me smack into his arms and walked with me to the bedroom where he lay me out and slowly licked the water from my body starting at my neck. He licked my breasts and sucked on my nipples, rolling his tongue all over them and sending electricity all throughout my body while simultaneously fucking with my mind because I know that he would soon have to go. He has to go home to his wife. All thoughts of him leaving to go home to his wife dissipated, when I felt his tongue touch my clit. Oh lawd a mercy! His tongue is golden; damn it's driving me out of my mind. I can't think.

"Oh Miles, lick that pussy baby. I have been saving it for youuuuuuuuuu… Aaaww!!"

"Mm mmmm." Was all he could muster with a full mouth.

Miles ate my pussy so good. Gentle. Rough. Not so rough. Lick, suck, swipe. I could not stand it any longer, I really could not help myself when my body started a slow tremble that turned into a violent rush of juices that Miles licked and swallowed. I took a deep long breath and before I could exhale he started stroking my pussy lips with his big fat dick and I could feel it touching against my too tender clit and I came once more. When he felt me cumming he quickly lifted my legs to his shoulders, kissing them hungrily. He put the tip of his hot rod on the entrance to my heavenly gift and slowly slid it inside me inch by inch until all nine and a half of it was being hugged by my sugar walls. There were no more words between us.

He had me in every position I can think of. I am not ashamed to say that man fucked me like I stole his prized possession. It was way more sweet than bitter, but the bitter was the icing on the cake. He has a way of making it hurt so fucking good I would never complain. It was too much but I couldn't get enough. When I felt his tremors coming on I was a little relieved in spite of how good he was laying it down because my little girl was tender.

He came and I could feel his babies moving up inside me with major force. He was grunting and acting like a man possessed. After making his deposit inside me he rolled off and was just totally breathless. So was I.

After catching his breath he pulls me close to his chest and just hugs me tight, very tight.

I was wrong about Miles leaving to go home to his wife after we made love. I want to say that God was smiling down on me but I will not get God mixed up in my adulterous life. Who is the real adulterer anyway? I would think its Miles; after all he is the one who is married. I don't have a marriage to violate so the term adulterer should not be so extensive. If I am an adulterer, however, it will not be for much longer.

Miles spent the night and the next morning he was still hanging around even went out and picked up pancakes and eggs breakfast. When he was still hanging around after midday I asked him what his wife would think.

"So Miles, what is your excuse gonna be for staying out overnight and way into the afternoon."

I was not prepared for his answer, but he had one ready.

"I no longer have a wife to go home to." He said with nonchalance.

We are in the living room. He is sitting on the couch and me standing beside him. My knees were turning jelly so I sat down next to him. I was speechless. I had so many questions but I could not verbalize a single one. I was relieved when Miles started talking again.

"She was having an affair. I found out that many of her long shopping sprees were a lot more than that. She was meeting her lover in numerous hotels in disguises. Her disguises included wigs, big hats and whatever the hell else."

I finally found my voice.

"How did you find out?" I asked sounding concerned but not exactly.

"Does it matter?"

"Well, if you don't want to talk about it you don't have to."

There was a long awkward silence and I could hear my heart beating out of context in my chest.

"I had her followed."

"What?"

"I had her followed."

"I heard you the first time. Why did you do that?" I really didn't know what else to say.

"I suspected she was cheating because so much about her had changed. She was no longer the kind, gentle woman I married."

I pulled up closer to him and took his hand in mine and caressed his finger with mine.

"Natasha I know you are probably thinking that I am a hypocritical bastard but she was not just cheating; she was cheating with one of my employees from another branch I opened in Coral Gables. That's unforgiveable."

"I am in no position to judge you babes, or her." I said with a little laugh. He kissed me on the forehead.

"Are you hurt or angry, or both?" I asked.

"Honestly, I am a little of both. Hurt that she would step out on me when I gave her everything. Nothing was too good for her. All she had to do was be a good wife. All she had to be was loyal. And yes I am angry because she chose to fuck with my fucking employee. She's out."

"I'm sorry."

"Why are you sorry? Now we don't have to hide."

I could not believe what I was hearing. All my organs were doing the happy dance. I had to make sure I heard what I thought I heard.

"What did you say?" I literally had my fingers crossed.

He pulled his body away from me and moved over on the couch. He then took my face in his hands and when he spoke I swear I heard my pussy clapping, literally cheering, rah, rah, rah.

"I said we don't have to hide anymore. This did not just happen. It happened over seven months ago and she is out of the house and I already got the divorce I asked for."

I was stunned.

"Oh shit. Miles. Miles. Miles."

I could not stop saying his name so he shut me up by pressing his lips to mine giving me just enough tongue to make me tingle. We made mad love right there on the carpet in front of the couch. The couch got its share of the action as well.

Miles stayed with me that night and I cried tears of joy. He was finally going to be mine. I was going to be Mrs. Miles Covington.

Chapter 20
KYLIE

I can't believe it's the end of July already and it's Melanie's birthday as well. The last day of the month, but we still have no clue where she could be or if she is even alive. When it was all good, when no one got killed and none of us were killers we would be getting all dolled up to go out and celebrate her birthday. Not this year.

So much has happened over the last year. We lost one friend by the hand of another. Keri left her two timing husband. Natasha is on her way to being Mrs. Miles Covington and her modeling career is moving full speed ahead. I got married to Mr. Movie Star Shane D'Marco and I just turned in my second novel. Life has been bitter-sweet.

It's a really hot Saturday and the air condition is on full blast. Shane and I had breakfast together earlier and he went on an errand and promised he would be back by noon so we can spend the rest of the day together.

He just finished shooting on his latest movie only three days before and he came home immediately after it wrapped. We have been holed up in the house for the entire three days just making crazy love in every room of the house. That adds up to a lot of pressure on my little baby girl but she is taking it like a woman.

Shane loves sex, he wants it all the time. It's a good thing that we have people to take care of us and our home because when Shane is around all my time is spent on my back. Well, that's not exactly true. I also spend a lot to time on my hands and knees, jacked up against the wall, hanging off the bed literally on my damn neck while Shane storm my pussy.

Before I married Shane I knew he was a freak in the bed. Deep down that is one of the reasons I married him. No one before him turned me out the way he does. And his pussy eating game is off the cliffs. He is passionate, I love that in a man; and he has a way of making me feel like I am the only woman in the world. I have to admit I get a little jealous when he is working with all those beautiful women, but he gives me no reason.

I did some research on him shortly after I met him and his life was pretty drama free. There are a couple of actresses that he dated before he met me, beautiful ones, but he married me so I am pretty confident that he knows what he wants, and that's me.

I never dreamed I would have a man like Shane in my life. Don't get it twisted, I knew I could get a good man, a husband, but I never thought I would be married to a movie star. I never expected to travel in that circle even though I wrote a book and became a semi celebrity myself.

I lay up in the sofa thinking about how fortunate I have been and it got me thinking again about Amanda and how unfortunate it was for her that her best friend would kill her and rob her of the opportunity to live her dream of running her very own high end boutique like Secrets. It made me so sad thinking about it that I had no idea when I fell asleep.

I was awakened out of my slumber when I felt a hand going up my dress and touching my wetness. I opened my eyes to see my husband naked in front of me except for some sexy silk boxers. The love in his eyes is apparent and I could feel the love I have for him moving inside of me.

I sat up in front of him and pulled down his boxers below his knees; his instrument was already erect and I could see the veins popping out.

I ran my fingers over it, gently touching it, caressing it. He took a couple of deep breaths and closed his eyes. I licked his nuts with feathery tongue and he moaned and called my name. I was on a roll, I took him in my mouth and slowly pulled him in as I licked and sucked him like my life depended on it. I sucked him deep into my throat and I could feel my lips touching the base of his cock.

Without any warning he busted inside my throat and I swallowed all of him licking him dry.

After a few minutes catching his breath, he bent me over the couch and fucked me so good I swear even though my closest neighbor is almost a city block away they could hear my screams and guttural moans. I have no idea where the hell Shane learned to fuck like this but I thank the holy heavens that he picked my pussy to torture. After having him inside me the sensation would last for days. All I have to do is close my eyes and think hard enough and I can feel him inside me all over again.

Shane and I went at it until we were both useless. We fell asleep on the couch.

Shane had to leave for California the next day so we went to South Beach for an early breakfast and made a stop in the Versace and Armani Exchange stores where I thought he was gonna empty the damn stores. As per always he had them deliver the packages to the house.

I drove him to the airport because I did not want to say goodbye just yet. He told me I didn't have to, that he could call his driver, but I insisted. On the way to the airport we talked and laughed and made fun of everything and everyone we saw on our way there.

After our goodbyes; hugging, kissing, more hugging, more kissing; I stood by the car and watched him till he was out of site. Before he disappeared behind the double doors he turned and blew me a kiss. I blew one back at him and he was gone.

I picked up some Jamaican curried chicken on the way home and dig right in soon as I got in the house. I was starving. Boy them Jamaicans can cook their asses off. I never met a plate of Jamaican food that I did not enjoy.

I cleaned up a little so the place wouldn't be such a terrible mess when the helper gets in the following day. I know, it's weird that I would be cleaning up before the cleaning lady gets in, but I would hate for them to think that I can't take care of my own home.

I had to fire one girl because she had the feeling that if I could sit around and don't do a damn thing she could do the same. I remember hearing her telling the gardener that if I can chill she can chill as well. Bitch had real nerve. I had to let her go cause only one HBIC (Head Bitch in Charge) in my house, and that bitch is me.

My phone rang as soon as I got up to put my bathing suit on to hang out by the pool.

"Hello." I did not bother checking the caller id.

"Kylie, come up for air girl." Keri hollered in my damn ear.

"I know, right?"

We both busted out laughing.

"So what's going on with you Miss Lady? We barely heard from you over the last few days."

"Girl, Shane had my ass up in the air for the past three days. I just dropped him off at the airport not too long ago."

"That's sweet ... well you know what I mean."

"Yes it was." I emphasized, and we had another bout of laughter.

"Hold on, I'm getting another call." Keri said and switched over to the other line.

She was gone for longer than I thought she would and I was about to hang up when she came back on the line.

"That was Miguel.'" She said with a hint of sadness in her voice that was definitely not there before.

"Oh, Okay." I did not want to say anything.

"Girl, he was on the fucking phone crying, begging me to take him back. Telling me shit like he was never in love with his side bitch and how he now realizes it was a big mistake. What the fuck he wants me to do?"

She was talking tough but I know Keri and I know that she loves Miguel and he loves her. And I believe that it was more the embarrassment that caused her to divorce Miguel. I sometimes think she regrets it.

"What do you want to do Keri?" I flat out asked.

"What you mean what I want to do? I already did what I want to do. I divorced him. Didn't I?"

"Keri listen, sometimes we do things in the heat of the moment and make decisions based on how we are feeling in the moment. But it's okay for us to change our minds. Sometimes bad things happen in our lives to change the paradigm and though those things cut us to the core, it can bring us back to a peaceful place."

"Girl, speak English. So what are you saying, I should give Miguel another chance?"

"It wouldn't be my place to tell you to give Miguel another chance. Only you can make that decision. What I am saying however is, if in your heart of hearts you want to give Miguel another chance then that's what you should do. You know him a lot better than I do."

Damn I'm good. Oprah should give me a show. I thought to myself.

"Kylie you have no idea how good it makes me feel to hear you say that. Miguel has been calling and begging for about a month now and I have been giving it a lot of thought. On one hand I want to take him back. I love him. Then on the other, I am scared to death that I will look weak to him. I love him Kylie. But I am so afraid of getting hurt again. What if he just wants to come back because he is miserable?"

All of what she was saying makes sense. What am I suppose to say. I said the first thing that came to mind.

"Sounds like you need more time to sort your feelings out so you should do that. Take time to figure it out."

I heard her take a deep breath.

"Thanks Kylie, I am so glad I called you. Thanks so much for your advice."

"Girl, don't go telling nobody I give you some damn advice." I said and we both laughed.

"You are a nut case, but I love you girl."

"I love you too chica." I said with a smile.

"I will call you later. I have to make a quick run. Thanks again."

"Ok babes. Catch you later."

I hung up from Keri and by then I no longer want to get in or hang out by the pool. I took my bathing suit off put one of Shane's shirt on and just lie on the couch and watch Lifetime until I fell asleep. I woke up thinking about Melanie and cannot for the life of me fathom how she could kill Amanda. What it is has to go way deeper than just a man. And where the hell is she anyway?

Chapter 21

KERI

My birthday party last night on the beach was a hit. Natasha and Kylie left no stones unturned when they planned this beach bash. I had no idea what was going on until I actually got to the beach. They had an entire five thousand foot stretch of the beach cordoned off just for us. Don't know how they did that. Those crazies even had tents put up on the beach and I have no idea how Natasha pulled it off but she had a Jamaican Rasta roasting fish and another guy with braids, Jamaican as well, jerking chicken.

A lot of people showed up including Jennifer, who still has not heard anything from Melanie and Kylie's housekeeper and her friends, the people from the flower shop and lots of other people I did not recognize.

I had a great time but today I am really tired and I want nothing more than to sit around the house and do nothing.

I was in the middle of watching Pretty Woman for the hundredth time when the doorbell rang. It was the mailman with a package. I took the package from his hands, rested it on a table near the door and signed the clip board he handed me. I thanked him and he turned and walked away. As I was about to close the door, I saw a car pull up in the drive way and a woman got out and walked up to me. I have no idea who she is.

"How can I help you?" Something about her immediately irritated me.

She looked me up and down like I was something on a market shelf. Then she spoke slowly.

"You don't know me but I know you" shaking her finger in front of my face.

I felt a sudden rush of blood to my head. I was not going to take a check from this bitch. How she gonna roll up on me like that then talk shit to me. What the fuck is she talking about?

"My bad!" She said while pretending to straighten out the white linen blouse she was wearing over black slacks and red mules.

"Let me introduce myself. I am Nina Perez. I am the widow of Paul Perez."

I went directly into "idiot" mode. I had to do some fast thinking.

"Who is Paul…? You mean Paul Perez that I went to school with?

"Yes, that Paul Perez" she said rolling her eyes.

"He's dead?" I put on my sad face.

"You don't know?"

"Why would I know? And why are you here?"

"So you are not going to invite me in?"

"Why would I invite you in my house? You pull up in my driveway and felt the need to tell me that you are Paul's wife, I mean widow and tell me that Paul, who I might add, I have not seen since high school and with that I should invite you in my home? Why are you here?

"I am not here to make trouble. I was going through my husband's things and I saw your number and address written on a sheet of paper. Then I saw that he called your flower shop a few times. You see, Paul died here in Miami, they found his body in some abandoned building and I am trying to figure it all out so I can get some closure."

She turned her head and wiped a tear that I was not even sure was there. I was almost starting to feel bad for her, but I have no time for emotions. This bitch showing up on my doorstep is not a good look.

"I had no idea he called my flower shop and if he did, he certainly did not talk to me. I have not seen or spoken to Paul since high school. So why do you think coming to see me will bring you closure? And what the fuck was he doing with my address and phone number?" That bitch was buying every bit of my anger and lies.

"I am so sorry. I should not have come here. It's just that he never told me he was coming to Miami and when they found him dead here all I could think was that he was here to see a woman. Then I found the paper with your information. I am sorry. I will go now." And she turned and walked away.

I suddenly feigned sympathy. For no other reason than to get on her good side and see where her head space is. I could not let her leave without making sure that she would not be getting me mixed up with her damn dead husband. Okay, so I killed him. But I don't want her talking to the police about me. I have to invite her in.

"Uhm, Nina." I called before she got to the car.

She turns and looks at me.

"Come on inside. I hate to see you leave like this. Please, come inside."

"I don't want to impose." She whispered.

"No, you are not imposing. Sorry, I came off the way I did earlier. I just didn't know who you were, but now that you explain, I can see you are hurting and looking for answers and from one woman to the next I don't think you should drive right now. Come in and have something to drink, just clear your head before you leave."

It took a few moments, but I was as happy as Dallas when Debbie was doing it when she took me up on the offer.

"Okay, thank you. I really don't know anyone here. Thank you." She said not even closely resembling the woman who pulled into my driveway and got out of the car. That woman was very confrontational. This one seems so vulnerable, even weak. I will have to work my mojo on this bitch. I did not invite her in to have her cry on my shoulder or feel sorry for her hard luck. I have to keep this bitch from going to the police. I can't have her talking to the police about me. Not ever.

"Don't worry about it. Come on in."

"Thank you." She said and followed me inside."

I let out the breath I was holding the entire time. I invited her to sit anywhere she pleased in the living room and handed her the remote to my 70 inch flat screen television while I went and fixed us a couple of long island ice tea.

I am not a big drinker so I made them separately and was sure to make hers way stronger than I did my own. After a couple of the devilish brew she cried and spilled her guts about Paul. Not that I wanted to hear a damn thing about the bastard, but I had to work on the bitch so she keep me out of her fucking drama.

In the four hours she spent at my house I learned that she met Paul at some restaurant and they dated for a couple of years before they got married. She said Paul immediately began cheating on her after they started living together as man and wife. She also said he had a drug problem and could not hold down a job.

She was at the end of her rope and was ready to divorce Paul if he did not start making some monitory contribution to the marriage. She told me that he told her that he had something big pending only weeks before his death. She said he told her he was working on a deal that would bring in at least a hundred thousand dollars.

I asked her if she knew what that deal was and she had no clue. I convinced her to go back home and stop stressing herself over a man that did not respect her enough to cheat on her while she is busy taking care of him. She was getting angrier at him by the minute and by the fourth hour I had her calling the airline and booking her flight back to wherever the hell she came from.

I told her how happy I was to make a new friend and told her how sorry I was that I did not get his calls when he called my flower shop. I feigned how maybe if he had gotten in touch with me how maybe he would still be alive.

She has no idea that Paul and I were involved in a relationship when we were young. I only admitted to knowing him from high school.

I offered to take her to the airport and she accepted. I followed her to her hotel to collect her belongings and drove her ass to the airport my damn self. I even parked and hung out with her inside the airport until it was time for her to board her flight.

I still did not leave the airport until I was sure that her plane had taken off and she was safely on it back to her life.

Boy did I dodge that bullet. After what is still going down with Melanie missing, a fugitive running from the law for killing her best friend; the last thing I need in my life is to be connected to a murder, especially one I actually committed. I cannot see me living the prison life. I do not look good in any of the popular prison colors, and though they say orange is the new black and orange goes well with my skin tone, I do not think prison orange is my shade.

I worry about my soul though. I feel absolutely no remorse and I am starting to think that there may be a real killer lurking inside of me. Can I kill again? Will I kill again? How is it that I feel no remorse? I asked myself all those questions and could not fathom an answer to any of it.

Those thoughts made me wonder if Melanie was feeling any remorse for killing Amanda. I quickly realize that no matter what Melanie's reason for killing Amanda I was no better than her. I am just as much a murderer as she is. Lord, have mercy on me.

It's been a whole three weeks since Nina showed up at my door. She called me a couple times and I called her a couple times. She told me how she is moving on with her life and has accepted Paul's death for what it's worth. I was more than happy to hear that. She also told me she is dating a doctor. Those words made me jump up; do back flips then fell on my knees and thanked God.

Way I see it, with a new man in Nina's life she will have no interest in finding out anything else about Paul's death which lessen the chance of her ever voluntarily talking with the police which in turn keeps my name out of their business.

There is no doubt in my mind that God gave me one extra. I would never make it in prison. I would die a slow death if one of those hard ass jail bird bitches doesn't put my lights out before that. I guess getting fucked by Big Bertha would not be my biggest issue.

I have been living my life as if I am the one keeping me here, and I think it's time I start going to church and getting closer to God. Growing up, church was always a big part of my life and when I went to college all that went out the door. I will make a concerted effort to start going back to church. I owe this to God and myself. I have to show him how grateful I am that he saved me. I prayed for forgiveness, though I feel no remorse. I don't know how that makes sense. What makes sense though is that I get a connection with God.

My issues with Miguel has also been centre stage in my thoughts and I figured if God can forgive me for killing Paul, then I can forgive Miguel for cheating on me. So I decided to take my husband back and give our marriage another try. The one thing I will not do however is ever admit to being a killer. That will be a secret that I take to my grave.

Chapter 22

NATASHA

I can't believe it's almost Christmas again. If someone had told me that I would be getting married before the year ends I would have laughed my butt off. First of all, Miles is the only man I have been seeing and he was married at the time so I had no real plan to marry him. I did not see him leaving his wife for me and in retrospect I was more than willing to keep being his side-bitch for as long as it felt good and as long as he was taking care of me.

But as fate would have it his wife's affair sent him running right into my arms and my life for good. Well, I know we have not sealed it with that piece of paper yet. We are getting married on the day after Christmas and its only days away.

Miles and I decided to do something small in Jamaica with my mom and dad, Kylie and Shane, Keri and Miguel, Margaret my manager from the agency and Jennifer who is still running Melanie's hair salon. Another four or five people from Miles' side will be there as well. We chose not to do anything thing big but instead something small and intimate.

My mom and dad and Margaret are already in Jamaica putting it all together and the rest of us are flying down tomorrow. Everyone wanted to get down there on the island a couple of days before the day of the ceremony for a little extra fun in the sun.

I still have quite a bit of packing left to do. I am taking two huge Louis Vuitton suitcases. My mom took my dress and veil with her. I am so glad she did, because that would take a whole suitcase all by itself.

All in all, everything is falling in place perfectly. I sold the big ass house that Donna left me and there is a lot of dough coming in from the apartment building she left me as well. I have a ton of money in the bank and is about to marry one of the richest, sexiest, most handsome man in South Florida. And let me not talk about the sex. Miles could certainly live in my pussy twenty four seven and I would never once complain. My life is fantastic. I have the best friends in the world. I try not to think too much about the Melanie and Amanda debacle. I miss them both. I struggled to push thoughts of them to the back of my head. I did not want any other emotions getting in the way of my happiness at this time.

Miles and I thought it best that we wait until after the wedding to live together. He bought a beautiful new seven bedroom seven bath, 20,000 square foot home for us on Star Island in Miami with acres of land to boot. I have never even driven pass a home like that before let alone dream of living in one. Not that I didn't have big dreams, but there is no way I dreamed that big and believe me I am a big dreamer.

My phone rang and snapped me out of my own head. It is my baby, Miles.

"Hello darling." I whispered in the phone.

"Hi there Mrs. Covington, how are you doing this evening?" He said and I could hear and see the big smile that must be spreading all over his face.

"I like the way it sounds on your lips."

"You do, uh?"

"Yes I do. It sounds really sexy when you say it."

"You want to hear something sexy?" he asked

"Yes." I said, barely audible.

"I want to whisper it in your ear." He said in that honey-drip voice.

"I'm listening baby."

"No Nat I want you to feel my breath on your skin when I tell you. I am getting in the car right now, so have that pussy ready for daddy. I want you really bad baby."

"Oh Miles, I want you so bad baby; Hurry."

"I'm on my way."

He was at my house in less than an hour and when I opened the door his eyes popped wide open and he seemed to freeze for a moment then he walked up to me, use his foot to close the door behind him, pulled me into his arms and pressed his lips against mine giving me officially the longest and sweetest kiss I have ever had in my life. I am experiencing a lot of firsts with Miles and I am just soaking it all in.

"Hello sweet lady." Miles said after finally wrestling his lips away from mine.

"Hello back sexy man." Our eyes locked and I could see the yearning embedded in them. What I was not sure about was; is it a yearning for sex or a yearning for something deeper? I know whatever it is I will have to step up to the plate and provide it.

He pushed his hand into his pocket and came up with a box about six by two inches in size. He hands it to me.

"Open it." He said

"What i…"

He jumped in before I could finish the question.

"Just open it." He said calmly.

I opened the box and was completely taken aback.

"Oh Miles, Oh, Oh, Oh… O…. Thank you so much baby. This is absolutely out of this world. Wow! Thank you."

Inside the box lays the most beautiful diamond necklace I have ever seen. I am sure it cost at least a couple hundred thousand.

"Well, that's about enough thank you to last a lifetime. I am glad you like it baby. I am hoping you will wear that around your neck when we get married, but only if you want to." He said kissing my lips gently. We were still standing in the doorway.

"Like it? No, I do not like it, I love it." I said excitedly.

"Come baby; let's go sit down or something. You know I can't stay, right? My flight leaves first thing in the morning and I have a few things left to pack."

"I know baby, but do you have a little time for me to spoil you just a little bit with a taste of cream pie that's still warm and moist." I said in a sultry, teasing tone as I reached out and gently grabbed his crotch.

"Of course I do. The necklace is just an excuse to come and take advantage of your warmth and moistness."

"We both laughed and he followed me to the bedroom where I put the box with the necklace on my dresser and before I could turn to walk to the bed he turned me around to him, knelt down in front of me and pulled my thong to one side using his hands to nudge my legs apart.

I held on to the dresser to keep my balance as he ran his tongue up and down the middle of my wetness and I felt the sweet tender sensation heating up my clit and sent my head in a spin.

"Wait baby, let go...o….o to the...e...e bed."

He did not say anything as he slowly moved me over to the bed with his lips on my pussy, walking on his knees. My man has skills.

Miles sucked and fucked me for way past an hour. When we were through he snuggled with me for only a few minutes before he got dressed and headed home.

I can't believe that man will be my husband in only a few days. I never even dreamed I would be marrying anyone let alone so soon.

The whole time I was cheating with Miles while he was still married, I never ever entertained the thought of being with another man. I never thought about a future with anyone else. I however dreamed many times of one day being his wife, but was more than willing to spend the rest of my life being the other woman. That arrangement was surprisingly fulfilling and I never felt the need to alter it. Miles more than took care of my emotional, financial and sexual needs and always treat me like a lady, with love and respect.

I met up with Keri, Kylie, Karen and Jennifer at the airport. Miles' private jet was waiting for us. It made several return trips from Fort Lauderdale to Jamaica and back in the last few days. All our guests went to Jamaica by private jet. The trip was uneventful, thank God for that. I hate flying.

We landed in Montego Bay and a limousine took us to our hotel which was only about twenty minutes away on rocky roads.

When we pulled into the resort the place seemed void of people except for the porters and waiters and the other staff members. We were headed to the front desk when I saw my mom coming toward me walking so damn fast you'd think she was being chased by bears.

"Hi mom." I said running up to her and giving her a big hug.

"Hi baby, I am so happy you are here."

"Where are all the people on the resort?" I asked her curiously.

"Well, I guess I can tell you now."

"Tell me what mom?"

She had this big grin on her face and she really looked happy about whatever it is she was about to tell.

"Your husband, I mean husband to be had the resort people close off the resort for the next three days, so we are the only ones here. Don't ask me how he did it, but he did."

"Are you serious? When did he have time to do all that?"

"That is a question you will have to ask him. Let me take you to him."

She gave instructions to the bellboy on where to put my luggage; instructed another, a woman, where to take the girls before taking me to see Miles.

She asked the young woman to show the girls where we will be once they put their luggage in their rooms. Reggae music was being played all throughout the resort and you could even hear it from speakers that were up in the trees, very creative.

My mom took me to an area toward the back of the resort that looked like one big massive porch with just a roof and no sides. There is an Olympic size swimming pool and only a few yards from the end of the pool is a beautiful beach with the ocean as far as the eyes can see. It is absolutely breathtaking. Off to one side is a secured area with the most delicious looking food I have ever seen in one place. Three people in uniform were standing in that area and one of them was serving a man. I take it with the resort reserved for just us; he has to be one of Miles' people. Aside from his sister Rhonda I had no idea who else he brought with him.

My mom took me into a large room with sofas and a bar with bartenders waiting to take orders and Miles who was laying back all relaxed saw me, jumped up and ran over to me, picked me up and spun me around. I wrapped my legs around his back and we kissed passionately.

"Hey, you are not married yet you know" my mom said laughing as she walked out of the room.

"Where's dad?" I asked Miles.

"Your dad decided he wanted to catch his own food so he and I a couple of my guys went fishing."

"Why would he do that with all this food here?"

"Oh, my wonderfully naïve wife to be" He said laughing.

"It's all about the experience. I get it."

"I get it too now that you explain it. All this talk about food is making me hungry." I said rubbing my stomach.

"Good, because as we speak they are setting up a special are for us to dine outdoors later."

"That's good. I like that." I said smiling and looking into his eyes.

I still can't believe that tomorrow he will officially be my husband. I'll have papers on this fine specie of a man and all the accolades that comes with him. Yes, I am totally happy that he is rich but I know in my gut that I could also live under a bus with him if necessary. I truly believe that he is probably the only man I would gladly spend my money on if he had none. Miles Covington is definitely the best thing that ever happened to me outside of my parents.

"Let's go up to our room until it's time to eat. They will notify us." Miles said and took my hand in his and we went to our suites, the best they have.

We occupy The Presidential suite. I had no idea they do it like that on the resorts in Jamaica. This is the freaking high life to the max. I walked around the place and it was one marvel after the next. Everything is in white with touches of black.

Miles went right into the shower and wants me to join him. I was getting out of my clothes when I noticed a newspaper, The Jamaica Observer on the table, I was blown away when I saw a huge photo of me and Miles on the front page announcing our wedding on the island.

I shouted to Miles in the bathroom.

"Babes, you didn't tell me we are on the front page of the newspaper here?"

"It thought I'd surprise you. Come on in the shower with me baby."

"I'm on my way baby." I said and joined him in the shower.

We got freaky in the shower and I think my happiness meter went up several notches. I love Miles so much. Even though tomorrow is only a day away, it seems way too long.

We had to make that one really short and luckily we did because as soon as we stepped out of the shower, the telephone at the side of the king bed rang.

"Hello." Miles said into the phone.

He then said "thank you" and hung up the phone.

"Get dressed; dinner will be in fifteen minutes."

"Yes sir." I said and was about to get something from one of my suitcases when someone knocked on the door.

Miles wrapped a towel around him and went to get the door. He came back with a package and handed it to me.

"I got you this to wear to dinner."

"Wow, thank you." I said and quickly took the cover off the box. I pulled out a beautiful red dress with the silhouette of a huge palm tree on the front in a deeper shade of red. Also inside the box was the perfect pair of wedges sandal about three inches tall matching the darker shade of red in the dress.

I was stunned.

"Miles.' Was all I could muster.

He smiled at me and said "Thank me later. Right now I want you to just put those on so I can go show you off."

"Anything you say boss."

I reached up and kissed him gently on the lips.

I got dressed and we walked hand in hand as we joined our guests for dinner.

Chapter 24
MELANIE

My new life here in Jamaica is not so bad after all. Hollywood and I are definitely an item and I can tell you that some of the Jamaican girls are not feeling that. Everyone is wondering how I came all the way from where I come from and snatched him while women down there who have been incessantly throwing themselves at him can't make any headway. Bitches don't know I am not the one to play loser.

Hollywood told me he can no longer travel to the United States because he caught a drug case the last time he was there and in lieu of a prison sentence his lawyer worked it out so he got deportation without serving time in prison. He does not seem too bothered by it and I definitely am not because now he would have no reason for wanting to go there and possibly invite me along. What reason would I have to say I don't want to go back? With the situation the way it is I can fly wherever I want to with my American passport, so it's easy for me to say I am taking a trip to the United States and beeline to Canada or any place I choose. I will have to pretend to go home at some point, so it's perfect that he can't travel to the America. I will never tell Hollywood or anyone my secret.

I was in the kitchen making dinner when I heard the newspaper boy coming down the street like the town crier. "Newspaypa! Newspaypa! … Neeeews…paypa!" with an accent so thick you could cut it with a knife.

That is one of the things I love about Jamaica. Everything is sold on the streets. On Sundays you can put your pot on and wait for the fish man to show up on your street with his wide assortment of fish. You can also hear the broom man verbally pedaling his ware on a Sunday as well; always on a Sunday. Most evenings and several times on Sundays you will find the ice cream man and the frozen ice man coming thru the neighborhoods and you just have to step outside your door to get what your heart desires. I think they love coming into our neighborhood where they make huge sales because everyone in this particular area has money and it shows.

I ran outside and got a copy of the newspaper and almost fainted when I looked at the front cover. What in the world? Natasha and Miles were looking back at me and the caption read; "American Business Mogul Miles Covington to Marry Supermodel Natasha Bell Here In Jamaica."

I ran inside the house and sat at the kitchen counter and read the article on the inside and found out that Miles Covington rented out an entire resort for their nuptials. Way to go Miles.

A rush of sadness immediately engulfed me, my throat tightened and tears rolled down my cheeks. I miss my friends so much. I would be there with them right now if I hadn't killed Amanda and ran away like the murderous fugitive that I am. I will never be able to call my friends and shoot the breeze with them the way I use to. I felt my heart break.

This is the closest I have ever come to feeling genuine regret for killing my best friend Amanda. It's too late now to wonder what would have happened if I had not gone on my killing rampage.

There were two other pictures inside the paper. One showing Miles, a woman and three fine ass men getting off a private jet, and the second showing Natasha, Keri, Kylie, Karen, Natasha's hairdresser and Jennifer from my salon exiting the same plane as well. I miss my friends. I miss the fun.

The paper said that the wedding will be at a private resort but it did not give the name of the place. Montego Bay is filled with resorts, so it could be one of any number of them. It should make no difference whether or not I know where it will be going down, it's not like I can pop up there and show my face.

I would have loved to be able to see all of them. I have been running so scared I abandoned the salon to Jennifer, but am too scared to contact her and make the paperwork straight. I do not want anything threatening my freedom. My life is so fulfilling here that I do not feel like a fugitive, yet I constantly remind myself that I am so as not to slip up, make any mistakes that would work against me.

My life has been pretty good. I take care of Hollywood and he takes care of me. I stay at home all the time; I guess you could call me a homebody now. I do not go the clubs and whenever I leave the house to do some shopping or run some errands I have a designated driver that is on Hollywood's payroll mainly for my protection. But for the most part I stay at home, exactly where I want to be under the circumstances. I have not made any new friends since I got here and all of Hollywood's staff is male; so no nosy bitches in my business or around my man.

Every damn day I find another reason to give Hollywood why I no longer like America and that I don't ever care to go back. I told him I have no family and how my friends all went their own way and I find myself alone. I told him if they did not want him in America, then America can kiss my ass as well. He told me he never knew that I felt so strongly about him. To be honest, as bright and intelligent as Hollywood is, he sure is an idiot when it comes to me. He eats up everything I tell him and just keep falling deeper and deeper in love with me. I am not going to pretend that I don't have feelings for him because I do, but I do not want to fall too deeply. With my present situation, one never know, I may have to just get up and run one day and if that worst case scenario presents itself I do not want to have to wrestle with my heart.

Luckily for me Hollywood is not much into television, social media or even computers so I don't have to worry about him seeing anything about my case or even if he does hopefully he won't recognize me. I made a drastic change in the way I look. I don't even remember my old self. In addition to my looks, the name Robin Goodison is latched in his brain now.

I was deep in my thoughts and did not hear Hollywood come in, but I heard him calling my name and running up the stairs. I quickly hid the newspaper in a drawer in the kitchen.

"Robin, where are you baby?"

"I'm down here in the kitchen hon." I answered

He came back running down the stairs with an envelope in his hand. He waved the envelope in the air.

"So you feel up to going to a wedding tomorrow?"

"A wedding? Just like that?"

"I know its short notice, but I am positive you have something awesome to wear." He said.

"Whose wedding is it anyway?' I asked not really prepared for the answer I got.

"I ran into a friend of mine today. I had a meeting in Montego Bay and I and a couple of the boys went over to the Riu Montego Bay Resorts. My friend is a friend of the groom. He is some filthy rich guy from the United States, Miles Covington. You may have heard of him. He is marrying this supermodel chick name Natasha Bell?"

"Yes, I would love to go. You don't have to worry. I have something to wear."

I know damn well as the words were falling off my tongue that I would not set foot on that resort for no damn wedding but I could not give him any reason to be suspicious. Now I will have to suddenly fall ill or something. I have to get sick enough that he won't even consider going by himself. That would be the last damn thing I would need. Just thinking about him going there and making conversation, talking about me; maybe even recognizing the girls from our previous trip together made me cringe. I can't have that. This is way too close for comfort. Why the fuck did they have to come here for their wedding anyway? Can't a girl run away in fucking peace? I have a lot of work to do.

"Great. So you have the rest of the day to get prepared."

"Yes daddy." I said and hugged him around his waist.

I guess he took that to mean something more than just a hug around the waist because he started kissing my neck and face and before I knew it he was leading me up the stairs to the bedroom. This is my chance to put my show in motion. Making him believe I was all for the wedding plans by fucking his brain out. Let me not lie, he is more likely to fuck my brain out. I swear this man is ten lions in one. A Rasta Lion.

When I first started fucking with Hollywood, I could not get him to taste my pussy for any amount of money in the world. But he must have really fallen in love because now he eats my pussy like he getting paid.

He laid me down on the bed and knelt in front of me then pulled my ass to the edge of the bed and spread my legs wide open. First he kissed the insides of my thighs as he caressed my pussy lips.

"Aah baby! This is sooo goooood." I managed through labored breaths.

"It's good for me too Robin. I love you."

This was not the first time Hollywood told me that he loves me. But this is definitely the first time I believe it. I could feel it in his touch and saw it in his eyes. And please don't let me verbalize the message he was sending is sending to my wet pussy.

We made love and I had multiple orgasms and so did he, but his dick would not stay down for long. Every time I think it was over that dick recharges itself and send shockwaves to my pussy that was numbing. After we were both spent we fell asleep and when I woke up he was gone.

I have no intention of going to that wedding. Going to the wedding would be no different than turning myself in to the police. I would not dare think that Natasha or any of the other girls would spare me. Amanda was just as much their friend as I was and if I should be honest with I know I was the least favorite.

I think they all secretly had a problem with my mouth and the fact that I had never been a one man girl. Why should I? I have never in my life found a man that could totally satisfy all my needs, so I did the next best thing; I get a couple of men or three to fill each other's gap. I don't see a damn thing wrong with that, but bitches act like they are holier than Jesus and I am sure they all have motherfucking skeletons in their closets like every other motherfucker they think they are better than.

I lucked out though since coming to Jamaica. Hollywood is all the man I need. He fills all the gaps by providing all my sexual, financial and emotional needs and I know before long I will have him going down the altar. Fuck Natasha and her wedding. I am sure those bitches don't have anything good to say about me right now, so on that note, fuck them.

That night I took a shower before Hollywood got home and rubbed myself all over with bleaching cream. A lot of women in Jamaica was using bleaching crème by mixing several brands together to make it more potent so it works faster, it seem to work really fast. My reason for using the bleaching cream is however very different. One of the things I noticed outside of its quick result is that it makes them sweat profusely, especially with the Jamaica sun so steamy hot.

When Hollywood made it home which was just after ten I was already in bed, which surprised him. I had turned down the air conditioner because I wanted the bleaching cream to get me sweating and it did.

He came up to bedroom and pushed his head in the door that was already slightly open.

"Bedding down so soon? He questioned with his brow furrowed.

This is my moment to shine. Time for me to play the damsel in distress and it can be nothing less than Oscar worthy.

"I'm not feeling well." I said all pitiful

He walked over to the bed and touched my forehead.

"Baby, you are burning up. You are sweating and your face feels clammy. Do you want to see the doctor?"

"No, I think it's just the flu. My throat doesn't feel good either, but it will pass." I was playing my role and that Oscar was looking more and more possible.

"Are you sure? Cause I can have a doctor friend of mine come over and see you."

Hollywood has a fix for every damn thing. I like that he is so resourceful but that shit was not working in my favor right now. I can't have no doctor coming over to see me when ain't shit wrong with me.

"No, it's not that bad. I don't think I need a doctor. A doctor would only tell me to get something over the counter. There is no need to bring one here just for that."

"You are a stubborn one, aren't you?" He asked sitting beside me and taking my hands in his.

I faked a laugh, brought is hands up to my lips and kissed on his fingers.

"Do you want me to turn the air conditioning up or is it more comfortable this way" he asked.

"I turned it down earlier, because I was hot then cold, then hot again. But you can turn it up a little now, 'cause I am hot again." I was lying through my pearly whites.

"Okay, I'll turn it up a little but if you change your mind later let me know. It's whatever makes you comfortable Miss Robin."

"Thank you for everything baby." I faked a weak smile.

"No need. You have been just as good to me as I have to you."

He stood there for a moment looking at me like he just hates to see me sick. Then he walked toward the door. He turned back around and said he would be in one of the guest rooms so I would have room to make myself as comfortable as I needed to be. I thought that was so sweet of him. He even handed me the remote for the television before leaving the room.

Less than an hour later he was back in the room with a tray that he put on the nightstand with orange juice, a glass with ice, a bottle of cold spring water and grapes. He went back out the room and returned once more with a bottle of Nyquil and a bottle of Aleve. I was impressed. He insisted on giving me some of the Nyquil himself and even had me take a couple of the Aleve. I had to play along but I swear it no longer felt like deceit; I was really into my sickness now.

He left me he said to sleep it off. I guess I still have some kind of conscience because I was feeling really bad about having to lie to Hollywood. He is such a sweet, caring, selfless man and it breaks my heart to know that everything he knows about me is a lie. I pray every day that he never find out about the life I was running from. There were a few occasions when he got so deep under my skin that I wanted to spill my guts to him. Those moments when I feel the love he gives me is so genuine that he would still love me even if he finds out that I am a murderer; and not just a random murderer, but one who killed her best friend. I wonder if Hollywood ever killed anyone before. With the life he is in anything is possible but I wouldn't dare ask him. Asking him something like that would open up the way for him to ask me shit like that so I would not even try to pry or entertain those particular kinds of conversations. Don't ask, don't tell, isn't that how the saying goes?

I had a really good night sleep and felt good enough for a jog, but I wouldn't dare. I lay up in bed and watched the Today Show on NBC while I waited for Hollywood to come and check in and check on me. The tray that he brought for me the night before is still on the nightstand with almost everything still on it except for the water and ice that I consumed. I was playing this out for real.

It was eight thirty when Hollywood knocked on the door then pushed it open without waiting for an answer. It was déjà vu all over again with the familiar scene that was playing out in front of me. Hollywood walked in with yet another tray in his hand with egg and bacon, toast, a Jamaican apple and a cup of tea that I later learned is called cerasse, bitter as hell; but Hollywood said it is good for cleaning out my insides by flushing out all the toxins. At first when I tasted it I wanted to spit it out but after a few sips I was starting to like it. I even asked for a second cup.

I ate just couple bites of everything that was on the tray, it was so good. I wanted to eat it all but I had to keep up my charade, that's a downer.

While I was on my second cup of cerasse tea Hollywood brought up the wedding.

"I guess we are goin' to miss the wedding today."

"I know. I am so sorry." I said with a little pout.

"Don't be sorry baby, it's not your fault you are not feeling well. It's just one of those things."

"You can go without me if you like." I said

I said that hoping that he would shoot the notion down and he did not disappoint.

"Why would I want to do dat? I only want to go with you. If you can't go then I can't go." He was looking at me like the world was in my eyes.

I reached out to him and pulled him closer to me and hugged him like my life depends on it. In a sense it does.

"I love you Rodney Fontaine. I love you so much." I meant every syllable of that.

Falling in love with Hollywood was not part of the game or the lies. I was in love with him for real, deep, strong feelings that I have never felt for any of the men I had been with and believe me there were quite a few. See, aside from wanting men for the purpose of taking care of me, blah, and blah, blah. I have a weakness for some good dick. Let me not lie, I have a weakness for dick period. Big dick, little dick, short dick, long dick, my pussy was at times like grand central station. I remember in one day I fucked Jerry, Jim and that fucking pastor Michael Langston. And there was another time I had sex with the entire football squad from another high school in my area. I just walked into their locker room and none of them knew who I was. I had this fantasy of wanting to get fucked by more than one guy at the same time and at that time it was a perfect situation for me because no one knew me. I remember each of them taking turns getting up inside me, making pathways to heaven. My pussy was having a party and I was the only girl invited. Some of the guys were just freaky as shit and wanted to suck my pussy out so I let them. I went home that night feeling like I had conquered the world. Truth be told I think that is where I developed the appetite for multiple dicks in my life. I later learned how to make them put their money where their dick is.

"I love you too baby. Don't worry your pretty little blond head about anything. Just relax and watch television all day in bed if you like. Since we are not going to the wedding I would like to go out to the fields see what they are doing there. Most of the staff is here so if you need anything just have one of them get it for you." He said and kissed me on the mouth though I did not brush my teeth all morning.

"Okay, I will do that. I still feel a little weak."

"Make sure you eat something. Tell the kitchen staff what you want to eat and they will fix it for you. If you want takeout just have one of the drivers get it for you. Okay?" He asked with concern written all over his face.

"Okay."

The rest of my day was uneventful and by evening I was almost back to my full strength, but I kept the show going for the entire weekend into Monday because I had the feeling that Natasha and her wedding party would be gone by then and there would be no chance of him wanting to go have a drink, or whatever else he can possibly do with me. I have no idea who is friend is in that bunch but I would hate to feel better just for him to want to take me to meet this friend.

I dodged many bullets and as bad as murder is, and even though God said "thou shall not kill" I think he has forgiven me and is maybe even helping me along my escape route. All I have to do is keep my trap shut. I can't let some dick get in the way of the rest of my life.

I read in the newspaper the following Monday that Miles Covington, his new bride and friends including the mother and father of the bride flew back to Miami on a private jet. I should be happy for Natasha, but something inside me just won't let me be. How can I be happy for anyone when every day I wake up I wonder if it's the day that I will be captured and forced to live the rest of my days in jail? I can't do jail, it's not in my DNA. What the fuck would I do in jail? I would rather die than live the rest of my life in jail.

It has been weeks since Natasha and her wedding party left the island and I have been breathing a little easier. I know dooms day is still hanging over my head, but so far so good.

Hollywood seem to have gotten the marriage bug because he just came home one evening and asked me to marry him while we were in bed. He simply got off the bed, knelt down beside me and asked me to marry him. I answered "yes" laying on my back and he got on top of me put the ring on my finger and we made love.

That would not sound like the most romantic proposal to most people but to me it was beautiful. Hollywood is mostly a simple guy in spite of the way he lives, beyond that he is pretty modest. We have not set a wedding date or anything like that but he was talking about me taking a trip to Miami to get my dress. I told him that would be perfect.

Being Robin Goodison is setting in and I know that in no time I will have erased all thoughts of being that other person; the fool who would kill her best friend. I think even my features have changed drastically; I have been maintaining my short blond look by getting a fresh color job every six weeks, but I am thinking of getting dread locks. Hollywood would like that. I am practically living like a Rastafarian anyway so it's only logical. I eat like a Rastafarian now, veggies and fish, and down here in Jamaica we get most of our food directly from the ground or the trees. I love this life.

I think I will be very happy down here in Jamaica as the wife of Rodney Fontaine. Mrs. Rodney Fontaine has a nice ring to it. I hope I will never have to find out if he would still want me if he knew my secret.

Chapter 25

NATASHA

I cannot believe a whole year has passed since Miles and I tied the knot and I must say I have been in marital bliss since with no sign of slowing down any time soon. Miles cut back on his schedule tremendously so we could spend more time together, but my modeling career has gone through the roof with me doing a lot of traveling with Miles right there with me. I could not ask for more. He spoils me rotten with gifts; he conveniently has one ready after every show. Life with Miles is my dreams come true.

The sex is off the chain, through the roof and meets the clouds kind of good. He pampers me like a baby, protects me fiercely and keeps a smile on my face with his warped sense of humor. To top it all off, all my friends love him, my family loves him and he loves them right back. In fact we are all doing well in our relationships; we are one happy bunch right now.

Kylie and Shane are doing their thing and doing it bigger than ever. She released another novel this year and it shot straight to best seller status in only days. Shane has about three movies in the theatre and more on the burner and you hardly see one without the other. Those two are attached at the hip and the media loves them.

Keri and Miguel got pass their baby mama drama and she is now expecting a little one of her own. She only found out recently but you know we already threw the first party. Miguel has really evolved into that doting wonderful husband that we knew before his closet door opened and all the bones spilled out. We are all happy about the baby and can't wait to become aunties and uncles.

With everyone doing well and being happy I am sure I am not the only one who has those moments of sadness and despair when I think about Amanda and Melanie. I miss Amanda so much and sometimes I lay up in bed at night thinking about her and how scared she must have been in her final moments at the hand of one of her best friends. The more I miss Amanda the more I pray they find Melanie and pull her from under whatever rock she is hiding and bring her to justice. What kind of person kills their best friend over a man? That simply tells me that in reality we were all in danger of being Melanie's victim. She was liable to kill any of us for saying or doing what she perceives to be the wrong thing.

I live in the belief that whatever you do in life has consequences. With that credence I know Melanie will be found and punished for the crime she committed. Maybe the punishment has already been exacted, but if it isn't, it will be sure to rear its ugly head one day in the future. I pray it will be the near future because as happy as I am now I don't think I will ever feel total happiness until Melanie is dragged before the court and forced to face all of us. She must pay for her crime and we will not stop until justice is served. I am certain that wherever she is hiding someone is bound to make the connection; Damn! Life is full of secrets.

www.ingramcontent.com/pod-product-compliance
Lightning Source LLC
Chambersburg PA
CBHW060935030726
47503CB00003B/603

* 9 7 8 0 6 9 2 4 1 9 6 9 4 *